With Her Boots On

LISA DOW

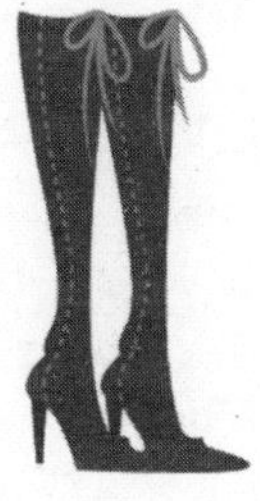

McArthur & Company
Toronto

First published in Canada in 2010 by
McArthur & Company
322 King Street West, Suite 402
Toronto, Ontario
M5V 1J2
www.mcarthur-co.com

Library and Archives Canada Cataloguing in Publication

Dow, Lisa
With her boots on / Lisa Dow.

ISBN 978-1-55278-874-5

I. Title.

PS8607.O9873W57 2010 C813'.6 C2010-903986-6

The publisher would like to acknowledge the financial support of the Government of Canada through the Canada Book Fund and the Canada Council for our publishing activities. The publisher further wishes to acknowledge the financial support of the Ontario Arts Council and the OMDC for our publishing program.

Cover and text design by Tania Craan
Cover image © Eastnine Inc. / Getty Images
Printed in Canada by Webcom

10 9 8 7 6 5 4 3 2 1

For my friend
Nicola (Nix) Galloway
Your laughter lives on in my heart

Acknowledgments

Very special thanks to:

Hilary McMahon, for being my brilliant and beautiful agent.

Kim McArthur, for bringing Mel's story to print.

Heather Lindsay, for the amazing website, ongoing encouragement and the occasional — much needed — kick in the butt to keep writing.

Kim (Roberts) Sands, for your infectious exercise drive and shared love of Australia.

Dr. Walter Heidary, for imparting some of your invaluable knowledge and twenty-plus years of friendship.

Jennifer Richter, for giving me insight into the inner-workings of the real estate world.

Larry Dow Jr., for bringing Molly, the Great Dane, into our family and the discounted car repairs.

Julie (Dow) Reid, for Stella and your ongoing support.

Sandy and The Original Kit, for decades of unwavering friendship. I can't imagine my life without either of you in it.

Cindy (Farquharson) MacPherson, for lending me a stingray story that I could not possibly have made up.

Michael D'Angelantonio, for your relentless promotion of *It Would Be Funny*.

Dorothy Dow, for being the most supportive mom in the world.

Gladys (McMahon) Giroux, for your constant support and unconditional love — and for being a little bit like Peggy!

Mary Kirkpatrick, for being "my people."

Julie Kirkpatrick, for your shared loved of the written word.

Trillium Lakelands District School Board, for employing me so I can support my writing habit.

And to all of my amazing family and friends who encourage, support and feed me during the lean times. I can never say thank you enough.

1

"Mother of Pearl." This can*not* be right. I am standing in the oversized change room at the Bedazzled Beauty Bridal Boutique wearing what can only be described as "the ugliest dress known to man" — or woman; especially this woman. I turn to Kit for support but can see she is shaking in silent laughter and wiping her tear-filled eyes.

"KIT!" I hiss in my strongest quiet voice because the dressing room has only a curtain separating us from the outside world. Kit looks up with a jolt and tries to pull herself together; she is so not helping at this point.

"Seriously, just one picture? On my cellphone, just *one*! Please?!" Kit pays no attention to my tone. She asked this same question a few moments ago and she knows the answer. I give her my steeliest "I'm not impressed" stare. We've been best friends since before kindergarten; you'd think she'd know me better by now.

"Okay, whatever! Fine." Kit starts to speak again but stops and looks down as the silent laughter starts again.

"Kathryn Jennings, you standing there laughing is really not helpful. Can you get the copy of the email out of my bag?" I should probably be laughing as well, but since it's me wearing the dress it hardly seems like a time for levity.

"Okay. Okay." Kit reaches into my Prada bag and finds the email. I love my Prada bag. It's beautiful, classic and streamlined. The dress I'm currently wearing cannot be described as any of those things. There are no words in the English language to describe what I am wearing.

Having a vocation seems to finally slow Kit's laughter. "Okay." Kit is scanning the page and starts to read, "Manufacturer number 4414, dress number 666096, colour 'Sunset Desire,'" Kit looks up at me, "and that's what the tag says."

"Well, check it again, there is no way this colour could ever be described as 'Sunset Desire' and this can*not* be the dress." Kit starts to dig in the billows of fabric encasing my upper arm, searching for the tag affixed to the armpit seam.

"No. Sadly, this *is* the dress. Number 666096, 'Sunset Desire.'"

"Six-six-six, indeed," is all I can mutter turning back to the mirror. "Didn't Sam say in the email she *likes* the dress?"

"She *loves* the dress actually." Kit scans the paper she is still holding in her hand. "Here," she points at the page and starts to read, "Mel, it's perfect. It's the colour the sky was on my first date with your brother. I knew the second I saw it that I had to have this dress in my wedding." Kit looks up and we make eye contact in the mirror. Kit is finally able to control her laughter. The situation is losing its humour quickly. I may be expected to actually wear this dress in public — forget Kit wanting one picture; there will be hundreds of pictures to prove it.

"Is Sam colour-blind? Deranged? Delusional?" I ask Kit sarcastically. A part of me hopes any of these things might be true. I'm standing in the change room on the little platform-thingy wearing a dress with massive three-quarter-length billowing sleeves, a three-inch-wide empire waistband covered in incandescent sequins, and a skirt that contains enough fabric to cover two sofas, even if one of them is a sectional. The yards of fabric that make up the skirt begin mid-ribcage, gathered under the sequined empire waist, and A-lines out to end mid-calf with a diameter of no less than four feet. The small portion of my calves, visible below the volumes of fabric, look like toothpicks, and my feet look too small to hold the dress up. The scoop neckline is edged with ruffles. I have determined that this is indeed a double ruffle, so the top ruffle sticks straight up in clown-outfit fashion and tickles my chin. I can't resist the urge to blow downwards and try to get it away from my skin, and have done so several times. Sadly, all of these elements, as bad as they are, are only accentuated by the fact that the dress can only be described as "Construction Cone Orange." You know, the plastic type used to indicate roadwork and film sites. Yes, I look like a common road pylon!

"Surely, this dress is a different dye lot than the one Sam saw in Georgia." Kit is trying to be hopeful. No subtle dye lot change is going to improve this little number, and I use the term "little" loosely. The underlying colour of this eyesore is orange.

"I can't be seen in public in this," I state. "The closest I've ever come to wearing orange is my tangerine handbag, and I don't wear it and it's not orange. It's *tangerine*." I turn to get a side view. "I can't do it. I can't!" The truth of the matter is that I look short and fat. I'm not exactly a willowy giant but I do have a nice figure — size four, well proportioned — and I don't want to run around at my brother's wedding looking like a pylon or, worse, a pumpkin. "I look like a sumo wrestler dressed in a clown suit."

"No. It's not *that* bad," Kit tries to downplay the dismal situation.

"Really? Would *you* want to wear this thing in public?" I retort, my voice dripping in sarcasm.

Kit visibly shudders at the thought of donning the Sunset Disaster before she tries to change the subject. "How many attendants are in the wedding?" Kit asks, and I realize she has jumped ahead to visualize how more than one person, wearing this particular dress, will look standing together. Worse, standing together for photos to be taken of us.

"Six. There are going to be six of these dresses in one place. Planes will start landing around us."

"Well, that's not likely." Kit tries to be pragmatic but immediately starts to giggle. She will soon be back in silent laughter mode again. Even I have to admit a single-engine Cessna landing between the photographer and six versions of this dress would be funny.

I hate my brother. I know the word "hate" is bad and I'm

not supposed to use it unless in the most dire of circumstances, but I have to say, right now, standing here in a horrible orange dress, this might indeed be one of those dire circumstances. I hate my brother. Mike, who has avoided all adult dating badly by marrying his university sweetheart, is now giving our wedding-obsessed-mother the wedding of her dreams — beating me to the punch — and is also going to manage to completely humiliate me in front of friends and family. Samantha, his fiancée, who I actually quite like, is showing a remarkable lack of fashion sense and is making me wonder if she isn't perhaps a little "off." Samantha is a redhead; why on earth would she want Construction Cone Orange attendants' dresses? My mind is reeling as I stare at my reflection in the oversized mirror.

"Kit…" I turn to my best friend, who is currently crouching in the corner wiping her tear-filled eyes again. I know she is about to fall into another laughing fit so I must get her help sooner than later. In answer, Kit looks up and the laughter starts all over again.

"KIT!" I have to hiss again because her laughter might get me started and this is no time for a fit of giggles. "Okay, you can take a picture. One picture. On *my* phone. I have to email Sam and get to the bottom of this. There is no way this is right." Kit, who has been rendered fairly useless up to this point, manages to pull herself together for a photo shoot and digs the cellphone out of my bag.

"I can't get the whole thing in," Kit states from the corner she is in and starts to move around me, pushing the skirt out of the way so she can walk past it, looking at the phone screen. I notice a laughter-tear still wet on her cheek. When Kit gets to the door of the change room — the curtain — she pushes it aside and steps out, backing up a few feet. "Okay, I've got most of it, but not the full skirt, it's going off the screen on both sides."

"Whatever. Just so I can email Sam and she can confirm but hopefully deny this fashion atrocity."

"Got it!" Kit sounds triumphant. "But you're right. There must be some mix-up. There is no way Samantha wants to have *this* dress in her wedding." Kit hands me the phone and I look at the photo on the screen and want to cry. The dress, if it is indeed possible, looks more orange in the photo than in the mirror. This outfit can*not* be in my future. I manage to stop dwelling on my impending doom long enough to text off a quick email to soon-to-be sister-in-law, Sam, attaching the godawful photo.

Sam, attached is a photo of the dress matching the details you gave

Please confirm/deny this is indeed the dress we still need to talk shoes

"There. All we can do now is wait for Sam's reply." I know waiting for this answer is going to seem interminably long, but the relief I will feel when I hear this is *not* the dress will be worth the wait.

"Well, let's get you out of this thing." Kit finally says something welcome and starts to close the door she had to open for the photo shoot. Just before the door closes, the overly helpful saleslady who found the abominable dress when we first arrived — how could she miss it really, it's the only orange dress in the store — pops her head into my change area.

"Oh, it's absolutely lovely on you! But wait, you don't have a crinoline! Let me run and get you one!" she offers with way too much enthusiasm, and leaves to retrieve the only remaining element that can make this particular creation more hideous.

Kit and I make eye contact. There is a crinoline.

"Mother of Pearl," we both say in unison.

2

"I'm never getting married," I remark to no one in particular, although Kit is the only one with me at the Firkin an hour after we've finally escaped the Bedazzled Beauty Bridal Boutique. I managed to get out of the dress and fully changed into my real clothes before the saleslady returned with the crinoline. I hustled Kit out of the store, pleading over my shoulder to the saleslady that I could "imagine how the dress will look with the crinoline," and, unfortunately, I can imagine it. Shudder.

"Don't be silly, of course you will, and you'll make me wear something hideous. That's what weddings are all about." Kit is ever the ray of sunshine.

"I used to think I would, but not anymore. Especially with the way things are going with bloody *Charlie Brown*! I don't think I'm cut out to even date anymore." In my frustration with wedding attire I've blurted out more than I meant to about my current boyfriend situation.

"What do you mean? You never call him Charlie Brown! What's he done?"

"Nothing. Don't worry about it. I'm sure it will be fine. Just a passing bad patch." I try to muster belief in what I'm saying, but I suspect Kit will see right through my feeble attempt. Calling John — my live-in boyfriend for fourteen months — "Charlie Brown" is a telltale sign something is amiss. Charlie Brown is Kit's nickname for John, stemming from his preferred striped t-shirt attire, and I never call him Charlie Brown. The slip today must be orange dress stress, induced.

"Okay, what's up? Now you're acting weird. First calling him Charlie Brown, then trying to pretend everything is fine when I can clearly tell it isn't, fess up!"

"I'm sure it's nothing. He's just being weird; some nonsense about wanting to take a modern dance class. I'm not encouraging him, but he seems bound and bent to do it." The modern dance class topic came up a few nights ago at dinner. The whole concept is confusing to me. John is an electrician — a manly man. John's idea of culture is watching the cheese in the refrigerator mutate from white to blue and green mould. We've had many discussions and arguments over mutating cheese and I personally have been given proper heck on several occasions for tossing away what I thought was cheese gone wrong when, in actual fact, John was considering that same piece of mould to be at its peak of perfection. Accepting a man's strange fascination with moulding cheese is one thing; embracing the same man as a modern dancer is quite another.

"Modern dance? Like in leotards-leaping-on-a-stage modern dance?" Kit looks a bit confused. "Surely you heard him wrong. Charlie Brown doesn't move off the couch unless his beer is empty, and only then if someone isn't around to hand him a full one."

"I *know*! I'm usually the 'someone' who replenishes the beer. He's making me crazy with this one. Okay, maybe if he wants to get fit I do encourage exercise. He is getting a bit flabby around the middle, but modern dance? John and modern dance are not two things you use in the same sentence. Well, in a *good* way, at any rate. I can hear someone saying, 'John threw up on himself outside the modern dance studio' but that's where those two things should meet and then depart."

"Okay, back up. What exactly did he say that makes you think he is really contemplating this most uncharacteristic move into culture and weirdness?"

"Mel, I'm going to join a modern dance class at the dance studio around the corner. You know, the one near the beer store." I repeat to Kit, word for word, what John had said to me a few evenings prior.

"But the dance studio is *past* the beer store. Surely he's never been that far down the block." Kit makes the same point I had raised with John during our discussion.

"I know! But apparently the *good* video game store is past the dance studio, so he has passed it and does know where it is. I guess he saw a flyer in the window and, suddenly, voilà, modern dance is his thing."

"Wow, it must have been some flyer." Kit takes a sip of beer looking a little shaken. "Charlie Brown always struck me as more of a pick-up hockey guy, you know? With beer in the change room after the game."

"I *know*, me too. This is why I haven't mentioned it to anyone until now. I thought maybe he was just trying to get me going. Until last night when I found a receipt on the bureau; seems he's actually paid money for a class. If he's trying to get me going, he's going to elaborate lengths."

"But he's an electrician! Do you think Marc and the guys at work know about his foray into modern dance? He must be keeping it quiet at work; they'll razz the heck out of him." Marc is John's boss and he contracts for the condominium developer Kit works for. That's how I met John in the first place. Marc has had a crush on Kit for years. We didn't see much of Marc for a while after Kit turned down his marriage proposal, but he and Kit have managed to remain friends despite all the goings-on and he occasionally joins us for beer.

"I have no idea what John's telling the guys at work. I hardly understand him anymore. All I know is this is very, very strange and I don't like it." I take a sip of beer and realize I'm glad I've told Kit about this latest escapade with John. Keeping this one to myself has been completely nerve-racking.

"Well, let's not panic. Surely once he gets into the class and realizes he has to move and jump around and, well, *dance*, he'll get it out of his system and this too shall pass. You know, like the toy race-car set? That wore off eventually." Kit's comment sparks a memory I've tried to suppress. Immediately after John and I had renovated our house and moved in together, John developed a fascination for all things toy race car. He had five hundred feet of track covering the living-room floor, wrapped around, under and over all of our furniture, and he ran it constantly. The first time I saw an episode of the series *Heroes* without the underlying whine of toy race cars I thought there was something wrong with the television.

"You're right. The living-room speedway only lasted three months. Maybe this too shall pass. I love him dearly, but let's face it, John isn't exactly a slave to his hobbies. Besides, there is no way he'll don a leotard. It's John! He is so *not* tights material!" Kit and I start to laugh. The thought of John in a leotard is quite funny, almost as funny as the thought of me in the Sunset Disaster from earlier this afternoon. Surely neither of these possible sartorial disasters will come to fruition.

3

"What happened to us?" I wonder as I'm driving home after dropping Kit off at her condo. Sitting in traffic, waiting for yet another construction delay on Bloor Street, my mind wanders back to happier days. John and I may not be the most obvious couple, but it works — or it did work. It worked for a long time and I know I didn't imagine it. It was real.

Our first night in our house, our first night of living together, was magical. We ordered in Chinese and had an intimate dinner, complete with candles, wine, and Hugh Dillon — John's favourite musician at the time — playing on the stereo. We sat at the table, long after we'd finished eating, and talked. We talked and laughed and just loved each other. We talked for hours and it wasn't forced or put on; we both really enjoyed each other's company. John pulled me up from the table and held me close as we danced around the dining room and kitchen. We christened the island in the kitchen shortly after that dance — well, it started during the dance — and left the dinner remains on the table to be dealt with in the morning. When was the last time we left dishes on the table overnight? Hell, when was the last time we even ate dinner together? It's been weeks.

John used to stare into my eyes back then. Back then? Back then was only a short time ago. Back then, John used to ask about my work, my new deals, my old deals. He used to tell me about his job and the guys he works with. I know their names, their wives' names. I know who has marital issues and how often they do, or don't, have sex. We talked about everything.

John used to go out of his way to ensure my happiness — almost going too far at times. When Kit and I were renovating the house we owned together, John almost killed himself with caffeine overload trying to get the renovation done quickly and efficiently. He was trying to impress me back then, and it worked.

He used to bring home fashion magazines for me if they contained pictures of exciting new boots. My boyfriend, who by all accounts — and Kit will back me up on this one — has very little fashion sense, bought me fashion magazines because he knew I liked them. How sweet is that?

Kings of Leon. He knows I love the band and left work early the day their *Because of the Times* album was released and brought it to my office. He wanted to get it for me before I picked it up myself.

We used to text and call whenever we had a moment to spare. If I didn't get a text from John during the day, it was only because his phone battery was dead. Even then, he would borrow Marc's phone and text me from it. Any texts from Marc's phone were generally very naughty, for Marc's benefit more than mine, and made me laugh.

I've never had to clean snow off my car since we moved in together. John leaves before me and he always cleans off my car when he's cleaning off his truck. John cleans my car every snowy day without fail. He's never once forgotten or run out of time. Taking the time to clean off my car is sweet and thoughtful and just plain nice. This is the man I love. The man holding the snowbrush and waving to me through the window is the man I love. This is the man I endure watching the Super Bowl for every year. This is the man I want to laugh with and cry with — well, I would, if I actually did that sort of thing — for the rest of my life.

I smile as I sit in my car and remember the warmth. I loved the feeling that I was exactly where I was meant to be when I was wrapped in John's arms and protected by his love.

Oh, don't get me wrong. It isn't all staring into each other's eyes, snowbrushes and undying love. There have been moments when I wanted to kill him — the mouldy cheese, the race track, the winter day he and his friends built a giant snow penis in the front yard. I have visualized John's demise at my hands on several occasions, but the good times have far outweighed the bad ones. I have been able to overlook his bone-headed moves because he's a solid boyfriend who loves me unconditionally. Well, he was solid. The past few weeks have been different. John seems to have pulled away from me and I can't figure it out. I thought it was just a blip — all relationships have those — sadly, now I think it's more than a blip. Dancing? My boyfriend who has never expressed any interest in the arts is suddenly curious about modern dance? As a participant? Big blip indeed.

The traffic starts to move and I wonder if there is an intervention for this sort of thing? Can you call a priest and have an exorcism to expel whatever manner of evil has possessed the man I love to make him want to become a dancer?

I'm still pondering the idea of an exorcism as I pull into the driveway and park beside John's truck. My phone starts to chime, indicating I have a text, as I gather up my purse and laptop from the backseat. The text is from Samantha in Georgia:

> Perfect. It's more beautiful than I remember but isn't there supposed to be a crinoline? Shoes—definitely satin, dyed to match! I can't wait

Wait! This is the dress? I read the text three more times and check the sender and subject. This is not possible. How can the dress I had on a few hours ago, with or without the crinoline, be the dress Samantha *wants* to feature at her wedding? She must know the attendants' dresses are a reflection of her and her apparently very bad taste. Matching shoes? I look down at my Prada-swaddled feet and almost cry at the thought of having to jam them into Pylon Orange satin shoes. I hike my computer bag's strap over my shoulder and slump defeated toward the house. This day cannot be over soon enough.

4

"Mother of Pearl! I could really use a beer, or *two*," I exclaim as I drop my purse beside the chair across from Kit and beside Marc at the Firkin two evenings after the bridesmaid dress adventure. I had spent the day running back and forth to City Hall in my four-inch heels, attempting to get a zoning permit expedited for one of my clients — with no tangible results — so I had called Kit to meet me for a beer.

"Okay, what's with the new saying?" Marc asks with a furrowed brow over his beer glass.

"We can't tell you or we'd have to kill you," Kit answers straight-faced.

"Yes. Kill you." I smile.

"No, seriously, what's up? 'Mother of Pearl' is a little too wholesome for either of you two. I've known you both to cuss like truckers, given the right circumstances." Marc looks concerned at our new-found wholesomeness.

Kit laughs, "Oh, we still cuss. It started completely by accident. Then when it irritated our mothers, it sort of caught on, and now I really like it." Kit starts to regale Marc with the tale of our mothers from a visit we made to our hometown of North Bay two Decembers ago.

Our mothers were stay-at-home moms when we were young. It seemed to Kit and me, throughout our formative years — and well beyond, actually — that our mothers' only true pleasure was derived from chastising and embarrassing us. Our mothers subscribed to the adage that "it takes a village to raise a child" and played equal roles in reprimanding us as required and deemed necessary. Kit and I rarely agreed with their ideas of necessary. I was just as likely to get scolded by Mrs. Jennings as I was by my own mother, and the same was true for Kit. It was quite convenient for them that Kit and I have been inseparable since birth; it saved them a lot of energy. I used to imagine them talking, high-fiving, and my mother giving Mrs. Jennings the thumbs-up after Kit and I caught trouble for something. "Thanks, Peggy, you got them this time. I'll make sure to catch them next time."

Mrs. Jennings is the more motherly of the two and insists on baking for Kit and the twins, while my mother is less Holly Homemaker and considers herself a bit of a fashion-accessory guru. While Mrs. Jennings is concocting new cookie recipes so she can mail care packages, my mother is out hunting down the perfect earrings or pendant accent. My mother has even taken jewellery-making classes and has produced some very unique, albeit outlandish. accessories. Kit and I both have jewellery boxes full of my mother's experiments to prove that not all things that glitter are gold.

During the visit, Mrs. Jennings had Kit and me helping with the preparation of her peanut butter chocolate chunk cookies for the church bazaar. Kit and I were placing the dough on the cookie trays and pressing the balls of dough with forks in the crisscross pattern Mrs. Jennings considers her "signature crisscross" — for the record, Kit and I still don't make the pattern properly even after all these years.

"Another dozen for the oven," Kit announces as she picks up the pan she is working on and turns to place the tray on the kitchen island. Unfortunately, she isn't paying full attention and bashes her elbow into the edge of the countertop. Kit shrieks, dropping the pan with its gooey contents onto the floor.

"Mother of God!" Kit yells over the clatter of the pan hitting the floor while hopping around and grabbing her funny bone.

"Language, ladies! Taking the Lord's name in vain while baking for the church bazaar, no less!" Mrs. Jennings is scolding Kit before the cookie dough has flattened between the tray and the floor.

"I'll clean it up." I grab a spatula, crouch down and start to scrape the dough off the floor back onto the cookie sheet.

"Kathryn! That is hardly ladylike language. And look at the mess you've made!" Mrs. Jennings continues her diatribe while stirring a batch of dough the size of a basketball in her giant cookie bowl.

"Ouch. Ouch. Ouch." Kit, still rubbing her elbow, bends down to help me with the mess and rolls her eyes at me.

"You wouldn't be talking like that..." Mrs. Jennings is just gearing into second when my mother walks into the Jennings' kitchen.

"What have they done now, Peggy? Good heavens, girls! Are you trying to give Peggy a heart attack? You know she takes her baking very seriously. Look at the mess..." My mother walks by Kit and me huddled on the floor while removing her jacket.

"I'm just telling the girls they have gutter mouths, Betty. You know we've discussed it."

"Oh, I know, Peggy! You don't have to tell me twice. What did they say this time?"

"Taking the Lord's name in vain..." Mrs. Jennings starts to reiterate.

"I could have said much worse!" Kit shouts from the floor beside me. Neither mother appears to be listening to her.

"I'll get a cloth to wipe the floor." I stand up from behind the island, stopping short when my eye catches my mother's newest accessory. Around my mother's neck is a 20-inch string of beads that appear to be coffee beans, at the end of which hangs a mother-of-pearl pendant the size of an Olympic discus — although obviously less weighty or she wouldn't be able to hold up her neck. The pendant is not easily missed as it covers most of my mother's average-sized torso. I stand staring, the cloth-and-batter-covered floor momentarily forgotten.

Kit, who has finished scooping cookie dough back onto the cookie sheet, stands up while continuing her defence "I could have said..." Kit places the cookie sheet on the countertop and is concentrating on getting cookie dough off her fingers when she lifts her head and looks toward our mothers. Kit does a startled double take at my mother's chest, forgets her chain of thought completely and the words "Mother of Pearl!" come floating out of her mouth.

Needless to say, I was immediately taken with the saying because Kit had said it so innocently, and its perfection was sealed when we made mischievous eye contact, then burst into laughter.

Kit takes a sip of her beer as she finishes telling Marc the story. "And because it was so ridiculous, yet wholesome, and our mothers were giving us grief, we said it all weekend to irritate them. We used it a bit but forgot about it until last week when Mrs. Melrose sent Mel a very large, rather expressive mother of pearl barrette. So it's been rejuvenated!"

"It will drive our mothers crazy and we aren't swearing. All in all, one of Kit's finest non-filtered moments, I'd say!" I high-five Kit across the table.

"But it sounds silly," Marc laughs.

"Oh, it's going to catch on. Trust me. Pretty soon all the guys on the jobsite will be saying it. You just remember that we started it!" I tell Marc with complete confidence.

"Exactly. Now you're going to start saying it." Kit looks seriously at Marc. "One day you'll be looking at blueprints and say, 'Mother of Pearl! This can't be right!' And then it will be official and Mother of Pearl will be an officially accepted saying and you'll..."

"....Ahhh, no. I don't think that's going to happen. We swear like men on the jobsite. The guys would beat me up if I ever came out with *that*!" Marc shakes his head and takes a drink of his beer.

"Well, your loss!" Kit chirps.

5

I get out of the car at home, after leaving Kit and Marc at the Firkin, and notice immediately that something is very badly amiss. My neighbour's yard, which this morning had appeared quite mid-May-morning normal, with green grass starting to show and the tops of tulips and daffodils poking their little buds through the garden soil, is now covered in lawn ornaments. Covered. Big gnomes, little gnomes, frog statues in various risqué poses, a family of skunks, what must qualify as a herd of sheep, three complete sets of Snow White and the Seven Dwarfs, a near-life-sized Disneyesque prince riding a horse and holding a shield-slash-platter, which appears to be full of birdseed, judging by the number of birds on and around him. Of course, the garishness would not be complete without the plywood silhouette of the fat lady's polka-dot-panty-covered bum bending over the garden of baby tulip buds. The display resembles the *It's a Small World* ride at Disneyland — only slightly more disturbing — you expect creepy little statues when you enter the Disney ride. You don't expect someone to vomit the same statues all over the adjacent yard.

Surely it must be a joke. I've met my neighbours. They seem so normal, young newlyweds, just starting out, early thirties with no kids. They moved in just after John and I celebrated Valentine's Day-slash-our living together anniversary. John and I went over to introduce ourselves. They are Cam and Pam. He's in insurance and she's a nurse. Despite the unfortunate rhyming names, which they could not have planned and no one can hold them responsible for, there is nothing in their demeanour to set off any crazy lawn ornament alarms. This has to be a joke. Pam or Cam must be having a big birthday and friends have covered the yard in an attempt to be funny. Whew! I breathe a sigh of relief because there is no way I can live next to this for the next three seasons. I wonder how long you are obliged to tolerate your friends' antics when they so badly defile your yard. Surely the display will be removed in a few days. You have to admire their handiwork though — a vast array like this must have taken months to amass. I should ask if they hire out. You never know when you'll want to litter a friend's yard just for laughs. If only Kit didn't live in a high-rise condo.

I walk towards the house. The walkway runs between our driveway and Cam and Pam's yard and I notice one of the lawn ornaments beside the walkway has fallen over. It is the groom squirrel of a fourteen-inch-tall bride-and-groom set of squirrels. Smiling squirrels standing on their hind legs, dressed in wedding garb, give me the creeps. But in the spirit of the occasion, I happily bend over and set the groom squirrel upright, pat his little ceramic head, snicker at the display, and think, "Excellent birthday prank."

I know John is not home because his truck is not in the driveway and I start to think about what to make for dinner as I step into the kitchen. I love our kitchen. The renovation was a lot of work, but absolutely worth it. Now I have clean, glossy new cupboards and shiny, stainless-steel appliances. I immediately notice the pink sticky note on the refrigerator. The stainless steel is off limits to magnets, tape, and sticky notes. John knows, and up until now has respected my fondness for the pristine, shiny stainless steel. He must have been in a real hurry to mar the otherwise sparkling surface, which he knows perfectly well is a "sticky-free zone." I rip the sticky off the refrigerator door.

At dance class. Home around 8:30.

This is not happening. Not only is he testing me with sticky notes on the stainless, he appears to be sincere about the "dance thing." The obnoxious, always-says-the-wrong-thing-at-the-wrong-time man I fell in love with is seriously attending modern dance lessons. My brain is swimming in questions, disbelief and horror. I don't want to make dinner. I want to go back to last week, when my sometimes abrasive boyfriend with the fondness for mouldy cheese was not a modern dancer. I must be dreaming. Hideous bridesmaid dress, scary lawn-ornament parade and now this whole modern-dance weirdness is a reality. I am losing control and I must get it back. I have no idea how to stop John's new dance plan, so I grab the phone to call Kit; we can figure it out together.

"No, I'm serious; he's at a class right now." I answer Kit's incredulous "Are you kidding me?" question after I filled her in on the latest dance troupe news.

"Wow. I'd hoped he was just trying to get you going, like you said. I didn't really believe he'd do it."

"I know, but he is doing it. I have to figure out how to get him to *stop* doing it." My brain is spinning. I'm a top-selling real estate agent, juggling needy and demanding clients with absolute skill and deftness at all times. I wear Prada boots and carry matching handbags. I'm always in complete control of my life. I'm in absolute control of, well, everything. Always. "I think I'm losing control of this situation. My boyfriend being a modern dancer is not in the plan. I can't handle this." I am starting to freak out just a little bit.

"Okay. You have to calm down. You are not losing control because it's not something you can control. Maybe Charlie Brown is acting out because you *are* always in control. This could be his way of taking a bit of his control back. I think you should just let this play out. Surely he'll tire of it. You know him better than anyone. Have any of his hobbies lasted very long? Just play along and he'll lose interest and you'll come out of this the supportive girlfriend. Who knows? You may even get enough ammunition to head off his next insane adventure."

"Do you think so? Really?"

"Really. It's Charlie Brown. As you know, I'm his most severe critic. And I'm sure this won't last. There is no way modern dance will ever become a huge part of his life. Just play along. Let him do his thing. Don't freak out and it'll all work out." Kit has a point. She did not like John at all when we first started dating. I don't like to use the word "despise" but it does come close to what Kit felt back in the day. She and John have actually warmed to each other considerably this past year. Kit's even gone so far as to introduce John as *her* friend on several occasions. If I can count on anyone to tell me the truth about John, it's Kit.

"I can do that. I don't have to be in control all the time, right?"

"No, you do have to be in control," Kit laughs into the phone. "*This* will be a great opportunity for you to learn not to be a freak about every little thing you can't control."

"I'm going to throw up." I start to panic because my stomach is flip-flopping in ways I've never known.

"Don't be silly. You won't throw up. You never throw up. Take some deep breaths. You'll be fine," Kit instructs me. I take three exaggerated breaths and I do feel better. If Kit knows anything, it's how to handle a nervous stomach.

I tell Kit about my neighbours' birthday lawn ornaments before hanging up. At least someone in my neighbourhood is having a good day.

6

I'm sitting up in bed reading a book when I hear the back door open and John come in from his dance class. I can't even think the words "dance class" in relation to my man without rolling my eyes. Calm. I must remain calm and play along. Like Kit says, I must try to ride the wave and this too shall pass. I am the calmest, coolest girlfriend ever. I don't need to be in control. I can roll with the punches and go with the flow. I am completely Zen. I'm a flippin' Zen master, in fact! Nothing John says can shake my calm.

"Hey," John pokes his head in the bedroom, "no dinner tonight? What are you doing in bed so early?"

"No, I didn't make anything, I wasn't hungry. Long day. How about you? How was your day?" I say with saccharine sweetness.

"Great. I really think dance is my thing. You'd love it; you should give it a try." It's official, my boyfriend has lost his tiny little mind. I don't break a sweat for any reason except to chase after a possible Brad Pitt sighting opportunity. Surely he knows this about me. Me attending a modern dance class would be more unrealistic than *him* participating in a dance class. My Zen is dissolving at a staggering rate.

"Sure, maybe I will," I lie less than convincingly looking back down at my book. "Did you meet anyone interesting?" I know in order to pull off the cool, calm, I-don't-have-to-be-in-control girlfriend, I am going to have to show interest — even though every fibre of my body is screaming otherwise and I really just want to get up and throttle him.

"Yeah, I have a really great instructor; her name is Ursula. She really knows her stuff."

Ursula? My head jerks up at the manner in which the name *Ursula* rolls off his tongue. Ursula who "knows her stuff"? How would Mr. One-Two-Hour-Dance-Class know what "stuff" is supposed to be and who does or doesn't know their "stuff"? I look into John's eyes and see something I haven't seen since he came home with the replica Dale Earnhardt Senior 1988 Monte Carlo Elite toy race car for the living-room speedway. Oh oh. My boyfriend has found something new all right, but I suspect it isn't entirely a love for modern dance. My first impulse is to scream and throw my book at the cheating bastard — okay, possibly cheating bastard — which would make quite an impression, as I'm reading Alex Haley's Thirtieth Anniversary Edition of *Roots* and even in paperback it's a formidable eight-hundred-eighty-eight pages and goes a good three pounds.

I manage to bite my tongue and tighten my grip on the book. "Must not throw the book," I tell myself. This too shall pass. Maybe I'm seeing something that just isn't there. I did have a stressful day at the planning department, I'm sure this is nothing and I'm just being touchy. I must stay calm and be the supportive girlfriend. John would never cheat on me. I'm being completely insane. John and I are happy. We live together in our newly renovated home. We're good together, we complement each other and we make it work. This is just a strange patch we're going through; I'm sure all couples experience this sort of thing. Well, not modern dance exactly, but things like this. Zen. I must locate and keep a firm grip on my Zen.

"Well, that's great. I'm glad you like her, err... it — the dance class, I mean. How many nights per week is this class?" I hate to ask this question, but since I haven't, until this evening, actually believed he'd follow through with the dance thing, I have no idea what sort of commitment I'm up against.

"It's two nights per week, Tuesday and Thursday, with extra practice classes any night — which I'm probably going to do because we are having a show in five weeks," John states matter-of-factly. A show? My brain starts to spin out of control again and I strengthen my grip on *Roots*.

"Sorry? A show?" I ask, hoping I had heard incorrectly. A show means he is planning to dance in front of an audience. There is no way I can contain this thing.

"Yeah. No point doing all this if no one gets to see the end result. It should be spectacular. Ursula has great vision."

I'll bet she does. "Sorry? So, when is this show?"

"Ursula is thinking the end of June if we're ready."

"Oh. Well, we do have my brother's wedding and that is a

priority. Don't double-book yourself," I say out loud but I am hoping beyond all hope John tires of this dance thing long before then or, failing that, hopefully the show will coincide with the wedding and it will not become common knowledge. Either way, Mel Melrose has no intention of sitting through Ursula's "vision," great or otherwise.

"Hopefully, it'll be around the same time as the wedding and your family can all come and see the show when they are in town. That would be great!" John's enthusiasm sends a shiver down my spine. Containing this thing is not going to be easy.

"Yeah. That would be great." I know the word "great" is dripping in sarcasm, but I can't help it. There is no way I can control all sarcastic comments. John starts to remove his t-shirt and I start to look back down at my book then stop and, blurt out, "John, this dance thing is very sudden and you are very… ahh… enthusiastic. Where did this sudden interest come from?"

John turns back toward me. "What do you mean?"

"I mean, what is actually going on here? Is there anything I should know?"

"No. I've just been feeling a bit lethargic. I'm not playing summer hockey so thought I'd try something different. Nothing to worry about." John walks over to me, tossing his t-shirt in the corner, leans down and kisses my forehead.

Nothing to worry about? Yeah, right. It's going to be a long month-and-a-half. The dance thing itself is stressful enough, now I think I'm also battling my man being smitten by this Ursula woman and her "vision."

"There's leftover lasagne in the fridge if you want to heat some up; you must be starving after all that exercise."

"Cool." John turns to go back to the kitchen. "Hey, babe, what happened to the yard next door?" John yells back over his shoulder as he heads toward the kitchen. My Zen finally admits defeat and slips quietly under the bed.

7

Work. Work is my one bastion. I have control at work, full and complete control. No one dances at work. No one mars my stainless-steel surfaces here. No one attends dance class. *His* dance class — somehow it just strikes me funny. When I think of "dance class," I always picture four- and five-year-old little girls in pink leotards and tutus. Imagining John standing amongst those little girls is quite humorous, and I'm smiling as I step into the foyer of the office. This is good. I feel in command of my ship. I'm carrying my favourite pink Prada bag and have exquisite boots swaddling my pampered feet. I have complete control of my life and my footwear. For a few short hours, I can forget the horror that is quickly becoming my orange-satin-shoe-filled life.

I say good morning to Astrid, our office administrative assistant — a title I use loosely — and am met with a steely stare. Astrid is really not cut out for the reception front-line game. She has a very difficult time getting work out in a timely fashion, which can be a problem when we are dealing with time-sensitive offers. Her telephone manner is wanting, and I always get the impression she'd rather be somewhere else. She definitely doesn't come across as friendly or helpful to staff or clients, and I've had to correct her work on several occasions. Unfortunately, Astrid is Grumpy Jim's niece, and Grumpy Jim is the owner of the company; well I believe his wife's father is the money behind the company, but Jim is the "owner" we know. It's Jim's wife, Margery, who insists Jim keep Astrid employed. Apparently, Astrid has had several "careers" and none of them have worked out. Grumpy Jim's wife is going to ensure this one does.

Grumpy Jim taps me on the shoulder as I am sorting my mail.

"Can I see you for a minute in my office?" Jim looks a bit frazzled. Frazzled is not something Jim ever looks. He looks grumpy, mean, miserable and sometimes beaten — never frazzled.

"Sure." I turn and follow Jim into his office. I notice there is a well-dressed, perky blonde sitting in one of the chairs in front of Jim's desk. She looks twenty-something and model pretty, like she might have just finished a gig as a briefcase girl on *Deal or No Deal*. My immediate thought is, "Yay, someone to replace Astrid!"

"Mel, this is Cecily. Cecily's going to be helping us out for a while," Jim states, looking very uncomfortable.

"Oh. At the front desk giving Astrid a hand?" I ask Grumpy Jim hopefully. The real estate agents all work independently and come and go with clients, so the front desk is really the only place we need help. Help for Astrid would benefit the entire office, in my opinion.

"Not exactly. Cecily is going to be working exclusively with you." Grumpy Jim looks a little bit afraid now and I would be starting to worry but my gut is pointing me down the path toward anger.

"Doing what?" I ask suspiciously.

"Well, it seems some people in the office are having a difficult time, ah… communicating with you, so I've hired Cecily to be your personal translator when you are relating to the office staff." Grumpy Jim physically takes a step back as I take a step forward and drop my purse in the empty chair beside Little Ms. *Deal or No Deal*.

"Excuse me?" I ask in my restrained voice on the verge of raising itself to a crescendo of expletives. My Zen has packed a bag and is on a speeding train out of town.

"It's nothing against you or the fabulous work you are doing here. We just want to ensure everyone in the office is happy." I can tell Grumpy Jim's foot is itching to take another step backwards but he is backed up against his credenza so has nowhere to go.

With my white-knuckled fists on the desk, I manage between clenched teeth, "Communicating? I think you and I are communicating perfectly well right now. In fact, I think you can tell by the look on my face this conversation is going downhill quickly. What the hell is a personal translator anyway? Is that even a real job?"

"If I might intervene," the perky Cecily has risen and taken a step forward, "I'm only here to help. Let's take this conversation, for example. I might say, at this point, Mr. Johnstone, Melanie does not understand what the communicating difficulties are. Could you please explain what you mean?"

The look of horror on my face would be priceless if I were able to see it.

This is not happening. I turn my attention to Cecily and start to turn on my heel with the trail of expletives starting to flow as Grumpy Jim finds his voice. "Some people feel you are a bit abrupt and harsh, Mel, and this seems like a way to smooth things out."

Turning back to Jim, I manage, "You have got to be kidding! By some people, I know you mean Astrid. And there is no way some twit at the front desk, who can't even send a fax, is going to dictate..." I start what is going to be a vicious diatribe with my voice clearly expressing my anger in every well-enunciated syllable when Cecily interrupts and speaks again.

"Mr. Johnstone, Melanie feels perhaps there has been a misunderstanding and would like further clarification about her role in this initiative."

The satisfied smirk on Cecily's face makes me wish I had my copy of *Roots* handy; that would change her expression in short order. I start to smile at this thought as Grumpy Jim starts to speak again. "Mel, I can't help it. Astrid has complained to Margery, and I'm stuck between a rock and a hard place. You're my best agent. I need you. But with Astrid running to Margery every time you upset her, my home life is becoming a disaster. Can't we make this work somehow?" Jim looks defeated and I would feel badly for him if it wasn't for Perky Cecily standing beside me, staring at me, waiting for me to speak.

"Jim, this is too demeaning for words..."

"Mr. Johnstone, Melanie is not completely satisfied with the new arrangement."

Ignoring Cecily's interruption, I continue, "You know I'm working on the biggest commercial deal of my career, and if I quit now Ryan is going to swoop in and take it. So I have to assume you planned this little ambush for today because you know I'd rather kill myself than give this one to Ryan."

"Mr. Johnstone, Melanie feels Ryan is a bit unsavoury and she herself is feeling a bit suicidal." Cecily's smug grin is back, along with my look of shock and horror. Calling Ryan Rysen "unsavoury" is like referring to a cornered poisonous snake that bites you as "misunderstood." Ryan is a cutthroat, wheeler-dealer who would sell his grandmother if he thought he'd make a profit. Okay, maybe not that bad, but he'd definitely sell the wheelchair out from under her geriatric butt. Ryan's shortcomings aside, having this overly enthusiastic twenty-something sugar-coating and incorrectly reverbalizing every word I say is making my skin crawl.

"Mel, this has nothing to do with your deal or Ryan. Margery is just being impossible at home. Can't we just try this for a couple of days? If it isn't working, then we can try something else," Jim pleads.

"Jim, you can't be serious?"

"Mr. Johnstone, Melanie is wondering if you are telling her a joke."

"Arrggh!" I shriek involuntarily after Cecily's translation and throw my hands up to press on my temples.

"Mr. Johnstone, Melanie is frustrated and has a headache."

"I'll headache you." I bring my hands down from my face and start towards Cecily, arms outstretched, fully planning to clasp them around her scrawny neck, as Grumpy Jim rushes around the desk between us and grabs me by the shoulders. "Mel, just for a couple of days and only in the office. Please. It won't be so bad and we can make Astrid and Margery happy, then hopefully we can go back to normal. Come on? What do you say?"

"No. She'll drive me crazy."

"Mr. Johnstone, Melanie has answered in the negative and feels unstable." Unstable, I'll unstable the little twit. I try reaching around Grumpy Jim, who is holding me back so I can't get hold of the game-show accessory.

"Mel! Please?!"

"Jim, could you live with someone trailing you around, manipulating everything you say?"

"Mr. Johnstone, Melanie asks if you would like a personal translator?"

If only my arms were longer, I'd have her emaciated neck in my hands and the satisfaction of squeezing the life out of her.

"Mel, just for a couple of days?"

Defeat. I have to recognize it when it slaps me in the face. I really want to finish the Blackwell deal I'm working on. Really. It's the biggest commercial deal I've ever had on my own. "Fine. But you have no idea how much you owe me!" I turn and start to open the door of Jim's office.

"Mr. Johnstone, Melanie has acquiesced to your request and feels remuneration is still open-ended."

I stop and turn back to Jim, "Jim, tell your overly enthusiastic twit translator if she calls me Melanie one more time I'm going to take off my boot and put a four-inch heel through her temple." I smile, satisfied I have made my point — no one, including close family members and best friends, calls me Melanie — and step out of Jim's office, slamming the door behind me.

8

"Personal translator?" I think to myself as I get back in my car and slam the door for good measure. I stare at the wall in front of me, still shocked at what has just transpired. What the hell? Me? Difficult to get along with? Okay, well, even if that is the case, I hardly think a personal translator is necessary — if it is even a real job? I make a mental note to Google that later and start the car. My original plan this morning — before I got sidetracked by Jim's insane new initiative — was to go over the proposal I had put together yesterday one more time before presenting it to my client. I glance at my watch and realize I have no time to double-check the numbers. I have to hope I did everything correctly yesterday.

I try to forget what had transpired at the office as I drive north towards Mrs. Dershowitz's house on Avenue Road. I was the listing agent for Dudley Dershowitz when he sold his home last year, and now his mother, a lovely lady in her seventies who wears bright red lipstick, matching nail polish, and is heavily jewelled, has asked me to prepare a proposal to sell her house. Mrs. Dershowitz is a widow and she's decided she'd like to have a home with less maintenance and is considering a condo. Her Avenue Road house has been very well maintained and will sell quickly.

When I arrive at Mrs. Dershowitz's house, Dudley is there as well.

"Hello, Mrs. Dershowitz." I shake her hand then turn to Dudley, "Hi, Dudley, how is the new house?" Dudley sold his condo on the Lakeshore just before he got married, and he and his wife bought in the Annex.

"Great! I love the new neighbourhood and I can walk to work. I couldn't be happier."

Mrs. Dershowitz has tea ready in the dining room and we sit around the table where I present my proposal. I have put together a comprehensive binder with four parts: my resumé and biography, current housing market sales trends, including comparable sales in the area, an in-depth description and analysis of Mrs. Dershowitz's home, including utility bills, and, finally, the proposal in which I detail how I will handle the sale of this particular house, including my commission rate.

"So, you and Dudley can look over this proposal and compare it to the other brokers you've met with, and we'll go from there. If you need any more information, just give me a call."

"No. I only met with one other agent. I didn't like him. He seemed slippery. My friend Agnes used him when she sold her house in High Park." Mrs. Dershowitz starts on a tangent, "Agnes has always had a thing for bad boys, you know? You should have met her second husband, Bryan; now, there was a swine. Sneaky as a fox..."

"Okay, Mom," Dudley interrupts. "If you're happy to have Mel sell the house, we should sign the agreement and then let her get on with her day."

"Oh, of course, certainly." Mrs. Dershowitz smiles and pats my hand. "Once I get started on Agnes, I just don't know when to stop."

"I think I'd like to meet Agnes," I laugh. "Is she still entertaining 'bad boys'?"

"Oh, I'm sure she is! She just doesn't tell me about it because she knows I don't approve of such goings-on!" Mrs. Dershowitz takes the pen and we sign the listing agreement.

"Great. If it's all right with you," I glance at Mrs. Dershowitz and then Dudley, "I'd like to do a bit of staging before I host an open house on…" I pause as I find my calendar and glance at it, "two Sundays from now? The staging won't take very long; I'll just pack up some of the knickknacks and family pictures so the potential owners can envision themselves in the space. I may have to rearrange the living-room furniture so the room looks bigger, but, honestly, I think the location is going to sell the house so I'm not going to do much."

"Oh, that's fine, dear. I know you'll do whatever it takes. Dudley said you worked wonders when you sold his condo. You actually made it look bigger than the shoebox it really was!" Mrs. Dershowitz pats my hand again.

We arrange for me to come by a week from Friday to stage the house and determine the open-house times. Despite the horrible start to the day, I smile as I drive back to the office. Of course, as I step back into the office and the personal-translator annoyance skitters up beside me, my smile dissipates and I groan under my breath.

9

"So, she follows you around and reiterates everything you say?" Marc asks with the fascinated look on his face I must have had on mine earlier. Kit, Marc and I are at the Firkin sitting at one of our regular tables. Steve, our favourite server, has just brought us our first round.

"Is personal translator even a proper job?" Kit is as amazed as I am about the made-up job title.

"No. I Googled it as soon as I got back to my office, and it isn't! Personal translators are for people working in countries where they don't speak the language, and they're just called translators. I think Jim or Margery made it up." I'm still seething from the humiliation of the whole experience. "Besides, *I'm* not hard to get along with. Astrid is the problem in the office, not me!"

"Okay... but you did try to physically accost this personal-translator person and told your boss you'd put your boot heel through her temple; those two things could be considered 'difficult to get along with.'" I honestly don't know why we let Marc come around at all. He really is such a "state the obvious" kind of guy. I thought we'd moved beyond discussing the threat part of this morning's meeting.

"Ha ha, Marc. You're a riot. This morning was the exception! I'm usually Mary-Flippin'-Sunshine, and you know it!" I have resorted to sarcasm for my defence because, sadly, I know there may be a grain of truth in what Marc is saying. "Okay. Admittedly, I'm a bit of a control freak. It's still no reason to make up a job, then fill the position with a twenty-something game-show reject who doesn't know the first thing about me. It's completely insane."

"It is a bit odd." Kit comes to my defence. "It seems like a lot of trouble and expense to keep nitwit Astrid happy."

"Tell me about it!" I snort and take a sip of beer.

"What are you going to do?" Marc asks. "If your first meeting is any indication, I can't see you tolerating this translator person for very long."

"I want to close the deals I'm working on, including the new listing agreement I signed today. Then, I guess, I'll have to move on." I try to sound confident, but the realization that I'm going to have to start over again — find a new company to work for, print new signs and new cards, and inform all my clients — seems like a daunting task.

"How long do you think it'll take to wrap up all the deals?" Kit asks sympathetically.

"If everything goes as hoped, the big deal should close and finish up the week of Mike's wedding. The Dershowitz house will sell fast, so it's not a worry. I guess I'll be free in five weeks or so." I explain the timeline I'd worked on this afternoon. "And, who knows, maybe this Cecily person will be long gone before then."

"I hope so, for her sake. Well, for all of our sakes really." Marc laughs and we join him.

"Me too, but who knows? The way everything is going in my life I might be in a padded room by then." I go on to explain to Kit and Marc how I had to order the Sunset Disaster with matching shoes this afternoon and the same helpful saleslady Kit and I met affirmed I would be getting the "fullest" crinoline made by man. She then went on to tell me if it isn't full enough, I should soak it in sugar and water to make it stiffer and fuller. Yeah, like that's going to happen. I can't get the dress through an average-sized doorway without the crinoline, so added girth will not be necessary. Since I know the sugar secret, I think I shall avoid all sugary drinks on the day of the wedding in order to keep the crinoline in check.

"Well, on a completely unrelated note, I got an email from Tia today and she's moving to Toronto," Kit mentions happily after my dress story. Tia is one of Kit's beautiful Barbie dollesque twin sisters. Tia and Taryn are ten years younger than Kit and me, and have just graduated from Queen's University.

"Wow, that's great. Is she going to live in your guest room until she gets established?" I ask Kit.

"Yep. She's already sent out several resumés and is hoping to have a job soon. I think it will be fun to have her here. I know Ben is excited about it." Ben is Tia's boyfriend and the drummer of the band *Kevin*. Ben works as a graphic designer when he's not practising or playing with *Kevin*. Kit and Kevin, the singer for the band, are dating and have been for about five months.

"The band is on the road right now, right?" I ask Kit because I vaguely remember her mentioning it and haven't seen Kevin on her arm lately.

"Yes, they've been gone for almost two weeks. They're back tomorrow for a show here." I can tell Kit is looking forward to seeing Kevin but isn't saying much because Marc is with us. Kit dating someone other than him is still a sore spot for Marc, so we don't dwell on the topic when he's around.

"What's Taryn up to?" I ask to get the subject off Kevin.

"Oh, she's waiting to hear if she's getting an internship in Australia. Tia says she's on pins and needles waiting for the reply," Kit fills us in.

"Good for her. That will be a fantastic trip," Marc comments.

"Absolutely! Tia says Mom is a complete mess and is all worried one of the nests will be halfway around the world. Dad seems to be taking it in stride. Taryn has her passport ready and can't wait. The plan, as I understand it, is to leave right after Mike's wedding and travel for a few months until the internship starts in October. Well, provided she gets one."

"What kind of internship is she looking for?" Marc asks.

"Marine sciences. She took biology at university and wants to specialize in fish. But I think if she doesn't get the marine science placement, she'll take anything they offer. Tia says she's pretty excited about the trip itself, so will accept any internship."

"Australia? Wow, that will be such a great experience.

Good for her." I am really happy for Taryn, and it might be good for the twins to separate for a while. They've been attached at the hip since birth.

"Completely off topic again," Marc starts to say, turning toward me. "Mel, are you taking dance lessons in preparation for your brother's wedding?"

"No, why?" I ask tentatively, not sure what Marc has heard about John's newest hobby.

"Oh, John mentioned something about a dance class and I only caught the end of the conversation. It was something about dancing and being show-worthy in a month? Are you guys going on one of those dance shows or something?"

"Nope, sorry, not me. For the next several weeks, my dancing will be limited to dancing around the office avoiding Cecily. Did John say anything else about it?" I ask Marc, curious if he's heard anything about Ursula "knowing her stuff."

"No, like I said, I just caught the tail end of a conversation the guys were having at lunch."

"Oh, make sure you ask him about it. I think you'll find his answer interesting." I don't want to fill Marc in on the off chance John doesn't want him to know. Although, it seems John has no problem telling the other guys at work. It's becoming painfully obvious any ideas I had about "containing" John's dancing to a limited few lessons are quickly evaporating. John's modern dancing is going to be common knowledge very soon.

10

“So, do you think this Ursula person is the real reason Charlie Brown has embraced the modern-dance thing?” Kit asks after Marc leaves us at the Firkin, and Steve has delivered us each another beer.

“I don’t know. But I do know I didn’t like the way his eyes lit up when he mentioned her name last night.” I had waited until Marc left before filling Kit in on Ursula and my budding suspicions. I don’t think Marc would go running to John with my concerns, but John is his employee and has been his friend longer, so I can’t take any chances. Besides, letting Marc in on Ursula would also be letting him in on the entire dance story, and telling Marc goes against my plan of dance damage control. “I’m starting to wonder what came first, the dance poster he supposedly saw or this Ursula floozy?”

“Well, not that I approve of his flirting with another woman, but it would explain the very sudden dance obsession.” Kit’s brow is furrowed and I can tell she’s thinking the same way I am.

“Whether it explains it or not, and I’m inclined to think it does, I can’t have my boyfriend running around after another woman, especially dressed in a leotard!” The realization that this may indeed be more than just a passing fancy for John is starting to settle in. "I'm not prepared to lose my relationship to some... some... dancing queen!"

"But it's a bit tricky. You aren't even sure there is anything going on, right? You're just suspicious about a couple of things John said last night."

"Yes. But if this Ursula person is the 'draw,' the whole dance thing makes much more sense."

"Well, your gut is generally bang-on, so if you think there's something fishy, there likely is. Which brings us to what are we going to do about it." Kit's statement reassures me she's volunteering to help me get to the bottom of the whole Ursula issue. I suddenly don't feel quite so overwhelmed by my spiralling-out-of-control life.

An hour later, at Kit's condo, we sit huddled in front of her computer. Google is our new best friend and ally. Almost all the information you'd ever require, plus a whole lot you never knew you'd need is immediately accessible at your fingertips. In the first thirteen seconds of our Ursula reconnaissance mission, we have discovered some very unsettling information. Ursula's blog name is Undulating Ursula. Obviously, Kit and I both find this tidbit hard to get our heads around, and we debate whether or not we have the correct Ursula. Her blog goes on to explain she is the owner/operator of the dance studio that has intrigued John, so we must have the correct woman. Apparently, again this is from *her* blog, she is a well-known dancer with a background in exotic dance. By "exotic," I mean seedy nightclubs having adjectives containing *X*s before the word "Club" and where poles and germs are not only mandatory, they are expected.

"So, that's *her*?" Kit incredulously asks the same question whirling around my brain. The photo of Undulating Ursula depicts a woman I can't imagine ever "undulating" or putting a sparkle in my boyfriend's eye. Ursula is very plain-looking, almost mousy. No makeup. Her earrings are average-sized dream catchers with feathers dangling over her shoulders. No hairstyle is discernible under her two-inch-wide floral headband. The blouse she is wearing is also floral, but not in the same design or colours as the headband, and has a scoop neck with a ruffle, not unlike the one adorning the bridesmaid's dress I've recently been forced to order. The front of her blouse is littered with slogan buttons, the largest reads, "I'm a dancer, what's it tutu you?" The photo is a head shot so I can't see her body, but her face is quite chubby, like she might be past the peak of her pole-dancing days. At a glance she appears to be much older than us — possibly mid- to late forties.

I am shocked. Did I imagine John's infatuation with this Ursula person? Maybe I am more stressed out by the Sunset Disaster with matching orange satin shoes than I thought. Surely the woman in this photo is not the object of my boyfriend's adoration. Maybe he does just respect her dancing vision? Okay. I have to shake my head at that thought. John wouldn't know a dance vision if it clogged across his forehead. I was just getting used to the idea of John being infatuated with another woman — which would explain the dance fascination. If he's not after Ursula, is he really a dancer?

"That can't be her. Or it's one really bad picture," I think aloud. No. I refuse to accept I imagined the gleam in John's eye. He spoke her name in such a way that I know there's more to this than just dancing. Men just don't pick up dance in their thirties, do they?

"It must be her. It's her blog and she didn't mention anyone else. Why would she put a picture of someone else on her blog?" Kit seems confused as well but, logically, she has a point.

"I don't know? Why would any woman be caught dead in that outfit, let alone have it captured forever in a photo?" I respond. Kit looks up at me and gives me a frown.

"Okay, that was a bit harsh. But seriously?" I say.

Again Kit frowns at me, but she also has no good explanation for the ensemble on the screen before us, so she says nothing to reprimand me.

"But you're so beautiful! Why would Charlie Brown be lusting after *this*?" Kit stretches her hand, palm up, towards Ursula's picture. "Who wears dream-catcher earrings? I ask you, *who*?" Kit is starting to get worked up on my behalf.

"Undulating Ursula, obviously." I start to pace behind Kit but keep glancing back to the photo on the screen. Kit is rereading the latest blog entry, pointing out bad grammar and typos by stabbing her finger at the screen. I can see Kit's lips moving and her animated hands, but I can't comprehend what she is saying.

This must be shock — real shock, not just surprise. I've never been in proper shock. Oh, I've been shocked, like when Kit received three engagement rings at the same time last year, but it didn't put me *into* shock. In fact, it made me laugh after I registered the conundrum she was in. But this, this is what shock is, I'm sure of it. I reach up and feel my forehead. Am I clammy? Is clammy a symptom of shock? What is the treatment for shock? Elevate feet? Drink tea? No, it's starve a fever, feed a cold. Good Lord! Why am I thinking about fevers and colds? My boyfriend is at a dance class with this… this… dream-catcher woman *right now*! Okay. I must calm down. There is something just not right about all this. Sure, John is acting strangely, but he can't be having an affair. Not with this Ursula, at any rate. I must have imagined all the glassy-eyed, silver-tongued business.

The John I know doesn't go chasing after other women. He called me seventy-six times over the course of a long weekend when he and his buddies went to Vegas. He came home and told me all about the other guys going after girls, but he didn't. He said he missed me too much to even contemplate being with another woman. Of course, Vegas was six months ago — six months before his sudden fascination with modern dance. I have no idea what to think.

"Kit," I start to talk, but Kit is pontificating on Ursula's incorrect use of one of the words there. I think Ursula used "their" instead of "they're," and Kit is not listening to me. "*Kit*!" I use my stern voice, like I had to at the Bedazzled Beauty Bridal Boutique.

"Oh, sorry. Her grammar is atrocious!"

"Whatever. I think I must be wrong about this one. Things just aren't making sense. What are you doing tomorrow night?"

"Kevin and the band are playing, but they don't go on until nine-thirty or so. Why?"

"John *dances* after work. I think we should go by the dance studio and see exactly what's going on. We can check up on John and this... this... *person*, then get to Kevin's show with time to spare."

"Absolutely. I'm so in! I can't wait to see the dancing queen up close and personal." Kit stands up and we high-five.

11

"You didn't exactly dress properly for this occasion." Kit points out my wardrobe faux pas a little too late. Kit came to my house after work, in part to meet for our dance studio mission but mostly to see the lawn ornament display next door before it is dissembled. Kit had to admit the lawn ornament display is something to behold, and she took a turn picking up the squirrel groom who had fallen over, yet again. I have had to pick him up every day since he arrived; he isn't very steady on his feet for a lawn ornament.

"Well, I didn't expect to be creeping around alleyways, did I?" I hiss back at Kit in a low whisper. "I thought I'd be looking in the front window at street level." The peeking-in-the-front-window plan had to be revised immediately upon arrival at the dance studio because the windows are frosted. Seeing the frosted windows made the hair on the back of my neck stand on end. Why would Ursula need frosted windows unless she is up to no good? What does she need privacy for? Man stealing? My imagination running wild is what sent me jogging down the alley beside the dance studio, determined to find a way to see inside.

"You're no lightweight, and the straight skirt isn't helping.

Any chance you could hike it up?" Kit grunts from a crouching level. She has my left, four-inch-heel-black-Prada-clad foot in her hands and is trying to hoist me up onto a large, metal garbage bin behind the dance studio. The garbage bin is placed directly under the only unfrosted window and, thankfully, is the kind with a lid, so, once I do manage to get on top of it, I will be able to stand normally and not have to balance precariously on an edge. Sadly, progress is slow and is being hindered by my skirt. The idea of hiking up the skirt is a good one, but I'm not completely sure I want to expose my butt, which I recall from dressing this morning is only partially covered by a white lace thong and sheer nylons, in the alley behind Ursula's dance studio. Kit's arms give out and we crumple to the ground. I hate to admit it, but I have broken a sweat and am quietly cursing the above-average temperature.

"Fine. The skirt goes up. I have to get on top of this bin." I announce as I shimmy my skirt up around my hips, giving my legs a bit of room to bend to get me on top of the bin.

"Okay, one more try. But it's probably all I've got left. You're going to have to throw a leg up, Mel." Kit bends over and grabs my foot again. "Ready? One, two, three..." Kit grunts and heaves me up. I try to lift my right leg but still don't have much range due to the skirt. I feel Kit's arms shaking, and I know she can't hold me much longer. In one last attempt, I throw my right leg up higher and my skirt slides upwards, bunching up around my waist. This allows my leg to swing up on top of the garbage bin and, with some of my weight off Kit, she is able to push my left leg up. I scamper to my feet on top of the garbage bin and immediately shimmy my skirt down. I hear the applause and hooting before I see movement out of the corner of my eye. I turn to see the house behind the alley has a balcony on the upper storey, which provides a perfect view into the alley behind Ursula's dance studio. The balcony is currently housing four beer-holding college-aged boys who have been following my struggle in climbing atop the garbage bin. Judging by the applause and hooting, I think I can safely assume they also had a pretty good look at my mostly naked butt in the air.

"Well, this is a bit embarrassing!" Kit laughs from ground level waving at the boys, "Helloooo, boys!"

"Don't encourage them!" I hiss.

"Oh, take a bow! Besides, they're clapping for me being able to get your butt up there. Now, how am I going to get up?" Kit's attention turns from the boys back to me on the garbage bin.

"I don't know if you can. I don't think I can lift you." I bend down and grab Kit's hands and try to pull her up while she scales the side of the garbage bin with her feet. Unfortunately, my lifelong avoidance of anything physical has left me with very little upper-body strength. I'm sure a preschool-aged child would be more help to Kit than I am at this point. My arms start to shake and I manage, "I… think… I… have… to… let… go" between clenched teeth, when suddenly Kit is as light as a feather and flies up beside me onto the garbage bin. Startled by Kit's sudden flight, it takes me a second to comprehend there are four muscled young men standing beside the bin looking up at us. I determine that one of them must have hoisted Kit up beside me. In another second, I am able to register that the four boys in front of me must be the same four from the balcony. They must have run around the corner at breakneck speed to be standing here now. Looking down at them, I realize one of them is actually quite attractive. He's about six feet tall, blond-brown hair that looks a bit too long but in a good way, sideburns, scruffy facial hair — I'd guess about three days' worth — smiling blue eyes with the straightest, whitest teeth in the biggest smile I've ever seen. He reminds me of someone but I can't think of who.

"You ladies aren't exactly dressed for breaking and entering, so what's the attraction?" the familiar one asks as he places both his hands on the top of the bin and swings himself up with the ease of an Olympic pommel-horse gymnast. Before I can answer, the other three boys swing up onto the garbage bin with the agility of monkeys and stand in very close proximity, looking at Kit and me. Waiting for us to do something.

"Ahhh..." I have no idea what to say. Telling complete strangers I'm spying on my boyfriend because I suspect he's having an affair with his brazen hussy dance teacher is something I can't bring myself to do. I turn to Kit but she seems equally puzzled.

We are let off the hook when one of the monkey boys, the redhead, turns to look in the window of the dance-studio and declares, "Holy crap! You guys have got to see this!" Saying nothing, the rest of us clamber to the window and stand shoulder to shoulder to see inside. Five of the six jaws on the faces pressed up against the dance studio window — which, I might add, has not seen a cleaning in a good long time — drop at the exact same moment.

12

"Mother of Pearl, I thought they were naked!" I hear Kit say, then start to giggle.

"So did I," the redheaded college boy says, and joins her laughter. I am torn between relief and complete embarrassment for John. At first glance, through the dirt-encrusted window, the six people dancing in a row did, indeed, appear to be naked. But upon closer inspection, they are wearing full-length flesh-coloured leotards. Whew. Well, sort of. Full flesh-coloured leotards are only slightly better than naked.

The class itself is made up of six people: John, one other man, and four women. From this vantage point, John looks to be the oldest and the rest of the class is in their late teens or early twenties. The teacher is definitely the same Ursula Kit and I found during our computer search. She is much shorter than anyone else in the class and is much plumper than I'd imagined. She is not dressed in a leotard but is wearing a gauzy floral skirt, reaching almost to her ankles, a mismatched floral blouse pulled tight across her ample bosom, and a paisley pashmina stole, which complements neither the skirt nor the blouse. Her mousy, stringy brown hair is in two short, messy braids, one of which is caught up in her dangling beaded earring. Ursula is leading the dancers in a nondescript jumping and leaping frenzy. None of the dancers seem aware of the others, as they trip over and bump into each other often. There seems to be no rhyme or reason to their movements. Despite the disorganization of it all, John is smiling and seems to be enjoying himself.

I turn away from the window after I don't know how long. I can't watch any more of what is going on inside, so I creep to the edge of the garbage bin. I want to jump off and run far from the scene I've just witnessed. I glance down to the ground and know I can't jump in my boots without breaking a heel or worse.

I turn my head back to the voyeurs, to see if Kit has had her fill. All the heads are looking in the window except the attractive-straight-teeth guy who is looking at me instead of the dancers. We make eye contact and he smiles at me. I suddenly feel even more uncomfortable and awkward. I feel my face start to redden and my desire to get off the garbage bin and miles away from here increases exponentially. I look back at the ground and am just about to throw caution to the wind, when I feel strong hands grab me around the waist. I look back and see it's the guy who was just smiling at me.

"Just a second, I'll help you down," he offers. "Here, Paul, grab this." He then lifts me, so I have to assume I'm the aforementioned "this," and hands me down to one of the dark-haired boys who has jumped down from the bin in one fluid motion. Apparently, God gave him an abundance of good looks but was quite sparing with the manners and charm. My awkwardness is quickly replaced with aversion; he wasn't looking at *me*, he was more likely staring at my ass.

Back on the ground, I watch as the boys help Kit dismount and soon we are all standing in the alley.

"Okay, that was worth the effort. I can see why you ladies were so anxious to see that!" the redhead laughs.

"Yes. Excellent entertainment," another one comments.

"Do you ladies know someone in the class?" the unmannered one asks.

"Ah…" I start but can't bring myself to explain any of this to a complete stranger, so extend my hand toward him, "Thanks for your help. I'm Mel and this is my friend, Kit."

"Chad, but my friends all call me Chazz. That's Chazz, with two *Zs*," he says as he shakes my hand. He keeps holding it as he introduces his friends. The redhead is Adam and the dark-haired boys are Paul and Dominic.

"But call me Dom," says Dominic. "No one uses my full name."

"I can relate," I say to Dom as I try unsuccessfully to shake myself free from Chazz's grip.

"Spying on a dance class? Doesn't seem like something two sophisticated ladies like you would be doing, if not for a pretty good reason. Are you sure you don't want to share?" Chazz with two *Zs* smirks like the Cheshire cat and squeezes my hand, which he's still gripping. He is far too cocky and sure of himself for a college kid.

"Ah, no…" I stammer. "Wrong building, actually." I lie ineffectively and start to search the ground for my purse, unable to make eye contact with Mr. Sure-of-Himself.

"So, what are you ladies up to for the rest of the evening?" Chazz asks, finally letting go of my hand.

"Oh, we have plans. Sorry," Kit chimes as she swoops down to get my purse off the ground. Kit grabs my hand and pulls me down the alleyway towards the street. "Thanks, guys," she yells back to the boys standing beside the garbage bin.

"Yeah, thanks!" I manage as we get to the street, around the building, and out of sight.

Sitting in a pub, not our usual Firkin, ten minutes later, Kit and I are able to talk about what we've just witnessed.

"That was disturbing." Kit verbalizes what I'm thinking.

"More than disturbing."

"Ursula is not what I expected, even after the blog preparation. She's just so…"

"So not John's type." I finish Kit's sentence.

"Well, that, but she doesn't strike me as much of a dancer either. She doesn't have the body type of a dancer. And from what I saw, she wasn't 'all that' or anything particularly special."

"I don't get it. The leotard, the disjointed leaping around, this Ursula woman. How can all that flailing around be something John is enjoying?"

"The weird thing is he did look happy. Well, it was difficult to tell through the dirty window, but he was smiling." Kit shares my wonder.

"Do you think he's attracted to that... that pashmina-scarf-wearing woman?" I finally blurt out the question most pressing on my mind — even more pressing than how John could wiggle himself into the flesh-coloured leotard.

"I don't know. I doubt it, but I don't know."

"Neither do I. I truly hope not, but my gut is still telling me something is up," I admit honestly.

"Well, we'll have to keep our eyes and ears open then. I'll pick Marc's brain the next time I see him at work. He might hear something on the job, and I'm sure he'll tell me if I ask. Don't worry. We'll figure this whole thing out," Kit tries to reassure me.

"I don't know if I want to figure it out. What if we figure it out and he is having an affair? What then?"

"Then we'll cross that bridge *if* we get there." Kit puts her hand on top of mine. "On the bright side, it was nice to meet four young men who were helpful. At least we know chivalry is not completely dead." Kit tries to change the subject to keep my mind off my boyfriend woes.

"Chivalry may not be dead, but cocky and rude are both alive and well. I think I caught the good-looking one with the ridiculous name staring at my ass!"

Kit laughs. "Yeah, but only because he was marvelling at how I managed to get it up onto the bin in the first place!"

"Remind me why I take you along on these little excursions?"

"Because only a *best* friend would hoist your butt up on a

garbage bin to spy on your boyfriend in his dance class. I dare you to find anyone else who would rise to the occasion!" Kit laughs again.

"Well, you haven't met my new friend Cecily yet. She'd follow me anywhere. She followed me into the washroom today at work."

"Really? The washroom? Who'd she think you'd be chatting up in there?"

"I have no idea what she was thinking. I sent her back to my office, then ducked out altogether before she caught on I was giving her the slip." I smile at my own success.

"You truly have your hands full right now." Kit states the obvious.

"I know. Between Cecily and the hippy dance instructor, I think I'm losing my mind."

"Oh, speaking of losing your mind, what is the plan for our parents when they come to deliver Tia next weekend? According to my mother, your parents are coming along for the delivery." Kit reminds me of the impending parental visit, which I had miraculously been able to forget with all the other goings-on.

Mother of Pearl. I should have jumped off the garbage bin. With any luck at all, I might have killed myself.

13

An hour later, parental visits and dancing-boyfriend woes aside for the time being, Kit and I strike off to see Kevin and the band *Kevin*. Kit is excited to see Kevin; I can tell by the jump in her step. Kevin is a wonderful guy who has hair that always looks like it needs to be combed even after it just has been. Unfortunately, being social after what I've just witnessed at the dance studio is the last thing I want to do. Hopefully the band will start playing loud music immediately upon our arrival so I don't have to make small talk. I would back out of going altogether, but I know Kit would never forgive me. Standing alone at a show, even when your boyfriend is in the band, seems a bit sad and pathetic so I have to go with Kit for support.

The club is already crowded when we arrive; seems the band's popularity is picking up. I look around from the door and spot a short, frumpy woman in an ill-fitting floral blouse with stringy brown hair. Oh, my God. The woman I just saw giving bad dance instruction to my boyfriend is *here*. I grab Kit's arm to get her attention and point out the woman I believe is Ursula, but Ursula starts to turn toward us and I panic. Instead of gently tugging on Kit's sleeve I shriek, squeeze her arm and drag her down to crouch behind the half-wall just inside the door.

"OUCH! Mel, what the *hell?*" Kit is not impressed with my less than stealthy move.

"It's *her*!" I hiss at Kit. I should apologize for hurting her, or at least let go of her, but I know if I do, she will stand up and draw attention to us.

"Her, who? What are you talking about? You've completely lost your mind!" Kit struggles to get free from my grip and upright, but I hold firm.

"HER! The badly dressed dance-instructor her!" I roll my eyes. Kit is being completely oblivious.

"Ursula?" Kit tries to pop her head up above the half-wall to see.

"*Don't look!*" I whisper harshly between clenched teeth and strengthen my grip on Kit's arm to keep her crouched down beside me.

"Mel, this is ridiculous! If it is her, she doesn't know us or that we were spying on her, besides how can it be her? Could they possibly have finished the dance lesson and got here before us?" Kit is making sense, but I'm sceptical and apparently slightly paranoid.

"Are you okay, now?" Kit continues. "Let's stand up and walk over to Kevin and see if it actually is Ursula. If it is, Charlie Brown should be here too, right?" Kit stands up slowly. I pop up beside her, still gripping her arm.

Prying my fingers from around her arm, Kit whispers, "Okay, who do you think is the person in question?" I look around the room and spot the woman I believe is the dance instructor we saw earlier.

"Her! That's her!" I start to point at the woman but realize pointing will draw attention to us, so I grab Kit's arm again. Unfortunately, my adrenaline must be pumping and I grab onto Kit with more vigour than intended.

"Ouch! What is wrong with you?" Kit hisses as she pries my fingers from her arm again. "Mel, I think you've lost your mind. That woman is about a foot-and-a-half taller than Ursula and has short, dark hair. There is nothing even remotely similar about the two except possibly the blouse faux pas but, let's face it, a lot of women wear floral blouses. Knock it off!"

Thankfully, before I can put together any words to defend my sanity — or lack thereof — Kevin walks up and hugs Kit. Honestly, I don't think I can defend my sanity at this point. I am behaving erratically. Mel Melrose, woman-in-control-of-it-all, is no more. I have completely lost control of my boyfriend, my job, and, now it appears, my eyesight and social skills. Honestly, what is wrong with me? I don't climb up on garbage bins. I don't crouch behind half-walls or shriek in public. I have to get my life back in order. I need something; perhaps a new vitamin regime. Yes, I'll just increase my vitamin D intake and I'll be back on track. I glance at my watch to see what time it is. I'm sure I can hit the late-hour drugstore on my way home. There. Erratic behaviour eradicated.

"Hey, Mel, where's John?" Kevin asks innocently.

"Oh, something came up. He might get here later though."

I try to answer casually and confidently, but suspect by the nervous laughter following my statement that my insane behaviour is not eradicated, as previously stated.

I'm standing with Kit and, when the band starts, the music is loud so I am able to get lost in my thoughts without Kit noticing I'm not really paying attention. John's new-found dance interest is the only thing I can think about. The idea of John pursuing a hobby so completely uncharacteristic is mind-boggling enough, but in reality his "interest" is completely interfering with my plans and long-range goals on the eve of my brother's wedding. I don't suppose I ever gave much thought to marriage before Mike announced his engagement — I guess I thought I had all the time in the world — but as Mike and Sam's wedding looms ever closer, I have to admit I have been thinking more about weddings, the white dress, and the idea of a partner for life. I do want to get married. I do want the wedding and the happily-ever-after, and I assumed John would be the person standing beside me at the altar and the partner standing beside me in life. If this dance nonsense keeps up, and John isn't the person with me, I'll have to start all over again. I don't want to start all over. I'm on the path to happily-ever-after, damn it, and I will not be side-tracked. I'm not going to take this Undulating Ursula thing lying down.

By the time the band has finished their first set, I'm in a slightly better state of mind. I'll figure this thing out, get my man back, and have the future I envision.

14

I keep a keen eye on John over the next week, but he continues his infatuation with dance and Ursula. I don't understand the attraction, but am now certain there is one. He does get glassy-eyed when he speaks of her — and I'm sure I'm not imagining it. Kit, Kevin, John and I meet at the Firkin for our usual Friday after-work beer. Even Kit, who has tried to remain open-minded, had to admit John does indeed seem very distracted and not his usual self. John, who usually gets very excited by baked goods, didn't even break a smile when Kit presented him with a box of Mrs. Jennings' mangled white chocolate macadamia nut cookies. John talks only about dance and Ursula now. He hasn't mentioned work or any other topic for days, including our neighbour's lawn ornaments, which, incidentially are growing in number. He has shown no interest in anything I tell him about what's going on at my office. When I told him about Cecily, he said, "Isn't that the name of a seed?" And I had to respond with "You're thinking of *sesame* seeds; Cecily is a woman's name." But by then it was fairly apparent he wasn't interested in what I was saying, so I stopped talking all together.

To further fuel my flames of suspicion, John hasn't made

one move towards me sexually since his first dance class. Okay, it's only been two weeks and no action for two weeks might be normal for some couples. But John is generally very amorous, so the lack of intimacy is noticeable and disturbing. I haven't filled Kit in on the lack of action, as I don't really want to admit it out loud. Once I tell Kit, I will have to deal with the fact that my boyfriend may indeed be having an affair. I can't bring myself to face the "affair" word; infatuation is difficult enough to wrap my head around.

The idea of my relationship careening toward a cliff makes my stomach knot and my palms sweat. I don't want to deal with a major change in my life. I like things just the way they are. I like my happy life — career, house, boyfriend, thinking about the next step toward marriage — I'm well on my way, right? If this turns out to be what I can't bring myself to say out loud, then what? So, I try not to think about it. I turn my attention to other things and sweep the Undulating Ursula thing under the carpet, pretending everything is fine.

I spent the Friday I had promised with Mrs. Dershowitz helping her stage her house. She is a remarkable lady. I spent the full day with her, when I could have been finished what I wanted to complete in a few hours. While we packed up knick-knacks and family photos — which Mrs. Dershowitz is more than happy to do as she has to pack for the move anyway — she told me about her life. Mrs. Dershowitz had survived her first husband, Dudley's father, whom she loved dearly before he succumbed to a cardiac arrest while on the golf course twenty years ago, as well as a scandalous second marriage.

"Well, Dudley never warmed to him — rightly so, he could be a bit of a prick!" Mrs. Dershowitz swears calmly.

"Mrs. Dershowitz!" I say, looking up from the bubble wrap in my hand and laughing nervously.

"Well, he was. And I've always said, 'If the shoe fits, strap it on and go for a stroll!'" Mrs. Dershowitz raises her eyebrow at me. "Anyway, back then, I was one of those girls who needed a man. I believed I couldn't make it on my own and I needed a man on my arm to be complete. Well, Mr. Abramsky soon made me realize I was dead wrong on that score." Mrs. Dershowitz wraps a framed picture of Dudley in his teens wearing a tennis outfit and holding a racquet.

"What did he do?" I know I probably shouldn't pry, but Mrs. Dershowitz has piqued my curiosity.

"Oh, I'm sure you've met the type. He takes you out for dinner to make up for his last indiscretion with the girl who books the courts at the club but lingers in the coat room a little too long with the coat-check girl. He was a randy one, that's for sure." Mrs. Dershowitz shakes her head. "I overlooked his shortcomings for as long as I could. I guess I hoped he would tire of his antics. It didn't work that way. He made *me* feel old and pathetic. I finally snapped when I arrived home one day to find him canoodling on the couch with Dudley's babysitter. What a scandal! She was young enough to be his daughter, not yet eighteen." Mrs. Dershowitz grows pale before my eyes.

After a short pause she continues. "Well, I'm not proud of what I did that day, but something *had* to be done. In hindsight, I probably shouldn't have gone after him with the cast-iron frying pan. I think the stainless-steel one would have gotten my point across just as well, but too late for regret now. I went after him with the frying pan. The babysitter was shrieking and jumping up and down. I caught a glimpse of Dudley laughing at the top of the stairs, but still I couldn't stop myself. I chased him around the house like I was caught by the devil, using words I'd only ever heard on late-night television. After five years of turning a blind eye, all I wanted to do was blacken his!" Mrs. Dershowitz stops and looks down at her hands.

"Wow! So, what happened to Mr. Abramsky? You didn't..." I can't bring myself to finish my question. I'm not sure I can represent a woman who killed her husband with a cast-iron frying pan.

"Oh, no," Mrs. Dershowitz laughs. "I broke his arm in three places and he had a nice goose egg on his head, but he survived."

"Well, that's good... right?" Working for an *attempted* murderess seems infinitely more acceptable.

"I suppose. He didn't learn a thing, though. He was flashing his smile and trying to make tracks with all the nurses at the hospital. Needless to say, after the frying-pan incident, I found the gumption to divorce him and I haven't looked to a man to complete me since." Mrs. Dershowitz smiles with calm satisfaction.

"Well, you don't seem to be lacking in any way, so maybe you're on to something," I laugh.

"Oh, you girls nowadays are much more self-sufficient than we were. When I was a girl, you got married — there was no question about it. Girls now are far more confident and self-reliant."

"It may look that way, Mrs. Dershowitz, but you'd be surprised what we *independent* women put up with." I look down at my hands and laugh nervously.

The office is a completely different work experience. The combination of Cecily — whom Kit and I now refer to as Sesame after I told Kit about John's ridiculous question — Astrid, and a healthy sprinkling of Grumpy Jim has been almost unbearable. Sesame's constant word manipulation is making me insane, but the satisfied grin on Astrid's face every time Sesame reiterates something I say is excruciating. Standing at Astrid's desk with Sesame invading my personal space, staring at me and waiting for me to utter a word, turns my stomach, but I must address Astrid's latest transgression.

"Mr. Blackwell didn't get the new zoning-permit application? You know? The one holding up the deal? Have you faxed it yet?" I ask Astrid, having to bite my tongue as she turns to Sesame instead of answering me.

"Mel is questioning your ability to send a fax," Sesame says to Astrid, and I find myself grinning a little. I didn't say what Sesame had translated, but this time her interpretation is inadvertently correct. Astrid has proven her inabilities in the faxing arena time and time again. So, in this case, I don't even try to interject.

"Tell Mel I did fax the application, and perhaps the problem is on Mr. Blackwell's end," Astrid says to Sesame, completely ignoring me.

"Astrid assures me she sent the fax." Sesame turns to me.

"Mother of Pearl. She's not even talking to you. She's supposed to be talking to me," I huff at Sesame, then turn to Astrid, "Could I please have the fax confirmation sheet?"

"Mel doesn't believe you and would like to see the confirmation sheet," Sesame states to Astrid. Astrid is looking at Sesame and still completely ignoring me. This is not an effective way to run an organization. This conversation is taking twice as long as it needs to, and my blood is starting to boil.

"Oh, for heaven's sake! Astrid, just hand me the confirmation sheet already!" I'm exasperated at this point.

"Tell Mel her attitude is not going to improve the situation," Astrid says to Sesame as I step around Astrid's desk to the basket of fax confirmations. I used to do Astrid's job before I became a selling agent, so I know my way around her workstation.

"You can't be back here!" Astrid shrieks directly at me as she tries to grab the fax confirmation basket out of my hands. I take the pile of paper, leaving her holding just the basket.

"You don't talk to me, remember. You'll have to go through Sesame..." I shake my head, "Sorry, Cecily, for this one." I turn my back to them both and riffle through the pile of confirmations, jostling to avoid Astrid's grabbing hands.

"Aha!" I find the Blackwell confirmation and hold it above my head. I'm taller than both Astrid and Sesame without my boots on; there's not a chance either of them can reach the paper in my hand when I'm standing in my lime green, four-inch heels. I toss the rest of the pile in the general direction of the basket they came from and turn, out of reach again, to read the confirmation sheet: Number of pages sent: 0 Status: N/G.

"I'm no rocket scientist, Astrid, but when the number of pages reads zero, doesn't zero mean the fax did not go through? And doesn't N/G stand for 'no good'?" I ask Astrid. This time the smug look is on my face.

"Well, I know I faxed it!" Astrid huffs directly at me. Again, ignoring Sesame.

"Ses, do you have anything to interject here?" I chirp at Sesame who has been standing dumbfounded while Astrid and I had our little tussle.

"Ahh... Astrid stands firm on her belief the fax went through as you requested." Sesame sounds slightly more timid than earlier.

"You two deserve each other," I state flatly. I remove the Blackwell file from the *To Be Filed* pile on Astrid's desk and march toward my office, ignoring the scamper of Sesame's feet behind me. When I get to my office, I close the door behind me without looking and hear a small "ouch" from the other side. I have to snicker because it isn't the first time I've clipped Sesame-Cecily with a door. You'd think she'd learn.

I'm scanning the last page of the Blackwell zoning application when my direct phone line rings. I can tell it's Kit calling from her office.

"Sesame Avoidance Headquarters, Mel speaking," I quip cheerfully into the receiver.

"They're *here*." Kit's voice sounds stressed and she doesn't acknowledge my cheery greeting.

"Who's here?" I have no idea what Kit is talking about, which is strange since we are generally on the same sentence of the same page. I can only assume aliens have taken over the offices of Sebring Development, where Kit works.

"Them! Our parents! Both sets. Yours and mine! They came early. They're here *already*! They're at my condo helping Tia unpack, then they are going to your house. They'll be there when you get home from work."

"Oh, crap, I'd completely forgotten they were coming today." My elevated satisfaction of clipping Sesame lessens. "No worries. I'm just going to email a permit application Astrid screwed up this morning, then I can get away for the day. Our parents will actually be a relief after my day at the office," I laugh into the phone.

"What? Have you lost your mind?" Kit is genuinely surprised.

"Probably, but hardly unexpected after the week I've had here with my annoying personal translator."

"You sound in a very good mood for someone dealing with Sesame — almost too good," Kit says suspiciously.

"Yeah, I just got her with the door again. It made my otherwise incredibly stressful day!" I laugh.

"Well, I'm glad you're able to laugh about it. I'll leave work early and head straight to your house. We shall be a united front." Kit has great intentions, but in reality I'm stuck with the parents all weekend since I have two guest rooms and Kit's guest room is now Tia's room. Kit and Tia will get to escape and go back to Kit's condo later tonight. I'm still going to be "entertaining" twenty-four/seven for the next two days. I much preferred the parental visits when Kit and I shared a house. At least then, it was us against them. The current situation is not as easy. My mother has never warmed to John, and John loves to get her riled, so I spend most of the parental visits trying to keep the peace. I smile as I wonder how my mother will take the news about John being a modern dancer. It ought to be an interesting conversation.

15

I arrive home with no additional cars in sight. Whew, at least I'll be able to tidy the breakfast mess in the kitchen before the parent-tornado arrives. Don't get me wrong I love my parents and Mr. and Mrs. Jennings very much, but I do find all four of them in my kitchen very hectic and a little bit nerve-wracking. As I walk toward the house, I notice the groom squirrel is again lying down. I stop and try to prop him up with my toe, my hands full of my purse, laptop and four bottles of wine. But he falls down again, so I abandon my attempt and continue to the house, smiling, and thinking, "Your squirrel wife must wonder why she married you." I'm putting my armful of belongings and wine bottles on the kitchen counter when the phone rings. Caller ID tells me it's John, calling on his cell.

"Hey, you. Tell me you're on your way home to help me entertain the parents," I laugh into the phone. I haven't talked to John all day. We haven't really spoken very much in the past few weeks actually and, honestly, I miss him.

"That's why I'm calling. I won't be home until late," John says matter-of-factly, even though he knows I am counting on him and he promised faithfully this morning over Count Chocula cereal that he would be here.

"Why? Are you working?" I ask suspiciously because John rarely works late on a Friday.

"Yeah, Marc has an emergency job and none of the other guys can do it. I'm all he has and I can't let him down." John's reply sounds rehearsed. The hairs on the back of my neck stand on end. I think he's lying to me.

"Oh. How long do you think you'll be? Should we hold dinner for you?" I ask, trying to sound casual and confident. I'm not feeling either of those things. I strongly suspect my boyfriend is blatantly lying to me. What if I'm wrong? Maybe the stress of the past few weeks and the nonsense at work with Astrid and Sesame is affecting my generally stellar judgment. If my parents and the Jennings were not currently en route to my house, I might give Mr. Not-A-Very-Good-Liar a piece of my already frayed mind. But there's no sense starting a fight over a suspicion.

"No, you guys go ahead. I shouldn't be too late, but no point in everyone starving."

"Okay, well, don't work too hard and I guess I'll see you later." I hang up the phone but I know something is amiss. The phone barely has time to disconnect before I'm dialling Kit at her office.

"Glad I caught you!" I exclaim into the receiver upon hearing Kit's voice.

"Just. I am on my way out the door. What's up? Are the parents getting to you already?" Kit laughs.

"No. They're not here yet, but I can handle them. I need you to do me a huge favour. Can you call Marc and discreetly find out if they are working overtime tonight?"

"Sure. So, Charlie Brown's working instead of hanging with us in our time of need?"

"He claims he is, but I don't believe him. Of course, I hope I'm just being paranoid."

"I'll check. Call you right back." Kit hangs up to call Marc, and I reach for a bottle of wine. I've just finished pouring a glass when the phone rings. It's Kit.

"And?" I ask without the normal telephone niceties.

"Well, the good news is you aren't paranoid," Kit says tentatively.

"I knew it. I could tell by his voice. Maybe all the guys from work are going out for drinks. No, that's insane. John would tell me if he was going out with the guys for a beer." I'm thinking out loud at this point.

"Marc didn't know any plans of going out. He said as far as he knows Charlie Brown is on his way home to you." Kit fills me in on the remainder of the conversation.

"You didn't tell Marc about my suspicion, did you?" I don't want Marc getting hold of John before I do.

"No. I let on I was trying to call him and warn him about the parents. I said his cellphone wasn't on and wondered if he was working."

"Okay. Good." I'm trying to formulate a thought, any thought, when I hear a commotion in the driveway.

"Darling! Oh, it's absolutely fabulous!"

"Perfect! Peggy, could anything be more precious?" I hear my mother and Mrs. Jennings declaring at the same time.

"I have to go, Kit. I believe they've arrived. See you soon." I hang up the phone, John's whereabouts momentarily pushed aside in my slightly overwhelmed mind.

I step out the door into the driveway, where I see Mrs. Jennings and my mother picking their way through the myriad of lawn ornaments on Cam and Pam's lawn. They are acknowledging the "darling-ness" of each and every one. Mr. Jennings, my dad and Tia are standing beside Dad's van with their mouths hanging open. I have to smile because I imagine I looked much like the dumbstruck dads when I first glimpsed the display.

"Dad!" I rush to where he is standing with Mr. Jennings and Tia to give him a hug. "How was the trip?"

"Mel," Dad hugs me back, but I can tell his heart isn't in it because he's staring at the ornaments. "What's on your neighbour's lawn? Why would anyone do that to such a lovely lawn?" My dad voices his disapproval of the display as I hug Mr. Jennings and Tia. My dad is a "lawn man." He believes a weed-free, well-maintained, golf-green lawn speaks volumes about the homeowner. His lawn is immaculate. Mr. Jennings, by virtue of being Dad's neighbour back home in North Bay, has had to embrace being a "lawn man" as well because my dad wouldn't stand for a neighbour not embracing his lawn perfection. To their credit, Dad and Mr. Jennings do have the best lawns in our old neighbourhood, and possibly the whole of northern Ontario. I do believe they are lawn snobs, if there is such a thing.

"Weed-whacking nightmare is what that is, Bob!" Mr. Jennings pipes up from behind the van, where he is unloading overnight bags. "They're going to have weeds popping up all around those things. Horrible waste of a yard."Tia laughs as our fathers continue to voice their disapproval as our mothers go farther afield on the neighbour's yard.

"*Mother*!" I hiss at my mom. "You can't be traipsing all over other people's yards. Get back here!"

"Mel, darling! Isn't this marvellous?" My mother stands up from beside one of the dwarfs — Grumpy, I think — and waves, totally ignoring my reprimand. "Peggy! You have to see this one!" Mrs. Jennings is carefully inspecting the life-sized Prince Charming birdfeeder and is not easily distracted.

"Good Lord. They think they're in Disney World!" I turn to Tia. "Tee, there's an open bottle of wine in the fridge. Can you go pour a couple of glasses and bring them here? Surely we can lure them back to my property with booze!" Tia laughs as she jogs up the walk toward the house. I can tell she's as embarrassed by our mothers as I am.

Mr. Jennings closes the back door of the van and he and Dad appear, carrying the overnight bags. "Tsk, tsk. Such a shame!" one of them mutters.

I take a bag from my dad and lead the way into the kitchen,

passing Tia carrying two glasses of wine to induce our mothers' return.

"Tee, if the wine doesn't work, tell them I'm going to make gravy." I yell to Tia, who is standing on the lot line, waving wineglasses in the air. My attempting gravy should get them scampering into the house to show me the proper way.

16

"They want refills," Kit announces as she steps in the door an hour later, "and why are we letting them talk to the neighbours?"

"What? Cam and Pam are home?" My head jerks up from the salad I'm making.

"Yep, well, Pam is anyway. Our mothers have her cornered." Kit rolls her eyes.

"Well, don't take them any more wine. They'll get thirsty eventually, and it will get dark at some point. They'll have to come in."

"Where have you been? You said you were en route when I spoke to you," I ask Kit quietly.

"I took a detour to do a little investigating before I got here," Kit starts to explain.

"And?" I put down the knife I'd been using to chop vegetables. I know intuitively she means she was checking up on John. I want to know if she saw him. A part of me hopes she didn't. Either way, it's best I don't have a sharp object in my hand.

Before Kit can answer me, our mothers come clambering

in the door. Mrs. Jennings plunks a Tupperware container full of cookies the size of my underwear drawer on the counter and exclaims, "Mel, we have such great plans for your yard. You're neighbour is delightful!"

"Yes, Peggy, you're right. She's a real sweetheart. Mel, you never mentioned how adorable Pammy is."

"Leave my yard alone. And I've only met the woman a few times, Mother. Why are you calling her Pammy? Surely no self-respecting woman wants to be called Pammy." I try to bring my mother back to reality, but for years I've suspected it's a losing battle.

"Mother of Pearl! What is around your neck?" My mother befriending my neighbour is momentarily put on the back burner when I see my mother's newest idea of fashion. It appears to be an old telephone spiral cord — I believe this particular shade is avocado — from which a child's plastic cellphone dangles.

My mother looks down at her chest and fondly pets the plastic cellphone. "Don't be so narrow-minded, Mel. Obviously, it's a symbol of the melding of old and new technology. How come you aren't more like Pammy? She's been collecting those lawn ornaments since she was a little girl. You never collect anything." My mother accepts the glass of wine Kit has poured for her.

"Too true, Betty. If our girls collected something, it would make Christmas and other occasion buying so much easier." Mrs. Jennings gives Kit an accusatory glare.

"Leave me out of this," Kit interjects, "and Mel does collect things; she collects boots and purses."

"Wait a second! Back up!" I raise my voice above the others to stop the conversation — my fascination with my mother's neckwear forgotten. "You mean the lawn ornaments aren't a joke? This Pam person didn't just turn thirty or pass the bar exam?"

"Of course not, dear. Don't be silly. It takes years to amass such an exquisite collection." My mother says "exquisite collection" like she just exited the Rembrandt Room at the Louvre. She rolls her eyes at me for good measure.

"So all of those… those… *things* are here to stay?" I've picked up the knife and am using it to point in the general direction of "Pammy's" yard.

"Of course, dear! And you should put some thought into sprucing up your own yard." Mrs. Jennings interjects and Kit grabs the knife from my hand before I can hurl it in our mothers' general direction.

Ignoring the tussle Kit and I are having over the knife, my mother continues, "Speaking of collecting things, where is John?"

"He's working, mother. He's productively working to bring electricity to people all over the city. He's practically the Emperor of Electricity, so give him a break." I release the knife to Kit and grab my glass to take a sip of wine. I'm a little sensitive to my mother's seemingly innocent question, given the fact John may currently be up to heaven-only-knows-what, and her low opinion of him may prove to be close to his true character. Kit, realizing the precariousness of my current mental state, takes over the salad-chopping duties altogether. She has no intention of returning the knife to me anytime soon.

"Oh, don't be ridiculous, Mel. There is no such thing as an Emperor of Electricity. How you girls carry on here in The City. Tia, I hope they don't rub off on you. So far, you're one of the good ones," my mother gives Tia a stern look. Tia just smiles politely while quietly sipping her wine. Tia is obviously self-medicating with some very good drugs. She's been back in North Bay, living with one of these lunatics and next door to the other, for a month and has just endured a four-hour car excursion with them. There's no way she's naturally this calm.

"Kathryn, what have you done to yourself? You have a rip in your skirt, a run in your hose, and you're covered in dirt. You look like a hobo. Is 'derelict' a new city fashion trend? I hope you plan on dressing a little nicer for Samantha's bridal shower." Mrs. Jennings has walked around the island to where Kit is chopping and is assessing her backside. I hadn't noticed Kit's dishevelled appearance until Mrs. Jennings pointed it out.

"Bridal shower?!" Kit and I shriek at the same time. We both ignore the comments about Kit's disarray. This is the first word either Kit or I have heard about a bridal shower so we are immediately very suspicious. Our mothers have been regaling us with every little wedding detail for over a year. Springing a bridal shower on us can only mean there's something about it we'd object to, ergo their last-minute announcement.

"Mother! You called me long distance to tell me Samantha had purchased new lingerie for the honeymoon! What the hell are you up to?" I am practically shaking. This can only be bad news.

"Language, Mel! And, of course, there's going to be a bridal shower. Weddings mean bridal showers!" my mother huffs, ignoring my question. She pours more wine into her glass and walks to where Mrs. Jennings and Kit are standing to pour the remainder of the bottle into Mrs. Jenning's glass, then continues, "Yes, Kathryn, you do look a bit dishevelled. Have you been scampering around in a garbage bin?"

"Where and when is this so-called bridal shower, and what horrific thing are we expected to do?" Kit completely ignores the garbage-bin comment, stands up taller, squints her eyes and tightens her grip on the knife.

"Tomorrow, dear. Samantha's mother is planning a little Southern-style tea and she'd like you girls to help serve. And it's here of course. You know, Samantha is from here. It's going to be just around the corner in the United Church basement. Do you know the one I mean?" Mrs. Jennings has no idea what "just around the corner" can mean in Toronto.

"Tomorrow? How come this is the first time we're hearing about this?" I hear Kit asking suspiciously, while at the same time I'm saying, "Serve? What do you mean 'serve'?"

"Oh, Mel! Serve. You know. As in bring little sandwiches and tea to tables. Like a waiter. Surely you know the concept!" My mother huffs again. I can tell she's hiding something.

"Oh, I know the concept, Mother. But what's the catch? You would have mentioned a bridal shower long before now if there wasn't a catch. What is it?" I set my wineglass down and lean on the island, glaring at my mother.

"Mel, you're being completely paranoid. There's no catch. Honestly, you girls! Now, let's see how the men are doing with dinner, shall we, Peggy?" My mom takes Mrs. Jenning's arm and they stroll past the island and out to the deck. Kit and I make eye contact. My brain is whirling. John is up to no good, the lawn ornaments are here to stay, and now the springing on us of a "Southern-style tea" bridal shower, whatever that means. I look up at Tia, who is still smiling and sipping wine.

"How can she be so calm?" I ask Kit.

"I have no idea, but I want whatever she's on," Kit huffs, then looks at Tia. "Tee..." she says, but Tia just stares at her. "TIA!" Kit raises her voice.

"Oh, I'm sorry. What?" Tia says as she reaches into her pocket with her wine-free hand. Kit walks to where Tia is standing and pushes her hair back from her ear to reveal the earbud of her iPod and the wire going down the back of her shirt.

"Have you heard a word of what's been going on?" Kit asks incredulously.

"Of course not!" Tia laughs and rolls her eyes. "I've been living with Mom for a month! I would be insane if I actually listened to anything she or Mrs. Melrose says!"

17

We manage to get through dinner with civil conversation, but the mothers remain mostly closed-lipped about what is expected of us at the bridal shower tomorrow. What we have figured out is that Mike and Samantha are in town for the weekend from Georgia and staying with Sam's parents; they arrived this afternoon. Taryn is driving here from North Bay early tomorrow morning and will be staying at the condo with Kit and Tia until Sunday. The location of the "Southern-style" bridal shower actually is just around the corner at the United Church across the street from the beer store and Ursula's dance studio. Convenient, and yet I'd really like to avoid the whole area since I have no idea what might be going on at the dance studio while I'm holed up in a church basement watching Samantha open gifts I may or may not recognize as having a use.

"So, aren't we supposed to give gifts at something like this? Surely you should have mentioned it so we could have been prepared," I confront our mothers over blueberry pie and coffee. I had picked up a blueberry pie because it's my dad's favourite.

"Exactly, we can't show up empty-handed. Do we have to go shopping tomorrow morning?" Kit asks.

"Oh, no, we took care of everything for you. We know how busy you girls are," Mrs. Jennings offers, but it just increases our suspicions. The hairs on the back of my neck are standing up again.

"What?" Kit and I exclaim together.

"What do you mean? What did you do?" I ask the mothers, trying to keep the anger out of my voice.

"Oh, just some wonderful little things. Nothing extravagant."

"Mother, are they wonderful little things we would *want* to give to Samantha as gifts?" Kit asks.

"Oh, absolutely. They're lovely. Besides, you won't have time to do any shopping. We have to get to the church early to help set up," my mother states matter-of-factly.

"What time is 'early,' Mother?" I ask, since my mother's internal time clock is much different than mine.

"We should be there by 11 a.m., I think." My mother downs the last bit of coffee from her cup and stands to start clearing the dinner dishes off the table, an indication that there will be no more information forthcoming on this topic.

After cleaning up the kitchen, Kit and Tia say their goodbyes. I walk them out to Kit's car and out of earshot of the parents. We've left the moms watching a rerun of *Supernanny*. Our fathers both doze on the couch while our mothers tell the parents on television how they would handle the situation and lament, "If only we were there, those children would be well behaved."

At the car, I am finally able to ask Kit what happened after work and what she knows about John's whereabouts.

"So, I assume from your skirt you went by the dance studio, and..." I am torn as to what I want the answer to be. I don't really want to know if he is with Ursula. But if he isn't there, where is he?

"And he was there." Kit looks down at the car keys in her hand.

"And? Don't hold back now, Kit. I need to know. I've been going crazy all through dinner — and not just because our mothers are nuts."

Kit looks at Tia instead of me. "And it was a private lesson; just John and Ursula." Tia says nothing. I'm not sure if Kit has filled her in on the particulars up to now, but I know she will bring Tia up to speed on the car ride back to the condo. I feel sick to my stomach but press forward, "Was it a private lesson or a *private lesson*?"

"They were just dancing, but..."

"But what?

"But they looked very intimate. I can't say anything for sure; maybe it was just part of whatever type of dance they were doing. It isn't like anything I've ever seen before, so I can't say. It could be some touchy-feely tango thing. I did not see any hard evidence of anything going on. They were *just* dancing." Kit tries to sugarcoat the delivery, but I can tell she thinks it's more than a dance.

"I don't get it. He's had no trouble telling me he's dancing up until today, so why the deception?" I bemoan my lot and register this situation is going to get exponentially more embarrassing before it gets better. Kit and Tia remain quiet, not knowing what to say. I hug Kit and Tia and return to *Supernanny* and my houseful of parents. This weekend can't end soon enough.

18

I wake up to John shaking my shoulder and whispering, "Mel, you'd better get up." I heard him come in around midnight last night; I glanced up at the clock when he crawled into bed beside me. I didn't say anything as I didn't know what to say in light of his untruth about working when he was at the dance studio.

I grab John's hand. "What are you doing up so early? Come back to bed. It feels like I haven't seen you in weeks." I do miss him. I can't believe we're falling apart. With all the dance nonsense, wedding hoopla and work stress, John and I haven't had a normal conversation in ages. We're living in the same house but hardly ever see each other, and I feel like he's slipping out of my hands. I don't know how to hold on. At this point, I don't care if he's done something stupid with Ursula, I just want my life back the way it was before. I want him to give me a hug and tell me I'll survive this parent weekend and the upcoming wedding. Hell, I'll even take the living-room raceway back if it means I get to spend time with my boyfriend; I just want to laugh and be happy again.

"Mel, you'd better come and see what your mom is up to. She's not listening to me — well, you know she doesn't like me — but you'd better see for yourself." John sounds afraid; John never sounds afraid. I jump out of bed and grab my robe. If John is afraid it must be bad.

"Where is she?" I shout back to John over my shoulder while fast-walking and groping for the tie of my robe.

"Outside. Front yard," I hear as I bolt out the door and run barefoot to the front yard.

"Stop!" I shriek when I see what has John so shaken up. "Mother! Put down the Statue of Liberty and step away!"

"Mel, darling! Did you know Home Depot is open twenty-four hours per day?" My mother ignores my directions completely, continuing to carry the four-foot-tall, plastic, mint green Statue of Liberty across the yard. Behind her, Mrs. Jennings is wrestling with what appears to be a garden gnome band. I'm sure I can make out an accordion and a banjo.

"Mother. Stop!" I demand again. "I will not have you defiling my yard! Dad?!" I shriek for my father as a last resort. There is no way Mr. Immaculate Lawn Man is going to allow my mother to litter my yard with godawful statues and gnomes.

"Isn't she perfect!" My mother exclaims as she centres the Statue of Liberty directly in front of the living-room picture window. "She's strong and independent, just like you, Mel. Perfect!" Mrs. Jennings is arranging the gnome band at Liberty's feet. There are four separate pieces, and they are indeed a band. An accordion player, a banjo player, one has a violin — in light of the ensemble, I suppose fiddle would be more accurate. The crowning glory is the harmonica-playing gnome who appears to be quite cross-eyed.

"Your dad's not here." John has caught up to me and is standing behind me. "I just got back from dropping him and Mr. Jennings off downtown. Apparently, they're going to the Hockey Hall of Fame while you girls are at a shower or something?"

"Yes, there's a bridal shower this afternoon, which my mother just sprang on me last night," I say to John, then turn back to my mother. "Mother. Enough. Get those things off of my lawn!"

"Mel, it's almost ten o'clock. I can't believe how long you've slept. Kit and the twins will be here in a few minutes and we have to go. You'd better get out of your pyjamas." She completely ignores me. I have lost control. I know I'll have to fight the ornament battle later, probably after they leave to return to North Bay, so I turn around to go back into the house to find a cup of coffee. As I'm pouring, Kit's car pulls into the driveway. I see Kit rush to where the mothers are and say, "Mother! What are you doing to Mel's yard?!" Tia and Taryn put their hands in their respective pockets, where I know they are turning on their iPods.

Twenty-five minutes later, I'm dressed, I've threatened John's life if he even thinks about not showing for dinner tonight, and am standing in the kitchen with my second cup of coffee. John has disappeared, no doubt to avoid any further lawn antics. Kit comes into the kitchen carrying the harmonica-playing gnome.

"Sorry. This was the only one I could wrestle from them." She places the scary, cross-eyed gnome on the island and starts to pour herself a cup of coffee. The twins come bounding into the kitchen, and Taryn rushes to me to give me a hug. I haven't seen her in ages.

"I got it! I got the internship in Australia!" Taryn announces and hugs me harder than usual before she and Tia start jumping up and down in unison.

"Wow! That's great news! The best news I've heard in a really long time, actually. Congratulations!" I am genuinely thrilled for Taryn.

"I just found out late last night. I'm so happy! I have to make firm flight and travel arrangements, but I'm hoping to leave right after Mike and Sam's wedding!" Taryn is talking fast and can't seem to keep from smiling.

Tia continues on her behalf, still jumping. "The internship doesn't start until October, so she's going to travel up Australia's east coast before she starts."

"I'm so happy for you!" It is nice to have some good news for a change.

"I asked Tia and Taryn what they know about the bridal shower and, apparently mom didn't tell them anything either." Kit starts to explain what she's deduced from the twins in the absence of the mothers.

"Nope, not a word until I was on my way to work yesterday morning, and then it was just that I *had* to get to Toronto before ten o'clock this morning. They haven't told us anything." Taryn explains why she's just arriving now instead of yesterday. We all look at each other with trepidation. If the mothers haven't told any of us what's going on, we're in for a long afternoon.

19

We have to drive to the church, because although it is just "around the corner," it is a Toronto corner and a fairly long walk, especially carrying gifts and serving trays and whatever else the mothers have loaded in the van. Kit, the twins, and I are all wearing respectable skirts and blouses, and our mothers have said nothing disparaging. Both Kit and I notice the lack of comment. Our mothers thrive on letting us know we are completely incapable of dressing ourselves. In fact, I had put on my lime green boots in anticipation of a comment. We brush off the mothers' acceptance of our ensembles as a by-product of their bridal-shower-brain overload.

Upon arrival at the church, Kit and I unload the van of serving trays, dessert squares and gaily wrapped presents. The twins are ushered inside to help set up tables and chairs. When Kit and I bring in our final armfuls from the van we are able to assess the situation. Samantha's mother, Mrs. Bennington-Hall, is a fiery redhead like Samantha, but is a little more tightly wound than Sam. She's whirling around the room pointing and directing the helpers, all of whom are women about my age so I assume at least some of them are the other wedding attendants. The table and chairs are set up and the twins and other helpers are draping the tables with white tablecloths and placing centrepieces, which are medium-sized topiary trees that have been spray-painted orange and have small, incandescent Christmas tree ornaments adorning them. I'm sure Mrs. Bennington-Hall was trying to match the Sunset Desire dresses, but the result is disturbing. We leave Mrs. Bennington-Hall to her tables and find the kitchen, where our mothers are arranging sandwiches and desserts on trays.

"Why does this room smell like mint?" Kit asks innocently, placing the last box of dessert squares on the counter.

"Garnish, dear, for the mint juleps. What else would you serve at a Southern tea?" Mrs. Jennings answers.

"Mint juleps? Aren't they straight alcohol? Like shooters?" Kit's eyes pop open wider.

"Don't be silly, dear. Of course, they aren't. No one serves shooters at a bridal shower!" Mrs. Jennings replies, accentuating with another eye roll.

I smile. To the best of my knowledge, mint juleps *are* mostly bourbon, and shooters at a bridal shower might be just what the occasion requires. The idea of an orange-topiary-treed church basement full of drunken women on a Saturday afternoon is far more appealing than the same church basement full of sober women playing shower games. Sadly, logic would dictate that Mrs. Bennington-Hall must have concocted some version of mock mint julep for the occasion. As much as the idea of a drunken bridal shower appeals to Kit and me, it surely isn't something Mrs. Bennington-Hall would knowingly organize.

Forty minutes later, Kit is placing the last sandwiches on serving trays and I'm muddling mint leaves when Mrs. Bennington-Hall rushes into the kitchen, panting, "Good heavens! Look at the time! Girls, you aren't even dressed yet!"

Kit and I both stop what we're doing and assess our fronts. We are both dressed. What is she taking about? Not only are we dressed, we both managed to do so without any interference from our mothers. I look up and give Mrs. Bennington-Hall my puzzled look in the politest way possible. She's obviously overstressed or the orange spray-paint fumes from the topiaries have muddled her mind in the same fashion I've muddled the mint leaves.

"Well, obviously you're dressed, but not for serving! Come along!" Mrs. Bennington-Hall grabs Kit and me each by an arm and ushers us towards the Sunday School room. I glance back at my mother, but she and Mrs. Jennings are nervously looking down at a serving tray of dessert squares, pretending not to see us being dragged from the kitchen.

Kit and I are pushed through the door of the Sunday School room where Tia and Taryn stand looking miserable.

"What the hell?!" Kit and I ask in unison trying to back up. But Mrs. Bennington-Hall is behind us pushing us into the room. The twins both look afraid and on the verge of tears. Tia is dressed in a long, blue, floor-length gown. The skirt is huge, complete with crinoline and a hoop. Her hair is tied up in a bun encircled by a matching blue headband and she's wearing elbow-length light blue gloves. Taryn's dress is also floor-length, the skirt is yellow and the tight bodice is a darker shade of blue than Tia's dress. The short sleeves are puffy blue with teardrop cut-outs so you can see the red fabric beneath. The dress has a white, ten-inch-wide collar, starched so severely it sticks straight up to frame the back of Taryn's head, not unlike the cone you see on a dog after a visit to the vet. Taryn's skirt isn't nearly as full as Tia's, having only a crinoline, no hoop. Taryn's long, blonde hair has been tucked into what appears to be a rubber wig of raven hair, complete with a red rubber bow on top. The twins are dressed like Snow White and Cinderella — Cinderella after she becomes a princess, not when she's scooping fireplace ashes.

"Perfect! Twins, you look lovely!" Mrs. Bennington-Hall, who can't distinguish which twin is which assesses them with satisfaction and reaches for two more gowns from a coat rack on wheels.

"Well, you have dark hair, Kathryn, so yellow is better for you." Mrs. Bennington-Hall hands Kit a massive, rustling, yellow gown. I am handed a gown of equal size that is predominantly Pepto-Bismol Pink in colour — I say "predominantly" because it's polka-dotted.

"And, Mel, you're fair-skinned, so this should work for you. Hurry, girls, the guests will be arriving any minute." Mrs. Bennington-Hall starts to leave the Sunday School room but then turns around. "Oh, dear. Mel, I almost forgot..." she says as she rummages in a large bag on the floor near the door. "Here it is," she announces, handing me a bonnet. It is also pink and has a very wide brim.

"And the final touch..." Mrs. Bennington-Hall then hands me what appears to be a staff like a shepherd might carry, only it's white-and-pink-striped, not unlike a candy cane. Kit will tell me later that the look on my face is priceless — and not in a good way.

"Of course, you won't be able to carry the staff when you're serving." Mrs. Bennington-Hall points at the staff, now in my hand, and then flies out of the room on the same whirlwind she's been riding since we arrived.

I stand, holding the pink gown, replete with massive crinoline and hoops, in one hand and my bonnet and staff in the other. I turn to Kit, who is dumbstruck, then to the twins. I see their sad little faces and I don't know whether to laugh or cry.

"Apparently, she was going for Southern belle when she rented them, but there was a mix up," Taryn explains from under the rubber raven wig.

"When the saleslady at the rental store heard 'Southern Belle,' she assumed Mrs. Bennington-Hall meant Belle from *Beauty and the Beast*, so that's who Kit is." Tia carries on with Taryn's explanation, pointing at the yellow gown in Kit's hand.

"Well, who the hell am I supposed to be?" I hold up the bonnet and staff.

"Little Bo Peep, I think," Taryn says and plops down onto one of the Sunday School's tiny, child-sized chairs.

20

"Not *one* word, Mother!" I hiss at my mother, who is just about to compliment me on the pink polka-dotted monstrosity I'm wearing, as Kit and I step out of the Sunday School room. "We will discuss your part in this when we get home!" I would love to let my mother have it but I can't due to guests in close proximity.

"Mel, dear, where is your bonnet?" Mrs. Bennington-Hall breezes up behind Kit and me but continues without waiting for my reply, which is probably a good thing. I have a few choice things I'd like to say about both the dress and the bonnet. I'm choosing to block the whole striped staff from my mind altogether. The bonnet is not on my head for two reasons, the first being my unbreakable rule of never wearing previously enjoyed headgear. Second, because the darned thing is ridiculously small and wouldn't fit on my head anyway.

"The twins are seating guests. Your mothers are helping with the gift table. So, if you girls would be so kind as to start serving beverages..." Mrs. Bennington-Hall continues and pushes our reluctant bodies toward the beverage table before rushing off to greet one of the guests. The beverage choices are coffee, tea and pitchers of pre-made punch meant to resemble mint juleps — in keeping with the Southern theme. The weather outside is quite warm, above normal temperatures for the end of May, and the church basement is heating up quickly, so the cool punch with its mint leaf garnish is a big seller. No one seems to want coffee or tea.

By the time Samantha arrives to yells of "Surprise," everyone in the room has had at least one glass of punch. Some of the early arrivals are onto their second or third glass. Kit and I are dripping in sweat — the dresses we are being forced to wear are definitely not conducive to staying cool. I wonder how ladies of the South and princesses do it. Looking over at Taryn in her rubber wig I see sweat running down her face from under it.

"Mother of Pearl, I'm hot!" Kit exclaims quietly to me as Samantha is being seated in the guest of honour's chair — a plastic chair the same as the rest in the room, only this one is overly decorated with orange balloons and streamers, framed by two very large, orange spray-painted topiaries.

"Punch?" I whisper in my most sarcastic tone as I hand Kit a glass and pick one up for myself. I don't normally sweat, but the combination of dress, crinoline and the sheer embarrassment of the ensemble — even without the bonnet — has me sporting a healthy glow and wondering if my deodorant is going to last the duration of this humiliating event.

"Here's to this soon being over!" Kit whispers, and we touch our plastic punch glasses together before downing the contents in one swallow. I register the look of horror on Kit's face and see her hands start to flap in front of her face before I register that my throat is on fire. I can feel the beverage burning every millimetre of my esophagus as it makes its way to my stomach, which is involuntarily clenched in anticipation of the impact the beverage is going to make upon arrival. I hear a high-pitched squeal I can't describe coming out of my mouth as I expel air in an attempt to make the burning stop. Kit seems unable to speak but grabs my arm and drags me around the corner into the kitchen, away from the other guests. We rush to the sink. Kit throws on the cold-water tap and drinks directly from it. Kit then steps aside so I can drink — which I do despite the thought of germs and years of my mother telling me it isn't appropriate.

"What the hell is in that stuff?" I finally manage to straighten up but still hold onto the sink for support.

"I don't know. Is it the mint that's burning my throat? I didn't know mint could be so offensive!" Kit exclaims, barely above a whisper. I notice her eyes are watering.

"What are you girls doing hiding in here?" Mrs. Bennington-Hall rounds the corner into the kitchen. "Samantha is going to start opening her gifts. You'll miss it."

"Mrs. Bennington-Hall, what's in the punch?" I ask point blank in a very hoarse whisper because I haven't regained my normal speaking voice yet.

"Oh, I'm not completely sure. Mr. Bennington-Hall found a recipe on the Internet. I believe he mixed sugar, water, mint leaves and... oh... some bourbon, maybe? It had to sit in the cold cellar for a month. It was his pet project. All I know is it's very refreshing on such a warm day!" Mrs. Bennington-Hall flits out of the kitchen and back to the main room as Kit and I make eye contact. Kit's eyes are as wide as mine feel. What have we done? We've just served fifteen possibly sixteen litres of only slightly watered-down bourbon to sixty unsuspecting, thirsty women.

"It's okay, right? Most of them are sipping. No one is downing it like we did!" Kit sounds hopeful, yet the situation still remains. We must find a way to rectify it. Most of these women are probably driving and haven't realized they are drinking a mighty potent punch. If you can call Mr. Bennington-Hall's concoction "punch"!

"We're going to have to water it down." I start to rummage through the cupboards in the church kitchen but quickly realize there is nothing suitable.

"Water it down? Pour it down the drain is more like it!" Kit exclaims as she searches the cupboards on the far side of the room, "Nothing over here."

I start fast thinking out loud. "Okay. There's a grocery store down the street, we can run there to get juice and soda, *anything* to water it down or, better yet, replace it."

Kit and I start to make our way to the Sunday School room, where our purses are stowed with our real clothes. We'll quickly change, run down the street and be back in a flash to stop the flow of alcohol to the unsuspecting guests. As we are trying to — quietly, without rustling our enormous dresses — make our way across the back of the main room, we hear, "Woo hoo!! That's not going to stay on long! Get a little nooky-nooky!" We both stop dead in our tracks. The voice predicting "nooky-nooky" is coming from Samantha's grandmother, Mrs. Bennington-Hall, Sr., a quiet, demure lady — probably in her late seventies — who wears pillbox hats and blushes at television commercials for women's razors because they show too much leg. Grandma Bennington-Hall is currently standing beside Samantha, holding up a risqué, red-tasselled, push-up bra and dancing in a circle. Samantha looks mortified and downs her glass of punch with the cringe only straight bourbon can produce.

"No time to change!" I grab Kit's arm and we run to retrieve our purses. Any ideas of a stealth mission dissolved with the phrase "nooky-nooky." As we flee the church basement, I glance back over my shoulder and see Grandma Bennington-Hall has put the bra on over her dress and is twirling the matching thong on her finger, while doing a clumsy version of the can-can. I can only hope she's wearing support hose.

21

The grocery store down the street from the now-drunken bridal shower is one of the more environmentally friendly sort, encouraging shoppers to bring their reusable carry-out bags in order to cut down on the number of plastic bags being thrown into the landfills. Normally, I embrace the idea, and the environment in general, but today is not one of those days. When I ask the cashier for eight bags — you have to purchase bags if you have not had the foresight to bring your own — she glares at me like I've just clubbed a baby seal and laid its bloody remains on her conveyor belt.

"Give me a break!" I huff at her. "Do we look like we planned this little shopping excursion?" I point at Kit in her yellow floor-length gown, standing at the end of the conveyor waiting to bag the juice and soda. Two minutes later, ignoring the stares and comments of fellow shoppers, Kit and I are running down the street as fast as our feet will carry us in our dress-up gowns, each laden down with four bags of heavy liquids. Running past Ursula's dance studio, I register a pang of sadness and want to stop to regroup and have Kit tell me everything is going to be okay. I glance over my shoulder to ensure Kit is okay — her hoop skirt got caught in the automatic door of the grocery store, so she is a few paces behind me. I slow down so she can catch up. Kit catches up to me in front of the beer store, where we prepare to jaywalk across the street to the church. I'm looking down the street for a break in the traffic when I hear, "You ladies really are slaves to fashion. What the hell are you wearing?" and I recognize the overconfident voice of Chazz with two *Z*s, before I turn around.

"Don't ask," I hear Kit reply.

"Here, give me those before you hurt yourselves," Chazz says as he takes two bags from each of us. As much as I want to argue, it feels really great to be two bags lighter. Adam is standing beside Chazz holding a case of beer he's obviously just purchased, and is appraising our attire with a confused look on his face.

"Oh, we're only going across the street. No worries." I try to get back the bags Chazz took.

"No. You *need* help," Chazz laughs, not giving back the bags, "unless your knight in shining armour is just around the corner? Parking his horse, perhaps?"

Based on Grandma Bennington-Hall's dance moves before we left the church basement, there is no time to waste in an argument over chivalry with sarcastic Chazz.

"Aren't you the funny one! Well, come on then," Kit says, starting to squeeze her enormous dress between two parked cars only to get stuck so I have to push her through.

The noise emanating from the women in the church basement is much louder than when we left. The quiet oohs and aahs for each wonderful gift Samantha opens have turned into rambunctious hoots and hollers, although not necessarily aimed at the gifts. Chazz and Adam duck into the kitchen after us. Adam puts the case of beer down on the floor, then peeks around the corner at the guests.

"There's a little old lady wearing a red bra outside her dress trying to get up on a table. That can't be safe!" Adam announces as I toss a can opener at Chazz. "Here," I say. "Can you please open the pineapple juice?"

Kit has already rinsed one of the empty 18-litre buckets the "punch" came in and has started to pour cranberry juice and soda water into it. I rush to the beverage table to retrieve the pitchers of bourbon, all of which are empty. Several pitchers are missing and I notice they are scattered around the room, also empty. I catch Tia's eye and motion for her to gather up the remaining pitchers.

"This is the wildest shower ever! Did someone spike the punch or something?" Tia asks as she and Taryn set eight empty pitchers on the counter in the kitchen.

"Who are the boys?" Taryn directs her question at me, ignoring the fact that Chazz and Adam are standing beside her.

"Well, Snow White, I'm not one of the dwarfs," Adam, who stands well over six feet tall, laughs. "So, I guess that makes me your Prince Charming!"

"Good one!" Chazz interjects his two cents' worth, and they laugh amongst themselves. Taryn just rolls her eyes at them.

"Mr. Bennington-Hall made the punch and, to the best of my knowledge, you can't spike straight alcohol. Well, I don't think you can. Why would you? Here..." I say and hand Tia two pitchers now full of juice and soda, no alcohol whatsoever. "Can you start pouring these, please? Start with Sam's grandmother, she needs it the most."

Kit and Taryn both grab two full pitchers and follow Tia into the main room.

"We can't go out there, Bo Peep, so you go with them," Chazz says to me as he starts to open another can of pineapple juice. "We'll make another bucket."

I'm in no position to argue but shoot him a glare for the "Bo Peep" comment and pick up two pitchers of the non-alcoholic punch and follow the princesses.

Kit slides up beside me and whispers, "Mother of Pearl!" I follow Kit's eyes to where our mothers are standing at the gift table with Samantha's mother, who appears to be their new best friend. They are laughing, snorting, and leaning on each other in such a way it is obvious they cannot stand independently. Our mothers have definitely imbibed the punch. Samantha herself is looking a bit bleary-eyed, but is still quite happily opening gifts, flanked by four of the members of the wedding party. Two of the wedding-party girls are holding pitchers still containing the potent punch, and I see one of them drink directly from the pitcher. I make a mental note to collect car keys from them at the end of this fiasco.

On my third trip from the kitchen, I'm pouring non-alcoholic punch at a table near where Samantha is opening gifts when I hear her say, "Kit. Mel. You shouldn't have! And I mean that. I wish you hadn't, actually." Oh, no. I forgot about the mystery gift the mothers had arranged on our behalf. I slowly turn around and see Samantha holding up an array of pink. In one hand, she holds a necklace — no doubt created by my mother especially for the occasion — which consists of a lime green, "flower power daisy" the size of a tea saucer hanging from a string of bright pink marble-sized beads. In the other hand, she holds what might be the scariest thing I've ever seen. It's a toilet-paper cozy, obviously new but made from a 1973 pattern book, crocheted with pink variegated wool, complete with a roll of toilet paper and a Barbie doll standing in the roll. Barbie's hair has been dyed red, in an obvious attempt to make her look like Samantha, and is wearing what I suspect Mrs. Jennings had hoped would look like a pink sunhat but more closely resembles a sombrero.

By the time I have registered the horror of the gifts and blushed with embarrassment accordingly, Kit is standing beside me, staring with the same shock I'm feeling.

"If they don't die of alcohol poisoning, I'm going to kill them!" I whisper under my breath, so only Kit can hear, and shoot our giggling mothers a glare for good measure

22

Three hours later, Kit and I have escaped our sweaty, dress-up gowns and are walking back toward my house. We had called our fathers and Mr. Bennington-Hall to come and help with the clean-up of the church basement and their respective giddy wives.

"Well, this puts a whole new light on bridal showers, doesn't it Mel?" My dad sees the humour in my mother's state of drunkenness.

"Yeah, I can pretty much do anything after this and look good in comparison. Right, Mom?" I ask as I help my mother, who ignores me because she is singing "Joy to the World" as she crawls into the van. "Thanks, Dad. I'll see you at home."

"Call if you need anything else, Mel." My dad waves as he pulls away from the church with my mother and Mr. and Mrs. Jennings.

Mike shows up to drive Samantha and the gifts back to her parents' house. I have no idea how they plan to get the gifts, including the tacky ones Kit and I are responsible for, back to Georgia. Kit enlists Kevin and Ben, who arrive at the church in record time, to call cabs and ferry some of the more inebriated guests who are well over the legal limit. Kevin is assigned the unhappy task of taking the four drinking-from-the-pitchers wedding-party girls home, and Margot — pronounced Mar-got as in "I *got* hit in the head with a football" — vomits out the window all over the side of his car. As Kevin reiterates the vomiting Margot story, I try to correct him, stating her name must be Margot (pronounced Mar-GO) but he says no, and Sam backs him up — she pronounces her name Mar-GOT. For some reason, it strikes me as particularly funny, probably because I don't have a past-tense verb in my given name.

Chazz and Adam were great sports about the whole thing and stuck around even after the new punch is made and distributed. I had even felt like I might be warming up to Chazz until he ruined it by stating, "Little Bo Beep? I had you pegged as more…Wonder Woman or Catwoman. Less sheep, more cleavage."

A couple of times during the clean-up, we had to get the twins back on task as they were spending more time chatting with Adam than cleaning. Chazz and Adam offered to take the bourbon punch off our hands for an upcoming keg party, and we willingly obliged them. At first, I wondered if we should return the punch to Mr. Bennington-Hall but decided it is the last thing Mrs. Bennington-Hall will want to see when she sobers up.

I tried to reach John to enlist his help during the clean-up, but he is nowhere to be found and he is not answering his cellphone. Kit noticed the dismay on my face each time I pounded the End button, with increasing force, but she didn't comment because so many people were around.

As Mike loaded the gifts into his car, he discovered the toilet-paper cozy and was immediately taken with it — in a bad way. Samantha told him that Kit and I were responsible for it, but he knew intuitively it was our mothers' doing. In true older-brother fashion, he insisted on tormenting us with it, refusing to pack it in the car with the rest of the gifts. He decided we should all revel in its uniqueness and carried it around for some time before depositing it on the kitchen counter for us all to admire during the clean-up. We had to field questions like "What the hell is *that*?" and "Why is she wearing a sombrero?" and "Does toilet paper get cold?"

"Well, I can see why our mothers didn't forewarn us," Kit laughs and bumps into my shoulder, pushing me off the sidewalk as we meander back toward my house.

"When the whole thing started, I thought it might be fun to have a drunken bridal shower. It wasn't as much fun as I'd thought it might be," I laugh. "It would have been better if we'd been part of the drunken crowd and not the sober ones cleaning up the mess."

"I feel a hundred pounds lighter getting that stupid dress off," Kit comments.

"Well, at least you were a princess, albeit a lesser princess," I laugh and poke Kit's shoulder. "I was Little Bo Peep! What the heck does *she* have to do with the South and mint juleps?"

"I don't know. Do they tend sheep in the South? And,

count your blessings; at least we didn't have to wear wigs like Taryn! Poor thing. Her hair was drenched when she took the thing off her head." Kit and I both fall into easy laughter for the first time all day. "It was nice of Chazz and Adam to help us," Kit states matter-of-factly.

"Maybe. I still think that Chazz is a complete know-it-all, though. Did you hear his 'cleavage' comment?" I scowl at the memory.

Kit laughs. "I think Chazz would like to get a better look at your cleavage, but I don't think he's all bad. You have to admit he is really nice to look at and he did help a lot."

"Yeah, yeah. Whatever. I think he's pretty cocky and too sure of himself for his own good." I huff but am actually momentarily happy. My world has been so topsy-turvy lately that I haven't had time to think about good things, like Kit, and how much fun we have together. I much prefer when Kit's world is insane. It's not so much fun when it's my world gone crazy. I'm much better at telling Kit how to fix her world than I am at assessing my own and making life-altering decisions affecting *me*.

Before the bridal-shower surprise, we had planned to have a barbeque this evening with Kevin and Ben to celebrate Tia's arrival in Toronto. We had no idea Mike and Samantha or Taryn would be in Toronto, but we subsequently added them to the guest list. Kevin, Ben and the twins were going to wash Kevin's car and pick up some wine for dinner before coming back to my house.

Kit and I round the corner, easily spotting Pam's yard of

horror from down the block. Our fathers were not very impressed with our mothers' inebriated state when they picked them up, so we suspect it could be a long evening. Thank goodness the bride and groom will be in attendance to take the pressure off us. As we approach my yard, I see John's truck is in the driveway and notice the Statue of Liberty and the gnome band are *not* prominently displayed in the front yard any longer. I say a silent "thank you" to the heavens. I'm sure my father removed the offending yard critters as soon as he saw them. More importantly, I'm really happy John did not let me down and take off again this evening.

Kit and I enter the kitchen, and John grabs me up into a big bear hug before I can even deposit my purse onto the counter. "I hear you girls had a big day!" John says as he puts me down on the floor and kisses my forehead.

"You could say that," I laugh.

"Tell me those are for us," Kit is pointing at two glasses of wine on the island countertop.

"Yep. I just poured them. I figured you could use a glass, or four," John laughs. "I put three more bottles in the fridge, but the way your mothers are going at it, that won't be enough."

"They're still awake?" I say at the same time Kit is saying, "I thought they'd be sleeping it off!"

"You'd think, but no! They are continuing the party in the backyard. Take a look." John hands us each a glass of wine and we walk to the garden doors leading to the deck off the kitchen. Our fathers are sitting in deck chairs, each holding a beer, looking dumbfounded and shaking their heads at our mothers, who are dancing in the backyard. My mother has a glass of wine in one hand and her dance partner, the Statue of Liberty, in the other. Mrs. Jennings seems to have taken a shine to the cross-eyed, harmonica-playing gnome. They are giggling and falling over themselves. They seem to be having a good time aside from the occasional lack of balance.

"Oh, dear God, please tell me they have acrylic glasses," I implore John. "They'll cut themselves to shreds if they fall over..."

Kit finishes my thought, "And it looks very likely at least one of them will."

"You bet. Acrylic all the way! I knew you wouldn't want them having the good glasses in their state. Your dads didn't even want me to give them any wine, but they started drinking straight from the bottle." John explains briefly what must have been a bit of a battle, in reality. I feel bad that I wasn't here to help him when the inebriated mothers arrived home.

"Well, at least they'll have really big headaches tomorrow!" Kit laughs. "That should be payment enough for the princess dresses and toilet-paper cozy, shouldn't it, Bo Peep?"

"Absolutely, Belle, absolutely!"

23

Kit and I have come to expect any evening with our parents, mothers more than fathers, will be stressful, but the remainder of Saturday turns out to be surprisingly relaxing, considering the start to the day. Needless to say, our mothers didn't eat much dinner and burned out quickly. They both ended up in bed by eight o'clock and the Statue of Liberty went with my mother. I peeked in at her at one point — Liberty was lying beside my mother, on my dad's side of the bed, with my mother's arm draped over her.

As soon as our mothers and Lady Liberty are tucked in, our dads seem to relax. I suppose knowing the mothers can't get up to any further antics helps. Mike and Sam are calm and happy to be here. I'm actually very glad they are here, as I'm sure getting any face-time with them during the few days they will be here for the wedding will be difficult. Sam seems to have sobered up from the afternoon's punch, but even sober she is still absolutely thrilled about the dresses she is making the wedding party wear. She describes them in detail to the twins, who nod politely despite having heard the "real story" from us and seeing the photo on my cellphone. There is no way they are buying what Sam is selling. After this afternoon's dress-up shenanigans, I'm starting to believe Sam gets her taste in dresses from her mother.

John, to his credit and my surprise, seems normal. Well, he's back to being *his* normal — often obnoxious, sometimes sweet — self. It's completely thrown me for a loop. The greeting this afternoon, having wine poured for me, kissing me at the door, picking on Kit mercilessly — it's just like before modern dance gripped him. I feel the knot in my stomach, which has been constant for the past couple of weeks, start to loosen. Maybe the whole modern-dance-Ursula-men-in-tights phase is nearing an end. It would be record-short time for one of his hobbies to wear thin, but, hey, I'll take it if it means I get my boyfriend back and at least one sector of my life is not careening off the toy race-car track.

Ben and Tia are attached at the hip, giggling and whispering like no one else is in the room. Taryn produces her *Lonely Planet – Australia* book moments after arriving from the car wash and plops herself down in-between Mr. Jennings and my dad to show them what she's planning to see on her trip. My dad has jumped on board immediately and is suggesting all manner of hiking and exotic excursions. Her father, Mr. Jennings, is a little more cautious and keeps asking, "Are you sure that's a good idea?" While I'm carrying glasses and dessert plates to the kitchen, I hear Mr. Jennings say, "Hang-gliding! For heaven's sake, Bob, don't encourage her!"

"Knock it off, you two," Kit laughs as she comes into the kitchen with more dishes in hand. John was in the kitchen when I arrived and is hugging me from behind and kissing my neck as I try to load the dishwasher. I'm not sure what's gotten into him, but it's good — whatever it is. He hasn't been amorous in weeks — toward me, at any rate.

"Yeah, yeah. I have to take Mike and Kevin more beer anyway, or I wouldn't be leaving," John punches Kit in the arm as he passes her. Ah, just like old times. I can't help but smile.

"Well, he's in a good mood tonight. Did he say why he wasn't answering his phone this afternoon?" Kit asks.

"He said he'd turned it off by accident. It's possible. But he seems back to normal, so I'm not going to force the phone issue. I hope this marks the end of our garbage-bin reconnaissance."

"Me too! I'm still really sore from yesterday," Kit whispers emphatically.

"You know, I've been thinking, maybe this episode is just a *Shall We Dance* sort of thing and John, like Richard Gere, is just expressing himself so we'll be a closer couple in the end?"

"Okay, no more wine or Sunday-night TV movies for you!" Kit laughs and returns to the living room.

I shoot Kit a glare. Well, it could be! John is the bored and tormented Richard Gere character — past his prime and Zack Mayo from *Officer and a Gentleman* days, I might add — who no longer finds fulfillment with his electrician career. I, of course, am the mature yet incredibly sexy Susan Sarandon character, who is perfect in every way and gets her man back in the end. It could *so* happen. The fact my life is currently running parallel to a really bad Richard Gere movie is a bit disturbing — okay, a lot disturbing — but I could be right about this. Kit's pessimism is not helping.

All I know is I'm happy John is acting attentive and in love with me again. Maybe he was all along and I was just being paranoid? Maybe he never had a thing for Ursula, the Jennifer Lopez character? I mean, honestly, she isn't exactly Jennifer Lopez — or even Ms. Mitzi, for that matter. I hope I'm not just nuts; being crazy would completely suck. No, crazy people never wonder if they're crazy; they think they are normal. I'm sure it was just momentary madness and now I've recognized my insanity and can get on with my life. I just have to get this wedding hoopla — biggest hurdle being to rise above the Construction Cone Orange ensemble — over with, figure out what I'm doing on the career front, and set up a series of anonymous, stealthy guerrilla-like attacks on my neighbours' yard, eliminating the disturbing lawn decorations. It should be doable. I should have my life back into its neat little controlled package as soon as the wedding is over. I mean my romantic life seems to be back in order, and that wasn't difficult at all.

24

Sunday morning, John and I stay in bed a little longer than I had planned, but it can't be helped. In his sleep, John puts his arm around me and spoons in behind me. I love the feeling of being surrounded by him. Even though I'm awake I don't make any attempt to get up, but instead concentrate on believing we are fine and everything is back to normal. Huddled with John under the covers, I even feel like I can face Sesame-Cecily at work tomorrow. I can leave the house and not cringe at the lawn ornaments next door. If I concentrate hard enough, I can make myself believe I'm in complete control again. Mel Melrose, control freak, back at the top of her game.

Unfortunately, my fantasy is short-lived as John wakes up, stretches and jumps out of bed with not even so much as a "Good morning." I get up and follow him to the kitchen, with my fantasies unceremoniously jolted back into reality, to greet my parents and Mr. and Mrs. Jennings. Immediately upon seeing my mother and Mrs. Jennings, I can tell they are harbouring some regret about the amount of alcohol consumed yesterday and a sense of satisfaction comes over me despite my reality check. I believe breakfast will be eggs.

Fried. Sunny-side-up and extra-runny. I know it may sound cruel, but please remember I've had my share of hungover mornings with dear, sweet Mother Melrose. Don't think she wouldn't do the same thing to Mike or me. This may well be the only chance I get for payback, because I strongly suspect my mother will never drink again. Well, I believe I can safely say she'll never drink bourbon again. Even when my mother and Mrs. Jennings drink wine, they never get out-of-control drunk like yesterday. It was definitely a first — and, I suspect, a last. So, runny eggs it is. I grin at my devious breakfast plan as I flip the bacon in the pan and take a sip of coffee. I hope Kit gets here early enough to share the joyous runny-egg experience.

The telephone rings. My dad picks it up and looks at caller ID. "Bennington-Hall," he says as he hits the Talk button.

"Sam. Calm down." Pause. "You have *what*?" I hear my dad say into the phone.

"I don't understand you. What is 'Pierre hair'?" My dad's forehead is crinkled and I can tell he's straining to understand what Sam is saying. For her part, Sam is shrieking into the phone. I am not able to make out the words, but I can tell it's her from across the kitchen.

"Mel, speak to your soon-to-be sister-in-law. She's not making a bit of sense." My dad has come around the island to hand me the phone. He removes the fork from my hand and takes over bacon duty.

"Sam, it's Mel. What's happened?" I say calmly into the phone.

"I've got him! I've got him!" Sam shrieks excitedly into the phone.

"Okay, but what exactly do you have?" I'm starting to worry Sam has finally flipped, what with all the wedding planning. What can she possibly have? I picture her holding up a leprechaun by his little green shorts. "Sam. Take a deep breath and tell me, without shrieking, what is going on."

"Mel. I have Jacques-Pierre!" Sam calms down enough to get out five words I can comprehend as words, but the sentence still makes no sense. What is Jacquepierre? Is it an illness? Is there a cure? Is it something affecting Sam's ability to select fashionable bridesmaid dresses? That would explain a lot. Hopefully, if there is a cure, we can remedy the Construction Cone Orange disasters. My heart skips a beat as I get lost in my thoughts of sleek, streamlined dresses in a normal shade of blue or green. I snap back to reality as Sam catches her breath and continues to speak.

"Jacques-Pierre Hair is available on the day of our wedding! I just got the call. Jacques-Pierre *himself* just called me. Jacques-Pierre! Do you believe it?" Sam manages to get the sentences out, but I can tell it almost kills her to calm down enough to speak.

"What exactly is a Jacquespierre?" I am completely confused. I can tell Sam is over the moon with excitement but I have no idea why. I'm starting to figure out she has not been inflicted with a curable bad-taste-in-dresses disease.

"Mel. It's not Jacquespierre — it's two names, hyphenated. Jacques-Pierre." Sam lengthens Jacques-Pierre out so I understand the two-name scenario. Sam sounds a bit angry with me, but I honestly have no idea who the hell Jacques-Pierre is, why he's calling Sam, or why I should know him. I'm quite sure I've never slept with any French men, let alone one who has *two* French names. Or is it considered one name when it's hyphenated? Surely I'd remember sleeping with a man with a hyphen in his name. A girl remembers something like that.

"Mel. Jacques-Pierre is an *artist*. He's the most sought-after hair artist in the world... okay, well, I'm exaggerating, probably not the world. But he did my friend's wedding last year." Sam is back to being gleeful and stresses the word "artist" as if I'm a foreign-exchange student and have no idea what the word means.

"Okay. So... this Jacques-Pierre person is going to do your hair for the wedding and that's a good thing?" I shrug my shoulders at my dad who is still minding the bacon, and try to muster some of the excitement Sam wants me to express. I honestly can't understand why this is so wonderful.

"Mel, you are so not getting it. I've been on the waiting list since the day we got engaged. Jacques-Pierre was originally booked for June 28th, but now he's free. Apparently, the wedding previously booked with him had to cancel. Seems the bride had a sex change the groom didn't know about but once he found out, he couldn't get past it. Anyway, that wedding is off. Jacques-Pierre and his team are now available for our wedding. We have Jacques-Pierre! We're all going to have Jacques-Pierre hair!"

"When you say 'team' and 'all,' do you really mean *all* of us are going to have Jacques-Pierre hair?" I cringe. I love my hair. I have beautiful, long, blonde, impeccably maintained hair. I don't deviate from the tried-and-true. I've had the same hairstyle, give or take a few inches in length, for the past five years. I do not deviate or experiment with my hair. I certainly have no intention of allowing someone named Jacques-Pierre, who refers to himself as a "hair artist" — or, worse, one of his less-than-artistic flunkies — near me with a backcombing comb. I don't do *artistic* hair.

"Of course, all of us! I can't imagine even one of us not having perfect hair. I can't wait. I wish the wedding was tomorrow!" Sam's voice is reaching crescendo pitch again. "Oh, I have to go and call Margot! She will be thrilled!"Then, click, the phone goes dead.

"So, what was all that then, dear?" my dad asks, concerned for Sam's sanity.

"Do you know who *Flock of Seagulls* are?" I ask my dad.

"No."

"I suspect you'll get a good idea in a couple of weeks." I put the phone down and get back to the business of making runny eggs to torment my mother and Mrs. Jennings. As much as I'm completely dreading the wedding outfit, and now the promise of bad hair, I share Sam's desire for the event to be tomorrow. At least then it would all be over on the day after tomorrow.

25

"Did you get a crazy call from Sam this morning?" Kit asks as she and the twins step in the door just after breakfast is finished. Well, when I say finished, I mean John, the dads and me. The mothers are still pushing runny eggs around on their plates, trying to pretend they aren't hungover.

"You mean the call warning me I'm going to have scary hair to accompany the bad outfit for the wedding?" I ask casually. As much as I'm dreading the whole thing, I know I can't change it so there's no point in dwelling on the horror.

"Yeah, apparently, since the twins are handing out programs at the church and I'm doing a reading, we all get to share in the Frank-Flare Hair experience." Kit is as confused as I was an hour earlier.

"Really?" I say a little too enthusiastically. If I have to go down with the Horrible Hair ship, it's good to know Kit and the twins are going down with me.

"Don't get too excited. I'm going to get out of it. He's not *my* brother, why should I have to suffer? I'm only doing a reading at the church! I believe my hair should be left alone." Kit is taking the bad-hair thing harder than I am. She has bad hair naturally, well, big hair — huge, actually — and has to work really hard to tame the insane mane. In fact, there was a phase a couple of years ago, during a particularly devastating breakup, when she insisted on bad hair. I should be the one more upset. I've *never* embraced bad hair.

"You're taking this pretty hard for someone who occasionally embraces bad hair. Why?"

"It's taken me thirty-two years to figure out how to manage this mop. Do you think Gordon-Glare will be able to figure it out in a few minutes?" Kit has a fairly valid point.

"Well, I shouldn't have to suffer alone!" I realize, as I make this declaration, I'm being decidedly immature.

"You have a whole wedding party to suffer with! Leave the poor gospel-reading girls out of it! Besides, my 'big hair' isn't necessarily 'bad hair.' It will be though when Darren-Dare gets his hands on it." Kit glances into the dining room at this point. She can't help but notice the mothers — sitting across from each other, both looking rather green — pushing runny eggs around their respective plates with the plastic Statue of Liberty standing at the end of the table "watching" them. Kit laughs. "Okay, good call on the eggs. I might suck up the hair if the eggs were your idea."

"My idea *all* the way, baby! John thought the eggs were mean and told me not to do it. When I set Liberty at the end of the table, he went out for a jog." Kit, the twins, and I all laugh at our small victory. Oh, we'll pay later, with bad, big hair and Lord knows what else but, right now, we're officially even with the mothers for the bad dress-up game yesterday.

"Charlie Brown is jogging? Weird," Kit states but doesn't

wait for any response. "We have to go shopping to get a proper shower gift for Mike and Sam, remember." Kit momentarily lets go of our horrible hair future.

"Absolutely. Although I'm sure all their married friends will ask what hideous gift they received and, when they produce toilet-paper Barbie, they'll be able to win any contest, hands-down."

"True, but is it a contest you *want* to win?" Kit laughs.

Two hours later, Taryn is on her way back to North Bay with plans of Australia running through her head. Our dads have our mothers loaded in the van. Both mothers still look very green and have been noticeably quiet all morning. Kit and I say our goodbyes and wave from the walkway as they pull out of the driveway. Kit bends down to pick up the groom squirrel, which is lying on his side yet again. He will be the death of us all, I'm sure.

John comes out of the house to wave just as the van is pulling out of sight. He is back from his jog and has showered, but is now carrying his gym bag.

"Where are you off to?" I ask. I had no idea John had plans to go anywhere and had hoped after last night we could spend some time together.

"Dance studio. I shouldn't be more than a couple of hours. Are you working today? Any open houses?"

Oh oh. The knot in my stomach starts to tighten again. I had hoped John's return to almost normal behaviour over the past eighteen hours had marked the end of his dance career, but obviously not. "Just for a couple of hours, I have the

Dershowitz open house," I manage to get out of my mouth without sounding ticked-off or stressed. I wonder how I'm going to get through the open house with thoughts of John in, or possibly out of, his leotard dancing in my head.

John kisses my cheek, punches Kit in the arm, then starts down the driveway. Apparently, he's going to walk to the dance studio. "I'll be home for dinner." He shouts back over his shoulder. I turn to Kit for words of support, but she's just standing wide-eyed, watching John stroll down the street.

"I'm..." I start to say something but can't formulate a sentence in my head. I suddenly feel very sad and completely out of control again.

"No, this is okay. Remember your *Shall We Dance* theory? John has to go to the big show, where your heart will burst with pride and you'll be a stronger couple for it. Right?"

"I hoped we could bypass 'the big show.' I don't need my heart to burst."

"You and me both," Kit laughs, "but we have to play this thing out. He's acting normal again. Maybe he's figured out how to balance being obnoxious Charlie Brown *while* embracing his inner dancing queen?"

"Yeah, and maybe the silly squirrel groom will someday be able to stand on his own squirrel feet for longer than ten minutes." Kit and I look down at the squirrel couple and, as if on cue, Mr. Squirrel slides sideways, in slow motion, rolling gently as he settles facedown onto the ground.

26

The next morning, I'm feeling on top of the world when I strut into the office. I received three offers on the Dershowitz house and it looks like Mrs. Dershowitz is going to get $10,000 more than we asked for. I've never had such a successful open house.

"Mel, in my office," Grumpy Jim demands. But I won't let him ruin my high spirits. It's been a long time since I've been happy, so I plan to enjoy every second.

"Sure." I stop to check my mail slot, then turn unexpectedly and quickly duck into Jim's office, closing the door on Sesame's nose just before she can squeeze in behind me. I smile to myself. I love it when I outmanoeuvre her. I'm grinning as I approach Jim's desk then sit in the chair across for him.

"Mel, I need you," Jim states bluntly.

"If I had a dime for every man who said that!" I blurt out lightly. Jim is constantly grumpy. Nothing I say can make him any more so.

Jim glares at me, and then continues, "We're making a commercial for the firm. All the other realtors are doing it, so we have to follow suit. Margery's insisting. I need you to meet with the producer."

"For what? I don't know anything about television commercials." I am completely taken aback. First he imposes Sesame on me, and now he wants my involvement in a television commercial? I suspect Jim's tipping toward the insanity side of the fine line between sanity and insanity he's been balancing on.

"To be the face of the company. You aren't completely unattractive and your head's big. You'll be fine."

"What?" I'm attractive! Big head? I am completely blindsided. Be the "face of the company"? I have a big head? What does the size of my head have to do with anything? And it isn't big, anyway.

"We were going to use Ryan, but he doesn't look right on film. His head's too small. You have a huge head. Surely they can work with that thing."

I am still speechless. Now my head has been elevated to "huge." My head is perfectly normal, thank you very much! The fact that Ryan has a tiny head is no surprise. He's a mental midget needing no headroom for brains. Ryan's pea-sized brain aside, I have no intention of "being the face" of any company — especially one I'm planning my escape from at this very minute. I can't believe Grumpy Jim hasn't picked up on my exit plan.

"I have a normal-sized head, and I'm not about to be a spokesperson for anything! Well, anything except possibly high-priced footwear." I stand up, preparing to leave, when the door crashes open. A very tall, heavy-set man who bears a strong resemblance to Grizzly Adams stands before me. I notice Sesame cowering behind him. She looks very afraid and for the first time since I've met her, she appears speechless.

"Jimbo," the voice of Grizzly booms, "who do you have for me? Time's money!"

"Calvin, this is Mel Melrose. Mel, Calvin Klein," Jim makes introductions.

I burst into a nervous laugh, "Calvin Klein? You're kidding me, right?" I shoot Grizzly a raised eyebrow in disbelief.

"Nope. I've had the name since long before some whipper-snapper from the Bronx slapped it on the ass of a pair of skinny jeans. I'm the real thing, Missy!" Just as I start to object to being referred to as "Missy," Calvin Klein's enormous hands are wrapped around my head, his thumbs meeting across my forehead. I struggle to escape his clutch, but he tightens his grip.

"She'll do, Jimbo. Huge head. Just what I'm looking for! I'll have her back in a couple of hours." Calvin then grabs my upper arm and pulls me along behind him as he ducks to get through Jim's office door.

"But..." I try to speak but am being dragged, my feet scampering double-time to keep up with Calvin's gigantic stride. Calvin Klein does *not* seem open to negotiation. Sesame backs up a step and tries to disappear into the wall. She looks at me with trepidation. I can tell she's glad it's not her being dragged out of the building by Grizzly in his oilskin coat, leather chaps over his holey jeans and furry boots.

Furry boots in June? Who, besides the occasional male stripper who's running late for work, wears chaps in downtown Toronto? Why is Jim allowing this man, who appears to be slightly if not completely insane, to drag me out of the building... oh, dear God! And manhandle me into a very old, black Suburban — circa 1989, I'd guess — with flames painted on the side of it?

Mr. Klein opens the door of the Suburban and shoves me into the back seat. I sidle across the seat just in time for Mr. Klein *not* to sit on top of me. Mr. Klein is a man who does things quickly — surprisingly quickly for his size. Mr. Klein has taken his iPhone out of his pocket and is sending emails frantically as the driver, who was sitting in the car while Mr. Klein was kidnapping me from the office, pulls away from the curb and starts driving. I have to assume he knows where he's going, as Mr. Klein has not given him any direction. I'm trying to remain calm while straining my neck to see what or who Mr. Klein is emailing, when I feel hot breath on my neck. Yes, the same neck managing to hold up my, apparently, huge head. Then something wet drips down my neck and onto my shoulder. I whip my head around and come face to face with a head much larger, and more hairy, than mine. The head belongs to the largest dog I've ever seen. Stowed in the back of Calvin Klein's vintage SUV is a very large, very wet-mouthed, harlequin Great Dane.

"Oh, my GOD!" I shriek. "What the hell is that?"

"Him? That's just Burton. He's a sweetheart. Sings like an opera star." Mr. Klein reaches up and pets Burton's huge head.

"Is he the biggest dog in the world?" At this point, I've given up any idea of putting on a seatbelt — did 1989 Suburbans even come equipped with seatbelts? — and am turned around backwards, with my back pressed against the driver's seat. I'm keeping an eye on the mammoth beast — well, on both of them actually.

"No. That Gibson fella is about an inch taller. But Gibson can't sing worth a damn. He's a no-talent, for sure. If there was an overall competition, like the Miss America pageant, Burton would win." Mr. Klein states calmly, while rubbing Burton's head with one hand and texting with the other. I realize I should start to panic. I'm sitting in the back of an SUV with a huge dog and his equally large, possibly insane, owner discussing dog talent. A large drool escapes Burton's mouth and rolls down the back of the seat where I was sitting moments ago.

"But Burton is harmless, right?" I've never seen a dog so large. Burton's head is much larger than mine.

"So long as he doesn't hear rap music. Or hip-hop. He doesn't like either of those. Ate a stereo once when he heard a song by that Slim Shady fella."

"Oh." I have no response to what Mr. Klein has just said.

"No, Burton only likes Burton Cummings. Has since he was a pup. That's how he got his name. Burton Cummings is the ultimate musical genius. Anyone will tell you that, Missy!"

"Oh… right," I answer tentatively. Of course, Burton Cummings is the ultimate. Who doesn't know that? "I Will Play A Rhapsody" must be in the Top 100 Best Songs, right?

"Mr. Klein," I start to ask the question that's been on my mind since this whole thing started, while still keeping a close eye on Burton, "Why is it necessary for me to have a… err… larger head than other people?"

"Better for television," Calvin Klein states matter-of-factly, still concentrating on his iPhone, as if everyone on the planet is aware of the aforementioned fact. "Walk down any street in L.A., you can spot them a mile away: average-sized bodies with huge heads. It's like walking around with a bunch of bobbleheads."

"But looking like a bobblehead in L.A. would be a good thing, right?"

"If you wanna look like a bobblehead. Sure." Mr. Klein shrugs, then continues, without looking up from his iPhone, "Burton likes you, despite your huge head."

"How can you tell?" The word "tell" is just out of my mouth when the world's second-largest dog extends his second-largest tongue and licks me from chin to forehead in one very wet, very hot Great Dane kiss.

"He doesn't kiss just everyone." At this point, Calvin Klein throws open the door and jumps out of the Suburban, which hasn't yet stopped completely. Before I can gather myself and follow him, Mr. Klein has opened the back hatch, Burton has jumped out and is standing in front of me, almost looking me in the eye.

Mr. Klein has started toward the door of a very seedy-looking warehouse in the west end of town and is several of his long strides ahead of me when he looks over his shoulder and yells, "Burton. Missy. Come!"

Burton and I, afraid to anger Grizzly Adams in chaps, trail behind obediently.

27

"Okay, so *you* are going to be on television?" Kit has asked the same question twice now. I wonder if she has started self-medicating after Tia moved in or has spent too much time at the construction site near toxic paint. What part of "so I filmed a television commercial this afternoon" isn't she understanding?

"You?! On television?" Marc, who is sitting beside Kit, across from me, at one of our usual tables at the Firkin, seems to share her disbelief.

"Isn't your head too big to be on television?" Tia, who is sitting beside me, asks innocently. I shoot her a look of complete disapproval. Tia should be on her best behaviour; it is her first beer-after-work-on-Friday outing. Besides, what is it with my head? If my head is so outrageously huge, how come no one has ever brought it to my attention? Better still, how come I've never noticed? It doesn't hang off both sides of the vanity mirror or anything.

"My head is *perfect* for television. Well, apparently. All the big names have large heads. Looks better on film." I spout my new-found knowledge like everyone should know it. Even though I just heard it this afternoon — and I honestly question its validity — it did come from a man who may, or may not, have been a close personal friend to the Unabomber.

"Okay, your head size aside. Aren't you quitting your job because of Sesame-Cecily? How can you be the 'face of the company'?" Kit finally asks a sensible question.

"Well, I am leaving, but I didn't exactly have time to explain before I was kidnapped for the filming." I start to tell them about my day with Calvin Klein and my first experience with film.

After Burton and I are summarily called to "come," we scurry after Mr. Klein into the warehouse where the filming is set up. It is all done against a green screen, so when it's edited, they can put any manner of scenery in the background. For all I know I'll be in a subway tunnel if and when this thing ever makes it onto television. The commercial is set up so a real actor does most of the talking and I only have to stand between the actor and a three-by-three-foot plinth for thirty seconds of screen time and get out one very short sentence. No problem. Easy, right? Well, unfortunately, it isn't as easy as it sounds. We practise several times. The actor's name is Rob. Nice guy. Seems to catch on much faster than I do — but he does act for a living, while I sell high-priced real estate. In my defence, Burton is lying at my feet and resting his head on my boots — my tangerine Jimmy Choos. I'm trying to get him to move, which isn't about to happen, while learning my line and staying on my mark — my mark is an X of masking tape on the floor. We finally get the words down and are good to go when Mr. Klein yells, "Okay, bring in the wrangler!"

Of course, the first thing through my mind is the theme song for the old Wrangler jeans commercial from the early 1980s: "Here comes Wrangler, he's one tough customer." So, while we were waiting for "wrangler," I started to hum the theme because it is all I can think about. And Rob says, "Hey! I remember that commercial," and then he starts to sing the jingle while shaking his butt, but then moves off his mark and gets yelled at by Calvin Klein. At this point, I gave a silent "thank you" to Burton because, due to the weight of his huge head, I am firmly planted on my mark and not being yelled at by scary Mr. Klein.

While I'm thanking my lucky stars that Rob is in trouble instead of me, four burly men walk toward us, carrying what appears to be a large dog carrier, but not large enough for Burton. They circle around behind Rob and me and hold the carrier up to the back edge of the plinth I'm standing beside. I turn to see what's going on, just as I hear a very loud "Arr Arr" and a seal — yes, like you see on the Discovery Channel and in Marineland — starts to wiggle and splat his way out of the carrier and onto the plinth, "Arr-arr'ing" the whole time. Burton's head or no Burton's head on my boots, I shriek and jump at least three feet into the air. My mark be damned and the wrath of Calvin Klein provoked. There was no mention of marine life when I signed up for — or, rather, when I was dragged to — this thing.

My disdain for all manner of sea creatures goes back to when I was a child — well, not exactly a child, I was thirteen, but thirteen is a formative year — and our family went to the Cayman Islands. My parents took Mike and me to Stingray City where we were allowed to swim with the stingrays. Of course, we had to take a twenty-minute boat ride to get to where you could swim with the creatures. All this sounds fine — almost exciting and fun — on paper. Sadly, it was not fun in reality. The sandbar that was described as "shallow and picturesque" in the brochure was neither. Okay, it may have been shallow to some, but not to me with my five-foot, four-inch stature. To me, it seemed deep and scary. Mike, because he's my older brother and big brothers do this sort of thing, grabbed a bit of stingray food — used to lure the stingrays to come and swim with people, because I'm sure they find swimming with humans demeaning and wouldn't do it without bribery — from a bucket on board the boat and slipped it into my bikini bottom. When I asked him what he was doing, he claimed he was tucking in the washing instruction tag. Needless to say, swimming with the stingrays — thanks to two particularly hungry ones named Hank and Sid — went very badly. I couldn't touch the bottom due to the water above the "picturesque sandbar" being well over my head, so when I was immediately pounced upon by Hank and Sid and a flurry of their stingray friends, I started to panic and flail. Hank and Sid slithered and slunk all over me, in-between my legs, over my back and stomach, while I shrieked, splashed and saw my very short life pass before my eyes. The stingrays were in a complete frenzy around me. I was flailing and screaming, positive I was going to drown. My mother was on the deck of the boat having a fit. My poor father was very confused and would have helped, but wasn't in the water; I'm not sure he could have kept Hank and Sid off of me anyway. Mike, in the meantime, was laughing his head off and not helping at all. I had to be hoisted up on the boat ladder by one attendant while the other one tried to keep Hank and Sid away from me. Both attendants were very apologetic and claimed Hank and Sid weren't generally so aggressive. Exhausted, lying on the deck of the boat, breathing into a paper bag — produced by my mother from her purse — and out of harm's way, I declared I would never again interfere, or be part of, any sea creature's world again. I swore off Marineland, all manner of fishing — including ice — and even the child's carnival game, Duck-pond, wherein children pick up plastic ducks floating past and read their bottoms to determine a prize. No. Marine life and I keep a very safe distance from each other.

So, my reaction to standing shoulder-to-snout with an honest-to-goodness seal may have appeared completely over the top to everyone around me, but to me it was completely justified. Unfortunately, my shrieking and panicking startles Burton, who jumps up faster than I could have imagined a Great Dane could move, and he is barking and jumping. The seal is prancing and "Arr-arr'ing." I am scratching against the green screen searching for an escape, while Rob, to his credit, stays on mark but is still humming, "Here comes Wrangler."

About this time, Calvin Klein completely loses it.

"Everyone *stop*!" I hear Calvin's voice through a megaphone. I freeze. My right foot still up in the air, clad in its soggy-from-Burton-drool tangerine boot.

"Missy! What the hell are you on about?" Mr. Klein directs his ire my way. I can't see him because Rob is blocking my view, but I can tell he's not impressed.

"I don't like marine life, Mr. Klein. I'm terrified of it, actually. No one said anything about a seal." I try to explain myself but, without the stingray background story, my phobia must seem silly and juvenile.

"Your line is 'And we'll seal the deal!' What the hell did you expect? A monkey?"

28

I share the remaining hours of the filming process with Kit, Marc and Tia. By the end of the story, I am physically exhausted from reliving the experience. Calvin Klein got his commercial, but it was no easy feat. My marine life phobia is much more ingrained than even I knew. Standing beside a seal, and letting the same seal "kiss" me, was absolutely debilitating. By the time Mr. Klein's driver drove me back to the office, I was pale, drawn and exhausted; I felt like I'd run a half-marathon — although, honestly, I have no idea what that really feels like. I'm just going by what Kit's told me.

"Well, that's exciting. I'm having beer with someone famous." Marc lifts his beer and nods in my direction.

"I didn't feel famous. Standing inches from a seal is not an experience I want to have ever again," I answer him sarcastically.

"But you're going to be on TV! That's so cool!" Tia grins.

"I'd rather it was Ryan, with his tiny head, wrangling the seal," I laugh.

"I bet Ryan does too!" Kit laughs. "You know he hates it when he's upstaged by you!"

"Speaking of stages," Marc jumps in, "what's up with John and this 'dance thing' I'm hearing about?"

"Your guess is as good as mine. He's been at it for a month now. I'd hoped it was a passing fancy, but he does seem determined. He's at practice right now, in fact." I explain to Marc the basic dance story. I don't feel inclined to share the spying-from-the-garbage-bin part of the story. I've been embarrassed enough today.

"I know. He is determined. He's invited all the guys from work to the show he's going to be in. Are you girls going?" Marc asks.

"I'm not sure. The so-called show isn't for two more weeks. I'm hoping the whole love of modern dance wanes by then, and he won't be in it. If he does participate, though, I suppose I don't have a choice," I shrug.

"I'm going!" Kit pipes up a little too enthusiastically. "I can't wait to see Charlie Brown in tights."

"Well, I've seen him in his tights. Believe me, I can wait — the rest of my life, if necessary!" I laugh.

"It will definitely be *interesting*," Tia mentions quietly, glancing down at the table. I'm fairly certain she is referring to the Ursula-possible-affair suspicions more than the dancing itself.

Marc takes his leave shortly after the dance discussion, and Tia catches a ride back to Kit's condo with him. Tia has worked her first full week as the temp receptionist for a financial investment firm and is very tired. Working full-time is a huge change from student life. Kevin and Ben are on the road with the band for the next week so Kit and I decide to have another beer.

"I ordered the Lagostina cookware today. It's going to be delivered to Mike and Sam in Georgia next week." Kit fills me in on our real shower-gift accomplishment.

"Excellent. What are you doing for a wedding gift?" I ask Kit. We've been so busy trying to figure out the belated shower gift, we've completely ignored the fact there's a wedding only two weeks away.

"I have no idea."

"Well, I'm thinking lawn ornaments. If they start their collection now, it will be quite formidable by their fifth wedding anniversary! Besides, I know where I can get a lovely gnome band and a previously enjoyed Statue of Liberty," I laugh.

"Yeah, but then both your parents would disown you!" Kit laughs back. "Your mom, for giving them away, and your dad for giving them to another family member!"

"Good point. They did register for china and crystal, so maybe china is the way to go."

"Oh, I don't think so. Sam and Mike selected Royal Doulton's Provence Rouge for their china, so no can do!" Kit states seriously. The Provence Rouge pattern wouldn't be my first choice — bright white china with rather ornate red flowers all over it — but I realize it won't ever grace my table so I don't share Kit's inability to purchase it as a gift for people who do want it.

"You don't have to use it. Heck, we may never even lay eyes on it. When was the last time you were in Georgia?" I laugh back.

"I know. It's completely insane. But you know how I feel about red dinnerware." Kit's dislike for red dinnerware goes back two-and-a-half years, when she and her then-boyfriend, Derek, purchased the condo together and were planning on living together. At the time, Kit had purchased bright red stoneware for the condo. Shortly after the stoneware purchase, Derek announced to Kit, over the phone, he was breaking up with her to marry a ditzy debutante. Needless to say, the stoneware was returned and Kit now has issues with all-red dinnerware and most red kitchen accessories. I had a red dish towel in my kitchen once that upset her so much we ended up burning it in a metal garbage can in my backyard — well, after we ingested two bottles of wine and said all manner of nasty things about Derek. I had assumed her dislike for red kitchenware would subside, but sitting across from her right now at the Firkin, I finally have to admit she may not ever outgrow this one.

"So, what are you going to get them?" I ask, admitting defeat in the art of china persuasion.

"Money, I guess. They can buy their own red china, if they must! Although I think it's a bad omen." Kit's sincerity makes this statement seem quite funny to me.

"I really don't think the colour of one's china makes or breaks a relationship," I laugh.

"Oh, we'll just see about that!" Kit laughs. I can only hope she someday realizes her red dinnerware aversion is completely insane on several levels.

29

Saturday, I awake to strong and constant rapping on the door. By the time I locate my robe and get my sleepy butt to the door, the knocking becomes more frantic. I open the door to a panicked, tired-looking neighbour wearing an incorrectly buttoned blouse.

"Have you seen them?" Pam blurts out the question before I even have time to register the person standing in front of me is indeed my lawn-ornament-loving neighbour.

"Sorry, Pam, seen who?" I really have no idea what she's looking for or why she picked such an early hour to be hunting for anything.

"Snow White and the Seven Dwarfs!" Pam huffs, almost hysterically. "They're *missing*!"

I can see from the stress written all over Pam's face that this is no time to mention she has three complete dwarf sets, so what does it matter if one goes missing?

"Are you sure some kids didn't just move them? I'll come out and help you look," I offer, but have to admit to myself that my heart is not really in the offer. I won't be able to tell the missing ones from the remaining ones, for heaven's sake.

"No, I've checked everywhere. You didn't move them by any chance, did you?" Pam asks, and I suspect by her tone she believes I had something to do with the disappearance.

"Pardon?! You think I took your dwarfs?" Since I've just woken up, I'm not completely firing on all cylinders but am awake enough to realize my neighbour is quietly accusing me, Mel Melrose, of petty theft.

"I did see you and your mother arguing over ornaments last weekend, so wondered if maybe you are anti-ornament enough to sabotage mine?"

"You've got to be kidding! If you saw me wrestling with my mother, then you know I have ornaments of my own I've tucked away in my shed. You're more than welcome to them, if you'd like, to replace the missing ones. I assure you I would never harm a lawn ornament not belonging to me." I am affronted by the accusation — mostly because her accusation immediately produces feelings of guilt about the number of times I have imagined doing unspeakable things to her vast collection.

"I'm sorry. I'm just so distraught. The missing dwarfs are my favourite. They were given to Cam and me for a wedding present. Who would do such a thing?" Pam looks on the verge of tears, but I can't feel too bad for her. Up until a nanosecond ago, she thought I was capable of taking her beloved dwarfs and doing Lord knows what to them.

"I'm sure it's just some kids playing a prank, and they will be returned in short order." I do reach out and pat Pam's shoulder at this point. "Would you like to have the gnome band until the dwarfs are returned?"

"No, it's okay. Your gnomes are a bit too tacky for me," Pam states, then turns to return to her yard, leaving me standing in the doorway, open-mouthed, on the verge of defending the hideous gnome band and wondering what exactly has just happened.

The rest of the weekend flies by in a rather uneventful fashion, nothing like last weekend with the drunken bridal shower, intoxicated mothers and tacky shower gifts. Kit, Tia and I spend Saturday shopping for wedding gifts while John spends the day at Ursula's dance studio. I'm still not comfortable with him fraternizing with her, but I'm trying my best to stay positive and not dwelling on my worst suspicions. For his part, his behaviour at home has returned to almost normal. He still talks about dancing more than I'd like, but he has mentioned work and will actually speak to me about other topics. I'm hopeful the whole dance thing disappears after the "show" he's still very determined to participate in. I just want my life back. I want off the roller coaster of wondering-if-John's-doing-something-he-should-not-be-doing.

Tia decides she, Ben and Taryn will go together on some wineglasses. Taryn has left all wedding details to Tia because she is far too wrapped up in travel plans and packing for her Australian adventure to really care what Tia purchases on her behalf. Kit is still holding firm on her no-red-china rule but did briefly consider a faux-bearskin rug Mike and Sam had put on their registry list. She was actually quite pro-rug until I mentioned what I thought Mike and Sam might *do* on it, at which point she reverted, very quickly, to her idea of giving money and letting them decide their own gift fate. For my part, I am quite determined to rid my garden shed of the gnome band. I'll give them the gnomes, but since it is really not an appropriate wedding gift, I decide to enhance the band with the $600 juicer they have on their registry. I have never seen Sam or Mike make juice, and vaguely remember Mike not even liking juice as a child but, hey, it's on the list and I feel obliged to go a bit overboard after the mothers sabotaged us giftwise at the bridal shower.

The pinnacle of the shopping excursion has nothing to do with my brother's wedding. After seeing the shape my tangerine boots were in post-Burton drool, I decided they had to be replaced. I really had no immediate plan to replace them; I had just made the mental note they would have to be replaced at some point. Then I saw them. Walking through the mall, I spotted the most fabulous boots, similar to the now-ruined tangerine ones, in the most passionate shade of pomegranate. I've never owned pomegranate boots before. Tia and Kit both maintain that my shriek upon spotting them was, in their words, deafening. I don't think it was as loud as they claim. I'm sure they are exaggerating. The boots, however, are perfect in every way and any loud shrieking would certainly be justified.

30

After John leaves for work on Monday morning, I decide not to rush into the office — Sesame-avoidance is fast becoming my only pastime. I stand beside the kitchen island, flipping through the newspaper, sipping coffee, wearing nothing but my robe and my new pomegranate boots. While exercising my boots to the coffee maker, I glance at the calendar and realize I have a doctor's appointment. My yearly checkup and Pap test. So soon? It feels like I just had that appointment. I look at the time and realize I'm going to have to hustle if I'm going to make the appointment.

I begrudgingly remove the pomegranate boots in favour of pink boots, as I don't have time to switch purses. I pet the soft leather of the new boots as I lean them up against the night table beside my bed and think, "I love boots."

Sitting in the waiting room of my doctor's office seventy-five minutes later, I realize my mad dash from the house — forsaking poor Mr. Groom squirrel, who was lying on his side again — was all for nothing. I should have picked the poor critter up. I had loads of time. I'm flipping through my third magazine by the time I hear my name called.

I follow the nurse practitioner into the exam room, not looking forward to the procedure. I've had it enough times to know you only really want to hear the words "Put your feet in these stirrups" when you're at a dude ranch and a swarthy cowboy is uttering them. When a doctor or nurse makes the same request, it has a completely different meaning. The procedure takes longer than usual because, after the "stirrup" request, which is followed closely by "Just skooch your butt to the edge of the table" and "This is going to be uncomfortable" — two things you don't generally hear at a dude ranch — I hear a clatter on the floor at the end of the examination table and Nurse Practitioner Olive exclaims, "Oops, butterfingers." Then she snickers and says, "Or, rather, cervical-jelly fingers!" and laughs to herself.

"Just stay still, I have to get another speculum," she commands as she stands up and moves towards the cupboard in the exam room.

I prop myself up on my elbow, which is not easy when you are in the stirrups, to see what exactly is going on. I notice one of my boots has fallen over near the end of the bed and it appears to have been on the receiving end of the fly-away speculum.

"Did that speculum drop on my..." I don't finish the sentence before Nurse Practitioner Olive returns to my nether region and continues where she had been interrupted with her cervical-jelly fingers.

"Okay, this is going to feel a little bit uncomfortable..."

I'm lying flat on my back again, possible jelly on boot forgotten momentarily.

I'm anxious to check my cellphone, which had started chiming with incoming texts shortly after I was in "the stirrups." I had thought it wasn't completely appropriate to be checking texts while the nurse practitioner did her thing. In light of her butterfingers I think I made the right choice.

While I'm hurriedly getting dressed, I see I have six new, urgent texts — all from Astrid. Astrid never contacts me. Ever. Lately, if she's needed anything, she's had the annoying Sesame contact me. I start checking the content: 1. Call office immediately 2. Where are you? Call 3. We need you NOW. Urgent 4. Mel this isn't funny! Call PLEASE 5. Enuff. Call me. 6. Help.

Dear Lord. One of my deals. Something was going horribly wrong while I was lying on my back with my legs in the air — and not in the good way! Nurse Practitioner Olive returns to the room and starts to sit down at her desk as I'm texting back frantically.

Am at dr. what is going on?

"Okay, Mel. I know you're busy, but I need to update your file before I can let you go." Nurse Practitioner Olive opens my file in front of her.

"Shoot. There's just an emergency at the office, so I need to keep an eye on this." I hold up my phone to underscore my statement.

"So you're still not married. Are you in the same relationship as last year?" Nurse Practitioner Olive asks.

"Yep. Still the same one," I hurriedly answer while glancing at my silent cellphone and picking up one of my boots to put it on.

"And you will want your birth-control pill prescription refilled? Not planning any babies just yet?"

"No to babies. Yes, to the… is this cervical jelly on my boot?" I glance up at Nurse Practitioner Olive with a raised eyebrow. The answer is obviously yes, because the dark spot on the ankle of my boot is in the distinct, duck-bill shape of a speculum.

"Oh, just rub it in. No harm done!" Nurse Practitioner Olive obviously does not own expensive boots. "Just a couple more questions," Nurse Practitioner Olive tries to change the subject while I try to rub the jelly into the leather of my boot and want to cry, the urgent texts from Astrid momentarily forgotten in light of my current boot catastrophe.

"How many sexual partners have you had?" Nurse Practitioner Olive asks casually, in the same fashion she would ask my address. I stop rubbing my boot. She finally has my full attention.

"Like, all my partners… ever?" I'm sure I've heard the question wrong. There is no way she wants a total number. I zip up my boot and assess the mark on the side noting how visible it is. Very.

"Yes."

"Ahhh… I don't know. I'm not eligible to marry the heir to a throne or anything, but I'm hardly promiscuous!"

Suddenly, the fact I've had sexual relations with more than one man is making me feel rather trampy. Having to justify my sex life to Nurse Practitioner Olive — who is about sixty-five and probably answers "one" to this particular question, ignoring the fact it was a "simpler time" when she hooked up with Mr. Nurse Practitioner Olive — just seems wrong. My brain is spinning out of control, on a tangent I'm sure Nurse Practitioner Olive had no intention of sending me on with her seemingly innocent question.

"Just a ballpark number will be fine, Mel," Nurse Practitioner Olive huffs.

"Ahhhh… ten, a dozen, maybe? University was a bit crazy… but twelve sounds like an incredibly large number, doesn't it?" I start to ramble. Twelve? Maybe I am a bit trampy? I look at Nurse Practitioner Olive for support, but she just stares at me. She could say, "Oh, twelve's not high we had a gal in here last week in the triple digits!" But, no. She calmly asks, "So, twelve then?"

Realizing compassionate bedside manner is definitely a thing of the past, I give the jelly spot on my boot another wipe and grab my bag. "Just fax my prescription to my pharmacy," I say over my shoulder as I storm out of Nurse Practitioner Olive's office, shaking my still-silent cellphone. How many sexual partners, indeed! Less than the average swinger or porn star, I'm sure! Porn stars have several every day… well, probably. I don't really know anything about that lifestyle except what I saw in *Porn Star: The Legend of Ron Jeremy*.

31

With my stomach in knots because I have no idea what is going on with my deal and the newly discovered knowledge that I may be considered a tramp by medical standards, I break almost every traffic law getting to the office. I squeal into my parking space and, leaving my car on an angle, am halfway to the office door before I hear my car door close.

"Astrid, what's going on?" I shriek as I run into the main reception area. I have to shriek very loudly, because Burton, Calvin Klein's Great Dane, is standing in front of the reception desk barking his huge head off. Astrid and Sesame are both pressed up against the credenza behind Astrid's desk, wearing looks of terror on their faces.

"Burton! Shut it!" I shout at Burton as I put my hand on his head. As if on command, Burton stops barking, sits down, and leans against me, almost pushing me over, but I manage to get my left foot out and steady myself. "Okay. Astrid. What's the emergency? How's my deal? Did Frank from the Planning Department call?" Burton, still leaning on me, is nudging my arm so I'll pet his head, which I start to do automatically. Anything to keep him quiet.

Astrid has yet to utter a word, and annoying, chatty

Sesame is equally speechless. I can't help but smile. A speechless Sesame is a bonus.

"Astrid. Any day now! What is the emergency? I ran out of my doctor's appointment for this!"

"That," Astrid states while pointing at Burton.

"Astrid. This is a dog, not an emergency. You just have to be firm with him. Where's Mr. Klein?" I hadn't given any thought to Burton taking up the entire front reception area of the office. I just assumed Mr. Klein was in Grumpy Jim's office.

"Mr. Klein left this for you." Sesame has found her voice and starts to walk away from the credenza behind Astrid's desk. But the second she moves, Burton jumps to attention and starts barking at her causing her to scurry back to where she had been standing, flattened, beside Astrid.

"See!" Astrid shrieks.

"Burton! Enough!" My voice, or Sesame being back in her original spot of fear, stops Burton mid-bark and he settles down again. "Sorry, Astrid. What did Mr. Klein leave?"

"The envelope. There on the desk." Astrid points at a manila envelope on her desk, but her movement brings Burton to his feet, so she quickly lowers her arm. With Burton standing at attention, I open the envelope. It contains a large number of $100 bills — which I will determine later total $3,000 — and a handwritten note that reads:

Missy. Have business out of town. Burton doesn't like kennels or being left alone but he does like you. Money is for incidentals. See you Friday. CK

Now, I'm speechless. Apparently, Mr. Klein has that effect on more than just Sesame. "So, my deal is fine? Nothing's gone wrong?"

"Yes. Everything is fine except that." Astrid points at Burton, who has settled down and is leaning on me again. "Mr. Klein came in, dropped the letter on the desk, and said, 'Tell the gal with the boots I'll see her when I get back' and walked out, leaving us with… with… *that*…" Astrid points at Burton, who has lowered his head and is sniffing the jelly stain on my boot.

"Yes, but that's not the scary part. The scary part was when that… *that*… ran here behind the desk and attacked the stereo!" Sesame interjects to fill me in on Burton's antics. "He grabbed it with his mouth, threw it on the ground, and jumped up and down on it until it stopped playing music." I take a step forward and look around Astrid's desk, where the remains of the office stereo receiver lie in bits on the floor.

"Burton, stop!" I lift my foot because Burton has started licking my boot. I turn back to the girls. "It probably doesn't matter, but do you remember what song it was playing at the time?" I ask tentatively.

"'Bringing Sexy Back,' by Justin Timberlake," Astrid replies. "I remember because I like Justin Timberlake."

"Of course. *Bad Burton*!" I say as sternly as possible to Burton, while shaking my finger at him. Burton, who seems oblivious to what I'm talking about, lifts his head from where he is again licking my boot, tilts it to the right and gives me a look that can only translate as "Huhhhh?"

"Okay, so Mr. Klein came in, left an envelope, and a giant dog, and just walked out?" I ask for clarification because the reality of the situation has not yet fully registered.

"Yes. And you are supposed to take care of the dog until he gets back." Astrid has a better grasp of the overall picture than I do at this point.

"But the note says he's out of town until Friday! Burton, stop licking my boot!" I try to sidestep Burton's enormous tongue.

"*Friday*!" Astrid parrots, obviously she didn't read the note before I arrived.

"What am I going to do with him? Burton! Enough licking!" My brain is ready to explode. I look down at my boot, where the side is now completely dark. I'm not equipped to care for a one-hundred-sixty-five-pound dog. The closest I've ever come to nurturing anything even remotely in this weight class is living with John and, well, look how that's going.

"Don't look at me!" Astrid pipes up, and Sesame does not translate for her. They both remain very still and keep their eyes on Burton. The upside to this situation is it has improved my otherwise dismal work environment.

"Okay. I get it. I'm dogsitting for a week, but Mr. Klein left me a *lot* of money. Way more than dog food can cost." I'm thinking out loud at this point.

"Not if stereos are his main source of sustenance!" Astrid glances at the stereo's remains on the floor. I'll never tell her so, but she has raised a very good point.

At this point, Jim steps out of his office and says, "Mel. Good. Take Brutus there home, but hurry back. I need you in a meeting this afternoon."

"How, Jim? *How*? I drive a Cadillac XLR. There isn't room in the backseat for my purse! Where am I supposed to put a Great Dane?"

"It's a convertible. Put the roof down!" Jim huffs and turns back into his office.

32

I take five $100 bills out of the envelope and put them down on Astrid's desk.

"Let me know if the receiver costs any more." I start toward my office with the remaining stack of money, thinking "This may not be enough if I have Burton for five days." I am about to call Burton to come along, but he follows my lead without being beckoned. Burton gives a low, throaty growl as he walks by the reception desk, then gives one authoritative bark causing both Astrid and Sesame to jump. As soon as I'm past where they can see me, a huge smile spreads across my face. I have to admit seeing them both mostly speechless is a beautiful thing to behold.

Settled in my office, I read Mr. Klein's note again. Burton doesn't like to be left alone. What am I supposed to do with a neurotic Great Dane? I can't take him home and leave him alone. Surely he'll do horrible things to my furniture, and what if John beats me home? I think I should be there when they meet, in case Burton takes a dislike to John like he did with the office staff. Burton, for his part, is quiet as a mouse and lying on the floor of my office — covering the entire area — with his huge head resting on my feet. Keeping

Astrid and Sesame in line must have exhausted him. I pick up the phone and call John, only to get his voicemail. I leave a brief message about Burton, thinking back to not so long ago when John actually used to take my calls. After the failed attempt to reach John, I call Kit; she always takes my calls.

"Mr. Klein left Burton for *you* to take care of?" Kit is as shocked as I was a few moments ago. "For *five* days? Your goldfish only lived for two days! You should take him to a kennel."

"Thanks for the vote of confidence, Kit. Besides the goldfish incident was five years ago, so it hardly counts."

"You killed two brand-new goldfish in forty-eight hours. Trust me, it counts!" Kit is dwelling on the deaths of Dolce and Gabbana just a little too strongly. Honestly, for all I know, they were really old in the store. You can never tell when you buy them. They all look the same. Dolce and Gabbana likely already had the ick, or whatever it is fish get when they live with other fish, when I purchased them. There's no way of knowing. The truth be known, I had purchased them in a fit of needing something to love. It was just after I'd moved to Toronto and my university boyfriend had dumped me for a bubble-gum-chewing brunette in a bright yellow Volkswagen Bug — complete with the "flower power" daisy on the front dashboard. I was hardly in good shape to be nurturing anything at that particular point in time. Poor Dolce and Gabbana were doomed before the twist tie closed the plastic travel bag they'd been dumped in. I still feel really bad about killing them.

"Kit, you know the fish fiasco still bothers me. I wish you wouldn't harp on it. Besides, Burton is more self-sufficient; he can get his own food whenever he wants. He seems to like JVC."

"Still, Mel, you and living things aren't exactly on the best terms."

"Well, it's not like I offered to dogsit, is it? Mr. Klein just left Burton here. What am I supposed to do?"

"Okay, good point. I guess you have to try. But a kennel is completely out of the question, right?"

"Apparently. After seeing what he did to Sesame and Astrid, I don't think I should attempt it. He is a bit scary when he wants to be. I'm just going to have to struggle through. How hard can it be? He's being quite precious right now."

"Precious is not the correct adjective to describe a Great Dane, Mel. Be afraid. Be very afraid."

My meeting with Jim goes well. Okay, it starts off badly but improves. Jim is not impressed at my still having Burton in tow. Burton, for his part, is not the least bit cooperative. He won't stay in my office alone — barked his massive head off — and, for obvious reasons, I can't leave him in reception with Astrid, so I have no choice but to bring him to the meeting. I actually agreed with Jim on this one. I was all for *not* bringing Burton to the meeting, but the barking from the hallway outside the boardroom was quite distracting, so we had to succumb to Burton's separation anxiety. Surprisingly, once he was allowed to sit beside me in the meeting, things improved greatly. Sitting, leaning on me, he was quiet as a mouse and may have gotten more out of the meeting than I did because my mind kept wandering back to the subject of how I am going to manage my life with a Great Dane for the next five days.

Burton and I say our goodbyes immediately following the meeting, at Jim's insistence. We proceed to my badly parked car. I stand beside the car — my beautiful immaculately clean car — and assess the situation. Burton's chin is level with the roof of the car and he rests it on the convertible roof as if to say, "Good luck getting me into this thing."

"I hear ya, Burton," I say out loud as I slip into the driver's seat and start the ignition. I leave the driver's door open so Burton won't freak out and think I'm leaving him. The only way I'm going to get Burton around is with the roof down, like Jim suggested. I start to put the roof down and, before it is even halfway down, Burton's front legs are standing beside me on the front passenger seat and his head is looking over the windshield. He gives one affirmative bark to let me know he's ready to roll. For my part, I am not impressed. When I purchased the black car with the shiny, black-leather upholstery, I had no intention of ever owning a dog — let alone a dog that outweighs me by fifty-five pounds and takes up more of the car than I do.

"No way, mister! You're in the back seat. No shotgun for you!" I try to push Burton's chest back with my arm, but he's not budging. I have to get out, walk around the car, grab his two-inch-wide, black-leather collar and start to haul on him to force him into the back seat. During the tugging and hauling, which results in nothing except tiring my arms and a look of disdain from Burton, I notice Burton's collar, which I thought was just randomly rhinestone-studded, is actually studded to read "Charlemagne." I stop trying to move the beast, let my arms flop down at my sides and think, "Father of a continent, my ass! More like the *size* of a continent!" In defeat, I walk back around the car, get in, buckle my seatbelt, and put the car in reverse. The second the car starts to move, Burton settles back in the back seat, sits and leans against the seat, looking forward. Of course, he does.

With the wind whipping Burton's ears back and drool flying, landing on the trunk of my car, we head for the nearest pet-supply store that allows pets *in* the store. I have no intention of leaving Burton in my car after his adventure this morning with the stereo receiver. I park the car in the giant-box store's parking lot and get out of the car. As I swing around, holding the car door open for Burton, he jumps out of the car over the door; very *Dukes of Hazzard* of him. When I reprimand Burton for jumping out over the door because "This isn't a hillbilly car, it's a Cadillac," he looks at me with the same head-tilt "Huhhhh?" I saw this morning at the office. He doesn't seem to understand English. I wonder what Mr. Klein's first language is?

I don't know what food Burton eats, so I walk up and down the dog-food aisle, trying to decide which kind to purchase while Burton sits, watching me. Finally, on my third trip between the two kinds I am comparing, Burton gets up and walks to a kind I hadn't even considered and puts his paw on it and barks. Okay. Now I have to decide if Burton is a superdog who can recognize his food brand — not likely, based on the head-tilt "Huhhhh?" looks he gives me — or if he's one of those kids who tells the sitter, "Yes, my mom lets me eat chocolate-chip cookies for breakfast all the time." I suspect the latter but, hey, it's not my dog and it's only for a week. Surely, even if it isn't his regular food, he'll survive. He ate a stereo for breakfast. Proper dog food must be better than stereos, nutritionally speaking. We don't escape with just food. Burton beats it down the toy aisle like a hundred-metre sprinter and selects a stuffed doll from the rack. I hadn't planned on buying him a stuffy, but since his goobery mouth was all over it, I don't think I have a choice. The doll is perhaps the ugliest thing I've ever seen. She's flat and appears to be tea-stained in an attempt to make her look vintage, but it just makes her look dirty. She has pencil-thin arms and legs and five bits of orange wool sticking out of the seam across the top of her head in an artistic attempt at hair. I grab a bag of rawhide bones as I'm walking by the end of an aisle. I'm not sure if Burton likes them, but I had noticed a few other pet shoppers with them and think "What the heck?"

At the checkout, I put the bag of food on the counter and Burton drops his doll for the cashier to scan its tag.

"Hi, Burton. Did you lose your other Stella?" the cashier directs her question to Burton and I look at him, half-expecting him to answer her.

"He has more than one of those things? Do you know Burton?" I asked the cute checkout girl.

"Yes. He shops here a lot. Where's Mr. Klein?"

"I'm not sure. He dropped Burton at my office with a note for me to look after him. Do you know if Burton eats this food?" I might as well take advantage of someone who seems to know and like Burton.

"Yep. That's the one. How long is Burton staying with you?"

"Until Friday," I answer, and try not to roll my eyes.

"Oh. You'll probably want to take the larger bag. I think he eats a big bag a week."

"Really? How often should I feed him?" I am shocked. I had selected the medium-sized bag as I knew the small one would be gone in no time. But the large bag is eighteen kilograms. Surely he can't eat a whole bag in one week.

"He probably eats twice per day, but you may want to just keep food in his bowl." The cashier is very helpful. I had no idea dog ownership could be so complex. I go back to the food aisle and reprimand Burton, who is following me with Stella in his mouth "If you're going to pick your food, the least you can do is select the correct size." Burton's response is his signature head-tilt "Huhhhh?"

The cashier rings up Burton's purchases and I ask her to

remove the tag from Stella, which is already soggy and rather disgusting. She hands the now tag-free Stella back to Burton and he follows me outside.

We leave the pet-supply store with the incidentals envelope $100 lighter.

Burton's legs are much longer than mine and he can travel much faster, so he and Stella have reached the car, leapt over the door and are standing with Burton's back legs on the back seat and front legs on the front passenger seat before I — weighed down with the food and rawhide bones — get anywhere near it. I start the car and pop my Kings of Leon "Because of the Times" CD into the stereo. Burton drops Stella, looks at the stereo and starts a low growl.

"Don't even *think* it, mister! If I have to put up with you for a week, you are going to have to put up with Kings of Leon." I believe I'm being firm but fair, and Burton must sense I'm not budging on this one, so he picks up Stella and settles into the back seat before the car starts to move.

33

Burton makes no further objection to Kings of Leon. But the calm doesn't last for long, as he seems to have some major objections to lawn ornaments. When we arrive home, I don't have the car in "Park" before Burton is out of it and barking and jumping nervously at my neighbour's yard. Before I can get out and around the car to grab his collar, he pounces on the life-sized Prince Charming bird feeder and has the Prince, horse and all, on the ground and is attacking the bird feeder's shield while jumping up and down on the Prince himself. Yelling and tugging on Burton's collar — when I say "tugging" I mean anchoring my feet and pulling on him with all my weight — I manage to get him off the Prince. Unfortunately, as soon as I have him off the Prince, Burton spots one of the two remaining Dopeys and picks the poor dwarf up by the head and starts gnawing and growling.

"Bad Burton! Drop the dwarf!" I yell while trying to get the dwarf out of Burton's mouth. Wrestling the dwarf from Burton is no easy feat, and I finally have to use both hands and wrench the dwarf back and forth. I understand Burton's dislike and his uncontrollable desire to attack the ornaments. I myself have spent many hours visualizing the demise of the display. But in reality, we can't just be running around attacking lawn ornaments belonging to other people — especially when I've already been accused of stealing a complete set of dwarfs.

"Burton! These are not toys! Let... go... of... the... dwarf!" I pant, still wrenching on the dwarf, trying to reason with the Great Dane. Burton is determined to keep the dwarf firmly in his mouth and is showing no signs of tiring, whereas I'm quickly becoming exhausted.

"Fine. You win." I let go of the dwarf and stand up, wiping my hands on the front of my skirt. "Bring it with you, I guess." I turn, wrestle Prince Charming and his horse back to a standing position, then start toward the car to retrieve my purse and Burton's supplies. Burton follows, the dwarf body and feet still sticking out of his mouth. Burton seems completely disoriented and a little bit afraid as he walks amongst the other ornaments, his head darting back and forth with low, slightly muffled growls coming out of him. I feel a bit bad for Burton. I'm sure he's never seen such a display in his entire dog-life, nor is he likely to anywhere else. But if he's here for a week, he's going to have to get used to it.

"I hear ya, Burton. I'm not used to it yet either, but you're going to have to try. They're here to stay, and I'm the No. 1 suspect for the missing ones."

It takes a bit to get Burton down the walkway and into the house. He takes an instant dislike to the squirrel bride and groom and has to drop Dopey, brace himself and bark at them. I let him bark as I unlock the door and wrestle his supplies into the kitchen. I'm filling bowls with water and dog food when I realize I hear nothing. No barking. I immediately panic. Burton has no idea where he is and, as much as I didn't go looking to dogsit a Great Dane, I certainly don't want to be responsible for losing the aforementioned Great Dane. I drop the bag of food and bolt outside. The dwarf is lying on the walkway, both squirrels are accounted for, but no Burton.

"Burton!" I yell. I can't believe I've lost the dog already.

"Burton! Where are you?" I rush to the front of the house to see if he's attacking more lawn ornaments. No. I look up and down the street. No very large dogs. I feel my heart pounding and my breath begin to get faster. I've lost the stupid dog.

"Burton!" I have no idea if he even comes to his name. He seemed to respond to Mr. Klein but so far hasn't really been very attentive toward me, so maybe he doesn't.

"Burton, you big bozo. Where are you?" I moan, just about to admit defeat, when I hear one loud, distinct bark behind me. Burton is standing by the back door, having just come from the backyard.

"Bad Burton! Don't take off on me. I'm new at this dog thing!" I try to be firm with him but I can tell by the head-tilt "Huhhhh?" that he has no clue what I'm saying.

"Where were you, anyway?" And, yes, I realize I'm talking to myself. Even if Burton could talk, I'm sure he wouldn't answer me.

I walk to where Burton is, then past him to the backyard to see what he's been up to. Burton follows me. That's when I see it. The pile. The largest mountain of doggie doo-doo you can imagine. It's larger than a softball, moist and very pungent. The size of Burton should have given me some forewarning about the potential size of his excrement but, in the flurry of being saddled with the horselike beast, figuring out food and supplies, and wrestling with lawn ornaments, Burton's bowel movements honestly hadn't crossed my mind; well, until now.

"Mother of Pearl." The idea of "scooping" that… that… stuff makes me instantly nauseous. I can suddenly relate to Kit and her overactive vomit response. "Why couldn't you be a purse-dog? I bet their crap is much easier to deal with!"

Burton follows me into the house, takes a few laps of water, picks up Stella, and heads for the sofa. He does three very awkward circles on the sofa before settling, dropping with a loud "Hmmpf" and closing his eyes. Dead to the world — four legs sticking straight off the sofa dangling in the air — oblivious to lawn ornaments and the pile of steaming doggie doo-doo waiting for me in the backyard.

Resigned to dealing with the backyard excrement, I locate an old pair of kitchen gloves and three of the plastic grocery bags from the environmentally friendly grocery store. I inspect the bags for holes. The last thing I need is the doggie doo-doo to work its way out of the bag and onto me. Bagging Burton's backyard deposit is excruciating. The smell, the texture — even through the triple-layer plastic bag and gloves — and the mammoth size all combine to make the experience one of the most demeaning of my life. Tied for first place with clambering onto a garbage bin to witness my boyfriend cavorting with Undulating Ursula. As I tie the bag and deposit it at the side of the house, trying not to gag, I wonder, "When did my life become so undignified?"

I return the Dopey dwarf to where it had been standing before Burton got hold of him. Thankfully, Cam and Pam are both at work, so they don't see me. As I set him back in place, I wonder if Pam will be dusting for prints and find out I was manhandling him? I must remember to bring over a towel and remove my fingerprint evidence, along with Burton's slobber.

In a pre-emptive strike, I spend the remainder of the afternoon downloading Burton Cummings' life's work. I figure if I can pipe music into Burton he will be less apt to eat stereos, speakers and other electronic equipment. I have no idea if my theory will work, but I can't have him growling at my car stereo all week. I had seen what he's capable of lying on the floor of the office this morning. Burton, meanwhile, sleeps peacefully on the sofa — the entire sofa, there's hardly room for Stella, let alone anything or anyone larger than a stuffed toy. I'm not sure if Burton likes only Burton Cummings' solo stuff or if he's open to The Guess Who's work as well, so I start to download it all.

34

The dinner hour comes and goes. I call John and text him, but he doesn't answer either. I fully suspect he is with Ursula but have no way of knowing, since he didn't have the decency to communicate his whereabouts. Since I have no one to cook for — Burton's food comes prepared in the bag — I don't bother fixing a meal. I couldn't eat if I wanted to. My stomach is constantly in knots these days, just in varying degrees of tightness. Walking by the lawn ornament display is one level, working with Sesame-Cecily tightens them a little, then, finally, dealing with dance and Ursula puts them into a whole new knot-tying category using one of those gigantic ropes that ties oceanliners to wharfs. I should be thankful I don't throw up like poor Kit. I, honestly, wonder if tossing my cookies would alleviate some of the tension; hanging over the toilet might be a welcome change of pace.

I spend the evening catching up on household chores. The laundry, in particular, has a nasty way of piling up. John used to do the laundry, since most of it is his — the majority of my work suits demand dry cleaning — but he's been so preoccupied, he hasn't gone near the laundry room in ages.

In between loads, while the iPod is charging — it's been

a while since I actually used it — I try to fit the earbuds into Burton's ears. Burton's ears are clipped, so they stick straight up. The earbuds could work but I fear will fall into his ear canals and get stuck. I can't imagine explaining to Mr. Klein how I managed to wedge an earphone into Burton's ears so I start to search the house for other options.

Finding workable headphones should be doable because John is a music and gadget freak — you don't know how many gadgets exist until you see John's stereo. I start looking for the small individual headphones with the plastic, curved arms that go over your ears to hold them in place. I figure if I can clip them to Burton's pointy ears, they'll stay put while he's travelling in the car or walking. I search, but, to no avail. I'm digging in one of the stereo-accessory cupboards, when Burton's "My Own Way to Rock" starts blaring from my laptop. Own way to rock, indeed! Burton is definitely his own dog. Arrggh. When the piano solo starts, I want to scream. I reach over to the laptop and press the Forward-to-Next button and "Break It to Them Gently" starts. Unfortunately, Burton must appreciate Burton's "My Own Way to Rock" because the mid-song forward prompts him to lift his head and start barking. Not moving or anything — Lord knows he doesn't get off the couch — but barking adamantly. I can't believe he can tell the difference between songs — in his sleep, no less — but I press the Back-to-Previous button and, the moment "My Own Way to Rock" begins, he yawns and lowers his head to rest on Stella again. This is ridiculous. I have to find some way for Burton to enjoy his choice of music independently.

I'm in the guest room, digging in the closet, when I hear Burton barking like mad. I register the silence of my laptop and assume Burton's issue is with the music being off, but I'm close to recovering John's Nike Aero neckband headphones — purchased last summer while he was wiring a cottage — but they'd never fit John properly so had been tossed in a miscellaneous box, in the closet. As I finally put my hand on the headphones and pull them out of the box I hear a frightened John yelling, "Mel! What the hell is this? Where are you?"

Oh oh. "Coming!" I rush out to the kitchen, where Burton is braced, barking at John, who's taken refuge on the opposite side of the kitchen island from Burton.

Quickly assessing the scene, I shriek at John, "Did you turn off the laptop?" Admittedly, it isn't the kindest way to greet my boyfriend, who is in fear of his life, but it can't be helped. It's not like dealing with a full-grown Great Dane hasn't been stressful but, honestly, several hours of Burton Cummings is really the catalyst for pushing me over the edge of compassion.

"What the hell is *that*?" John is pointing at Burton.

"It's a dog, John. I left you a voicemail and a text about him. Do you even check the messages I leave you?" I yell back and walk over to Burton. "*Bad* Burton! Sit and shut up!"

On command, Burton sits and stops barking but still maintains eye contact with John and lets out a low growl.

John stays put on the other side of the island. I walk over to the laptop, locate "My Own Way to Rock" and hit Play. Burton's head shifts and he turns to look at me. Satisfied, Burton stands up, barks at John one more time, and returns to the couch and Stella.

"Why are you listening to Burton Cummings? I thought you were into Kings of Leon?" John ignores my reprimand for not checking his messages and stops questioning the presence of a one-hundred-sixty-five-pound Great Dane on our couch holding an ugly stuffed doll. Odd, it's not like he arrives home every day to a scene like this one. I should worry at his immediate acceptance and deliberate avoidance of my questions, but, honestly, I can hardly work up the energy.

"It's not for my benefit! It soothes the giant beast, as you can see. I was looking for headphones when you came in, so I can hook him up independently. Where the hell have you been anyway?" I glance at the clock. It's almost ten-thirty. Marc said John left work early for dance class, and here he is not showing up until ten-thirty at night. I'm no ballerina but, even in my limited understanding, that's one mighty long dance class.

"We went late. Getting ready for the show. It's fast approaching, you know?" John states the last bit of his thought emphatically, then turns his head quickly to look at the floor. Like I could forget when the *show* is? But, wait, did I detect a quick double-blink just before he turned his head? The quick double-blink is a sure sign of deception. John's not telling me the truth. Well, he is telling the truth about the show approaching, so he must be deceiving me about what he was doing. This is not happening! No. We have this thing figured out. He's been acting fairly normal lately. He's not having an affair. I must have imagined the double-blink. The combination of the two Burtons is finally making me completely insane. I can't deal with this right now.

I start toward the cabinet under the sink to retrieve my rubber gloves and three plastic shopping bags. When I stand up, gloves in hand, John asks, "What are you doing now?"

"Walking the dog!" I roll my eyes. I haven't been a dog person very long, but John really isn't catching on at all. I have to assume Undulating Ursula doesn't have a dog. "Come on, Burton!"

Burton, on command, gets up from his couch and follows me out the door, giving John a low growl as he walks past him.

I turn back to John as I prop open the door for Burton to go out. "And, John, you may want to lose the attitude since you haven't been a contributing member of this household for weeks. Perhaps you can switch up some laundry instead of being a complete ass!"

35

Life with Burton is busy. If anyone had told me last week that one dog could command so much attention, I would have laughed. I'm not laughing now; I'm exhausted. I keep Burton with me constantly on Tuesday, afraid to leave him alone. The iPod is charged by the morning and I manage to get the headphones to fit over his ears and he seems content, sleeping on the couch. Napping after his morning walk and required excrement deposit. It must be tiring, making such vast amounts of waste.

I'm in the washroom, doing my hair, when Burton starts barking.

"The dog's barking!" John yells from his chair in front of *Breakfast Television*.

"Yeah, I hear him. What does he…?" I don't get my question out when Burton appears at the washroom door, pawing at his left ear and barking. I check the earpiece; it's in place. "What?" I ask the Great Dane, knowing how ridiculous I appear. Burton barks again. I take the headphones off and place them near my ears — not on my ears since they are now Burton's property and have been in his dog-ears — the iPod still firmly affixed to Burton's collar over the "m" in

Charlemagne. To his credit, the left earphone is cutting out and crackling occasionally through The Guess Who's "American Woman." Burton's barking continues steadily and he follows me around the house as I search for replacement headphones that will work on his awkwardly shaped head. The fact he has been an iPod-carrying dog for only an hour seems to escape his tiny mind. Now, it seems, he can't exist without two functioning earpieces. I try the earbuds again, but they definitely won't stay put when he's moving around — and we have a meeting to attend. Finally, in desperation, I pick up John's Bang & Olufsen A8 earphones, which are earbuds with ear wraparounds. They fit Burton perfectly, and he finally stops barking and returns to Stella on the couch.

"*Hey*, those earphones are mine and they cost $200!" John expresses his displeasure with my solution to the barking.

"Of course, they do." I reach into my purse and pull two $100 bills out of Mr. Klein's incidentals envelope and place them on the arm of the chair where John is sitting, watching *Breakfast Television* and eating Captain Crunch.

"Cool." John's "undying attachment" to *his* headphones is obviously not as undying as he originally let on.

"Speaking of insanity, have you spoken to Cam or Pam lately?" I ask John.

"No, why?" John manages between bites of cereal.

"Apparently, some of their lawn ornaments have gone missing. I think Pam believes I'm responsible. You don't know anything about missing dwarfs, do you?"

"Nah. No idea." John mutters into his cereal bowl while reaching for the TV converter. Apparently *Breakfast Television* isn't as interesting as it was thirty seconds ago.

When I'm finished getting ready for work, I come out to the kitchen and find John has left — without so much as a goodbye — and Burton, Bang & Olufsen headphones in place, is lapping up the milk from the cereal bowl John has left on the counter. "Can't take two seconds to put that in the dishwasher," I think as Burton turns to me and licks his drooling mouth.

"Let's go, mister," I grab my purse and motion toward the door. Burton trots over to me and out the door, then stands beside the car, growling at the neighbour's Prince Charming bird feeder while I put the roof down.

"Don't even think about it! I'm in enough trouble as it is!" I realize I'm talking to a dog, who, even if he did care what I was saying, probably can't hear me over his music.

When the roof is half-down, Burton jumps into the car, over the door like an Olympic high jumper, and settles into the back seat. The stereo starts up Kings of Leon, but Burton shows no interest and seems to be bopping his head to the sounds coming out of his iPod.

The day starts off well. At the office, Astrid and Sesame avoid me — which almost makes picking up Burton's excrement worth it — and I get confirmation that two of my smaller deals have closed. Only one more small deal and the big Blackwell deal to go. The day starts to go sideways when

Burton's iPod quits due to constant playing, it has run out of charge. I had charged it overnight, leaving the laptop playing for him, but the charge doesn't last forever and it's been playing constantly since his morning walk and breakfast. Charging the iPod is an issue. The only solution is to get another iPod that can be charging while the first one is playing. I need an Apple Store.

Leaving Burton in my office, with my laptop playing his Burton Cummings playlist, I rush to the Eaton Centre and the closest Apple Store. When I say "rush" I mean as fast as one can travel while downtown on a busy Toronto afternoon. With Calvin Klein's incidentals envelope almost $400 lighter, I leave the Apple Store with two 2GB iPods — a green one and a blue one. I thought the pink and orange were a bit too feminine for Burton — capable of holding 500 songs each and another set of Bang & Olufsen A8 headphones. You never know when the first set might go crackly, and I'm now well aware of Burton's take on crackly headphones.

Burton's needs fulfilled for at least the next half-hour, I return to the office to retrieve him and take him home. On my way back to the office I receive a call from the Bedazzled Beauty Bridal Boutique. Yes, the Construction Cone Orange dress has arrived and they require me to come in as soon as possible so the alterations can be completed in time for the wedding. With caring for Burton and trying to convince myself nothing is going on between John and his dance instructor, I had all but forgotten about the Sunset Disaster — with matching shoes, which are also apparently in. I don't think taking Burton to a bridal shop is a good idea, even with his new headphones and calmer demeanour. I think it's best to take him home and attend the dress fitting alone.

I drop Burton off, although I have to stand at the door calling him repeatedly, as his dislike for Prince Charming has not waned one bit. After Burton barks himself out — apparently the Prince has learned whatever lesson Burton is intent on teaching him — Burton walks over and pees on the horse's leg, then comes to meet me at the door. "I hear ya, Burton. There's no such thing as a Prince Charming, is there? You know make-believe when you see it." Burton settles on the couch with Stella as I start the laptop and unwrap one of his new iPod Shuffles to start the charging process. With any luck, I can have three iPods charged by tomorrow morning and ready to go, thereby being prepared for any Burton emergency. I pet Burton and give him a kiss on the top of his head. Despite his insane music fascination and questionable artist preference, I do rather enjoy having him around. Weird, I know. I'm not a pet person but somehow Burton transcends the average pet. Maybe it's his size and the fact he can almost look me in the eye. He behaves more human than some people I know.

Standing at the Bedazzled Beauty Boutique, wearing the Sunset Disaster, complete with Construction Cone Orange satin shoes, being pinned by the helpful saleslady, I almost start to cry. What has my life become? I've been very calm about the orange dress. I keep telling myself things like "It is not my wedding. The dress is not a reflection of me. It is not about me." But standing here now, wearing the offending dress, I realize it is a little bit about me. I have to wear the stupid thing, and the shoes are hideous and cruel. Standing completely still, the left shoe is digging into my foot in at least three places, and the right shoe has already caused a blister on my heel. Dyed satin shoes are the creation of Satan. Orange-dyed satin shoes prove Satan does indeed have a sense of humour. The only thing separating satin and Satan is one letter. Coincidence? I think not. I'm mentally congratulating myself on my theory and smiling into the mirror, when the helpful saleslady pops up from pinning the hem and sees my grin.

"It *is* lovely, isn't it?" she comments, mistaking my grin of evil genius for approval of the ensemble.

"Oh, it's something, all right!" I don't have the heart to tell her I'm actually feeling a bit nauseous and would rather attend my brother's wedding in a string bikini than wear this atrocity.

As I'm leaving the Bedazzled Beauty Bridal Boutique, a breathtaking wedding dress catches my eye. The dress is on a mannequin just inside the door, so I hadn't noticed it when I came in. The dress is remarkably unadorned with a straight cut, floor-length skirt, tight bodice with very thin spaghetti straps. Neither time I've been to this boutique have any of the wedding dresses ever caught my eye. Now this very simple dress is threatening to evoke a host of emotions I rarely acknowledge in myself. I reach out to touch the fabric of the skirt but think better of it and quickly turn to leave. Sitting in my car, I realize I do want to get married. I want the white dress and the big party. I want it to be me, and not my brother, who is getting married. I want John to snap out of whatever phase he's in and step up to the plate and ask me to marry him. I do want the fairy-tale ending. Obviously, I also hope I'll never display my fairy tale on the front yard in miniature ceramic. But, hey, I like to think I could if I so desired — with the hope that someone would slap me and save me from my insane self. Kit, presumably. Driving home, I turn the stereo up very loud and try to leave all thoughts of weddings, orange dresses and Satan's shoes behind me.

36

Apparently — and Mr. Klein failed to explain this fully in the short, cryptic note he had left at my office — "Burton doesn't like being left alone" is the understatement of the year. Burton has some dog version of separation anxiety. I, of course, had to Google Burton's behaviour after the fact in order to reach the "separation anxiety" conclusion. From my research, I conclude Burton is not a classic example but does exhibit some of the tendencies. The most obvious tendency is the destruction of personal items belonging to the "abandoner." In Burton's case, I am the abandoner and the personal items are my favourite pink boots — the same boots I still love even with the jelly stain.

"*Buuuurrrrtttonnn*!" I shriek immediately upon seeing the shredded bits of boots all over the living-room carpet. One sole and heel — well, half of the heel — completely mangled. The other sole and heel nonexistent. I have no idea what ingesting the sole and four-inch heel of a Size 7 boot will do to a Great Dane, but I suspect I will find out in the days to come. I yell at Burton, pointing and shaking my finger at him. I'm not sure if Burton has heard cuss words before, but he knows them now. Burton feels bad. Well, I think he does.

He cowers and keeps coming to me and leaning on me as I crawl around the floor picking up bits of torn leather. For my part, I'm not inclined to forgive him immediately and turn off the laptop to show him just who is boss. Why should I have to pick up the remains of my beloved boots while he enjoys the music of his choice? In fact, after a few minutes of no music and only the sounds of my cussing, I find my Kings of Leon playlist and press Play, scowling at Burton and defying him to make one sound — my thought process being if he objects too adamantly, I'll haul his Burton-Cummings-loving butt to the nearest kennel whether he likes it or not. Burton, obviously sensing my displeasure, creeps to the couch and cautiously watches me pick up boot bits, making no indication he's even registered my music selection.

I grab the telephone and plop down on the carpet, surrounded by shredded boots, and call Kit at work.

"Mel, is that you?" Kit asks, because I'm just breathing hard into the phone and can't say anything.

"I'm… going… to… kill… him." I finally get the sentence out in very slowly enunciated words.

"Who? Why? Where are you?" Kit sounds worried, and with good reason.

I'm still not able to give Kit a full explanation. My anger over the boots — which were technically ruined anyway — is inexplicably much more intense than I ever would have expected. It's just a pair of boots. Surely, I'm overreacting.

"Mel. Are you at your house? Just say yes or no." I haven't

answered Kit's questions, so she's resorted to the yes/no game.

"Uh huh." I'd love to expand my answer, but it isn't going to happen. I'm too angry to form complete thoughts.

"It's almost five o'clock, so I'll leave work right now and I'll be there as soon as I can. Just hold tight and don't do anything crazy." Kit is sincerely worried. I turn off the phone and lie back on the carpet amongst the boot remains. By the time Kit arrives, I'm in the fetal position, clutching the plastic bag I had started to fill with the remains of my boots.

"Mel?" Kit crouches down and puts her hand on my leg. "Mel. Are you okay?"

I sit up but can't make words yet. I open the plastic bag so Kit can examine the contents. Kit looks in the bag, and then around the carpet at the pink shreds I haven't picked up. Burton, for his part, is lying on the sofa with his paws over his eyes.

"I assume Burton did this." Kit looks up at Burton and continues, "BAD Burton!" I just nod.

"So, it's Burton you're going to kill and not Charlie Brown?" Kit sounds relieved. "You may be overreacting just a little. Didn't Mr. Klein leave more than enough money to replace the boots?"

"But these were my favourite pink ones." I slump back down to the carpet, my face still red with anger.

"I get it, but we can't change what's done. Let's get the rest of this mess cleaned up." Kit takes the bag from my hand and starts picking up shreds of leather. She crawls around me, picking up remains from the carpet. When she has all the visible bits, she pokes my side. "You have to get up so I can pick up the stuff you're lying on. And since you have to move, why don't you go to the kitchen and open a bottle of wine? Do you have the Merlot from Chile we like? We can have a chat on the deck. What do you say?" I am tired of being paralyzed with anger, so I stagger to standing and head to the kitchen, leaving Kit to finish picking up the remains of my boots.

Half an hour later, Kit and I are sitting on the back deck, holding glasses of Merlot. My anger has subsided, and Kit has placed the boot remains in the outside garbage container, vacuumed all the tiny traces from the carpet, and changed the playlist on the laptop for Burton, who is still cowering on the sofa.

"So, do you want to talk about what's really going on?" Kit asks quietly.

"Not really," I state matter-of-factly and look at my glass instead of at Kit.

"Well, I know it's not a pair of boots making you so angry, especially since they are the ones that were ruined at the doctor's office. What else happened today? How is the Blackwell deal?"

"It's not the boots. I knew Burton had acquired a taste for cervical jelly, so it's probably my fault for leaving them where he could get them. The deal is fine, thanks to Marc, actually. Marc was able to get me two three-day passes for the Canadian

Open, and I gave them to Frank at the Planning Department. Apparently, the Canadian Open's a big deal in golf or something, and Mr. Blackwell's permits were finally approved and filed yesterday. The deal will close Friday as planned."

"Wait a second! You bribed a Planning Department employee?" Kit stammers.

"No! Well, not technically. The permits are fine — they were just buried in a pile on his desk. And the tickets were encouragement for him to go and dig until he found them and get them processed in time for the deal to close."

"Whew! I was worried for a second you'd crossed over to the dark side," Kit smiles.

"Speaking of the dark side, I had a dress fitting for the wedding; it's being altered as we speak. The shoes are horrible, just like we suspected. I got blisters just standing still." I manage to fill Kit in on the Sunset Disaster fitting.

"Well, I can see where trying the Disaster on would be upsetting. Maybe we can..."

"John's having an affair." The words blurt out of my mouth, cutting Kit off mid-sentence. I haven't even let myself *think* those words, and now here they are — hanging in the air like streamers at a surprise party.

"What? I thought you said things were better?" Kit is visibly shocked and hasn't even noticed I have cut her off — she hates it when I do that.

"I've been deluding myself. I think I've known all along, but I didn't want to admit it. I've known in my head since the first garbage-bin adventure. It's just taken this long for my heart to catch up." Saying what I've known but couldn't admit to myself is good. I'm exhausted from the past few weeks, and telling Kit makes me feel better. "He doesn't get home any night before ten. And when he is with me, he's always 'somewhere else.' It certainly isn't here. He doesn't even read my texts or pick up my voicemails. Even if it's not an affair, it might as well be. His heart certainly isn't here anymore."

"What are you going to do?" Kit asks quietly.

"Nothing until after the wedding. I don't want anything to upset my brother's special day. Do you want to hear something funny? I had hoped I might be the next wedding. Can you believe it?" I laugh, slightly embarrassed.

"That isn't funny. It makes sense, actually. I'm nowhere near getting married and the twins are a decade behind us. You being next is still probable; even with this little hiccup." Kit smiles.

"Little hiccup, indeed." I pause, take an unladylike gulp of wine, then continue, "Oh well, I'll stick it out with John until the wedding is over, then deal with it. I'll have to figure out what to do about the house and all the logistics of breaking up, but I can't think about all that right now."

"This is a bad week for you to have Burton. Do you want me to take him?" Kit asks.

"No. Surprisingly, he's one of the things keeping me sane. I'm so busy watching him, it takes my mind off of John and the mess of my relationship," I laugh. "And he's more attentive than John has been lately. He *ate* my boots! John doesn't even know one was ruined in the doctor's office incident. Maybe I should stick to dogs instead of boyfriends."

As if on cue, Burton appears at the door and starts walking toward me with his head down. He drops Stella in my lap, sits and leans on me, putting his head against my chest. I pet him and say, "Thank you" for the Stella gesture so he knows we are friends again.

37

Burton has a digestive system of steel. Passing the Size 7 boot sole and heel didn't even faze him. It did take the remainder of the week to complete the process, but there were no emergency vet calls and he actually seemed livelier than before he ingested the boots. Maybe expensive leather is a metabolism booster for mammoth dogs. The rotating iPods are a stroke of genius and go a long way in controlling Burton's separation-anxiety issues. After the boot day, Burton starts destroying John's possessions instead of mine. And, honestly, I don't find this behaviour nearly as difficult to tolerate. The toy race-car speedway track is now eighty or ninety feet shorter, and as soon as the cool weather gets here, John will notice he's several sweatshirts and two jackets lighter. I did have to give John one of the $100 bills to replace his flesh-coloured, one-piece leotard. He noticed the holes in it immediately — well, the holes and it was missing a leg. Aside from the leotard, I make no attempt to replace John's other "missing" items because he isn't even aware they are missing yet and my voiced revelation of his affair is keeping me from feeling too much responsibility for his belongings.

Wednesday of Burton Week, Pam confronts me again.

Seems Goldilocks, the three bears, plus two sheep are missing. This time she wasn't quite so discreet in accusing me of stealing her lawn ornaments. The conversation went downhill until I finally told her to "search my house if she really thinks I have her tacky ornaments!" My relationship with the neighbours is very quickly evaporating.

Shortly after the lawn-ornament confrontation, Mr. Klein's incidentals envelope becomes $1,400 lighter when I go to replace my pink boots and find a sale, so purchase two pairs. The pale green is lovely — nothing like my lime green ones — and who would have guessed the yellow ones would be so cute? The new boots remain stowed in the trunk of my car, just in case Burton tires of eating John's things and goes back to mine, but I can't wait to start wearing them. Maybe Burton did me a favour; the new boots are fresh and crisp, and both pairs are dog saliva-free.

At ten p.m. of Burton's last night with me, I set him up on the sofa with one of his charged iPods as usual, then head to bed — alone. John's not home yet and hasn't responded to either of my calls. I only wonder if I'll be able to tolerate John's antics for another nine days until the wedding is over. I shake my head and try not to think about it. I crawl into bed and have just turned off the light, when I feel the weight of Burton climbing onto the bed.

"Uh uh, mister. No Great Danes in the bed. You're a couch dog, remember?" I turn the light back on and try to be firm with Burton. Burton doesn't seem to be listening and circles three times before dropping like a boulder onto the bed, his head on John's pillow. I try to push him off the bed, but he doesn't budge. There's no way I'm moving the brute. I could get up and coax him back to the sofa, but I can't be bothered. It's his last night, and John's not here anyway. Burton might as well sleep in his spot. Resigned, I turn off the light, lie back down, and throw my arm over Burton. Dogs are better than boyfriends; more reliable, at any rate.

I don't hear John come in. He must have seen Burton and quietly crept to the guest room. Heck, for all I know, he didn't even come home at all. There is a cereal bowl beside the sink in the morning and a sticky note on the fridge stating, "work early" — which I rip off and crumble immediately. Affair or no affair, he's taking the stickys on the stainless-steel too far. I may be holding my tongue about the Ursula thing, but the stainless-steel liberties will not be tolerated.

I take Burton for an extra-long walk, then leave him outside while I go inside to gather his things. I've found I can leave Burton outside on his own for short lengths of time and he's good not to run away. He mostly just stands in the driveway growling at the neighbour's lawn ornaments. After a week, he has yet to embrace them. But I can't blame him, I don't like them much either, and I've had much longer to get used to the idea. I'm locking the door, loaded down with my purse, laptop, the remains of Burton's food, bones, Stella, the iPods, and extra headphones when Burton trots up to me carrying what appears to be a large branch in his mouth.

"Hey, mister, what do you have?" In response, Burton seems to grin at me in a most satisfied fashion. Okay, I know dogs don't exactly have the ability to do that sort of thing, but I swear it looked like he was smirking.

"BAD BURTON!" Upon closer inspection, I realize what had appeared to be a branch is indeed one of the plastic legs belonging to Prince Charming's horse from next door.

"Burton! You've been so good and not touched him since the first day! What's gotten into you? You know Pam thinks I'm sabotaging her. This is *not* going to help my defence." Either Burton knows he's being reunited with Calvin Klein today and feels he's safe from my reprimand or he's been plotting his attack on the Prince all week and finally thought this was the perfect moment. Whatever the case, I now have to deal with a three-legged horse and further neighbour-relations damage control.

"Get in the car, mister!" I shout at Burton, who immediately jumps into the back seat, still holding the horse leg in his mouth. I deposit Burton's belongings on the seat beside him and throw my laptop and purse on the front passenger seat before digging in my purse for the incidentals envelope. Upon inspection I see there are three $100 bills remaining so I scribble a note on the outside of the envelope,

Sorry. Burton broke your horse. I hope this is enough to replace it. If not please come over and I'll make up the difference. Sorry again. Mel, next door.

I then yank the leg out of Burton's mouth, shake it at him,

repeating "Bad dog" several times. I make my way through Cam and Pam's ornaments to the mailbox, where I deposit the money, then return to the Prince and precariously prop the Prince's horse up on the broken leg. I get the Prince and horse so they are standing, but the broken leg will likely prove useless in even the most mild wind gust. I lecture Burton on the virtue of respecting other people's property — even if it is very, very tacky property — for the entire ride to the office, but I strongly suspect he isn't listening to one thing I'm saying because he seems to be nodding his head in tune to the music coming through his headphones.

Arriving at the office is strange. No one is at the front desk. Astrid often strays away from her post but, since Sesame's been around, waiting to pounce on me the moment I arrive, I can always count on seeing her face immediately upon arrival. Dare I hope Sesame's translation is a thing of the past? Has Grumpy Jim finally realized I'm working to rule and as soon as all my current deals are closed I'm flying the coop? Can I afford to fly the coop, now that John and I appear to be on the road to separation? My mind starts to take a turn down a road I'm certainly not ready to examine at the office with Burton in tow. Back to reality, I hear laughter coming from the boardroom and Burton and I start towards it.

The entire office staff appears to be crammed into the boardroom, watching the forty-two-inch television. There, on the screen, is a close-up of me. Me being kissed by a seal.

TV Mel doesn't look like me, but she doesn't appear nearly as stiff and nervous as I thought she would. The most redeeming factor is my head looks perfectly proportioned; quite normal, in fact. I had worried my huge cranium would shadow the entire production but for the most part, the finished product is much better than I expected it would be. The DVD is clicked back a chapter to replay my line — "And we'll seal the deal!" — again, and the room erupts in laughter. While the DVD is being reversed a second time, I clear my throat and Burton supports me with one loud bark. Everyone turns to the doorway where I'm standing, and the television turns off.

"Here's the superstar! Burton!" Calvin Klein makes his way through the crowd toward me and starts to wrestle with Burton in the hallway outside the boardroom. I'm not sure by his greeting if I'm the superstar or if Burton is. The staff starts to disperse. Grumpy Jim walks over and stands beside me with the remote still in his hand.

"How was my little man? What's up with the ear-things?" Calvin turns to me and asks. I don't register for a moment as I'm still absorbing the fact that my head has just been on a forty-two-inch television screen.

"Ahhh... good. He was fine. He likes iPods. The music keeps him calm. Is that the commercial?" I direct the question to Jim.

"Yep! Goes out this week. You're going to be a star, Mel!" Jim grins.

"Your head is perfect!" Calvin Klein seems impressed with himself and pats my head for effect.

"Are you sure? I don't think the seal idea is..." I knew this was coming but had managed to forget about it while taking care of Burton. I haven't addressed with Jim that I'm actively considering leaving the company and I probably shouldn't be the spokesperson.

"Seal's perfect. You look great!" Calvin cuts me off. "Did I leave you enough money? Burton has the ability to rack up expenses." Mr. Klein completely changes the topic.

"Tell me about it! And you left just enough. I spent the last of it on a lawn ornament this morning." I turn to Jim. "Are you completely sure you want a seal and, well... me... representing the company?"

"Margery loves it. She gave her approval last night. It's a go," Jim replies with a satisfied grin; so few things he does actually impress Margery.

"But..." I want to explain my leaving, but Jim looks so happy with his accomplishment I can't do it.

"Missy, you're going to have to fill me in on this ear-thing. If you say Burton likes it, then Burton shall have it." Calvin Klein rubs Burton's giant head.

"Oh, ah..." I'm still wrestling with what to say to Jim.

"Here." Calvin Klein hands me an envelope. I peek inside, a bit afraid. The last time he gave me an envelope, I was saddled with the care and nurturing of a Great Dane for a week. This envelope is much friendlier, however. It contains a cheque, payable to me, in the amount of $8,000.

"Okay, what's the catch? What's this for?" I ask suspiciously.

"Payment for being in the commercial. You didn't think you were working for free, did you?" Mr. Klein laughs. "Now, fill me in on these ear thingamajigs!"

38

Kit, Kevin and Marc stand around my laptop and burst into laughter for the tenth time. Kit's cheeks are wet from laughter tears, just like when I was trying on the Sunset Disaster for the first time. Only Kevin has the good taste not to laugh out loud. He is, however, having difficulty holding it in.

"Yeah, yeah. I think we've seen enough." I reach around Marc and stop the commercial, which I had downloaded from the DVD at the office.

"Just one more time?" Kit is laughing. "I just love when the seal kisses you!"

"No. You've seen enough!" I power down the laptop and put it back into the carry bag.

"Well, it's not as bad as I imagined after you described the filming, but it will be funny to anyone who knows you." Marc wipes a tear from his eye.

"Speaking of wildlife, did Mr. Klein pick up Burton?" Kit manages to pull herself together to ask an unrelated question.

"Yep, he's no longer my problem, although I did offer to watch him again any time. The big, lazy brute grew on me."

"Was anything said about the money you spent?" Marc asks, surprised.

"No. Mr. Klein didn't even bat an eye and... and this is the great part — he gave me another healthy chunk of change for the commercial! Seems I'm a paid celebrity now!" I laugh. "Oh, and he really liked the iPod idea. Apparently, he's tired of Burton's music himself so the iPods are a win-win situation. Unfortunately, he mentioned something about Celine Dion, so, if that is really the case, I'm glad Burton has his own iPod. Sorry, iPods. He has three now; I threw in mine when I was packing his stuff. I'm going to replace it. There's a new generation of Shuffle coming soon anyway."

"I thought the one you *had* was the new generation?" Marc asks.

"It was, but now there's going to be a third generation. Mine will be old news in a few months."

"I can't keep up. I have a cellphone that's just a phone! It doesn't take pictures or get email. It's just a phone!" Marc announces.

"That's because you're 'old school'!" Kit laughs and takes a sip of beer.

"Yeah, yeah. Are you going to John's dance show thing next Thursday?" Marc asks innocently.

"It's next Thursday?" I am completely shocked. John has not mentioned one thing to me. Mind you, I haven't seen him much and he doesn't answer my calls or texts, so how could I possibly know? I've had better conversations with Burton this past week. Sadly, most of those conversations were completely one-sided and revolved around Burton's excrement.

"Apparently. John is getting us all tickets. I personally can't wait to see it," Marc laughs. "You girls have to come!"

"Oh, I'm all over it!" Kit announces.

"We're playing out of town. But, Kit, you'll video it for me, won't you?" Kevin asks.

"Absolutely! It'll be something we can enjoy again and again!"

"Wait a second. Kit, the wedding is next Saturday. Aren't our parents arriving on Thursday?" I'm horrified. If John's crazy dance show is on Thursday night, I might be obliged to invite the parents. Or, worse, risk offending them by not inviting them. Obviously, in light of my suspicions, the last place I want to put my parents is in a dance studio with John and his floozy-headband-wearing-other-girlfriend. I feel my eyes open wider and know my face is giving away far too much information.

"Bring them along!" Marc offers. "The more, the merrier!"

"I don't think my parents are ready for a display of modern dance, especially if John's participating. He isn't exactly their favourite *sin*-in-law." I turn to Kit for support; she is the only one here aware of the whole situation.

"Well, I don't want to take my parents either! We'll have to think of something to distract them. Maybe they'll be busy with Mike and Sam, doing wedding stuff."

"Here's hoping." I take a sip of beer. "Oh, a much happier

note — well two happier notes, actually — the Blackwell deal closed today!"

"Cheers!" Marc says, and we all raise our glasses.

"Congratulations. Wow, that was a hard-earned commission!" Kit looks relieved after having lived the ups and downs of the deal second-hand.

"Absolutely, and I made some enquiries this afternoon with other companies. I'm meeting with my first choice on Monday morning. I'm going to meet the owner and, if everything goes well, I'm going to order signs and cards and be part of a Sesame-free organization!" I force a laugh. Inside, my stomach is churning and I feel completely uneasy. The idea of changing companies for work is stressful enough, but combined with John's looming public dance display, I feel completely out of control. I have never been able to relate to Kit's nervous stomach and her frequent bouts of distress. I never vomit from anything but stomach flu and occasional motion sickness. Boats are not my friend — probably because they take me near sea life, and you know where I stand on that particular topic. Suddenly, sitting at the Firkin beside a laptop containing my thirty seconds of television fame — which I had to share with a seal — while contemplating my probably cheating boyfriend's dance premiere, I understand what Kit lives with on an almost daily basis. How does she do it? I look up from my beer at Kit, who is laughing, sitting beside her boyfriend and across from Marc, the man who worships her and would do anything for her. I realize we've suddenly changed places.

Tonight, Kit is the self-assured, strong one and I'm the nervous, nauseous one. I want my confident life back. I reach down and stroke the leather of my right yellow boot. I love my new boots. Petting my boot gives me a renewed sense of calm. Kit maintains expensive footwear is not the answer to all of life's problems. I strongly beg to differ.

39

After I finish my beer, I have to head home to face the neighbours. I knock on Cam and Pam's door with flowers and a pie in hand. To my relief, Cam answers. To date, Cam has not accused me of stealing his property, like Pam has on two separate occasions.

"Hi, Cam. I just wanted to stop by to apologize for the horse thing. I'm really, really sorry. I only left Burton alone for a few seconds. I don't know what got into him..." I start talking fast, hoping to keep some semblance of a relationship with the neighbours.

"Hey, no worries. Pam's a bit upset about... well... everything these days. I should apologize if she's accused you of stealing the lawn ornaments; she's blaming everyone on the block, not just you."

"Oh." I really hadn't imagined Pam was blaming everyone; I thought she had her sights set only on me.

"Yeah, she's a bit emotional these days; she's taking the missing lawn ornaments quite personally..." Then, without stopping, Cam blurts out, "We're trying to get pregnant and it's not going very well."

I suddenly feel very awkward, like I'm overhearing a personal conversation I should not be party to. "Oh. I'm so sorry to hear that." I am sincerely sorry. I can't imagine wanting children but, if I did, I can't imagine not being able to have them. Heck, the control freak I am, I'm sure I'd do more than accuse my neighbours of lawn-ornament theft. "I brought these as a peace offering, and I'll keep my eyes open for anyone acting strange around your yard." I hand Cam the pie and flowers, and head back to my house. Wow, I guess it's not just me going through a tough time right now.

Kit and I go to the Bedazzled Beauty Bridal Boutique to pick up the Sunset Disaster the next day. I keep checking my purse, looking for something, but not knowing what. I realize halfway though the day I'm missing Burton. Not that he was ever able to fit into my purse. I just feel at loose ends without having to worry about him. The Sunset Disaster try-on is every bit as amusing for Kit this time as it was the first time. I, on the other hand, don't find it at all amusing. The shoes still hurt my feet, and I suspect I'm going to have to have a spare pair the day of the wedding if I hope to be walking and not crawling around the reception. I still have no idea what Jacques-Pierre and his crack team of hair designers will be doing with my hair, but at this point I realize nothing will improve the ensemble and it can't get much worse — so bring it on. I leave the boutique with the dress, which now fits, the nasty shoes and the crinoline. I plan to burn both the shoes and crinoline next Sunday, if not immediately following the ceremony. The dress I'm going to keep until I find a way to bring it back to torment Mike and Sam. I'm not sure what that might be, but I'm positive I'll think of something — placemats to clash with their red dinnerware, perhaps?

I don't see John for most of the weekend. He's gone to the dance studio before I get up and I'm in bed before he gets home. We are like two ships passing in the night. Unfortunately, or maybe fortunately for my sanity, I find myself smiling at the thought of him being the *Titanic* smacking into an iceberg.

Monday morning, I wake up with butterflies in my stomach. I have to go to the office first thing to resign my position officially with Jim; I have my letter of resignation ready and dated for today. Then I will go to meet with one of Jim's competitors to, hopefully, sign on as their newest sales associate. I'm not totally gripped by fear; I am, after all, a qualified agent with a good client base. But the fear of the unknown still lurks in my mind, interjecting doubt where I require complete confidence. I don't know what I'm worried about — I love the competitive thrill of making deals, selling properties and putting people together with the right homes for them. I love being able to get the job done, get the permits approved and haggle to get the best price. I'm good at my job, very good. A change of company could be just the thing I need; well, it better be just the thing — because it's happening.

I look over at the sofa while I'm pouring my coffee and miss Burton's big old butt lying on it. Maybe I should get a puppy after I kick John out. Hey, I could be a dog breeder. "Okay, probably not," I smile at my own joke.

I notice an envelope mixed in with the newspaper John has left strewn all over the island. John's handwriting reads,

Babe. Tickets for the show. Thursday. Bring your family. It'll be fun.

Babe. Who calls his girlfriend "babe"? I used to think it was cute, but now it makes my skin crawl. I wonder what he calls Undulating Ursula? Urs? Arse is more like it; she has a big enough one. I shake my head. I must stop thinking about John and Ursula and whatever it is they do together. I look inside the envelope and it contains ten tickets; enough for parents, twins, Kit, Ben, Kevin and me. There is no way I'm taking my parents to Ursula's vision. Whatever the hell else it might be, I suspect it will not be "fun."

I call Kit, and we agree we have to attend John's dance exhibit. But we also agree it would be best not to take the families. We aren't quite sure how we're going to accomplish the feat of keeping them away, but maybe they will have some wedding function to attend with Sam and Mike. If they are legitimately tied up with wedding stuff, then it will work out for everyone involved — but mostly for me. Of course, the idea of keeping the parents away and the actual ability to pull that off are two very different things.

Trying to put the idea of the parents witnessing John's dance recital out of my head, I get ready to face the reality at hand: resigning my position with Grumpy Jim. I dress in my black Armani power suit, light green blouse and my new green boots. Assessing myself in the mirror, I decide I look good enough to resign. Heck, I look good enough to get the new job — which hopefully I will.

When I walk into the office, the reasons I'm resigning come flooding back. There had been a week of reprieve, when I had Burton in tow. Both Astrid and Sesame had been terrified of him, so I was given a wide berth and didn't have to tolerate any Cecily-Sesame translation or Astrid attitude. Sadly, Burton isn't with me and, even in the power suit, the nonsense starts immediately. The moment I'm in the office, Astrid scowls at me and Sesame is standing within six inches of me, waiting for me to speak. I've made speaking to Grumpy Jim my first priority and must do it without Sesame's interference.

"Astrid, is Jim in his office?" I ask, knowing full well he is because I can see him through the glass wall.

"Astrid, Mel would like to know if Mr. Johnstone is in?" says Sesame. My head is going to explode. I have not missed her singsong voice at all. In fact, I'd forgotten how annoying it was while I had the protection of Burton.

"Tell Mel Mr. Johnstone is not seeing anyone right now," Astrid says to Sesame, even though I'm standing in front of her. She really seems to enjoy this talk-through-Sesame business — too bad the party's ending.

"Mr. Johnstone is not seeing anyone," Sesame says to me.

"I can see him!" I point at the glass wall of Grumpy Jim's office. "He's not with anyone. Can you please ask if he has a few moments for me?" I plead with Astrid, even though it's killing me.

"Astrid, Mel does not believe Mr. Johnstone has left instructions not to be disturbed," Sesame interjects.

"Astrid didn't say Jim left instructions not to be disturbed!" I raise my voice directly to Sesame, ignoring Astrid at this point.

"Cecily, please tell Mel that Mr. Johnstone *did* leave instructions not be disturbed, as you said." Astrid leers from behind her desk.

"This is insane! Can you two hear yourselves?" I am completely exasperated. "What are you? Twelve?" I then turn to Sesame and realize she probably isn't much more than twelve. "Well, you might be. But, Astrid, there is no excuse for your juvenile behaviour!"

"Astrid, Mel is wondering about the acoustics of the room and seems to be getting frustrated. Perhaps she's..."

"Enough!" I cut Sesame's translation short, storm to Grumpy Jim's office, open the door, and walk in. I slam the door behind me, noticing if I'd been half a second later, I would have whacked Sesame with it. Her ability to stay with me would be commendable if it wasn't so irritating.

"She has to go!" I growl at Grumpy Jim. "I can't work like this!"

"Who?" Jim must be playing dumb; there's no way he can't see Sesame's nose pressed against the glass wall, looking at us.

"Her! That's who!" I point at Sesame's squished face, then walk over and close the blinds so she can't see in.

"Not getting on then?" Grumpy Jim asks sarcastically.

"I can't work like this. Sesame... I mean Cecily may be making Astrid's life easier, but neither of them is making mine any easier. Astrid still can't fax properly and she still isn't doing her job. Surely the other agents are complaining as well. It can't just be me. The whole situation is driving me crazy, and it's a very short drive these days." I blurt out without drawing breath.

"I know." Grumpy Jim puts his head in his hands in defeat. "She is totally annoying. When you aren't here, or even when you were here with the giant dog, she follows me around. It's enough to drive anyone batty."

"So, you *know* how irritating she is and you still keep her?" I am shocked to hear Jim has had to endure Sesame translation and has not completely snapped. Grumpy Jim isn't nearly as easygoing as I am. And let's face it, I'm not easygoing at all.

"Margery won't let me get rid of her. Seems Cecily is the daughter of one of her Knit-Wit friends..."

"Nitwit, indeed..." I start to interrupt.

"No, they call themselves the Knit-Wits. It's Margery's knitting group," Grumpy Jim explains.

"Knitting group? Isn't knitting by nature an independent activity? Okay, whatever! Forget the Knit-Wits, Cecily doesn't *do* anything. How can you pay someone to walk around the office irritating people? Let her follow Margery around for a day!" At my last suggestion, Grumpy Jim's head pops up and I see what resembles a smile — or the closest thing to a smile I've ever seen on his face.

"Ohhh, that would be funny!" Grumpy Jim likes the idea of setting Sesame loose on Margery and the Knit-Wits.

"But it's never going to happen," I state matter-of-factly, as I plunk down in the chair across from Jim's desk. I can recognize defeat when it's right in front of me. Grumpy Jim does not have the spine required to take on Margery in any capacity.

"No, probably not in this lifetime. What happened to me, Mel? I used to be a formidable force. I was a top-selling agent, like you. When did I lose my drive and ambition? When did I become a doormat?" Grumpy Jim's plea makes me feel bad about my outburst. Knowing he also has had to endure the annoying Sesame, then go home to Margery every night makes my heart ache a little for him.

"I can't answer that question for you, Jim. I do know the situation here with Astrid and the lovely and vivacious Cecily has become completely unbearable for me."

"I know. I know." Grumpy Jim sounds defeated.

"The only feasible option for me is to resign. I know you've seen it coming. I haven't taken on any new clients in weeks. Besides, my personal life needs some attention, so I'm moving on." I take my resignation letter out of my bag and place it on Grumpy Jim's desk.

Grumpy Jim looks up, "Mel, we've had a great run, you and me. I know I'm not always the most approachable person, but I think we did some great work together." Grumpy Jim stands up and walks around his desk. I stand up beside him.

"You're doing the right thing, Mel. You're doing what I wish I had the guts to do. I'll miss you. Of course, I'll miss my sanity as well. You know it won't be around long if Cecily takes to following me around."

"Thanks, Jim. Good luck. You should consider making her an agent. She's a talker. I bet she could sell." I shake Jim's hand, then walk out of his office, where Sesame picks up my stride and follows me back to my office.

40

Arriving at my office door with Sesame in tow, I take extreme pleasure in telling her I am no longer affiliated with the company, so she should go find someone else to bother. I also plant the seed of her pursuing a career in another field. I believe my exact words are "This annoying thing you do? It isn't a real job, you know? Why don't you put your thinking cap on and come up with something less annoying to do on a full-time basis. Perfume-spray girl at The Bay, perhaps?"

After Sesame slumps away from my office door, I step into my office and look around. I never planned to leave this office. I made a good living, love the clients, found Grumpy Jim interesting, and even got along with most of the other agents — except, of course, Ryan the Snake. Strange how life works — one day, you're going along fine, the next you're packing up bankers boxes while picturing your future ex-boyfriend in a flesh-coloured leotard embracing an overweight woman in dream-catcher earrings — okay, maybe not everyone who leaves a job does that last part. I shudder at the thought and throw the framed photograph of John and me from last New Year's Eve into a box. Last New Year's Eve, John didn't know modern dance existed and I was his only romantic interest. We were out with Kit and Kevin, Kevin's band was playing, and we had an amazing time. Kit and I took turns dancing with John because Kevin was otherwise occupied, providing the music. Everyone was dressed in nice, normal clothes. Not a leotard in sight. Hell, six months ago, we all — including John — would have had a good laugh over someone wearing a flesh-coloured leotard. Things have certainly changed.

I spend the rest of the afternoon locked in my office, packing up my personal effects and determining how much money it's going to cost me to get John out of my house and out of my life. I start to scribble down numbers on a pad of paper. The sale price we'll fetch if we sell now, less the initial purchase price plus cost of renovation, less down payment — made entirely by me, as John had no money at the time and probably still doesn't because he's missing work to dance with Ursula — divided by two — $30,000. It's going to cost me $30,000 to buy John out. Good lord! My choices are rather bleak: $30,000 to keep the house, or we sell and I have to start all over again. At this point, even with the commercial money and my latest commissions, I don't have $30,000. The idea of leaving the neighbours' lawn ornaments in the dust is appealing, but I love my house and don't want to sell it. "At least, I have an idea of what I'm looking at," I think sadly.

I pull my laptop out of my bag and start to type a proposal, in the event I magically locate vast amounts of money between now and the day I confront John. Dear Dumb —

Ass...backspace, backspace, backspace — John. Yes, I'm writing a "Dear John" letter. I'm sure I'll find humour in this at some point later in my life, but today it's just frustrating. If *dear* John hadn't discovered modern dance I wouldn't be creating this little spreadsheet to propose how much money I'll give him to go away. *He's* having the affair and I'm going to have to pay him to go away. What was I thinking, moving in with him? Why did we put the house in both our names? Where did it all go so terribly wrong? I finish the financial settlement proposal, close my laptop, gather my boxes and bid my office goodbye.

Walking past Astrid's desk, I hear her say into the telephone, "Hello? Hello? Oh, well, I guess I lost the call!" Sesame is standing outside Jim's closed door, looking lost and panicked. Not having anyone to mimic must be killing her. I can see Jim through his glass wall, sitting with his head in his hands, a bottle of antacid on his desk. I smile to myself as I walk out the door towards my car. Whatever else this week brings, however financially destitute I become after confronting John, I will not ever have to tolerate another of Sesame's translations.

I immediately drive to the office of Jim's nemesis, Morty The Man. Morty's real name is Melvin Morton and he is the face for his company. Morty refers to himself often in his advertising and always in the third person as Morty The Man. My experience at Morty's office is refreshing. When I arrive, the reception desk has two women sitting behind it and both seem competent. One is on the telephone — presumably, she was able to pick up the call and keep the caller connected — while the other one takes my name and notifies Mr. Morton that I am here. A positive first impression, indeed.

Morty himself is everything I expect, and more. He's very gregarious, with a loud voice and exaggerated hand gestures. He shakes my hand with the strength of a lumberjack; he seems to know a great deal about me and my selling history. I assume he has taken the time to ask my industry peers about me. I like him immediately. My meeting with Morty is short and pleasant. Morty explains he is going to place an ad in the two major papers announcing my new affiliation with his company in two weeks' time — it gives me time to let my clients know and get over the hoopla of my brother's wedding — and the meeting ends with a second lumberjack handshake and a hearty, "Welcome aboard, Mel!" I leave with the name of the printer that has the company artwork, a signed contract, and, best of all, no personal translator trailing after me.

My next stop is at the printer to order new cards and signs, which are going to take a week to complete, then I'm free to do anything I please. I decide shopping is the only way to celebrate my new-found translator-freedom so I head downtown.

Unfortunately, my freedom is short-lived. Before I am able to make even one purchase, my brother calls me on my cell, announcing he and Samantha are in Toronto to prepare for the wedding and he requests my helping hands if they are available. I spend the remainder of Monday afternoon and evening in Mr. and Mrs. Bennington-Hall's living room, sticking Mike and Sam's personalized labels on bottles of homemade wine. Apparently, Mr. Bennington-Hall had insisted on making the wine and, even after the mint julep fiasco Mrs. Bennington-Hall allowed it. I guess she had a better time at the shower than I did. Sam and Mike think Mr. Bennington-Hall can't go too wrong with wine, but I have my suspicions. If anyone could go wrong in the homemade-wine department, it's Mr. Bennington-Hall. The fact Mr. Bennington-Hall won't let us sample any of the wine — his argument being there will not be enough for the wedding reception if we do — raises my suspicions even further. I make a mental note to avoid the wine at the wedding.

Tuesday and Wednesday fly by with more wedding preparations. I am glad I'm not working. I don't know when I would have found time to go to the office. I spend two days tying orange ribbons on bottles of bubbles — the guests are meant to blow bubbles at the newlyweds instead of throwing rice — boxing the chocolate-orange truffle giveaways and spray-painting topiary trees for centrepieces. It seems Mrs. Bennington-Hall was so pleased with the topiary decorations at the shower that she convinced Samantha to have them at the wedding. I believe I'd like to marry someday, but if the price is orange topiaries I may reconsider.

Our biggest challenge of the week is locating every party-supply store in the Greater Toronto Area trying to match the colour of the Sunset Disaster dresses to streamers and balloons. Samantha gets quite discouraged at the fourth party-supply store. I'd like to point out she should have planned her wedding closer to Halloween if she wanted to find the perfect decorations, but I manage to bite my tongue. Again, it's not my wedding. "It's not my wedding" actually becomes my mantra for the week. At one point, I suggest balloons and streamers might not be the way to go, decoration-wise. The reception hall is lovely and doesn't require extra decoration. An angry, puffy-eyed bride, whose desire for tacky decorations will be fulfilled, shoots me down. Samantha finally settles — at the seventh party-supply store — on the only orange streamers and balloons available. The colour does not match the bridesmaid dresses — but unless the streamers were made of recycled construction cones, how could it? Samantha is semi-defeated but pleased to have streamers and balloons — even in the incorrect shade of orange. I can picture the lovely reception hall all "tacky-ed up" with streamers, balloons and bright orange topiaries, on every table. I visibly shudder. "It's not my wedding, it's not my wedding," I chant to myself repeatedly. At one point, I start to think, "My wedding will be a small, intimate affair with very few attendants, none of whom will be wearing anything orange…" My thought stops quickly when I realize I am further from having a wedding than I was a few months ago. At the rate I'm backsliding, I may never have a wedding — tacky, topiaried or otherwise.

By Wednesday afternoon, John's dance recital, or show, or whatever it's called, is looming large in my head and I can hardly think of anything else. The parents are scheduled to arrive tomorrow morning — Thursday — and I have yet to come up with a plan to keep them from attending. The only idea I have is to persuade one or both of the twins to invent an illness. I strongly suspect, even if the twins would agree, that only the Jennings will stay home with them. My mother will likely still insist on attending. To keep my mother away, I consider doing something to sabotage my brother's wedding, thereby causing my mother to rush to Mike and Sam in support and sympathy. But after spending several days with the stressed-out bride, I can't bring myself to do anything so sinister. She's fairly close to the breaking point without a fabricated disaster, just days before the big event.

I decide the only possible way to keep my mother occupied while John dances his heart out is a jewellery emergency. Lame? Absolutely. But Betty Melrose is very passionate about her creations. If I need something "restrung" she will put her own art above John's. I riffle through my jewellery box and find the least flamboyant piece she's gifted me — a starfish dangling from a string of small seashells and rocks that she created during her Seashore phase — and cut the string, letting the pieces clatter into a cereal bowl.

"There!" I say with satisfaction as I toss the string into the garbage and make a mental note to take the garbage bag out before my mother arrives. "There's no way she'll leave the house until it's put back together!"

A little underhanded and devious? Probably. But it's for a good cause, and I will definitely be punished accordingly for my deed — I'll likely have to wear the thing at some point over the course of her visit to justify the urgent need for its repair.

41

"Are you kidding? I'm not pretending to be sick because then *I'll* miss John's dance thing too!" Taryn is not going along with my plan. Kit and I have been trying for twenty minutes to persuade her but she's not playing along. Seems she's become quite determined since accepting the internship in Australia — not the same child Kit and I used to know.

"Tia laughed and refused flatly as well," Kit reports.

What happened to the sweet little girls Kit and I could persuade to do anything? Times have certainly changed.

"I say 'Bring them along!' If John wants to dance in front of people, why not Mom and Dad?" Taryn is enjoying my predicament a little too much.

"Taryn, I've seen him in his leotard. Twice! Believe me, it isn't something Mom, Dad or the Melroses want to see. Trust me!" Kit is on my side. I love Kit.

"Nope. I'm going. John *wants* me to attend. He left me a ticket. I found the envelope." Taryn smirks and holds up the envelope I had tucked behind the coffee maker. "My ticket is already in my pocket. I've got Tia's too." Taryn laughs and pours herself another coffee. I grab the envelope and count the tickets. She did take two tickets.

"Taryn, this is *not* funny." I try to put on my best unimpressed face but I have to admit if it were Ben or Kevin doing something so ridiculous, I too would insist on attending.

"I liked the twins better when they admired us and would do whatever we asked," I state flatly to Kit.

"You have no idea. Try living with one of them now!" Kit groans. Tia isn't here arguing with us because she's working today. Kit has today and tomorrow off. Taryn arrived last night and is staying with Kit and Tia at the condo over the weekend during the wedding festivities.

"Well, the starfish fiasco should keep my mother busy. But if your parents insist on coming my mother might postpone the repair! We need something… something…" I look around the kitchen.

"The only thing that will distract my mother is a baking emergency…" Kit is using her brain now.

Kit and I have our heads buried in my baking-ingredients cupboard — which is bare because the constant supply of mailed care packages from Mrs. Jennings ensures I'll never need to bake anything — when the parents arrive in the usual chaos. The kitchen erupts in a flurry of suitcases, garment bags, gaily-wrapped gifts and two hatboxes. Unloading the van takes longer than their last visit due to the sheer volume of stuff. Taryn is leaving for Australia next week and doesn't have a fraction of the luggage the parents brought for one weekend.

"Where are your lovely lawn ornaments?" my mother asks incredulously.

"In the shed. I don't want to outshine the neighbours.

Besides, there's been a rash of lawn-ornament thefts in the area," I answer firmly.

"Well, the shed is no place for them. Who would steal lawn..." my mother gets cut off by John's entrance into the kitchen.

"Mother Melrose!" John hugs my mother. John startles her and it makes her crazy when he calls her Mother Melrose but it also stops her train of lawn-ornament thought. Seeing John makes me stop and pause. What's he doing home so early? Before I can stop him, it's out there.

"So, are you all coming to the dance recital tonight?" John has grabbed my mother by her shoulders and is speaking directly to her. "No!" I shriek in my mind. "No. Shut up!"

"What dance recital?" Mrs. Jennings asks innocently.

"Mine. I'm in a show, and it's tonight. I got tickets for everyone. Mel, didn't you tell them?" John glares at me.

"Not yet. As you can see, they've just arrived. I haven't even said, 'Hello.'" I glare back at him. Why he thinks I would want my family to attend his dance exhibit — where he'll be performing with the woman I suspect is his other girlfriend — is beyond me. Surely he must know I suspect something's up. This is the first sentence he's uttered to me all week. In fact, this is the first time I've seen him during daylight hours. He hasn't even verbally invited me to the stupid recital.

"Do you really think my parents will enjoy the recital? I'm not sure if modern dance is their thing." I try to sound casual, as if it doesn't matter to me one way or the other. I suspect I'm not pulling it off. I search the countertop for the cereal bowl full of broken Seashore-themed necklace.

"Sure! It'll be great. They'll love it!" John replies to me, then turns to my mother "My teacher has great vision. She's amazing." Before anyone can respond to his declarations, he continues, "Well, I'm off for the last practice before tonight. Can't wait to see you guys there." John then proceeds to the laundry room to gather his dance bag and leotard.

"Well, isn't this a nice surprise. I didn't know John was into community theatre," Mrs. Jennings states.

John comes back through the kitchen, shouts, "See you later," and heads out the door.

"And we do love to support the community. What time is the..." My mother starts to ask before I interrupt her by thrusting the cereal bowl into her hands and start towards the door.

"Good heavens, Mel! What...?" I hear my mother as she registers the contents of the cereal bowl, but I'm already out the door on my way to John's truck.

"Hey, just a second." I catch up to John at his driver's door. "What's going on with us? I haven't seen you all week. You don't return my calls. Is there anything I should know?" I had not planned on having this discussion, or any other discussion like this one, before the wedding. I find myself currently on autopilot, unable to stop the flood of questions. Perhaps in the back of my mind, I know that by having this discussion, I may be able to avoid the dance recital. If John confesses his infidelity, I'll have the perfect out.

"No. Don't be silly, we're fine." John seems shocked that I've noticed his behaviour. Or maybe he's shocked I mentioned it. "Sorry, babe. I've just been so wrapped up in the recital, I haven't been a very good boyfriend." John grabs my shoulders and kisses me on the cheek, then hugs me. A nice hug, like those he used to give me before all this dance nonsense started. He briefly seems sincere. Am I completely losing my mind? I give him the opportunity to 'fess up and not only does he not confess, he seems back to normal again.

"Are you sure? There is absolutely nothing you want to tell me?" I pull away from him so I can look him in the eyes. If he's lying, I can tell in his eyes.

"Babe! I'm sure." He manages eye contact for a nanosecond, then glances at his watch and continues, "I've got to run. I won't be home before the recital. We're all going out for dinner together, but I'll see you after." He jumps into his truck and backs out of the driveway.

John is telling me things are okay, but my gut is telling me something is just not right. He did make eye contact, but it was fleeting. Now, I *have* to go to the dance recital, with or without the parents in tow. I have to see if what my gut is telling me translates to the stage.

Back in the house, the hubbub continues. Kit and Taryn have shuttled the parents' numerous bags into their respective guest rooms. The mothers are "oohing" and "aahing" over the Sunset Disaster, which Kit took out of my closet to show them upon their request. The mothers seem to love the

Disaster enough to forget momentarily John's dance announcement and the necklace's remains. Samantha loves the orange dress. Now the mothers love the dress. Perhaps Kit and I are completely off the mark on this one. Maybe too bright, too big, too hideous is the new black? Looking down at my green boots I smile to myself. No matter what my mother and Mrs. Jennings think, even if hideous is the new black, I'm not about to embrace it!

42

The rest of the day flies. Getting the parents settled, watching my mother deftly restring the seashells with the speed of an Olympic sprinter, while being told the details for all the wedding events — starting with the rehearsal dinner on Friday evening — keeps my mind occupied. I don't have time to dwell on my boyfriend or future ex-boyfriend or whatever he is right now because I'm just too preoccupied. Kit corners me at one point and we decide if the parents are determined to go to John's dance recital-slash-Ursula's vision, no jewellery or baking emergency will stop them. The mothers actually seem quite interested and enthralled with the whole thing, to the point that my mother comments, "Well, this is a nicer side of John. It's just such a shame Mel never showed any interest in dance."

Ursula's vision has a name. The tickets indicate she's called the show *Freedom Speaks — A Premiere Experiment Theatre Exhibition*. I'm not sure how much I want to hear or see freedom actually say, but here I am, in front of centre stage at a rundown west-end theatre, three rows back. I'm sitting between Kit and Tia; Taryn is on the other side of Tia. The parents are sitting in the four seats behind us; Kevin's and Ben's seats remain empty because the band is playing in Kingston this evening. Kit has her camera ready, poised on her lap to video the performance for them. I suppose the five seats here and five behind makes for easier chatting but, aside from the mothers chatting about wedding plans, we girls remain remarkably quiet while waiting for the "vision" to begin. Marc and five of John's co-workers are in seats to my left. I had to climb over them to get to my seat. Apparently, they all went out for dinner and arrived early for the seven o'clock performance, so as not to miss anything. Marc is sitting beside Kit and they whisper back and forth a bit. I don't ask what about. I can only imagine.

"It won't be so bad," Kit grabs my hand and whispers. "It'll all be over in a couple of hours, then we can get back to wedding preparations! Yay!" She laughs at her own sarcasm.

All I can think of is how badly I want this to be over. I tell myself, "I'm calm. I'm cool. I'm collected. This is John's thing. Not mine. This is no reflection on me. I'm my own person. I'm Mel Melrose. Nothing fazes me. This will not shake me. I'm strong and independent. I'm bigger than this, whatever *this* is." I actually get to a point at which the nausea has faded. I can do this. I smile to myself. I can do this.

Then it begins.

Ursula steps out on the stage and introduces herself. She is wearing a pink bathrobe, a red fabric headband, and her signature dream-catcher earrings. Her hair looks as bad as it does on her website photo. She appears a few pounds heavier than when we spied on her through the dance-studio window — although the bathrobe could be exaggerating her girth. She explains the presentation this evening is "something I've been percolating for several years but never had the perfect group of students until now. I love this group of students more than any I've ever had before."

My hand reaches over and squeezes Kit's arm. Hard. I'm going to lose it. Forget the mantras and Mel Melrose being above all this nonsense. Mel Melrose is going to kick some Ursula ass. Kit, who is trying to video the exhibition, realizes she won't be able to video and also keep me in my seat, so she leans over me and hands the camera to Tia, then removes my hand from her arm letting me squeeze her now freed-up hands, which have inadvertently become fists. I suspect Kit is almost as disturbed by Ursula's "love for her students" as I am. Ursula gushes a bit longer, then the lights go low. In the darkness, I feel my face start to turn red. I'm the opposite of calm, and no amount of petting the soft leather of my boots will get me back to calm. I'm ready to blow a gasket.

In the dimness, the curtain rises and the music starts. I know the song but can't place it. I find myself humming along, trying to determine the song title. It sounds very familiar. The lights flash on and I see Ursula start to strut across the stage, entering stage right, wearing a very clingy red dress — not the same red as her headband — a red boa and red sequined shoes. The first line of the song is "She got a red dress / Kicking up pretty heels" and I realize the song is Burton Cummings' "Charlemagne." Ursula is opening her vision with my Burton's favourite song. The stage is devoid of any scenery except three separate clusters of lawn ornaments. My mouth drops open as I realize the stage decorations must be the missing items from Cam and Pam's lawn. I lean over to Kit to express my shock and horror about the ornaments but don't get to say anything as the rest of the dance troupe, including John, come scampering onto the stage from stage left. I don't comprehend the entire ridiculousness of the scene until much later, after seeing the video several times; for now, it's mostly surreal. There are two male dancers — one is John — and three female dancers. I hear my mother gasp and say, "Oh, good Lord! I thought they were naked." To her credit, at first glance they *do* appear to be mostly naked, like the first time I spied on them. They are wearing flesh-coloured leotards, red tutus and red headbands. The dancing itself isn't so much dancing as flailing and disorganized "expression" — the term John will use tomorrow in response to Marc's question "What the hell was that?"

I hear Mrs. Jennings say, "Jezebel, *indeed*!" when the lyrics "she could not change her name to Jezebel" play. But all I can do is grip Kit's hands even harder. Logically, I know John's actions are not a reflection of me, but, emotionally, I'm having difficulty separating myself from the person in a flesh-coloured leotard and red tutu pulling on both ends of the boa around Ursula's neck and "shimmying" to the ground in front of her. After the shimmy move, the dancers all fall in behind Ursula in what looks like an attempted conga line and weave around the lawn ornaments, drawing a great deal of attention to the stolen goods. I have no idea what the combined lawn ornaments cost, but I wonder if John could be charged with theft over or under $500.

"Charlemagne" ends and the lights dim. Silence. There is quiet applause from a small group to my right — presumably, people who understand Ursula's vision — but, for the most part, the theatre is silent. Most of the audience doesn't know what to think. I look over at Kit in the dimness and all I can see are the whites of her wide-open, shocked eyes. I hear a very quiet "What the hell?" from someone to the left of me. I believe the quiet voice belongs to Marc. Fortunately or unfortunately — I'm not sure which really — the speakers burst alive with music again. I recognize the new song immediately as "Don't Cha" by the Pussycat Dolls. The dancers have shed their red tutus and headbands and are wearing nothing but the leotards. Ursula is still wearing the red dress ensemble and seems to be the "hoochie mama" trying to steal the male dancers, as per the song lyrics — which accurately represent her general demeanour if you ask me. This number seems to be a little more choreographed than the previous one, but that really isn't saying much. At one point, the dancers are able to form a line and perform the moves in unison, well, sort of — they all seem to be aware of what they are meant to be doing. The attempted choreography appears to be a takeoff of a

Michael Jackson video from the eighties although I can't determine which one. The crotch grabbing points towards the "Bad" video, but the terrible attempt at moonwalking makes me think more "Wanna Be Startin' Somethin'." In actual fact, the amateur moves of the dancers make me think that a group of Grade 2 schoolchildren could do a better job. And they would be much cuter.

The crotch grabbing and gyrating causes grief for the mothers and I can hear the "tutting" from behind me. I assume there is a good deal of eye rolling to accompany the "tutting." My dad, who has remained quite silent up to this point, gives a loud "Oh dear!" when John shimmies — down to his knees this time — in front to Ursula, caressing her sides as he lowers himself to the ground. I must say, in the two-plus years since I've known John, he's never moved so fluidly for me. About the time John shimmies to the ground, Kit gets squirmy and buries her eyes in Marc's shirt. I know her reaction is embarrassment because I'm experiencing a very similar reaction myself. The number ends to very light applause, not unlike the subdued applause you hear at golf matches.

"It can't get much worse, can it?" I whisper to Kit in the dimness between numbers. Kit and I make frightened eye contact just before our eyes snap back to the stage as the first notes of Lynyrd Skynyrd's "Free Bird" break the silence. The dancers scurry onto the stage and things do, indeed, get immediately and immensely worse. I register the flapping of arms and the shrieks of my mother and Mrs. Jennings behind me before my eyes are able to send the message of what I'm seeing on the stage to my brain. The music is loud, but the mothers are louder. Arms are reaching beside me to cover Tia's eyes. Tia is standing — well, being dragged, actually — from behind, over the seat and over me, to my left. She manages to pass Kit's camera to Marc as she is hauled over top of him. Taryn is close behind, being dragged by Mrs. Jennings. I feel the commotion behind me, and know the parents are vacating the premises and taking the twins with them. I hear, "Good Lord, this is no place for children!" "Bob, save the twins!" "What are they thinking?" "Bill, grab Kathryn! We're leaving!"

Rightly so.

This time, the entire dance ensemble is completely naked.

43

I am in shock, possibly real shock this time. I feel Kit being lifted, hauled out of her seat, and dragged over Marc and his employees. A part of me knows I should follow, but I can't take my eyes off the scene before me. John is completely naked and standing on a stage, showing the whole theatre parts of him I thought I alone was allowed to see. Ursula, also naked except for the dream-catcher earrings, steps up to John and kisses him. On the mouth — open mouth. It's like a train wreck; you know you shouldn't look, but you can't help yourself. After the parents are gone, the remaining audience is unnaturally silent save a few nervous giggles coming from John's co-workers, who have obviously never seen this side of John either. For the most part, the audience is sitting completely still, mouths gaping open. Ursula's vision is indeed something none of us will forget — without years of therapy, at any rate.

The human body is beautiful, or not. Fine-tuned athletes with zero percent body fat, six-packs and sculpted bodies — possibly. Middle-aged, flabby bodies that have spent the past decade sitting in front of televisions, watching reality shows and scarfing back sugary snack food — absolutely *not*. Flabby, jiggly bodies, riddled with cellulite, gyrating on a stage amongst innocent lawn ornaments are bad enough. But there is one part of the male anatomy no one wants to see dancing around a stage — or anywhere else, for that matter. No matter how you look at it — and, unfortunately, the entire audience is getting up close and personal with two — male genitalia is floppy. Even the most fit of male athletes cannot control the actions — or reactions — of the unrestrained genitals. Dangling "boy bits" have minds of their own and flop and flap willy-nilly according to gravity, motion and, apparently, their own free will. No amount of concentration can make the "wiener and beans" behave in any sort of choreographed manner. The resonance of male genitalia slapping on skin during the frenzied guitar solo of "Free Bird" is something you will never mistake for any other sound on the planet — trust me. At one point, John and Ursula are groping together — in what I'm sure they consider a dance move but in reality looks more like wrestling — and John's protruding manliness, for lack of a better word, is visibly squished between his leg and Ursula's flabby stomach in what *should* be the most embarrassing manner. But neither of them seems to notice. The flailing and disjointed movements were upsetting enough when the participants were clad in leotards and tutus. Once the clothing is removed and there is a stage full of loose flesh performing similar flailing moves, it's infinitely more disconcerting. John's manliness slurps away from Ursula's stomach and he throws his leg up. Ursula grabs his foot at waist level then she skips in a circle around him so the entire audience gets a good view of him from *every* angle. Shortly after the circle move, John trips while leaping across the stage and topples, in a very undignified manner, landing entwined with Goldilocks and two of the bears. I hear Marc say quietly, "He's going to feel that in the morning!" For my part, I'll never be able to look Goldie in the eyes again.

For the finale — as if one is really required — John scrambles up from his entanglement with the fairytale creatures and he and Ursula attempt what I think is meant to be a lift. Ursula runs at John, then jumps, and John is meant to lift Ursula over his head. But the move fails miserably on many levels. Ursula is far too short and chubby to get any speed in her run or height in her jump; John has very limited dance experience, and probably has never lifted anything as heavy as Ursula — and certainly not over his head. The attempted lift ends in a jumble of naked John lying on the stage, Ursula straddling him, her most private woman parts splotched squarely on John's sweaty, naked chest in a very unseemly mélange.

The theatre erupts in a crescendo of standing applause, hoots and hollers — mostly from John's co-workers — as Ursula clambers off John and to her feet. When the final notes of "Free Bird" fade, John sits on the stage, breathing heavily from the exertion, clinging to Ursula's leg. Even in my shocked state, I am able to register that the leg John is clinging to is very hairy. Until now, my focus had been mostly on

John and his naked, flapping body parts — well, the one embarrassing part, anyway. Seeing John embracing Ursula's hairy lower leg is enough to bring me back to reality. The lights dim again, and I try to stand. My legs are shaking. I stumble into Marc, who stands up beside me and helps me make my way out of the row of seats. I notice the theatre is about half full and wonder how so many people heard about this exhibition of horror and why so many would actually attend. The applause dies down as we make our way to the back of the theatre. After a moment of silence the music starts up for the next number — "My Humps" by the Black Eyed Peas. I don't look back. No amount of curiosity can make me turn around to view Ursula's naked interpretation of "My Humps."

Outside isn't much of a reprieve. The parents are still completely frantic and speaking all at once. Kit is trying to quell the mothers. Mr. Jennings and my dad are protectively guarding the twins. Taryn tries to squirm out of Mr. Jennings' grip, but he's holding onto her like a drowning man clinging to a life preserver.

"Melanie Melrose! What were you thinking bringing the twins to something so vile?" My mother attacks me the second she sees me. Calling me Melanie is a sure sign I won't be living this one down for some time to come.

"Good God, Mother! I tried to tell you not to come. Do you think if I knew what was going to happen I would have let any of you attend this… this *thing*?" I reply with more venom than I intend.

I am angry. I'm angry with John for his antics over the past two months. I'm angry with my mother for her accusation. I'm angry with my brother, Mike, for getting married and making me wear a Construction Cone Orange dress and nasty shoes. I'm angry with John for parading naked in front of my family and friends. I'm angry with Ursula for stealing my boyfriend and not having the decency to shave her legs while doing it. But, mostly, I'm angry with myself for even being here in the first place. I should have dealt with the John situation long before now. I should have confronted him and ended the relationship after the first garbage-bin escapade. I was clambering up onto a garbage bin for heaven's sake. I obviously knew, on some level, he was cheating on me. Why didn't I do something about it?

My angry retort to my mother stops the frantic parent commentary. I stand up taller, flatten my blouse and skirt, and continue, "Mom. Dad. Mr. and Mrs. Jennings. Why don't you take the twins out for a coffee?" As if on cue, Marc reaches in his pocket, takes out two $20 bills and hands them to Tia. "Thank you, Marc," I continue. "You guys go, and we'll meet you at home later. Okay? Kit and I are in good hands with Marc."

My mother starts to object, but Tia, who has been freed from Dad's grip, takes my mother's arm, steering her towards the parking lot. "Mel doesn't need us aggravating an already awkward situation. Let's go get that coffee or maybe even a proper drink," she says. Taryn follows with Mrs. Jennings, and the dumbfounded dads look happy just to be putting distance between themselves and the theatre. I hear Mrs. Jennings say, "Why is Mel dating that horrible exhibitionist? She needs to meet someone nice like that Marc fellow. He seems very nice. He's always been very good to Kathryn."

I'd laugh if I had the strength.

"Thanks for the money, Marc. I owe you," I say more calmly than I'm feeling.

"You owe me nothing. You did well, but I saw you were shaking too much to manage your wallet."

"I don't know about you guys, but I could use one of those proper drinks Tia mentioned. Anyone?" Kit takes her camera from Marc and puts it in her purse. Marc leads Kit and me across the street to a pub.

Marc, Kit and I are sitting in the window of the pub so we can see when the theatre lets out and Ursula's vision is just a memory for all the poor people who are still witnessing the train wreck. Marc orders beer for us but before the server walks away from the table, I add, "And three tequila shooters, please."

Marc and Kit both look at me, surprised, but say nothing. Neither of them has ever seen me in a situation like this one; well, I don't expect many people to find themselves in a situation exactly like this one. I excuse myself to go to the ladies' room and notice a seal, then myself, on the television screen in the corner. I have heard the commercial is being televised on a regular basis, but this is the first time I've actually seen it.

Standing in the washroom, looking at myself in the mirror, I hardly recognize myself. I am a shadow of the in-control woman I was three months ago. I am currently between jobs, I get to relive the humiliation of my television début with a seal over and over, my boyfriend and his other girlfriend are dancing naked in a theatre across the street, and I'm an unwitting accomplice in the neighbourhood lawn-ornament theft ring. My hopes and dreams of an engagement, wedding and the entire fairytale ending came crashing to the ground with John when he got tripped up with Goldilocks. For the first time in my life, I have absolutely no idea what to do next.

After a few more minutes of standing in front of the mirror, trying to get my bearings and come up with a plan or direction, my mind remains completely blank. I have nothing. No plan, no next move. The shreds of the relationship I've been clinging to have officially unravelled. John's not coming back; I won't take him back even if he wants to come back. The embarrassment of what I, and my family and friends, have just witnessed makes "getting over this hump" completely impossible. I feel a wave of nausea starting just as Kit comes into the ladies' room.

"Hey, are you okay?" Kit puts her hand on my back as I lean over the sink.

"Yeah. Good. I just need a few minutes." Luckily talking lessens the nausea.

"Do you want to go home? Get out of here?" Kit asks.

"No. I want to go back to this afternoon and dump John

before he gets the opportunity to embarrass me in front of everyone I know. I knew he was lying, when I asked him about us this afternoon. Why didn't I just end it? What is wrong with me?" I moan into the sink.

"Nothing's wrong with you. You love the guy and you wanted it to work out. There is nothing wrong with wanting your relationship to work."

"No, but there is something wrong with knowing it isn't working and not leaving. I should have been the one to end this thing, not him."

"Well, technically, it hasn't ended yet, has it?" Kit's face brightens up. "You gave him the opportunity this afternoon, and he didn't take it. You can still be the one to end it. Well, if you want to end it?"

"I want my life back. I want to be moving forward, not sliding back to single. I want a lot of things I can't have. But if I can't have the happy ending then controlling *this* ending will be a start to getting back on track, right?"

"Right!" Kit says, and gives me a hug.

I reapply my lipstick with a shaky hand, and Kit and I return to Marc and the table, now adorned with beer and tequila shots.

"Are you okay?" Marc asks.

"No, but it's nothing my friend tequila can't fix." I laugh half-heartedly and sit down. I lick the side of my hand, sprinkle salt on the licked area, lick the salt, down the tequila, and then jam the lemon wedge into my mouth. Tequila. It may not solve all your problems, but after enough of it, you can forget you *have* problems — for a short while, at least. Marc shoves his tequila over to me, and Kit and I shoot the remaining two together. Marc, Kit and I sit and sip beer. I don't say much as Kit and Marc carry on a light conversation, consciously steering away from any mention of John or the spectacle we have all just witnessed. We order three more tequila shooters and make short order of them.

As I swallow the dregs of my beer, I glance out the window and see people starting to flow from the theatre and onto the sidewalk.

"I think this is my cue to confront my future ex-boyfriend. Kit, will you watch my purse until I get back?" I hand my purse to Kit, stand up, flatten my blouse and skirt, throw my shoulders back.

"Do you want me to come?" Kit asks after me.

"Nope. I think I've got this one." I stride out the pub door towards the theatre. I have no idea what I'm going to say or do, but I know I'm going to do it in confident, Mel Melrose style.

44

Walking across the street, I meet John's co-workers, who seem to be in incredibly happy states of mind. They are laughing and high-fiving, no doubt in anticipation of the razzing they are going to give John tomorrow at work.

"Marc's at the pub across the street," I say to John's co-worker, Greg. "Tell him the next round of tequila shooters is on me. Kit has my purse." I hear the hoots of approval behind me as I open the door and start into the now empty theatre. I walk down the aisle towards the stage and meet two of John's fellow exhibitionists, fully dressed at this point, leaving.

"Is John still around?" I ask, trying to sound calm instead of angry.

"Yep, in the back. Just go up on the stage and around to the left."

"Thanks." I walk up the four steps at the side of the stage and across to stage left. I hear voices and assume I'm on the right track. I come around the curtain, to what appears to be the costume change area for the performers, although the segment of the production I just witnessed involved more disrobing than anything else.

I see them before they see me.

John is sitting on what appears to be an ottoman, obviously from another production because the only props used in Ursula's vision were stolen lawn ornaments. Much later, I will wonder if the use of miniatures was to make the male dancers appear "larger" in their naked state. Ursula is kneeling behind John, giving him a back rub. Thankfully, they are dressed. John is wearing the same jeans and t-shirt he was wearing when he left the house this afternoon, and Ursula is wearing the clingy red dress — dream-catcher earrings still firmly in place. Their demeanour eliminates even the tiniest residual hope I had of the affair being all in my mind. There is something far too intimate to ignore in the way they are sitting together.

"You were fabulous this evening. Best performance yet!" I hear Ursula say, then she messes John's hair. My stomach flops. If I had Kit's propensity for retching this would be the perfect occasion to vomit.

"No, I tripped. You were the best. You made the entire performance," John responds as he reaches back and caresses Ursula's hip. I feel bile rising in my throat. I *will* throw up if I have to witness any more of this nonsense.

"Ahem." I clear my throat and try to look calm. "I hate to interrupt you lovebirds…" I feel bile rising in my throat, "but I need to speak to John." John's head snaps toward my voice and he scrambles to stand up, which throws Ursula backwards and she lands with a satisfying thud on the floor.

"Ahhhh…" John is flustered, and rightly so. I've just caught him red-handed — no pun intended.

"No need to say anything, John. I just wanted to tell you, in light of your new attachment to *all* things dance," I glare at Ursula, who has scampered to her feet and is standing beside John, staring at me indignantly, "your presence will no longer be required in our relationship or in my home. I'd like the key back please." I put my right hand out, palm up, waiting for the key. I am not feeling one hundred percent calm, but I'm holding it together. I just need to get out of here quickly. I refuse to break down in front of John. I won't give him the satisfaction of seeing me upset.

"Mel. Don't be crazy. Where am I going to go?" John asks. I notice he makes no attempt to deny he's moved on.

"I don't care where you go. Hell, perhaps? Just give me the key."

"Mel, you're being hasty." John is not winning any points with this comment.

"Hasty? Hasty, my ass! I've tolerated your nonsense for weeks, and now you've embarrassed me in front of my whole family." I wiggle my fingers. "The key. NOW!" The raised voice on the word "now" hastens John's reach into his pocket. He pulls out his keyring and starts to remove the house key.

"I'd like to explain…" John says as he places the key in my outstretched hand.

"Really? I gave you a chance to explain this afternoon, but

you didn't take it. You're obviously having an affair, and have been lying to me for weeks."

"Well, I wouldn't have had an affair if you weren't so needy. God, you completely smothered me. It was like you stopped living *your* life the second we moved in together and started just being part of *us*. So, when I met Ursula and she is just so... so..." John pauses and looks at Ursula, his eyes lighting up as they fall on her, "strong. She's so independent and sure of herself." John looks back at me and puts the key in my hand.

My mind starts to spin like one of the giant teacups at an amusement park; if John is still speaking, the words are not getting from my ears to my brain. Needy? Mel Melrose, needy? And smothering? I stand, gobsmacked, staring at the man I had believed I would marry and not recognizing one thing about him that I used to find redeeming. Unable to speak, in defence of myself or otherwise, I simply move the house key from my right hand to my left, raise my right hand, and slap John across the face with all the pent-up frustration, anger and embarrassment I've been storing up for the past two months.

I take a deep breath, drop my stinging hand, and, as calmly as possible, deal with the remaining details of our breakup. "I'll arrange with Marc to have some of the guys pick up your things tomorrow." I turn to leave but stop and turn back to John. "Oh, and I'm sure Cam and Pam would like their lawn ornaments back. I have video proof of them in your possession, so please return them in a timely fashion." I then turn to Ursula. "He's all yours. Good luck. You're going to need it."

Satisfied I've handled this encounter with as much poise as I could, considering the circumstances and the "needy" slur, I turn my perfect size 4 frame on my exquisite Prada boot heel and start to leave, ensuring my steps are slow and even. It takes all my strength not to break into a run. I will remain calm — at least, until I get away from the adulterous, free-loving couple. I manage to get out of the theatre, and lean against the wall outside the door trying to regain my composure. Kit, who must have been watching for me, walks up to me and puts her arm around me. "Are you okay?" Kit asks and rubs my back as I double over, holding my churning stomach.

"I don't know," I state calmly.

"You actually look pretty calm. What happened?"

"I saw them. They were all over each other," I shudder visibly and continue. "But I handled it well. You would have been proud." I smile weakly.

"I'm always proud of you. I would have started vomiting long before I could handle anything if I caught my boyfriend with a handful of red-sequined butt," Kit laughs.

"I almost did. I still might, actually." I cross my arms tighter over my stomach. Kit rubs my shoulder.

"Do you want to go home? Or go somewhere else? You probably don't want to stay with Marc and the guys."

"Nope. I will not let him win. I will *not* lose."

"It's okay to be upset, you know? It's not losing. It's normal." Kit tries the diplomatic approach.

"He said I'm needy. Needy? Me!" I feel tears starting but hold them back and lean against the wall, still clutching my stomach.

"Charlie Brown called you needy?" Kit stops rubbing my shoulder and stands up straight. "You're one of the most independent women I know! What the hell is he talking about? I have half a mind to go in there and kick his ass!"

"I don't know. He said I was smothering him and I stopped living my own life when we moved in together." I ignore Kit's threat of violence because I know she won't do anything of the sort. But I love her for defending my honour.

"He's just being a complete idiot and trying to save face by putting his infidelity back on you. Do not give him the satisfaction of even entertaining his comments! He's just a big jerk. A big, bad-striped-shirt-wearing jerk." Kit steps forward and hugs me. "You can do way better than John in his ridiculous leotard!"

"I know." I smile at Kit's last comment, "But what if he's right?" I squeeze Kit. "What if he's right?"

The number of tears I shed at the immediate end of my relationship was nine. The tears all escaped while leaning on the wall of the theatre in which my ex-boyfriend had become an exhibitionist; four from my left eye and five from my right eye. Don't get me wrong — I am sad, very sad, but crying just isn't a part of my makeup. I am sad for my relationship ending. I'm sad I'm single again. I'm sad for the embarrassment and humiliation John has put me through. Mostly I am sad because I didn't deal with the problem as soon as I suspected it was a problem. Why didn't I deal with John and his philandering ways long before now? Do I place so much importance on being in a relationship that I will tolerate bad behaviour? Did I lose my confidence? Was I needy? If so, why?

After my "cry," I feel much better, and rejoining the party of John's co-workers seems like a very good idea. I don't want to go home to face my parents; I might as well enjoy some more tequila. Tequila doesn't care if I'm needy. Tequila likes me just the way I am — needy and misguided but with clean-shaven legs.

45

My head is throbbing. I am vaguely aware of the surroundings. I can hear my parents' voices far off, but I can't make myself open my eyes. I don't want to wake up. Without opening my eyes, I pat myself down and realize I am fully dressed in the blouse and skirt I was wearing last night. I can freely wiggle my toes — ouch, even small toe movements hurt my head — so I know I managed to get my boots off. I'm completely and utterly hungover. Tequila is not my friend, as previously believed.

"Are they being exceptionally noisy?" I hear Kit mumble from beside me.

"Probably. They want us to know they aren't impressed, and now we know. Do you think they'll stop?" I answer without opening my eyes. I know opening them will cause severe pain and suffering.

"Not on your life. It's only going to get louder."

"Don't they have stuff to do for the wedding? Surely we can get rid of them." In all the detailed planning the mothers made us listen to yesterday, I can't for the life of me remember if they have anything planned for today.

"We'll have to get up and let them yell at us. After they've had their fill, they might find something to do and we can come back to bed."

"Okay. You first." My eyes have still not opened, and I know I'm going to get the spins as soon as I move a muscle. I feel Kit push herself up, I hear an "Oh no!" then hear her hurried escape to the washroom. Kit is throwing up. Oh no, indeed. If Kit's throwing up, I'm going to be in worse shape. Tequila may have been Kit's friend last night, but tequila was my *best* friend last night. I listen for Kit to finish vomiting, then open my eyes, despite the pain, to see her crawling on her hands and knees out of the washroom before collapsing on the floor beside my bed.

"I think that went pretty well," Kit laughs from the floor.

"Well, you two aren't making any friends the way you look today." Close-eyed, I recognize my mother's voice from the doorway of the bedroom.

"Kathryn, get up off the floor. Good Lord, *what* are you doing down there? Did I hear you vomiting?" Apparently, Mrs. Jennings is standing with my mother.

"What time did you girls come in last night? Hardly responsible behaviour when there's a wedding rehearsal this evening."

"Enough," I hear Kit moan from the floor. "We were late. We are irresponsible. We are the worst daughters ever. Maybe you can trade us in on better models."

"You forgot bad influence on the twins. And don't you get snippy with us, Kathryn!" Mrs. Jennings refers to any form of self-defence as snippy. I personally am cheering Kit on, quietly, inside my very sore head, "Yay! Go, Kit!"

"Mel Melrose, don't think I don't know you're awake and ignoring us. We want to speak to you about what happened last night. We talked about it, and we don't think it would be appropriate to bring John to the wedding after his... his... *exhibition* last evening. I see he had the decency to go into hiding after his performance!"

My mother's favourite question to me when I was a child was "How can you be so heartless?" I was always half-tempted to answer that, honestly, I believe I got the trait from her. But I never have. I may before this weekend is over.

"Mother, John won't be bothering us anymore. We broke up last night after his *exhibition*, and the breakup is the reason I went out and got stinking drunk. The getting stinking drunk is the reason I'm so hung over right now. So, you may want to rethink your timing of this little inquisition."

"Broke up? Well, your timing is most inconvenient. Mike and Samantha have already paid for the wedding meals. I can't believe you broke up before the wedding! It's not fair to your brother."

I cannot win. My mother doesn't want to see or have anything to do with John but she also wants me to bring him to the wedding? I really must determine what type of barbiturate my mother is on and get some for myself.

"Mother! He's having an affair with the red-dress dance woman. I had to break up with him for my own sanity. As soon as I can open my eyes, I promise I'll call around and hire a male escort for the wedding. Will you be happy then?"

"Are you sure he's having an affair with *that* woman? She doesn't even shave her armpits!"

I would laugh if I had the strength. "Yes, I'm sure. Kit can confirm it."

"He is." I hear Kit's muffled voice from the floor beside my bed. She must have something over her head.

"Apparently, John loves her strong independence and the passion she has for her art," I state matter-of-factly.

"Oh well, I never really did warm to him. Maybe it's for the best."

"I don't feel like it's for the best right now, Mom. Can we talk about this later?" My head is throbbing and I have a hollow, sick feeling in my stomach, the one you get when someone dies or you get dumped. I don't have the strength to defend John or myself to my mother.

"Okay, but I want you girls to promise to get it together before the rehearsal," my mother concedes, but she still has to let us know she's not impressed.

"We promise," Kit and I mutter in unison. After our mothers leave the room, Kit crawls back onto the bed and we return to fitful, hungover sleep.

46

I love Kit's sisters. Tia and Taryn wake us up at one o'clock in the afternoon with burgers, fries and Coke Classics. There is nothing finer than a greasy hamburger and a sugary soft drink to improve the state of a hangover. The parents are spending the afternoon at the Bennington-Halls'. This leaves Kit, the twins, and me at my house alone. The parents' absence is perfect timing. I have arranged with Marc and Greg to come by this afternoon to pick up all of John's belongings. I told them that if John has not suggested a place to drop his things, dropping them at Ursula's dance studio would likely be a fine idea.

After eating our burgers, we have a little over two hours to get all John's belongings packed up. I ask the twins to go to the grocery store and get some boxes. Kit and I start piling John's things in the kitchen near the door. I look around the house and am surprised by the amount of crap one man can accumulate in a year and a half. It will actually be refreshing to have it all gone. When the twins return they begin to box the items Kit and I have dumped in the kitchen, while Kit and I tackle the basement and all of John's tools. We are still boxing items when Marc and Greg arrive with their trucks to collect John's belongings. Through the window I see Marc start toward Cam and Pam's yard with an armful of dwarfs. I rush outside in case Pam confronts him.

"Hey, Mel, where should I put these?" Marc asks when he sees me come out the door.

"I'll take them." I take the four dwarfs from Marc and place them carefully in one of the empty spaces, breathing a sigh of relief that neither Cam's nor Pam's car is in their driveway. Marc and Greg help me with the remaining dwarfs, sheep, bears and fairytale females.

"No parents around?" Marc laughs.

"Nope, wedding stuff called them away. But, trust me, it's a very good thing!" Kit laughs.

"Did dumbass John give you a place to dump all this stuff?" I ask Marc.

"I'm going to store it in my basement. I came home last night and found him sitting on my front steps," Greg offers.

"I'm surprised," I say. "I thought he'd be shacking up with Ursula now he's totally free to do so."

"Apparently, Ursula's husband has a problem with them shacking up," Marc laughs.

"She's married?" Kit and I ask in unison.

"Yep. And apparently her husband is the money behind the studio, so she's taking money and security over love and passion. John's pretty broken up about it," Marc says as straight-faced as possible, but I know he wants to laugh.

"Well, that's a refreshing bit of irony, isn't it, Mel?" Kit starts to laugh.

For my part, I'm dumbfounded and feel slightly nauseous. The woman John left me for, Little Miss Not-Needy-And-Independent, actually relies on a husband for financial security? John fooling around with another woman is one thing, but with a married woman? John is a much bigger idiot than even I gave him credit for.

"It is pretty funny, but apparently he spent a lot of money on her," Greg says. "His credit cards are all maxed out and he's in a pretty bad way. He couldn't even get a hotel room last night after you told him not to come home and Ursula went home to her husband." Greg looks a bit sorry for John but I'm not moved. John had a perfectly good home here if he'd just been able to control his dream-catcher-loving libido. As for spending money on Ursula, I can't even remember the last time he picked up a tab in which I was included.

"Really? He's broke *and* he's been dumped?" My brain, which had been hungover-fuzzy until just now, is racing and the perpetual real estate agent in me takes over. I instantly have the outline for a money-saving plan.

"He's fairly messy. He kept saying he was stupid to get involved with Ursula, and he wished he hadn't," Greg says.

"He was useless at work today. I had to send him home, well, back to Greg's house," Marc adds. "He asked me to feel you out about having dinner with him to contemplate reconciliation. Any thoughts?"

"None I can say out loud, in the event something unexpected happens to our stupid little friend," I state, my mind churning. "Kit, grab the guys a beer. I'll be back in a few minutes." I turn to start back up the driveway to the house, then stop. "Marc, can I borrow $15,000?"

"Depends on what for. I'm not paying to hire a hit man, if that's what you're thinking? He's a fairly good worker when his mind's on his job," Marc laughs.

"Ha ha. Have a beer. Don't leave!" I sprint to the house as fast as my hungover body will carry me and locate my laptop. I find the proposal I put together for buying John out of the house. The original proposal would require me to refinance the house in order to get the money to pay John off, and it could take months before John sees a cent. Since John is in a bit of a pickle — thanks to his aforementioned raging, dream-catching libido — and I can get a loan from Marc, I can offer to pay John a smaller amount immediately. John may take the offer, thereby saving me thousands of dollars and getting him gone for good much faster. I print off the original proposal with a cover page stating, "Payment in six months" then throw together a second proposal, with a buy-out figure for $15,000 instead of $30,000, and change the cover page to read, "Payment in seven days." Is it cruel to exploit John's weakened state? Absolutely. But I will leave the ball in his court. He can have money now or more money later. I'll be fine either way, and he will get to make the ultimate decision.

Marc and Greg are having beer on the deck with Kit and the twins — well, Kit isn't drinking beer as she's still a bit under the weather, so she's sipping on another Coke Classic. I ask Marc to join me in the kitchen. I explain the proposals to him and ask him if he'd be willing to lend me $15,000 if John takes the latest offer. Marc is one of my wealthiest friends — well, honestly, probably my most wealthy friend. He had helped Kit out when she was buying her condo and got dumped by her co-owner just before the deal closed. I know he's always investing in property. Marc and I discuss an interest rate and repayment of the potential $15,000 loan.

"Are you sure about this, Mel?" Marc asks seriously. "You guys had a pretty good thing going for a long time."

"I'm sure," I state quietly. "I'm not even quite sure what happened to us. He said I'm needy. What does that mean? I can support myself, I make more money than he does, and I work independently. I can't fix something I don't know is broken. Besides, I can't be with someone I can't trust, and John made sure I'll never trust him again."

"Okay, as long as you're sure." Marc gives me a hug.

By the end of the conversation and of Marc's beer, we've struck a deal. Marc is going to present the offers to John this evening. I call my lawyer and leave a message telling her about my change in situation, asking if we can get John off the title of the house — Monday, if possible — provided he accepts the lower-priced proposal.

After Marc and Greg leave with John's possessions and my buyout offers, Kit, the twins, and I start getting ready for the wedding rehearsal and dinner. Kit and I shower and do our best to look human. Last night's friendship with tequila is still taking its toll. We both look like we've seen better days, which undisputedly we have. I looked better the day after my wisdom teeth were pulled.

"Mom isn't going to be happy with you, Kit. You look like shit," Taryn, ever so helpfully, comments.

"Yeah, yeah. You're just gloating because you're escaping to Australia for a year," Kit laughs.

"Here." Tia comes into the washroom, where Kit and I are frantically trying to do hair and makeup, juggling two shooter glasses containing dark liquid and two highball glasses containing darker liquid.

"No!" I say adamantly. "No way. No how. Booze is what got me into this mess."

"You weren't drinking these. You'll feel better. I promise. It's what Taryn and I always drink the day after a rough night. Nice necklace, Mel!" Tia nods at the starfish lying on my chest then giggles.

"Absolutely, it will help. It's Jägermeister. It's herbal," says Taryn, backing up Tia's argument.

"Oh, what the hell. I'll try it," Kit concedes. "I can't feel much worse."

"Mel?" Tia looks at me, holding the shooter glasses above the highball glasses.

"What the hell, indeed? I'm single, at least $15,000 in debt and I have to wear the Sunset Disaster with orange satin shoes tomorrow. Bring it on!"

"Get ready!" Kit and I each take hold of a highball glass and Tia drops the shooter glasses into them. Kit and I down the contents of what we will discover afterwards is called a Jägerbomb. A shot of Jägermeister in a glass of Red Bull. Mother of Pearl! Kit is gagging beside me, and I shudder uncontrollably. Jägerbombs make Mr. Bennington-Hall's mint julep concoction seem like Kool-Aid. The twins are laughing at our reactions.

"You drink this voluntarily?" I ask in a raspy voice as soon as I am able to speak.

"Yep! You'll feel better in a bit. Trust us!" Taryn says, handing Kit and I each an open beer. "This will help take the taste out of your mouth, and you'll be right as rain before we face the rehearsal."

"Hurry up! If we're late for the rehearsal you know the mothers will kill us," says Tia, taking her iPod earbuds out of her pocket and then asking Taryn to help her run the cord up the back of her shirt.

The twins are preparing in advance for the preservation of their respective sanities during the family evening ahead. If only Kit and I had been so ingenious at their age.

47

After the rehearsal, on our way back to the Bennington-Hall residence for dinner, I have to admit the twins are more resourceful than I ever suspected. The Jägerbomb was indeed an amazing cure for my hangover. After recovering from the taste of it, I did indeed feel much better and was able to face the rehearsal with new-found energy. The iPods are also quite creative. The parents have yet to catch on to the fact that they are being completely ignored by the twins on most occasions. I suppose the parents don't notice because they never really require a response.

At the Bennington-Halls' house, Kit and I decline Mr. Bennington-Hall's offer of blender margaritas. After witnessing his work at the bridal shower, and on the heels of our tequila outing last evening, Kit and I play it safe, opting to sip slowly from bottles of beer we open ourselves. Samantha and Mike seem excited although they both look tired. I'm sure planning a wedding is absolutely no fun, especially when you factor in all the well-meaning parents and homemade alcoholic beverages. I approach Mike about attending the wedding dateless and costing him a dinner. I offer to pay for it, but he takes my announcement in stride, laughs and tells me our mother had informed him about my breakup this afternoon.

"You've probably heard about the dance recital as well?" I ask, even though I'm ninety-nine percent sure of the answer.

"Oh yeah. I hear Kit has video. I can't wait to see it. If it was half as bad as Mom said it was, I bet the video is hilarious." Mike is his ever helpful self.

"Hilarious, all right," I state matter-of-factly. "I'll share it with you when this whole thing isn't quite so new."

"Don't worry about the dinner. I think Samantha was able to find someone to fill the seat, so it won't be wasted."

"That's good news." I am genuinely happy the meal won't be wasted. "How does it feel to be on the eve of 'happily ever after'?" I ask Mike, and punch him in the shoulder.

"Great. Well, busy and a bit nerve-racking but good. There's just so much to do and think about. Sam and I haven't had fun for ages. It's been all wedding, wedding and more wedding. I'll be glad when it's over, actually," Mike laughs.

"Well, you've both done a great job. I'm sure it will all go smoothly tomorrow and you'll be on the honeymoon before you know it."

"It better go smoothly, or Sam will lose it," Mike laughs again. "She's been pretty touchy these past few weeks. I don't know how she'll handle it if things don't go off perfectly."

"Oh dear, well, let's pray there are no mishaps," I laugh and cross my fingers for good measure. As I walk away from Mike, he comments with a laugh, "Nice starfish, Mel. Mom's work, I assume?"

During dinner I receive a text message from Marc stating John is willing to accept the $15,000 proposal and he'll ferry

John around on Monday to get the paperwork signed and money arranged. I breathe a sigh of relief and hand Kit my phone so she can read the text. I don't want to say too much out loud with my parents in earshot. This is Mike and Sam's rehearsal dinner; no need to bring my issues into it.

The dinner party breaks up relatively early. The parents want to be rested for tomorrow, and Kit and I have to concur. A good night's sleep is in order since we are both very tired after our encounter with tequila last night. Tia, Taryn and I cannot leave the Bennington-Hall residence until we have promised faithfully we will be back in the morning by nine o'clock sharp in order to ensure Jacques-Pierre and his band of scary hair designers have time to "do all our heads" — a phrase that sounds really bad when spoken out of the context of hair design. Kit — and I'm not sure how she managed to pull this off — is being excused from having Jacques-Pierre "do her head." The twins and I are not so lucky.

I arrive at the Bennington-Halls' the next morning just after the twins. We arrive separately since I am part of the wedding party and the twins are greeters at the church so we have to travel separately to the actual ceremony. I wrestle the Sunset Disaster, matching orange shoes, and massive crinoline into the house where I am directed to deposit them on the bed in what I assume was Sam's high-school bedroom — her track-and-field awards still sit prominently displayed on shelves. Sam's old bed already contains four other Sunset Disasters, so I deduce I am the second-last one to arrive. I meet up with the twins and three other wedding attendants in the kitchen, all drinking champagne and orange juice. In the adjacent dining room Sam is gushing over a tall, extra-slim man in skinny jeans. "I assume that's the 'world famous' Jacques-Pierre?" I ask the twins who are also watching the thin man's exaggerated arm movements.

"Presumably. But I overheard Sam last night saying she had to have him because her archrival at high school used him. I think his fame starts and ends in his own head!" Taryn whispers to me.

The thin man claps his hands and three equally stick-skinny people appear at his side — one man and two women — each carrying large cosmetic cases. Jacques-Pierre and his staff all have jet black hair, in various lengths, combed completely flat to their heads. As they walk to the table and start unpacking their cosmetic cases, not one hair on any of their heads moves. I have no idea what product they use but it must be super-strong. I lift up my hand and pet my hair. It may be the last time I can feel my hair in its natural state.

"I shall do the bride. Bride!" Jacques-Pierre summons Sam with a snap of his fingers and sits her at the head of the dining table. Jacques-Pierre then points at three of the attendants and says, "Three, wedding party. Sit!"

The twins and I let out audible sighs of relief and the fourth attendant involuntarily grabs my arm, I can tell she's thankful not to have been selected for the first round of hair. Tia pours another round of champagne and orange juice — heavy on the champagne.

"Mel, can you please call Margot? She isn't here yet, and

she's usually early for these things," Sam asks from under a head of backcombed hair.

"Sure." I pick up my cell and dial the number Sam yells out to me. Ring, ring, ring. Voicemail.

"Sorry, Sam. It's going to voicemail. I'm sure she'll be here. She's no doubt just held up with something. Don't worry. She would never miss your wedding." I think sarcastically to myself, "I have no idea what would keep Margot away from Jacques-Pierre."

The twins and I have distributed champagne and orange juice around the table twice before the Bennington-Hall house phone rings. Sam asks me to grab the phone because she is still under Jacques-Pierre's creative hands — and "creative" is the word to describe what he's doing to her poor head. The call is for Sam, so I hand her the portable phone and watch as her expression changes from happy to horrified before my eyes.

"No. No. It can't be!" Sam keeps repeating. "It's my wedding day. Margot has to be here. She's my maid of honour."

Oh oh. It appears Margot has met with something to keep her away from the festivities of the day and, lucky for her, Jacques-Pierre's artistic expression. Turns out Margot was struck with an attack of appendicitis during the night. Her roommate took her to the hospital, where she is now lying in a bed, after emergency surgery, unable to leave, walk or, most important, stand up beside Sam on her wedding day. Sam gets off the phone in a panic of tears, but Jacques-Pierre will not let her move, so I hand her a tissue, remembering what my brother said last night about her fragile state.

"Okay. It's a terrible tragedy, but let's stay focused, Sam. One of the other girls can stand up for you. Right?" I look around the table at three of Sam's other friends, who are all sporting very scary hair. One is definitely sporting what is a beehive (circa 1962). The second one is less beehive, more Mike Score from *Flock of Seagulls* — high, backcombed hair at the back, front pushed forward over her forehead. She looks like Cyclops because her right eye is completely covered. Surely, despite the scary hair, one of them can move up in the procession line to be a witness.

"Yeah..." Sam blubbers between sobs.

"And there are six attendants; one less won't make too much difference. Right?" I hope for a positive response similar to that I received on the first idea.

"No. I can't have five. Five won't work. I need six attendants for pictures. I need balance in the pictures!" Sam isn't so positive anymore and drags the word "pictures" out in another blubbery sob.

"Okay. Well, we'll find someone. One of the twins could step in?" I drag Tia and Taryn out of the kitchen and into the dining room. The twins smile on cue and wave.

"NO. I need two greeters. They match and have matching dresses. I must have balance." The sobbing increases. Sam totally misses the irony of her current, unbalanced breakdown.

"Not to worry. What size is Margot's dress?" I ask the

other girls at the table because Sam is fast becoming unable to answer my questions.

"Ahhh, six, I think?" The girl whose hair now resembles the cone on top of a rooster's head answers helpfully.

"Yep, she's a six. We ordered the dresses together, and we were both the same size," *Flock of Seagulls*-hair adds.

"Perfect." I walk over to Sam and take her hand. "Sam, I know it's not going to be Margot, but Kit's a size six. She's already doing a reading and she's like a sister to Mike. What do you think?" I smile and nod at Sam, hoping my positive influence will help her warm to the idea.

"But Margot's dress is different than everyone else. Kit can't wear the different dress!" The sobbing is seconds away from beginning again.

"Okay… okay…" I point at the girl with the *Flock of Seagulls* hair because I'm not sure of her name. "But Kit and… Kelly?" *Flock of Seagulls* hair nods, "are both size sixes. And they can switch dresses and Kelly can stand up for you! Kelly, would switching be okay with you?"

"Sure. I just don't know if I'll be able to see to sign the register," Kelly looks back at the stick-skinny girl doing her hair. "Is there any way we could move my bangs so I can use *both* of my eyes today?"

48

After a harried twenty minutes, I find myself pacing in the front foyer of the Bennington-Hall residence, waiting for Kit to show up. The fourth attendant — I found out her name is Jenn — is sitting in the chair in front of the skinny male hair designer; the twins are sitting in front of the female hair designers. Jacques-Pierre is still "doing" Sam's head. After it is decided Kelly will move up the line to become the maid of honour — Kit will wear Kelly's dress and Kelly will wear Margot's dress — we need to do some fast organizing. The girls with the beehive hair and the rooster hair are sent to meet Margot's roommate and retrieve Margot's dress for Kelly. They are given a stern lecture from Jacques-Pierre on how to hold their heads to ensure their hair remains in place. It is on the tip of my tongue to tell them their hair isn't going anywhere — you can knock on their hair with a baseball bat and nothing is going to move. I am given the unhappy task of calling Kit on her cell to inform her of her elevation in rank.

Kit takes the news in stride — well, after she says a few things I can't repeat and "No! There is *no* way I'm going to be caught *dead* in one of those dresses!" Her reaction goes on but most of her statements contain a lot of profanity. Kit's opinion about Jacques-Pierre hair is also very well articulated, and she hasn't even seen what he's capable of yet. In response, I just nod and answer affirmatively into my cellphone. I give Sam the thumbs-up to let her know everything is under control. When Mr. Jennings arrives to drop Kit off at the Bennington-Hall residence, I have to go to the van to drag her out if it, prying her grip from her father's arm. In the middle of our struggle, I think Kit pleads, "Please don't make me go, Daddy!" I'm sure I must have heard her incorrectly.

"I'm *so* sorry. Sam was beside herself and I needed to think of someone. And you are a size six!" I say at the front step, where I have a tumbler full of champagne — no orange juice required — waiting for Kit. Putting champagne in a tumbler goes against everything I believe in. I always have the proper glass for the drink, and I have been using an appropriate flute all morning. Kit's reluctance to be elevated to a member of the wedding party calls for drastic measures; I have to set my stemware convictions aside.

In reply, Kit lets out a low growl, frowns at me and downs the champagne in one swallow. I think she's warming up to the idea of wearing the Sunset Disaster.

"Mother of Pearl!" are the first words Kit utters at the Bennington-Hall residence. She walks into the kitchen, where I pour her another tumbler of champagne and hand it to her. From the kitchen, she can see into the dining room, where Jenn and the twins are sitting facing her. The twins have been graced with similar hairstyles. Their hair has been combed tight to their heads and knotted to the back, where the hair has been divided into five braids and the braids then bent and affixed so they look like they are wearing elaborate headpieces. There are occasional hairs, cemented with product, sticking out amongst the braids. If Heidi — yes, Heidi of the children's story set in the Swiss Alps — had had a high-end hairstyle, I suspect it would resemble what the two skinny females have done to the twins.

Kit downs the second tumbler of champagne then I take her by the shoulders and step with her into the dining room so she can see Sam. "Hey, Sam. No worries, Kit's here," I say.

Kit just smiles and gives a little wave. I don't think she can articulate words, as she digests the outrageous hairstyles. I'm glad the beehive and rooster dos are out picking up Margot's dress. Jenn looks to be getting the windblown look. All of her hair has been swept to the left and treated with product. It looks like she's in a strong windstorm, but there's no wind in the dining room.

"Ta da!" Jacques-Pierre announces with flair as Sam stands up from her place at the table. Sam actually doesn't look too bad. Her hair has been swept up and is sticking out in little wisps all over her head. Jacques-Pierre has affixed small pearls and flowers throughout the mess of hair, and Sam actually looks quite nice — well, compared to the rest of the hairdos I've witnessed today.

Kelly and Sam excuse themselves to go upstairs and work on Sam's makeup. The twins, with their braided Heidi hair, leave to go back to the condo and finish getting ready. They have to be at the church earlier than the rest of us to greet the guests. Beehive hair and rooster hair enter in a flurry of orange dresses and shoes and go to find Sam and Kelly to ensure Margot's dress is going to fit. Kit and I are alone with Jacques-Pierre and his team.

"You two!" Jacques-Pierre points, "Sit!" Kit looks afraid, grabs the open bottle of champagne and two glasses, and sits in front of the two female designers who have just transformed the twins into matching Heidis. I sit in front of Jacques-Pierre and accept a glass of champagne from Kit.

"Mother of Pearl" is the only thought I can formulate forty-five minutes later, as I stand in the downstairs washroom of the Bennington-Hall residence. All of my hair is pulled back into a very tight bun, at the back of my head, from which five prongs of hair, about as thick as my finger but several inches longer, stick straight up. The prongs of hair are hard with product. I gently touch one of the prongs and it yields nothing. Crunchy hair would be a welcome relief. I have no idea how I'm ever going to get back to my normal hair. I wonder if Jacques-Pierre used Crazy Glue to get this effect.

Kit is standing beside me at the mirror. I follow her eyes and she is fixated on my hair. Her hair is tame compared to mine. Kit has a two-inch section of bangs lying flat against the right side of her face, and the rest of her hair has been braided in small braids — like you get when you are travelling to a Caribbean island — with only the ends sticking up in a structured yet messy way all over her head.

"It's just so... so... patriotic," Kit finally blurts out.

"Yes, because it's an exact replica of the Statue of Liberty!" I answer sarcastically. This day cannot be over soon enough.

Kit reaches up to touch one of the prongs. "Wow!" She is as fascinated as I am.

"My life is in the toilet. I have to change the company I work for, I'm single, now this! Could my life get any worse?" I turn to Kit for support but, before she can say anything, Kelly, the upgraded maid of honour, limps to the bathroom door and answers my rhetorical question.

"Is this over the top, or is it just me?" Kelly asks straight-faced, but I have no idea how she's able to do it. The poor girl not only has *Flock of Seagulls* hair — although the compromised version, so we can see part of her right eye — she is also wearing a modified version of the Sunset Disaster. Kelly's dress, which was Margot's dress, has a double row of very large, incandescent-sequined rosettes affixed around the bottom hem of the dress. The incandescent roses match the three-inch-wide empire waistband, and the skirt appears to be fuller than I remember mine being.

"Is there a hoop in your skirt?" Kit asks the question I'm starting to formulate in my mind.

"Yep! Like it wasn't big enough before!" Kelly answers sarcastically. "I bet Margot isn't sick at all. She just woke up, took one look at this thing, and knew she couldn't wear it in public."

"Can't wear the shoes?" I look down and nod at the orange satin shoes in Kelly's hand.

"I had them on for about thirty seconds. Putting my feet in a barrel full of razor blades would be more comfortable. I have another pair I'm going to wear for everything but the ceremony. I need champagne. Anyone want any?"

"Yes, please," Kit answers at the same time I say, "Absolutely!"

"Okay, to answer your question, yes your life could be worse. *You* could have been elevated to maid of honour," Kit whispers, starting to laugh.

49

The Bennington-Halls, who had been decorating the church and reception hall all morning with my parents and the Jennings, return home as we are all in the backyard being photographed by the photographer named Lars, who appears to speak limited English. He's more of a pointer/grunter than a speaker.

Kit, who had understandable reservations about being in the wedding party, seems to embrace the whole experience after her fourth large tumbler of champagne. Kit's shoes don't hurt her feet because they are a size too big; Margot has larger feet than Kit. So, instead of excruciating pain with every step, slightly inebriated Kit must ensure her shoes don't flip off. Mr. Bennington-Hall looks shocked when he sees us lined up in the backyard. I am standing closest to him, and hear him ask Mrs. Bennington-Hall, "Do they *want* their hair to look like that?" Mrs. Bennington-Hall smacks Mr. Bennington-Hall on the shoulder, then drags him inside to get ready for the wedding.

"Girls, I've put two more bottles of champagne in the refrigerator for you," Mr. Bennington-Hall yells over his shoulder on his way into the house. Kelly immediately breaks up the photo by kicking off her shoes, tossing her bouquet of white and orange lilies up in the air for beehive-hair girl to catch, and heading to the refrigerator.

"I'll just grab those bottles, shall I, ladies?" Kelly says over her shoulder as she sprints to the kitchen. Shortly after Kelly's exit, Lars decides to photograph the bride alone, so we attendants are free to remove our horrible shoes and join Kelly in the kitchen for champagne. Lars poses Sam under the large tree in the backyard, and I have to admit she looks stunning. Even with the questionable hairstyle, she is quite beautiful in her slim-fitting, beaded dress with the square neckline and tiny-capped sleeves. I glance down at the billowing fabric around my arms and wonder why we couldn't have tiny-capped sleeves.

"How come Sam's dress is so tight-fitting and we all look like construction cones?" I say out loud to no one in particular.

"So, she looks good and we look like hell!" I hear from a mostly inebriated Kelly. "Look at the thing I'm stuck in! You hear about brides making the wedding party dress horribly so they look better. But, honestly, I didn't think it was true until I saw what she did to Margot's dress."

"Do you think maybe she just has bad big-dress taste?" Kit asks. "Mrs. Bennington-Hall did make us wear hideous dresses at the bridal shower. Maybe it's a family thing."

"Possibly," rooster-hair girl says from the living-room. "Check these out."

We all tromp into the living room, after we break up the

bottleneck in the doorway by pushing Kelly and her hoop skirt through, to the family's "wall of shame." Of the nine photographs on the wall spanning the lifetime of the Bennington-Halls, Mrs. Bennington-Hall has massive-skirted dresses in seven of them.

"Hmmpf. I guess they do consider large skirts the height of fashion. You'd never know to look at them. They look so normal," Jenn, who looks like she's standing in a wind tunnel even though the air isn't moving at all, comments.

"You think your family's completely messed up. But then you meet someone else's family, and yours looks pretty darn good!" rooster-hair girl laughs.

As if on cue, Mr. Bennington-Hall enters the living room, wearing a purple tuxedo.

Yep, poor Samantha cannot be held responsible for her idea of fashion. "The gene pool is a scary place to swim!" Kit whispers to me as she accepts another glass of champagne from Mr. Bennington-Hall in his purple tuxedo.

"Especially if there's no deep end!" Kelly whispers in response to Kit's comment.

We cut Kelly off all alcoholic beverages shortly after this comment. In order to have her walk down the aisle and sign the register, she's going to have to sober up a bit. We arrive at the church a few minutes ahead of schedule, so we have some time to assemble and try to flatten out the skirts of our dresses — well, flatten them out as much as you can in light of the massive crinolines. The six orange-clad attendants standing on the stairs of the church must be a sight for any passerby. My heart raced when I heard a plane overhead, and I looked up to ensure it wasn't trying to land on us.

By the time we are all limping down the aisle in our cruel orange shoes, we've consumed more champagne than a group of underaged Hollywood starlets so we aren't nearly as self-conscious about our ensembles as we might be. Kelly is in better form than I suspected she might be and the bystanders would be hard-pressed to tell how much champagne she has consumed. The only mishap getting down the aisle to the front of the church is Kit slipping a shoe, but she managed to pull it off. The shoe flew ahead of her, stopping when it hit the back of rooster-hair's dress and dropping to the ground. When Kit got to the shoe, she stooped and scooped it up in one fluid motion. Aside from continuing to the altar with a limp, wearing one shoe and carrying the other behind her bouquet, it was all very well orchestrated.

When Sam walks down the aisle with her dad, I can't believe how incredible she looks. She appears completely calm, having fully recovered from losing Margot from the wedding party, her balance fully regained. I turn to look at Mike, and he is smiling from ear to ear. I've never seen him look so genuinely happy. I see Kit wipe her eyes, so I know she's thinking the same thing I am. My brother looks so handsome and grown up — his tuxedo is a lovely shade of black. I can't believe the man saying his wedding vows without a stammer or bit of nervousness is the same guy who used to break out in hives if a girl spoke to him in high school. He's come a long way. I'm so happy for him I have to steal Kit's tissue to wipe my own eyes. I seem to be making a habit of this crying thing.

Kelly manages to sign the register and stand for the obligatory pictures without falling over or getting into a fit of giggles. When the pastor announces Mr. and Mrs. Michael Melrose, I feel like I might start to cry again, with a combination of happiness for my brother and his new wife and sadness for me. Just as Mike's life is starting down a wonderful, blissful path leading to couples, kids and carpooling, my life is floundering in the cesspool of "Holy hell?! What am I supposed to do now?"

I wish it was me getting married and having everything under control. I am not good at having no idea where my life is going; I am good at being in complete control. I look down at my dress, remember how my hair looked in the rear-view mirror of the limousine, and think, "Well, wherever I'm headed, I'm certainly not dressed for success."

We take limousines to High Park for photographs. Lars is his normal chatty self but somehow manages to convey what he wants us to do. I watch him with fascination. He rarely speaks, yet we all know what he's conveying with his grunts and pointing. When the six Sunset Disasters topped with bad hair are in a row, we are a formidable force. People walking their dogs and pushing their baby strollers stop and look on with varying degrees of shock, awe and sorrow. I can tell the young mothers, who have obviously had weddings in the recent past, are thinking, "Wow, there will be some regrets when they get those pictures back."

I suggest we take a shoulder/headshot of all the girls, and Lars grunts in agreement. It's difficult to squash our skirts together enough to have all of our heads and outrageous hairstyles in one shot, but we manage to do it. I know this is one photo I'm going to insist on getting a copy of for my memento box. I don't actually have a memento box, but I will start one as soon as I have this bad-hair photo in my hot little hands.

50

All the orange-dressed attendants brought comfortable shoes for the reception, except me. I brought my favourite black, knee-high, four-inch-heel Prada boots. No matter what the evening is going to hand me, I'm going to be ready. I always feel more confident in boots. Upon entering the reception hall, making my way to the bar with Kit, my mother stops me, "Melanie Melrose! You can't wear boots with your beautiful dress. Where are your lovely satin shoes?"

"Mom, is there a bird on your hat?" I saw my mother at the picture-taking session in High Park but I didn't really pay attention to her hat. There is definitely a bird — a fake chickadee, I believe, in foliage — affixed to the side of her outrageously large, floppy hat.

"Birds are calming." My mother expressing herself with a hat instead of a necklace is a refreshing change, but I momentarily wonder if she's going to start adding hats to all of her outfits or if it's just a special wedding thing. "I think the wedding went very well, don't you?"

"Amazingly well. I'm so happy for Mike and Sam." I smile because I am genuinely happy for them.

"How are you doing? With the breakup and everything?"

"Fine. Well, not fine, really. But I'll be okay."

"Well, if you need anything, you can always call your father and me. We talked about it, and we won't see you lose your lovely house over all this naked-dancing business." My mom touches my arm, and I feel a sudden rise of emotion and my throat start to constrict. The wonderful, supportive mother I occasionally see has picked a bad time to show up. I know if I don't change the subject, I may start to cry. And if that happens, I may not be able to stop. I clear my throat and change the subject. "Thank you, but I'm fine. Really. How's Dad doing? Does he have his speech ready?"

"Oh, good point. I better go and check in on him, to ensure he doesn't have too much wine before dinner." My emotions stand down as my mom returns to the "normal" I know and love. Just as my mother turns to find my father, Mrs. Jennings walks up to her and hands her a glass of wine. I can tell immediately that my mother has "expressed" herself with Mrs. Jennings' hat as well as her own.

"Mom, is that a salamander on Mrs. Jennings' hat?" I ask as I crane my neck trying to get a better look.

"Gecko, dear. Gecko!" My mother rolls her eyes, takes Mrs. Jennings by the arm, and walks away — presumably, to fine-tune my father's speech.

Knowing the head table will be stocked with Mr. Bennington-Hall's homemade wine, Kit and I get a glass of champagne and a beer each from the bar. We don't want to mix the copious amounts of champagne already consumed with whatever Mr. Bennington-Hall has bottled during what is apt to be lengthy speeches. After the trip to the bar, we devour some appetizers while waiting for dinner and the speeches to begin. The few handfuls of trail mix and Ritz crackers I grabbed at the Bennington-Hall house earlier today had worn off long ago.

Dinner is divine, or I'm just starving. I've never tasted a roast beef meal I've enjoyed more. The carrots, and there are plenty, are a lovely complement to the Sunset Disaster dresses. Sitting beside Kit at the head table is a bonus. Before Kit was elevated to bridesmaid, I was going to be sitting with veritable strangers. The guest tables are circular, so I am able to see only the back of the person sitting in what would have been John's seat. It's a woman with big hair — obviously heartily backcombed for the occasion — in a lime green dress, which may or may not have sequins on it. I can't tell from the head table. The table is full of boyfriends and girlfriends of the wedding attendants. Kevin is sitting with the twins and Ben at another table. I'm just happy Mike and Sam found someone to fill John's empty seat.

Thinking about John starts a flood of emotions I don't want to think about or deal with right now. I've been so busy since the confrontation-slash-breakup, I haven't had time to give the whole thing much thought. I shake my head and come back to reality in time to listen to Mr. Bennington-Hall, in his purple tuxedo, welcome Mike to his family.

The speeches continue through dessert, which is carrot

cake — I wonder if Sam just adores all things carrot? An insane love for carrots would explain the orange theme. The speeches finish up shortly after the dessert dishes are cleared. I notice the room is much noisier than it was before the meal. I have to assume Mr. Bennington-Hall's potent wine is starting to take its toll on the guests. I'm glad I'm sticking to beer.

At the bar Kit and I join up with Kelly and her boyfriend, Phil, after the speeches. Kelly is quite tipsy from the wine at dinner but is still in fairly good form considering the amount of alcohol she's consumed in total today. Phil seems very nice. He's dressed head to toe in black leather, including a black leather Harley-Davidson baseball cap. Phil's all-black, plain, biker outfit only underscores the exaggerated floral theme of Kelly's maid-of-honour dress — to their credit, the orange of her dress is a shade very similar to the Harley logo.

The DJ introduces Mike and Sam for their first dance, and the music of Harry Connick, Jr.'s, "It Had to Be You" starts to play. I have to admit, as first songs go, this one is as good as any. And when Mike and Sam start to dance, it is obvious they've taken dance lessons for the occasion. I've never seen Mike so graceful. Up until today, he was more of a stand-still, bend-over-like-a-robot kind of dancer. During Celine Dion's "Because You Loved Me," which Sam has selected for her father/daughter dance, there is a ruckus near the door. I turn toward the noise and see Kevin, Ben and Kit — who had been going to the bar for another round of beer — standing in front of a very intoxicated John, trying to halt his entrance.

"Oh no!" I did not anticipate John showing up at the wedding. I honestly thought he took the breakup in stride. I hurry toward the group, hoping I can get John outside before too many people notice, and Mike and Sam's reception is marred due to my naked-dance-obsessed ex-boyfriend.

"*John*!" I hiss. "What are you doing here?" I break in between Kit and Kevin and grab John by the shoulders — stopping short, only briefly, when the billows of my skirt get caught behind Kit's equally massive skirt and Kevin, causing them to have to move left and right respectfully to make room for me to get through.

"Why is my girlfriend at the wedding and I'm not?" John slurs, obviously very drunk. He loses his balance, so Kevin has to reach out and catch him.

"He's my brother, you idiot. And this is not the appropriate time or place for your antics!" I answer in a hissed whisper. I try to manoeuvre John so he's facing the door, and not the room full of guests.

"No!" John pulls back around to face Kit and Kevin. "I'm not leaving until I talk to my girlfriend."

"This is going to have to wait for another time..." I am getting exasperated with drunken John.

"It's been four months, and I won't give up without a fight..." John points at my chest and stumbles again.

Four months? What the hell is he talking about?

Just then, I hear a voice from behind me and I stop short. "I'm right here, precious! What's all the commotion?"

This is *not* happening.

The same voice I heard announcing her "vision" not forty-eight hours ago is now speaking over my shoulder at *my* brother's wedding reception. I spin around in stunned disbelief at the same time that Kevin and Kit turn to follow the voice. I let go of John's shoulders and, since Kevin's attention is also drawn to the voice behind us, he doesn't see John toppling over, ending up on the floor in a heap behind my voluminous skirt.

Standing before me is the woman with the bad back-combed hair and lime green dress — which does indeed have many lime green sequins on it, as I suspected — who utilized John's empty chair and ate John's dinner. Yes, Undulating Ursula is at my brother's wedding reception.

51

"YOU!" I hiss. I am instantly mad. More mad than I've ever been in fact. All the emotions I've been suppressing since John first started this entire dance nonsense rise to the surface, and I can't help myself. My heart is racing; I notice my palms are instantly drenched in sweat as I clench my hands into fists. I want to punch this woman. I am not an advocate of senseless violence, but this isn't senseless, is it? I don't consider myself a fighter, in light of my belief in non-violence, but I've seen my fair share of television programs with the "discretionary viewing" warnings. I've seen a few punches thrown. Just as I start to raise my arm and step into the punch — I know enough to know I'll get more oomph with stepping into it — John wraps his arms around my ankles and pulls me toward him, uttering, "A little help here!"

Instead of connecting with my target, which is Ursula's face, I end up on the floor, dress and crinoline billowing, with John's arms firmly gripping my Prada-boot-covered ankles. I look up to see Kevin and Ben on either side of Ursula, escorting her from the building. I'm punching the air in Ursula's general direction, trying to get a piece of her while kicking at John to get away from his grip. Kit is standing by, waiting for me to tire myself out before coming anywhere near my flailing arms. I hear a voice from my feet. “Hey, stop kicking me. Ouch!” So, I give another kick — with more feeling.

A small crowd forms as I tire myself out punching into the air and kicking at John. Every time my foot makes contact and John lets out a yelp, I feel a strange sense of satisfaction and fulfillment I never had while John and I were a couple. Kelly’s biker boyfriend, Phil, and one of the other attendant’s boyfriends pick John up under the arms and carry him from the building, following Kevin, Ben and Ursula. Kit and Kelly help me up and hustle me into the ladies’ room. I don’t see my mother or Mrs. Jennings, and silently count my blessings. Having to defend my juvenile behaviour would be too much to take at this particular juncture.

“So, you handled yourself pretty well!” Kit laughs as she checks the stalls to ensure we are alone in the ladies’ room.

“Too bad you got muddled up with the drunk guy; you could have taken her — or at least poked her in the eye with your hair,” Kelly pipes up as she empties the wine from her wineglass and then pours more from the bottle in her other hand. “Here. You need this more than me!” Kelly then hands me the glass. I down its contents while Kit gives Kelly the Coles Notes version of the John and Ursula saga.

“More.” I hand the glass back to Kelly, who obligingly refills it and then scampers from the washroom — presumably, to get another bottle.

“I really wanted to hit her. I did. What is wrong with me?

And what the hell was she even doing here? Did you hear John say, 'Four months'? Have they been together for four months?" I slide down the wall and end up sitting on the bathroom floor, repeatedly trying to flatten my skirt, which keeps popping up to almost chin level due to the volume of crinoline underneath it. "Stupid skirt! I hate this skirt!" I shriek and then shake the billowing fabric angrily.

"Okay, calm down. Let's just remove the silly crinoline," Kit says. "You know what? I'm going to take mine off as well."

Kelly comes back with another bottle of homemade wine and two more glasses. "Okay. I got the scoop." Kelly starts to say while she pours wine into the three glasses handing Kit and me one each. "Apparently, the woman — Ulysses, is it? The one in the horrible green dress was Sam's dance teacher when Sam was young. Sam ran into her yesterday, and Uvula, or whatever her name is, was crying and told Sam a sob story about breaking up with her boyfriend, so Sam invited her to come to the wedding to cheer her up."

"No, Ursula broke up with John..." Kit starts.

"Because she has a husband and needs his money!" I finish Kit's thought.

Kit, Kelly and I all sip our wine pondering the story Kelly has just shared. Two women come in to use the washroom, so we sip wine casually, like women always sip wine in the washrooms at these events.

"The wedding was lovely. You girls looked marvellous!" One of the ladies pats Kit's hand while Kit is removing our crinolines from two of the sinks so the ladies can wash their hands.

"Thank you," Kit answers politely while jamming the crinolines behind the garbage can.

After the ladies leave, I continue, "I guess they've reconciled. John was referring to her as his girlfriend, and I believe she called him *precious*!"

"John is a lot of things, but precious is not one of them!" Kit comments.

Kit is halfway through her sentence when it starts. A feeling like I've never had. My heart feels like someone is squeezing it, and I can't breathe. Am I having a heart attack? I'm still wondering about the heart attack and clutching at my chest when I hear the primal scream erupting from somewhere very deep inside of me. Then the tears start. Tears. *Me* crying and sobbing in the ladies' room at my brother's wedding reception. *Me*. Mel Melrose. Sobbing.

Kelly hasn't known me very long, so she takes my sobbing in stride. Kit, on the other hand, is completely shocked. Kit has known me for three decades, and she's never seen me cry more than a handful of tears — let alone, sob — so she takes a noticeable step back from me.

"It's going to be okay." Kelly pats my shoulder.

"*Noooooo*..." I manage through the sobbing while I slide back down to the floor — I had had to stand to remove the irritating crinoline — I register the door opening, then quickly closing. Apparently the person who thought she needed the ladies' room is willing to wait rather than walk in on my scene. The door opening and closing brings Kit back to the reality at hand. I'm an unprecedented mess. She is the only one who can help me.

"Kelly, can you please go and get us a couple more bottles of wine?" Kit asks as she grabs some industrial-grade paper towel and wets it from the tap. Kit presses the damp paper towel on my forehead and tries to calm me down, "It's going to be okay. John and Ursula are going to do whatever they're going do and you're going to be fine. I promise."

"No, I won't!" I protest. "I'm a loser!"

"What?" Kit gives me her best confused-raised-eyebrow look. "*You* are *not* a loser! You're Mel Melrose. What are you talking about?"

"I don't have a job. Remember, I quit because the people at work didn't like me, so they had to hire a translator to deal with my personality? My boyfriend has been having an affair with a flabby dance instructor who has terrible fashion sense for *four months*! I owe Marc $15,000! My neighbours thought I was the person stealing their lawn ornaments. People think I'm capable of petty theft! I look like the Statue of Liberty would if someone dressed her in a construction cone... Four months... I was hoping to marry him, and he's been fooling around for four months..." I gulp for breath, then continue, "I miss Buurrrton!" Tears and sobbing follow, and I take the paper towel from Kit's hand and cover my leaking eyes.

"Sweetie, don't you mean you miss John?" Kit asks quietly.

"*No*. I miss *Burton*. I want a puuuuupppppppy…" I sob out the word "puppy" and I hear nervous laughter. Kit, Kelly and the twins are all crouched around me. I had been so wrapped up in telling Kit my troubles, I didn't hear Kelly return with two more bottles of wine and the twins as reinforcements.

"You can probably visit Burton anytime you want. And we can get you a puppy… if you really think you want one." Kit then gets a puzzled look on her face and adds, "And don't be silly. You're an amazing woman; of course you'll get married."

"No, I won't. I'm needy, remember?" I blubber.

"You are a lot of things, Mel, but you are not needy." Kit wipes tears from my face with a paper towel. "If you want to get married, you will! You're Mel Melrose. I've never seen you not achieve what you strive for."

"I'm not a balleriiiiina!" I blubber, almost incoherently. I'm not even making sense to myself anymore. I've never felt so distraught or disoriented.

"Ballerina? Ballerinas aren't allowed to eat. No one wants to be a ballerina!" Kelly comments to no one in particular.

"Yeah, and we're all different." Taryn starts to speak. "Look at Tia and me — we're identical twins but we love different things. I love marine life and Tia loves rock bands. It's okay to be different."

"And Ursula's no ballerina! You don't want to be like stupid Ursula anyway," Tia adds and hands me a full glass of wine. I take a sip between sobs.

"How great can she be? She has the same name as the evil octopus in *The Little Mermaid* cartoon!"

"Hey, yeah! I knew she reminded me of someone! Good call!" Kelly comments seriously. I have to laugh despite my self-pity.

52

Two hours — and more bottles of homemade wine than I can count — later, I'm still reeling in shock over John's inadvertent "four-month affair" confession, when Kit asks a question I've never heard her ask before.

"Mel. What would Jackie do?"

"Pardon?" I have had a lot of Mr. Bennington-Hall's homemade wine, so I may easily have lost track of the conversation. I have no idea who Jackie is or what Kit is talking about.

"Jackie O. You know, JFK's wife. What would Jackie do?" Kit explains.

"About what?" I'm a little less confused but still not entirely aware of the direction Kit is taking.

"Your situation. If Jackie O found herself recently single due to a philandering boyfriend and chunky mistress, leaving her to feel less than adequate, what would she do?" Kit asks triumphantly.

"I have no idea. No one ever dumped Jackie."

"No, but she was no stranger to philandering husbands. And she always handled herself with all the grace imaginable." Kit has a point.

"Okay, I'll bite. What *would* Jackie do?" I ask suspiciously, knowing Kit already has an answer she wants to share with me.

"I think Jackie would take a hiatus and get away from it all for a while. Returning triumphant, refreshed, and back in complete control." Kit grins at me.

"Hiatus to where?" I'm hardly the jet-setting type; I'm more the workaholic type.

"Australia. Why don't you go with Taryn? She's travelling for a few months before her internship starts. You could go along, get some sun, and get away from all things Charlie Brown!"

"Okay, back up. I have to start work with a new company in a couple of weeks. And Taryn certainly does not want me tagging along on her trip. I'm ten years older than her. Won't I cramp her style?"

"Cramp whose style?" Tia asks as she and Ben and Taryn walk up to the table.

"Taryn. She doesn't want me to tag along on her trip to Australia," I state matter-of-factly.

"What?! No, it will be so cool. Do you want to come, Mel? I'd love for you to come along!" Taryn answers, jumping up and down. She is much more enthusiastic than I imagined she'd be over me encroaching on her trip. "Oh, please come!"

"Why? Do you have dastardly things planned to do to me?" I laugh suspiciously. For the life of me, I can't imagine Taryn *wanting* me to travel with her.

"No. But I've never been away from Tia for longer than a few days. I've never been anywhere alone. I'm a bit afraid I'll be lonely. But if you come along, I won't be lonely at all!" Taryn presents her argument.

I suppose it is true the twins have never been apart for very long. They shared a bedroom until Kit moved out; they went to the same university, where they shared a room; and aside from the past few weeks of Tia living here in Toronto, they haven't been apart — ever.

"But I'm not exactly a backpacker," I state honestly. I really am more of a five-star-hotel gal on the rare occasions I do travel.

"You'll be great. I'll help you pack. You can get a ticket and travel visa on Monday and fly with me on Tuesday. Oh, please? It will be so great!" Taryn is pleading her case now.

"I have a new job to start. A new job with a new company. I can't just be running off to Australia. Besides, how irresponsible would that be when I just borrowed money from Marc?" I try to quell the excitement of the animated faces in front of me.

"Okay, firstly, Marc won't care if you don't start paying him back for a couple of months. And secondly, new company maybe, but it's the same job really. You're taking your clients with you. I'm sure Morty The Man would postpone your start date. Honestly, Mel, a change is as good as a rest. The timing is actually quite perfect!" Kit really seems intent on getting me on a plane out of here.

"Kit!" I grab Kit by the shoulders and stare into her eyes, "you've known me my whole life. Is running off to Australia something Mel Melrose would do? No. I am not spontaneous and, in my world, backpack is a noun, not a verb."

Kit laughs and takes my hands off her shoulders, "Verb. Noun. Whatever. I think it would do you a world of good to get away from here for a while. Who knows? Getting away might allow you to figure out what happened with the whole Charlie Brown thing."

"Why are you trying to get rid of me?" I start to become paranoid.

"I'm not! Are you kidding, I'll go crazy without you here every day. I just think you could use the break. I mean, I've never seen you as upset as you were earlier. I really just think you could use some time away from here and… well… everything."

Kit's last sentence seals the deal — without the actual mammal being present and kissing my face. I know she means "get away from the vicinity of John and his new dancing partner."

"Really? Do you think it would be good for me?" I look from Kit to the twins. "I can always come home if I hate it, right?" I ask Taryn.

"Absolutely," she replies. "We'll get you an open-ended ticket! You can come home anytime."

Before I can give a definite, verbal "yes," the shrieks being emitted from the twins are deafening. I get caught up in their excitement as the three of us hug and jump in a circle. It seems I'm going to Australia.

The remainder of the wedding celebration is more enjoyable for me. Having a plan, albeit not a traditional plan, is comforting. The thought of waking up tomorrow being single, in debt and "needy," was wearing me thin. Now with a plan, even if it doesn't address any of my immediate concerns, I can concentrate on all the logistics and preparation, thereby putting my self-esteem busters on the back burner.

When I told Kelly I am planning to go to Australia with Taryn, she hugs me and says, "Great news. Don't let a cheating ex-boyfriend keep you down." She also mentions, quietly, "John stumbled into Kevin's fist while being escorted out of the reception, and will have a very nice black eye in the morning." I must admit, my heart does feel a little warmer after she tells me.

Mike and Sam leave the reception to great fanfare and little bubbles, blissfully unaware of the kafuffle John and Ursula caused. I turn to Kit as the newlyweds leave the building, "We'll have all this one day, right?"

"Absolutely. Only, hopefully, with nicer attire!"

I'm going to Australia. The truth of the statement doesn't settle in until the next morning, when I'm in the shower trying to remove the nasty hair products that were so liberally applied yesterday by Jacques-Pierre. During the third application of shampoo, I start to wonder if I can pull off bald. Do all wedding attendants have to shave their heads after standing up for someone? Surely not! No one would ever volunteer to be wedding attendants. Shaving your head is a pretty tall order. Just as I am starting to panic, the last of the Crazy Glue-like hair product finally releases its hold and I'm able to run my fingers through my hair. It feels really dry and brittle, but it's no longer in knots. I liberally apply conditioner, twice.

I'm going to Australia. What have I agreed to? I'm no traveller; I'm certainly no backpacker. How much wine did I drink last night?

My longer than usual shower allows me to miss breakfast preparation with the parents. By the time I enter the kitchen, a complete big breakfast — bacon, eggs, home fries, toast — is ready and waiting. Excellent. I'm starving due to my mid-grade hangover. I sit down to breakfast, and the parents are chatting about how wonderful the wedding was and how happy they are for Mike and Sam. Just as my mother mentions we have been invited to the Bennington-Hall residence this afternoon to watch Mike and Sam open their gifts, Kit and the twins come into the kitchen. Kit's hair is still wet and looks like it will be huge once it dries. The twins' hair is dry but looks frizzy.

"How was your hair?" I ask Kit, hoping she had the same difficulty removing the product that I did.

"Nasty. Whatever product was in there was impossible to get out," Kit comments as she pours a mug of coffee.

"I know! Horrible stuff," Tia comments as she takes a mug from Kit.

Mrs. Jennings, who has finished her breakfast, gets up to make eggs for the twins. Kit asks for just toast. I guess Kit is feeling the effects of Mr. Bennington-Hall's wine. We should have stuck to the beer, as planned.

"So, are you girls coming to the gift opening?" Mrs. Jennings asks the twins.

"I can't," Taryn answers. "I have to get Mel packed for Australia."

"Pardon? What did you say?" My mother is visibly shocked.

"Mel's coming to Australia with me. We decided late last night. I have to pick up a knapsack and loads of travel stuff for her. Tia's going to help me, freeing Mel up to go to the Bennington-Halls," Taryn answers while eating a piece of bacon.

"Mel is *not* going to Australia!" My mother is obviously not embracing the idea. I wonder why?

"What do you mean, I'm *not* going?" What does she care where I go?

"I have just watched my son get married, and he and Sam are going to go back to Georgia and Lord knows how long it will be before I see them again. So I will not let you leave me to go traipsing all over a continent halfway around the world! Bob, talk some sense into your daughter." My mom turns her head and is on the verge of tears.

"Mom, I'm not doing this to upset you. I just think I need to get away for a while after all that has happened in the past few weeks. I won't be gone very long, only a couple of months." I touch my mom's shoulder. I had no idea she would even care about what I do, let alone get upset about it.

"Betty, Mel will be back in no time. And we can go and visit Mike and Sam any time you'd like." My dad seems a little more accepting of my travel plans.

"But anything can happen in a couple of months, and both of my children will be so far away." My mom looks depleted, and everyone is staring at the two of us.

I had expected some flak from my mother, but not in the caring way. I had expected her to tell me I wouldn't be capable of backpacking, which would have cemented my resolve. I have no comeback to genuine concern.

"Well, I think Mel will be good company for Taryn. I, for one, am glad they will be travelling together," Mr. Jennings says, breaking the awkward tension.

"I know *I'm* glad. I think Mel and I will have an amazing time together!" Taryn is animated and sincere in her affirmation. "And, Mrs. Melrose, I promise we'll email every day and stay in touch. It'll be like Mel's still here in Toronto."

"But it's still a bad idea," my mother states, then turns to me. "Mel, aren't you still prone to motion sickness. Surely the flight to Australia will do you in."

Everyone laughs, including me, although I think quietly to myself, "Mom may have a point there!"

53

The next two and a half days whiz by at a surreal pace. After I announce to my parents and Mr. and Mrs. Jennings I am indeed going to Australia, I am completely committed. Kit, the twins, and I clean up the kitchen, then Tia and Taryn lead the way through Mountain Equipment Co-op like they work there. Apparently, they had spent ages doing research and comparative shopping for Taryn's trip, so they know exactly what I need to purchase. Forty-five minutes and $550 later, I am equipped with a knapsack, sleeping bag, Swiss Army knife — I opted for the one with the corkscrew, knowing full well wine will, at some point, be involved in my travels — and godawful hiking boots. I had argued with Taryn about the boots. Honestly, I wouldn't be caught dead in them, so why do I need to purchase them? Taryn strongly believes the weight of my knapsack will make the boots imperative; I, on the other hand, think she must be overstating. How heavy can a knapsack be?

After Mountain Equipment Co-op, we part ways. I had promised my mother I would attend the gift opening so she could have both her children together "one last time" —

you'd swear I was going off to war instead of travelling in Australia. I leave the twins with a wad of cash, and Kit and I head to the Bennington-Hall residence.

The gift opening is more fun than I thought it would be. Kit gets a real workout, tensing her entire body every time Mike and Sam open another piece of red dinnerware. I think her head is going to pop off when they open the Royal Doulton Provence Rouge gravy boat.

"Kit, you really must get some therapy for this red china thing you have going on," I whisper to Kit while we're sipping Mr. Bennington-Hall's homemade wine — which actually has grown on me since I consumed so much of it last night — and Mike unwraps a bearskin rug.

"I don't need therapy. I need to be surrounded by nice white plates. Don't tell me you'll be able to look at a full-length flesh-coloured leotard anytime soon and not cringe!" Kit laughs.

"Good point." I hadn't considered Kit's aversion might be justified, like my now adverse reaction to all things modern dance. Hmm?

Our mothers' both shoot us glares when Mike and Sam open the gnome band I regifted. Kit and I can't stifle our giggles and we ignore our parents' disapproval.

After the gift opening, we meet the twins back at my house for a barbecue. Our parents are planning to return to North Bay after dinner and, apparently, I have a lot of packing to do. While the burgers are cooking, I'm in the kitchen preparing a salad. The twins are presumably going through my bedroom finding suitable travel wear.

My mom starts helping me cut vegetables. "I'm sorry about this morning. You're right. If you want to go to Australia, you should go. I just didn't think travelling was ever high on your priority list."

"It wasn't until yesterday. Heck, it still isn't really but I believe the change will do me good. I have the rest of my life to work. Maybe a break is exactly what I need," I answer honestly.

"I'm sorry about what happened with John. I know you cared about him — and what he did is inexcusable."

"I did care about him, Mom. I still do. Trust me, being single at this point wasn't in my plan. I really thought I might be the next wedding. But now I am single again and I have to figure out what's next."

My mom walks to me and hugs me. "Well, Bill and Peggy are very glad you will be travelling with Taryn. They've been terribly worried about her being halfway around the world on her own. But it doesn't make it any easier for me to let you go."

I hug my mom back and laugh. "The way Taryn's set me up for the trip, I think it's me they should worry about. Thank goodness Taryn will be there to take care of me!"

Our parents pack up the van after dinner. My dad gives me a long hug and slips two $100 bills into my hand. I laugh and try to give the money back, but he shoves it into my pocket and whispers, "Just take care of yourself."

After our parents depart, Kit and the twins return to Kit's condo, leaving me alone in my house for the first time since I broke up with John. I've never been single in this house. I look around and realize how large and quiet my house is when I'm the only one in it. John was always good for making noise. He can only watch television if the volume is too loud to hear yourself think; he walks loud and he talks loud. The silence is deafening, so I find Kings of Leon on my laptop — making a mental note to replace the stereo that was John's and is now an empty spot in the entertainment unit — and make a list of things I must accomplish before the plane takes off in forty-one hours. Rereading the list, I realize completing everything on it may not happen. I should prioritize but I yawn at the thought. I walk into my bedroom, where Taryn and Tia have started packing my backpack. I should take a look at what they've chosen for me, but lie down on my bed instead. I'm asleep in seconds, without washing my face or brushing my teeth.

The phone is ringing. I reach blindly for it on the nightstand, banging my hand several times before making contact. I realize I'm still in my jeans from yesterday.

"Hey, we have to get an early start. This is your wake-up call," Taryn announces into the phone before I even say, "Hello."

"What time is it?" I moan.

"Seven o'clock. Kit's already called Marc to update him on the trip and to ensure he's got John on standby to meet you at the lawyer's to get him off the house documents. The Australian Consulate opens at nine, and we should be there as soon as it opens to get your travel visa. You need to call your bank about getting some Australian money if they have any. Are you listening?" Taryn is talking a mile a minute.

"Yes, I'm listening. I hope you aren't going to be Little Miss Sunshine every morning when we're travelling," I manage to say, finally waking up.

"I can't say; I've never travelled before. I guess we'll find out together. Now get up! We'll be there in forty-five minutes." Then, click — she's gone.

To my own surprise, by the time Kit arrives with the cheery twins in tow, I'm up, showered, have eaten, have located John's key for the house, started a load of laundry, organized my bank accounts online — thank goodness for the huge commission from the Blackwell deal and my television début pay — and have signed several cheques from my chequebook so Kit can pay bills while I'm away.

Taryn starts her internship in October, but I only plan to travel with her for the first month or two, depending on my backpacking abilities. The latest I'll be back is Labour Day, but I am leaving enough money to cover three months of living expenses "just in case." Kit's going to be checking my house, picking up mail and paying my bills while I'm gone. I explain that the red cheques are from my line of credit and that those cheques should be used to pay my credit-card bills, as I'll be using those while travelling.

Nine hours later, Kit, the twins, Marc, and I are sitting at our regular Firkin, waiting for a round of beer to toast this crazy day being over.

"Okay, and Send." I press the button on my laptop and raise my hands triumphantly. "That was my last major task; I'm ready to go." I've just sent an email to all my clients, letting them know I'll be away, back by Labour Day, and working for Morty when I do return.

The day had come together much better than I could have hoped. We checked the visa and money exchange off the list first thing. Taryn called the travel agent she used, and I got the identical ticket and trip plan. My lawyer had the papers to take John off the title of the house ready by noon. I called Morty and explained my travel plans, and he took the news better than I ever could have hoped. He wished me luck and told me that "happy, well-rounded people make the best agents." The twins went off to complete my shopping while Kit came with me to sign the papers with the lawyer. Marc took John to the lawyer's office after we'd left, to ensure John did the same. As soon as my lawyer informed me the new title was registered in my name alone, I called Marc and he gave John the $15,000 cheque. Aside from owing Marc a mittfull of money, it's a relief to know the house is completely mine and there's nothing to tie John and me together any longer.

I'm exhausted again but a little bit excited, as I've had no time to dwell on the fact I'm leaving Toronto for an extended period of time. I give Marc the extra key to the house —

John's key — and tell him he can have use of the house while I'm away. Kit already has a key, so I know the house will be safe in my absence with both Kit and Marc checking in.

Marc fills us in on John's black eye, which apparently is turning a lovely shade of yellow now, and tells us John and Ursula have reconciled. Apparently, Ursula's husband got wind of the affair, and despite her desire to keep him for financial security, he chose not to keep her. John is going to buy into the dance studio with the $15,000. Marc thinks John and Ursula actually have to live at the dance studio until they find something affordable.

"Where's Kevin?" I ask Kit. I was hoping to see him before I leave. The trip was planned so quickly I haven't been able to think, let alone try to see people before I leave.

"He's at home, packing. With the last-minute trip planning, I haven't had a chance to tell you. Apparently, the band is getting some radio time in New York, so they've booked two weeks of shows and are going on the road to the U.S.," Kit explains. "Tia and I might drive down next weekend and catch up with them for a couple of days."

"Wow. Congratulations to the band. I'm so happy for them. Give them all my best. Who knows, they might be famous soon," I laugh.

"I don't know if I want them to be famous. I like having Ben around, he's one of the reasons I moved here," Tia laments. "And you guys are leaving tomorrow. It's just going to be Kit and me left."

"Hey! What am I? Invisible?" Marc laughs.

"Oh, sorry, Marc. No. But it sucks that everyone is leaving us." Tia takes another sip of beer.

I know she is going to miss Taryn desperately. I'm only away for a few months; Taryn is away for over a year, and possibly longer.

54

Tears. I've cried more in the past six days than I have in the rest of my entire life, infancy included. Standing at the departure drop-off at Pearson International, I'm crying, Kit's crying, the twins are crying — well, Tia is weeping, really.

I manage to wipe most of the mascara and reminders of the tearful goodbye off of my face while we are standing in the check-in line. Taryn is getting excited after the tearful goodbye, and there's even a bit of a jump in her step. I'm just nervous and wondering what the "heck am I doing here?" Check-in goes smoothly until the lady behind the desk says, "So, change planes in L.A. then on to Fiji?"

I panic. Fiji? This is the first I've heard about Fiji. I almost snap my head off my neck turning to look at Taryn who is casually nodding and saying, "Yes."

Fiji? I manage to hold it together and not freak out on the spot. No one said anything about Fiji. Where is Fiji? Don't barbaric headshrinkers live in Fiji? Maybe it's a good thing I have a giant head; it will take longer to shrink.

I quiz Taryn after we get our boarding passes. "Taryn, are *we* going to Fiji?"

"Yes," she laughs. "We're stopping there for six days on our way to Australia. Didn't you look at the itinerary I left with your ticket?"

"I haven't had time to look at the silly ticket. I didn't have time to pack for myself, remember?"

"We're staying at Beachcomber Island, and you'll love it. I hear the island is beautiful and the people are amazing. It'll be a fun adventure. Come on, we have to go through security."

Getting through security is an adventure but no fun. I have to remove my tall turquoise boots so they can ensure I don't have any weapons in the soles. Like I would purposely ruin an outrageously expensive pair of boots to put a box cutter in the sole! Who would do such a thing? I'm sure terrorists shop at Payless. Terrorists are just going to ruin the boots anyway, so why pay top dollar for them?

Walking to our gate, with my boots back, safely secured to my feet, I give Taryn my "terrorists shop at Payless" theory, to which she answers, "I told you to wear your hiking boots anyway." She really is going on about the hiking boots.

"But they are *ugly*," I state for about the fifth time.

"But functional. We are backpacking. Aren't your feet killing you in those heels, even after just walking from the car to the check-in desk with your heavy backpack?" Taryn asks.

"No!" I answer in the manner of a child in Grade 3. My feet *are* killing me but I won't give Taryn the satisfaction of knowing it. She may have a point about the hiking boots but, in my defence, they are really ugly. As if to underscore her point, Taryn picks up the pace she is walking at as we near the boarding gate.

As we approach our boarding gate, Taryn several strides ahead of me, I glimpse the profile of Brad Pitt. Could it be? My heart jumps and I strain to look around the man walking in front of me. Brad Pitt at our gate? Well, it makes sense; he's going to L.A.

I'm so intent on getting a better look at Brad that I don't notice Taryn turning her head side to side, scanning the passengers.

"Eek!" Taryn lets out a small squeal and grabs my arm. "He's here!"

"Who is? Brad Pitt? I think I saw him too." I didn't know Taryn had a thing for Brad, and I turn to where I spotted Brad moments prior.

"No, Adam!" Taryn lets go of my arm and starts off in Brad's general direction. Adam? My heart sinks. If Adam is here, then I can only assume the person I had hoped was Brad Pitt is indeed obnoxious Chazz. The absolute last person I want to see is Chazz with two *Z*s. It's bad enough he's seen me on a garbage bin, then dressed like Little Bo Peep. I never seem to have any composure when he's in my general vicinity. And starting off on my first backpack adventure hardly gives me the confidence to improve my track record.

"Good afternoon, ladies." Adam does seem very nice despite his unfortunate taste in friends.

"You made it! I thought you couldn't get away yet!" Taryn

is completely enthralled with Adam, and seems far too familiar with him than she should be after seeing him for a short time at the bridal shower.

"I couldn't, but I worked my tail off — and here I am!"

"I thought Chazz wasn't going to come? Didn't you say he was starting a job?" Taryn asks as I listen in.

"He was supposed to, but he managed to postpone it."

Of course, he was able to postpone it; I'm sure he doesn't even have a job. I'm momentarily distracted from my aching feet by thinking lazy thoughts about Chazz, when Chazz walks up to us.

"Mel Melrose! I saw you on television the other day. Nice seal!" Grrrr. This guy can get under my skin so fast.

"He wasn't that nice actually, but thanks for commenting. Did your mother raise any polite children?"

"Nope! Just me. Once they had perfection, why try again?" Chazz laughs, completely sure of himself.

"Well, one of you is plenty." I stare, unblinking, at Chazz. I swear there is something wrong with this man! "Taryn, let's go sit down." I grab Taryn's arm but she seems reluctant to move away from Adam. Good Lord, this is all I need. If Taryn likes Adam, I might be stuck in Chazz's general vicinity for the whole trip.

"Mel, did you hear what Adam said? They're going to Beachcomber as well! It's so cool!" Taryn is grinning from ear to ear.

"Oh, it's cool, all right." I cannot believe my luck — my

bad luck. This calendar year cannot be over fast enough. Surely the black cloud following me will dissipate soon.

"Yeah, Mel? How cool is *that*?" Sarcastic Chazz is relentless.

I stare at Chazz and remember the Marvin the Martian line from the Bugs Bunny cartoon. "Earthlings," in this case Chazz, "are so naughty and so complex, I could pinch them." I could pinch Chazz although I don't know how complex he is. More arrogant than complex I suspect.

Chazz puts his arm around me and wrestles my small travel knapsack off my shoulder — I don't want him to touch me or my things — then grabs my arm and leads me to where he and Adam were sitting. "Come on, ladies, you might as well wait with us for the plane to board."

I glance over at Taryn but she's giggling with Adam, totally ignoring the dynamic between Chazz and me. I'm going to have to fill her in post-haste. I can*not* spend any amount of time with this man. He's so irritating.

I sit down beside Taryn, who is oblivious of the kerfuffle I have with Chazz to get my small knapsack back. Once it's in my hands, I open the pack and pull out my book. I will read and completely ignore Chazz. He will get bored and leave to find some other unsuspecting woman to torment.

"Whatcha reading?" Chazz is not going along with my plan.

"*Three Day Road* by Joseph Boyden." I open the book and hold it up so it covers my face and Chazz can't see me.

"What's it about?" Chazz puts two fingers on the top of the book and forces it down so he can see me.

"World War One. I'm hoping to get some trench-warfare techniques; maybe I'll practice my bayonet skills on you," I huff and put the book back up.

"Why don't you like me?" Chazz isn't the sharpest knife in the drawer, but he finally seems to be catching on.

"You're arrogant and far too self-assured. It's not normal," I state from behind my book.

"You don't even know me. And from what I remember I've helped you on every occasion I've been in your presence. Doesn't that count for something?" Chazz says.

"Well, I never *asked* for your help!" I retort in a most childish manner.

"And yet I helped you. You'd think I'd get credit for being a gentleman or something?"

"Hummpf!" I snort, unable to come up with anything to say as a comeback. I always have a comeback. This Chazz character makes me crazy; my brain refuses to come up with any cutting, sarcastic comments in his presence.

"Or maybe you just can't ever admit you *need* help, and you actually like it when I help you?" Chazz grins and tilts his head to the right as he pushes the book upwards with his finger to cover my face again. I then feel him stand up and walk away. Ohhhh, I *could* just pinch him!

55

Taryn and I board the plane before Chazz and Adam. Taryn and I get settled in — we have a window and a middle seat. Taryn is sitting by the window for the takeoff; we've agreed to take turns.

"Don't you think Adam is just the nicest guy?" Taryn is excited. I've never seen her excited about a man before. I'm happy for her, but wish he were anyone other than Chazz's friend.

"He is very nice. Unfortunately, his choice in friends is a bit questionable," I comment quietly.

"Chazz? Oh, my God! He's so cute! How could you *not* think he's cute?"

"Well, for the record, Chazz is not cute nor is he amiable in any way," I huff.

"Yeah, whatever! He is really cute, and what's with the big words?" Taryn laughs and picks up her *Lonely Planet* and starts to read.

"Isn't it a bit strange that Adam is on the same flight on the same day as you?" I push Taryn's book down so I can see her.

Taryn laughs. "Not really. We've sort of been in touch since the shower for Sam." The smile on Taryn's face, combined with her dancing eyes, makes me think they've been more than "sort of in touch."

"So, you knew he'd be here today?"

"No, that was a surprise. I did know I'd see him at some point. Originally, he didn't think he could get away until next week." Taryn's expression almost makes me believe in love again. Almost, that is, until a flash of grinning Chazz pops into my head and I shudder.

I open my book but can't concentrate on the words. My mind starts to register that I'm sitting in a plane, on a runway, waiting to take off and leave everything I know for an extended period of time. Weeks. Months, even. Taryn had said she and Tia have never been apart for more than a couple of days. When I think about it, Kit and I have never been apart for more than two weeks at a time. When we were younger and took vacations with our families, we'd be apart but by the time we were in high school and had part-time jobs we had stopped travelling with our parents and often stayed home — with each other. We went to the same university, as the twins did, and had lived together. I moved to Toronto before Kit, but she visited twice in those six weeks, so we still saw each other and spoke on the phone almost every day. Being in Australia, halfway around the world for at least two months, will be the longest I've been away from Kit. I start to feel sick. What am I doing?

Just before I start to completely panic, the plane jolts and starts to move. I take the plane moving at just this moment as a sign I'm not suppose to jump up screaming to get off the plane. Not only would it be impossible at this point, it would also be very embarrassing. I'm stuck on this plane but know if the panic doesn't subside I can always come back from L.A. and never leave the continent.

The plane takes off, I manage to start reading my book and the initial panic subsides. I can do this. I can travel. I can leave Kit for a few weeks. I'm a woman of the world! Besides, if stupid Chazz can do it, so can I!

Landing in Fiji is amazing. The heat from outside seems to permeate the plane, and it is still very late at night, Fiji time. Taryn is excited. I'm more tired than anything else. I didn't sleep well on the plane. Taryn tells me we will be hanging out at the airport until the Beachcomber representative gets to the airport. The wait is going to be several hours. We deplane and end up in the customs line with Adam and Chazz. They are as tired as I am, so Chazz doesn't antagonize me very much. We get through customs. The airport is basically one very large room with no front wall — the airport is open-air concept. We are technically outside, and it's incredible. The air is heavy and humid, but it's a refreshing change from being cooped up in the airplane.

There are a group of four — two girls and two guys — who appear to be settling in for a long wait. Adam walks over to them and discovers they are also camping out until morning. They are Canadians from Montreal. We do the introductions and join their campout. I put both my knapsacks against the wall, and sit down beside them. I take my boots off — my feet are killing me. I curl up against my bags. I feel Taryn settling in beside me but am asleep before I register where Adam and Chazz are setting up their camp for what's left of the night.

I open my eyes, registering that my hip is asleep — and not in the restful way, more in the pins-and-needles sort of way. "Ouch, ouch, ouch," I think in my head, then I start to lift myself up to move off the offending area. I manage to take the pressure off my hip and blood starts to return to the area, alleviating some of the numbness. I look to my left and see Taryn, sleeping on her knapsack. I then turn to my right, where the airport is open to the air, and see the sun starting to peek over the horizon behind a row of palm trees.

Wow. If I see nothing more beautiful for the rest of the trip, this moment makes me glad I'm here and didn't turn back at L.A.

"Makes you think we've got it all wrong back home, doesn't it?" I hear his voice before I'm fully aware Chazz is lying on the ground beside me. I was so caught up in the sunrise, I didn't notice he was beside me.

"Oh. It's you," I state. I look back toward the horizon not wanting to ruin the peaceful moment.

"Of course it's me. A day without me is like a day without sunshine!" Chazz has managed to ruin the moment, despite my attempts to ignore him.

I look down at him as he laughs at me. I reach over and pinch the back of his arm — really hard, with a twist. I smile when he shrieks, then I stand up and brush off the jean capri pants I've been wearing for almost twenty-four hours. Marvin the Martian is one smart cartoon character.

We all stay together, but I manage to ignore Chazz while we wait for the Beachcomber representative. Taryn seems completely smitten with Adam. If I'm honest, I have to admit I'm happy for her. Adam does seem like a really nice guy, and I've never known her to be infatuated with anyone. The other Canadians are really nice, but I quickly calculate I am the oldest, by far, in our group. As we load onto the bus that will take us to the boat, which will then take us to Beachcomber — a tiny island off the west coast of Viti Levu, Fiji, in the middle of the South Pacific — I conclude most backpack travellers are students or recent graduates like Taryn.

Boats. For the most part, I consider all boats vile and evil and the source of vomit and queasiness. The boat to Beachcomber, however, is actually not vomit-producing at all. I start to think maybe I am growing as a person; maybe I'll be able to embrace the things that torment me. Just as I ponder this, I glance to where Taryn is sitting with Adam and Chazz and shake my head. "No. I am definitely not growing as a person, and I'm not embracing the things that torment me."

Unfortunately, the boat is too large to take us right to the island, so we have to transfer to smaller boats. My boat dislike settles back immediately upon setting foot on the smaller, much rockier boat. Taryn hands me my large backpack, and I cling to it with all my strength. Adam and Chazz are in the same small boat as we are, so I am determined not to vomit in front of them.

"You look a bit green there, Boots!" Apparently, Chazz lacks all forms of discretion. I give him my best scowl to show my displeasure.

I try to ignore him and growl under my breath. Boots? How annoying can one man be?

"Boooots? Earth to Boooooots." He just won't stop.

"I don't like boats," I manage, trying to keep my eye on the island. It is only a few hundred metres away.

"You were fine on the big boat!" Chazz points over his shoulder.

"This boat is more tippy and much closer to the fish. I don't like marine life either, if you must know."Why am I talking to this man?

"You picked a strange place to vacation if you don't like boats or fish. You're going to hate snorkelling."

"I don't snorkel. Why would anyone want to see fish up close?" I shudder at the thought of snorkelling. Talking to Chazz is frustrating, but it does keep my mind off vomiting until I feel the bottom of the boat bump on the sand of the beach. Land. Sweet wonderful land.

The bow of the boat is resting on the beach, but there is no dock in sight. I look over the side of the boat and realize I'm going to get wet. I let go of the backpack I've been clinging to and start to unzip my boots. I will not ruin a perfectly good pair of boots on my first day of travelling in order to get to the beach.

All the other boat passengers have jumped over the side and are on the beach as I continue to remove my boots. I hear Chazz huff, "Oh, for heaven's sake," and come splashing back to the boat. "Adam, grab Boots' bags please."

Then I feel arms around my waist and I'm being lifted out of the boat. I grab the boot I've already removed before I'm hoisted. I hear the splash of Chazz's feet, then he drops me unceremoniously on my butt on the beach sand.

"Nice!" I look up at Chazz with a sneer. "I was doing okay on my own, but thank you for your help." I say the last part as sarcastically as possible.

"No worries, Boots. You may want to rethink your footwear."

"Hmmpft," I huff emphatically as I remove my second boot and stand up. Taryn helps me put my large backpack on, then hands me my small pack and my boots — I can't bend over once the large backpack is secured to me. We had discovered my lack of balance back in Toronto, when I was trying to get from the car to the airport terminal.

Adam and Chazz are walking ahead of us and I quietly say to Taryn, "He's so egotistical! Why is he calling me 'Boots' anyway?"

"Boots? I think it's kind of cute and well..." Taryn looks down at the turquoise boots in my hand.

"You're *not* helping." I quicken my pace because the sand is really hot and burning my bare feet.

56

Hostel. It's a word I know and a concept I understand, but I've never actually had a hostel experience. I'm more experienced in "hostile" than "hostel." The housing on Beachcomber Island is in *bura*s. There are several small *buras* for one or two people and one huge *bura* housing about fifty people — in bunk beds. Taryn has booked us into the large *bura*.

In the whirlwind between my decision to join Taryn and our leaving, it hadn't occurred to me to wonder about our accommodations once we had arrived. In hindsight, as I stand at the side of my bunk bed — I claimed bottom because there's no way I'm climbing up to the top one — I have to wonder why accommodations hadn't crossed my mind. I've never shared a room with forty-nine other people.

"Oh, come on, Mel. You're here to get away from all the stuff going on back home. It'll be an adventure. You need more adventure in your life." Taryn is perpetually Mary Sunshine; it's enough to drive me crazy.

"Get your swimsuit on, we're going snorkelling. And no, you don't have to snorkel, but you should come and sit on the beach and at least watch us. When was the last time you sat on a beach and did nothing? Come on." Taryn reaches into my small daypack and immediately pulls out my swimsuit and hands it to me. I suppose it makes sense; she did pack my bags. I couldn't have found it so fast, if at all.

"Fine, but I won't like it." I tromp off to the washroom to change.

"Good attitude, Mel. I think you're starting to come around," Taryn laughs behind me.

Sitting on my towel on the beach alone, while Taryn and Adam swim and snorkel, I start to panic. I feel beads of sweat start to form on my forehead and my hands grow instantly clammy. My breath quickens and I feel like there is an elephant sitting on my chest. I have to stand up and pace around my towel. What am I doing halfway around the world from my life? My real life. This isn't real life. Who sits on a beach all day? Who? Lazy people, and homeless people who live in warm climates — that's who! I should be at home working. I've never "not worked." Never. I had part-time jobs until I finished school, then I started working for a real estate firm in North Bay before I decided real estate would be my life and I moved to Toronto to "do it right." I have a house. I drive a convertible. I've just walked away from everything. I walked away from my structured, crazy, busy world. I'm completely lost. I have no structure. I have nothing to do *right now*. I reach to my hip for my BlackBerry. It's not there. Taryn didn't let me bring it. I'm completely out of touch! I stand up and start to pace. Is there Wi-Fi on this island?

Taryn, Adam and I had walked around the island before

deciding where they'd like to snorkel. It only took ten minutes. I'm on the tiniest island in the world. What if there's a tsunami? We'll be wiped out for sure, and I won't be able to contact anyone!

"You look a bit flustered, Boots." It's him.

"Chazz, I'm having a panic attack right now; can you torment me later?" I start to wave my hands in front of my face in an attempt to cool down. I've never been so clammy.

"Hey. Sit down." Chazz takes my arm and lowers me to my towel. "Put your head between your knees and just breathe." He is actually being nice and his voice is calming. Why is he always showing up and helping me? "You're in a tropical paradise. What can you possibly panic about?"

"You wouldn't understand." I do feel better sitting with my head between my legs, but I'm not about to share my concerns and problems with the likes of Chazz, with or without two *Z*s.

"Try me. I'm not a complete moron." Chazz starts to laugh but I lift my head and give him my raised eyebrow, "Wanna bet?" look. Chazz palms the back of my head, turns it, and shoves it back down between my legs.

"Yeah, whatever! Keep your head down."

When I maintain silence, Chazz continues, "Okay, let me guess then, since you won't tell me. You're sitting on a beautiful beach in the most beautiful place in the world and you're feeling bad because you aren't back home, running around like a madwoman, in your crazy boots, furthering your career and making more money."

I look up at Chazz again, but this time with a shocked look. How does he know what I'm thinking?

"I was just walking around thinking the same thing," Chazz laughs. "We've been so busy travelling to get here, making flights and meeting buses and boats, the second we haven't got something to do according to a clock, it hits us — we don't have *anything* to do — so we panic. It will take a couple of days to get used to it. It happened to me last year, when I went to Bali."

"What if it doesn't go away?" I lift my head now, feeling like I can finally hold it up.

"It will, and when the trip's over and you get off the plane back in Toronto, you'll remember this and laugh because you'll know for sure what we do back home is no way to live. You'll want to turn around and come back."

"Thanks," I say quietly into my arms, which are folded around my knees.

"Come on. Let's get your feet wet. You'll cool down from all the panic." Chazz grabs my hand and starts to pull me up.

"No. I'm good."

"Come on, it'll get your mind onto something else and you'll feel better. Trust me."

"Yeah, it'll keep my mind on how many fish want to nibble on me."

"No fish want to nibble on you. You probably aren't very tasty. Come on, or I'll carry you again."

I hate him. I get up voluntarily because I can tell by

Chazz's voice that he will carry me into the water and drop me in over my head.

We spend the rest of the afternoon splashing and swimming. I try Taryn's snorkel and mask, but only briefly and while my feet are planted firmly on the ocean floor.

"You'd have more fun with the mask if you weren't just looking at your own toes!" Chazz yells from where he's standing with Adam.

"Bite me!" I yell back as maturely as one can while giving a most juvenile direction.

"Nah, biting is what the fish want to do to you, Boots. Remember?"

I shriek, toss the mask and snorkel in Taryn's general direction, and trudge back to the beach, Chazz's laughter ringing in my ears.

57

We spend three nights at Beachcomber and, much to my pleasure and dismay — because I hate when Chazz is right — I do stop panicking about not being back at home making money to pay Marc back. The island has no Internet, so we are completely cut off from everyone except the people on the island with us. At first, I worry we will have a *Lord of the Flies* situation. But so far, except for Chazz tormenting me, it's all been fine. No hostile — or hostel — takeovers.

The first afternoon, after my initial panic attack subsides, I participate in beach activities; well, I use the word "participate" liberally. I'm not exactly a top-notch athlete — or an any-notch athlete, really. I was enrolled in physical education classes during my elementary and high-school education but none of it seems to have stuck. I excelled at business and math class. My physical education at university started and ended with walking between buildings to business-related classes. I'm quite dismal at beach volleyball, but since Adam and Taryn insist on being on the same side, I am often paired with Chazz, who, as I'm sure we all suspected, excels at *all* sporting activities — of course, he does. He single-handedly, because I'm not much help, beats Taryn and Adam three games in a row.

I'm mostly there to make the court look even. I'm like an accessory really. The thought of accessories makes me miss my Prada handbags. Taryn didn't let me bring even one.

The island is well equipped for young adults who like to party. The Barefoot Bar is exactly what the name boasts and is located on the beach. Taryn wants to meet Adam at the bar on our first evening, so we head back to the *bura* after swimming and volleyball to shower and change out of our swimsuits. Going through my large backpack for the first time — we had our swimsuits in our small bags in the event of lost luggage — I am completely in shock. I take out the first item. It is an Old Navy t-shirt with the tag still on it. This can't be right. I don't wear Old Navy. I start removing items at a harried pace. This is not my backpack. Or rather, this can*not* be my backpack. Old Navy, Garage, Suzy Shier. My bag is full of shorts, t-shirts and sundresses all with tags still affixed and all from, what I consider to be, less-than-fashionable stores. At the bottom, I find a pair of flip-flops from Payless — flip-flops with plastic flowers across the strap. That's when I completely lose it.

"Taryn! Where are my things?" I corner her in the washroom, Payless flip-flops in hand.

"In your backpack. What are you talking about?" Taryn looks innocent, but I know she's part of a diabolical plan to ruin me.

"These are flip-flops! From *Payless*!" I point the plastic shoes at her for effect.

"Yeeessss… and?" Taryn looks expectantly at me.

"And I don't wear flip-flops from Payless!"

She is completely playing dumb. She must know my feet wouldn't stand for such treatment.

"Mel, Tia and I went through your entire closet. You had nothing suitable for backpacking except your bathing suits. Remember, Tia and I went shopping for you?" Taryn puts her hand on my shoulder and speaks slowly to me, as if I'm mentally deficient.

"I know I gave you money for shopping, but I assumed you'd buy me things I could actually wear!" I am poking her in the shoulder with a flip-flop.

Taryn starts to laugh. "Well, you're here now and you have a backpack full of clothes you can choose to wear or not. But since there's nothing on this island except us, you might want to reconsider your expensive and somewhat snooty taste." She laughs again and turns back to applying her mascara in the mirror. "Mel, you are so funny!"

Snooty? I look down at the counter and see that her makeup bag only contains a few items. "Dread" is the only word to describe the feeling rising from the pit of my stomach to my throat. My skin-care ritual at home is lengthy and two-part — morning and night before bed. I have face wash, pore toner, skin firmer, special wrinkle-fighting eye cream, line corrector for morning, and skin smoother, then the same anti-aging routine for evening, only I add a heavier moisturizer. I use high-end, very expensive cosmetics applied just so.

I don't leave home without my coverup and a mixture of two lipsticks with glossy overcoat. In a panic, I hurry to my bunk bed and search the contents of my backpack for my cosmetics. All I find is one small blue cosmetic bag, its contents meagre.

"Taryn? Where did you put my makeup?" I ask as I return to the washroom.

"It's in your blue cosmetic bag," she states calmly, combing her hair.

"No, my blue cosmetic bag," I hold it up for effect, "contains one face wash, one daytime face cream, one waterproof mascara and one ChapStick — SPF 30. Where is the rest of it? You know, night cream, line eliminator, eye cream, foundation, coverup, bronzer?"

"You don't need that stuff; you're backpacking, in a sunny climate. You hardly need bronzer. You'll bronze naturally," Taryn laughs.

Mother of Pearl. She didn't pack my cosmetic staples on purpose.

"But I can't be running around in bad clothing with no makeup. I'm thirty-two. My skin isn't line-free, like yours. I need help!" I grab Taryn's shoulders. I feel the panic rising again.

"Mel," Taryn says calmly, "you are a beautiful woman, and you don't need cosmetics to enhance it. Come on, throw on some mascara and let's get going. Besides, no one wears makeup when backpacking; you'd look completely ridiculous."

I look into Taryn's cosmetic bag, which contains fewer items than mine, and realize I don't have a choice. She brought less for herself than she packed for me. She obviously doesn't understand my confidence comes from *appearing* to be in control even when I'm not. I need high-end clothing, perfect makeup, perfect hair and exquisite footwear. How can I look "in control" while wearing plastic-flowered flip-flops, mascara and clear ChapStick?

Getting ready takes much less time than usual, in light of the lack of cosmetics and very limited clothing choices. The longest amount of time is taken in deciding which sundress to wear, the one from Old Navy or the one from Suzy Shier? I opt for the one from Old Navy because it has turquoise in it, so it matches my boots. I refuse to wear the Payless flip-flops. I assess myself in the mirror upon completion of my very short getting-ready ritual. Seeing myself, I feel like I could cry — if I was prone to that sort of thing. Arrggh. "What am I doing here?" I ask myself as Taryn grabs my arm and leads me into the world wearing Old Navy.

Taryn and I get to the Barefoot Bar, where Adam and Chazz are sitting with the Canadians we met at the airport, sipping Fiji Bitter beer — which is very good after the third one — comparing stories of our Beachcomber adventures so far. Adam squeezes over on the bench he's sitting on to make room for Taryn, but I choose to sit at the other end of the table, away from Chazz. I sit across from Jack and Jake, who have both just graduated from McGill University and are travelling before they start to work in the real world. Travelling after graduation seems to be a very strong trend. I don't know how Kit and I missed it actually. I suppose financially it wasn't an option back then. I think Taryn only got parental approval because Kit and I wore our mothers down. The mothers lost it when Kit and I moved to Toronto; I can't imagine if we'd come home and announced we were going to start travelling the world.

I'm filling Jake and Jack in about my life back in Toronto, when Chazz plunks himself down beside me and states, "I met Mel when she and a friend of hers were in a dingy back alley, trying to clamber onto a garbage bin. What exactly were you doing that day, Mel? You never did tell me. As I recall, you ran out of there as soon as you could."

"Wouldn't you like to know?" I laugh and try to avoid the subject.

"I would, in fact. Guys..." Chazz looks at Jake and Jack across the table, "wouldn't you like to know what a sophisticated woman like Mel was doing hiking up her skirt and climbing onto a garbage bin behind a dance studio?"

"Hmmm? I think we would be interested," Jake laughs.

I glower at Chazz and try to think up a reason, besides the truth, that I might have been in the aforementioned situation. But nothing comes to me that wouldn't embarrass me just as much as the truth, so I give them the short 'n' sweet version.

"Okay. My boyfriend took a very sudden interest in modern dance, and I suspected he was more interested in the dance instructor than the dancing itself. So I was doing some spying, and the garbage bin was the only way to accomplish the investigation. There. Satisfied?" I turn to Chazz and take a sip of my beer.

"Really? You have a boyfriend? I've only ever seen you with your friend Kit." Chazz looks puzzled.

"I did. Not anymore." I moan and take a gulp of beer this time. I really don't want to discuss my personal life with the likes of Chazz.

"So, he was, then?" Jack asks.

"He was what?" I ask.

"He was having an affair?" Jake explains Jack's question.

"Yes. We broke up just before I decided to come here with Taryn. This whole trip is very last-minute for me — a bit of a rebound thing actually."

"Well, at least yours left you for someone else," Jack says. "My ex-girlfriend is a trapeze artist who broke up with me to join the circus. I was left for a bunch of clowns. Literally." He goes on to lament missing the contortions his ex-girlfriend was able to manage, so I was able to escape the John-dancing-naked portion of my recent breakup tale.

I'm tired after sleeping on the airport floor last night and spending a full day on the beach. I'm not used to so much fresh air. Sleeping in one huge room with forty-nine other people, however, is not something I'll sign up for again. The *bura* is noisy with snoring and chatting and, well, the sound of people having sex. I'm no prude or anything, but there are sounds you want to hear and sounds you don't want to hear.

And people having sex falls into the latter category. I hear a particularly loud coupling in the corner where Chazz and Adam are bunked and wonder if Chazz had made a new friend after I left the Barefoot Bar. It wouldn't surprise me. I'm sure he can't be alone for more than forty-eight hours. He's just that type, and I know his type. John didn't even wait forty-eight hours between women; he overlapped us. I pound my pillow with my fist, determined not to think about John. I'm travelling to get over him and his frumpy girlfriend with her skewed dance vision.

The next morning, I stumble out of bed to the washroom with my face wash, silently thanking Taryn for at least giving me the ability to wash my face every day, when I see it. I shriek, louder than I should in shared accommodations. My face is covered in a rash. I search my arms — rash — I lift my t-shirt — rash — I'm covered head to toe in a bright red rash. Forgetting my face, I rush to Taryn's bunk and shake her awake.

"Taryn!" I hiss.

"What?" she opens her eyes, and then bolts up to a sitting position. "What the hell happened to you?" She's awake and standing on the floor beside me in seconds.

"I don't know!" I was fine last night.

Taryn lifts my shirt to look at my belly. "Is it all over?"

"Yes!" I point down to my legs, where the rash seems to be concentrated around my calves. It's not so bad on my upper legs.

"Ladies!" I hear his voice behind me and am surprised he's up so early what with all the action I presume he got last night.

"Adam. Chazz. Thank goodness. Look at Mel!" Taryn turns me around to face Adam and Mr. Annoying in all my rash glory.

"Wow! Mel that is some heat rash you've got going!" Chazz answers casually like he's seen hundreds of cases of heat rash. Rug burn, more like it. Adam lifts my arm to take a closer look.

"Heat rash?" Taryn and I ask together.

"Yes," Adam answers.

"Yep, it appears to be a classic case. You don't sweat much at home, do you?"

"Of course not!" I huff. Why would anyone voluntarily sweat?

"Well, as undignified as it is, you may want to start. Heat rash occurs because sweat ducts become plugged and the sweat leaks into the skin instead of out of it," Chazz explains.

"He's right," Adam shrugs. "The only thing to do is stay out of the heat for a few days. Won't be easy here. But if you stay in shaded areas, it'll clear up in a couple of days."

"So, I'm fine?" I ask Adam, ignoring Chazz.

"Yep. You'll be back to normal in a few days," Adam reassures me.

"Yeah, but you might want to strive for something other than *your* normal!" Chazz sneers.

"Ha ha." I curse my slow-thinking brain. Why don't I have any good comebacks for this infuriating man? He gets me so flustered.

58

On the last full day of our Beachcomber experience — the second day of me seeking constant shade in order to combat the heat rash — the boat brings in the new guests, including a group of beautiful Swedish girls. They are stunning actually. Six of the most runway, pageant-worthy, buxom women I've ever seen. I am sitting in the Barefoot Bar with a handful of other guests, when the boat carrying the goddesses bumps up onto the beach. The next several seconds are surreal. Men from every direction hurry toward the boat. The men sitting near me are the first to stand up and beeline for the boat. But others, from every corner of the island, are right behind them. The Swedish women are giggly, touchy-feely and wearing full makeup — I make a point of noticing how ridiculous makeup looks when you are backpacking. None of the women get their feet wet or have to haul their own backpacks. Their perfect Swedish feet are gently deposited on the beach, and they stand together with their twenty-two-inch waists being shaded by their D cups. The rest of the boat is unloaded by the male minions, who carry the bags and follow behind while the girls settle in and are assigned beds.

I look down at my lean, red-rash-speckled body and average-sized B-cup bikini top. The word "average" is actually a step up from the way I feel about myself right now.

"Hmmpf! Did you see that?" Taryn flops down on the bench beside me, tossing three snorkels and three masks on the table in front of us.

"How could I miss it?"

"Adam and Chazz took off like moths to a flame the second that boat came in. Did you see Adam carrying two backpacks? He didn't carry *my* backpack! I'm getting a beer, do you want one?"

"Absolutely. I think it's going to be a long night."

It's a good thing Taryn brought a pitcher of beer back to our table, because right after sitting down the goddesses arrived with their entourage — the number of men has grown and they are all thirsty. The men clamber over themselves to buy beer for the Swedish girls, who continue to giggle and blush. It would actually be quite an interesting study in male behaviour if it wasn't so pathetic.

"I bet they don't ever have to have money on them. They can probably travel the world on thirty-six Canadian cents," Taryn huffs and gulps her beer.

"Less, I imagine," I laugh.

Slowly, our table fills up with the girls on the island who aren't Swedish. Three of the girls are fit to be tied, because their boyfriends are among the goddess worshippers. One of the English girls goes so far as to announce, "If he thinks I'm going to let my dad give him a job when we get back, he's sadly mistaken!"

We hear snippets of conversation from the goddess table. The women all have amazing accents and names like Sonja, Petra and Frieda. From what we can deduce, they aren't a travelling pageant but are, instead, just average Swedish girls travelling the same as we are. Same as we are, my ass! I assess my rash again. I bet Swedish girls don't get head-to-toe heat rash and, on the off chance they did, they'd have a team of men fanning them with palm leaves and feeding them grapes.

Taryn drinks far too much beer and gets a bit teary.

"Men are such fickle jerks," Taryn blubbers between gulps of beer. "Just take off with the first woman who comes along with a cutesy accent and enormous breasts!"

I have to admit, seeing Taryn in the throes of emotion is new for me. She's always just been one of Kit's little sisters and so far behind me in age I failed to notice she's grown into a beautiful woman with all the problems that go along with that — career, love, heartbreak, all of it. I marvel at how I haven't noticed but also realize it is time to help Taryn get to bed before she does something she'll regret in the morning. I start to help Taryn up, with the intention of taking her back to the *bura* to bed, when I notice the snorkels and masks. I'm not sure which one is Taryn's, but I know they belong to Taryn, Adam and Chazz. I grab one of the sets and toss it into my backpack when we get to the *bura*. Taryn's in no shape to wash her face as she spirals into a pity party because "Adam seemed so nice. Why would he take off after the first Swedish girl who comes along?"

I don't comment, because John didn't even wait for a Swedish girl; he just took off after the first girl, and she is frumpy with no discernable fashion sense.

I tuck Taryn into my bunk — not trusting her ability to get safely off the top one should she awake disoriented — and throw a sundress over my bathing suit and return to the non-Swedish table at the Barefoot Bar. During the course of the evening, I notice Adam isn't with any one Swedish girl in particular, he's just hovering around the table like a drone to the girls' queen-bee magnetic draw. Chazz has definitely coupled up. The arm languishing over Chazz's shoulder belongs to Annika, the tallest and most attractive of the group. She is perfectly proportioned, with lean, long limbs, perfect blonde hair and huge, see-through blue eyes. She is stunning, and they make an attractive couple. I'm sure any language barrier will only benefit Annika; she won't have to listen to know-it-all Chazz.

Taryn's hungover inability to move without vomiting — an inherited trait, it would seem — means I have to pack for both of us the next day, and manhandle Taryn and all our bags to the beach before we miss the boat back to Nadi. Taryn is lying on the beach when I return with the last of the backpacks.

"You can't call me snooty now, Taryn!" I exclaim as I throw the last bag down on the beach beside her. "Look at me hauling bags and being organized!"

"You're a saviour, Mel. But could you speak more quietly, please. I have a killer headache, and the sun beating down on my head is not helping," Taryn moans from under her hat.

The captain of the little boat helps me load the last bag and is ready to take us to the big boat. I look around for Adam. I'm sure he wouldn't let Taryn leave without saying goodbye, would he? At one point, he and Chazz had spoken about leaving with us today. At the time I had dreaded the prospect of further travel with Chazz, but I now wish they were walking down the beach toward us with their backpacks, for Taryn's sake. I am completely jaded about men since John's antics, but there is no reason Taryn should start to be disheartened so young. She should have a few more years of hoping they aren't all jerks.

I look up and down the beach, but there is no sign of him and we have to board the boat. I manhandle Taryn into the boat and then jump in myself. All my boat concerns are set aside as I worry about Taryn who, after making the switch to the big boat, sits slumped in a corner for the whole ride back to Nadi. I feel bad for her. It is so disheartening when you like someone who clearly isn't into you. Unfortunately for Adam, I think he *was* into Taryn; the draw of the Swedish girls is just too much for his young, feeble man-brain to resist.

I am able to get enough information out of Taryn, between vomiting and sleeping, to make our way to Hideaway Resort. Hideaway is an amazing family-owned resort on Viti Levu, where we are assigned a *bura* on the beach facing the ocean. The *bura* sleeps four, but we are the only ones in it. Taryn rallies enough to eat a little bit and go for a swim. We are both tired, mostly hangover-related, so after dinner we settle on the beach to watch the sunset.

"Men are total idiots, aren't they?" Taryn asks out of the blue.

"Not all of them maybe. But you saw John in action last week — and we were living together."

"Why?"

"Why are they idiots? Or why was I living with John?" I laugh. "I have no idea or answer for either question. I guess they're programmed differently than we are."

I really don't know the answer to Taryn's question. John isn't the first "dating badly" I've done. I'm thirty-two, single with no hopes of settling down anytime soon. If I spend too much time thinking about it I get depressed. Kit's had several proposals of marriage; I've had none. Not being proposed to never bothered me before. But now, after what John did, it strikes me maybe I'm simply not "marriage material." Maybe I *am* needy, like John said, and everyone can tell immediately upon meeting me so no man will ever want to marry me.

"I thought Adam was different. You know, nice and sweet and a bit shy. I didn't think he was the type to take off after the first pretty girl who came along. I thought he liked me too," Taryn laments.

"He does like you. A lot, I think. He didn't hook up with

any of them last night, in case you were wondering." I try to make her feel better.

"Yeah, but he didn't see me after they arrived, and he didn't come to say goodbye to me this morning either."

I can't comfort Taryn on this point. We sit silently for a while, watching the sun fall in the sky. I look at Taryn's profile and am surprised again by the woman I see sitting beside me.

"Have you ever been in love, Mel?"Taryn asks the million-dollar question.

"I had thought John and I were in love, but I guess not. Have you?"

"No. Tia is totally in love with Ben. She said she knew he was the one for her the first time she saw him playing the drums. She said it was like magic. She just knew he would be a big part of her life."

"If he loves her back then I guess she's one of the lucky ones."

"It's funny, we're identical twins and so different. I've never even really noticed any man until Adam. Isn't it strange? I dated a bit in high school and university, but no one even remotely special. And Tia's falling in love at first sight."

"You are different, and there's nothing wrong with being independent. You have other goals besides being in love. A marine science internship is no small feat. Besides, if you had met someone before now, you may not have accepted the internship and you wouldn't be sitting on a beach beside my sorry, old, rash-covered butt," I laugh.

The sun has completely set; Taryn stands up and offers a hand to help me up. “The rash is looking better, by the way.” she comments as I put my arm around her shoulder and we make our way back to the *bura*.

59

The resort has Internet and a computer we can use, so Taryn and I send messages to our respective parents, and then to Kit and Tia telling them we are alive and well. We keep it short and don't mention heartbreaks or heat rashes. I write a few postcards on the beach, which I plan to mail to myself. Kit is picking up my mail, so she'll be able to read them, plus, I'll have a diary of sorts when I get back. We spend the day relaxing by the pool — pools I like, as there are no unseen fish to nibble on me — and resting because we are scheduled to fly to Sydney tomorrow. The plan for Sydney is to check out the Aquarium where Taryn will be interning and see the sights. Taryn tells me we won't be spending too much time in Sydney but will instead be heading up the coast to enjoy beaches instead of the big city. Taryn feels she'll get to spend more than enough time in Sydney when she's there for a year and, for her, if you've seen one big city, like Toronto, you've seen them all.

Taryn is repacking her backpack and stops. "Oh crap. I lost my snorkel. I threw it on the table, remember? After the guys took off with the Swedish brigade and I proceeded to get falling-down drunk. I must have forgotten to grab it. Stupid Swedish girls." Taryn punches her backpack in frustration.

"Who do you love?" I reach into my pack and pull out the snorkel-mask combo. "You can have it back. My bag is full enough."

"It's not mine, but, hey, it'll do!" Taryn laughs. "I don't want to buy a new one."

Our flight to Sydney is long but uneventful. I actually take some interest in my future travels and pick up Taryn's *Lonely Planet* to try to get familiar with the places we'll be going. I don't know much about Australia. I've seen photos of the beautiful opera house and I know the country hosted the 2000 Olympics, when Canadian boy Simon Whitfield won the gold medal for the triathlon. Strange, I'm not athletic and don't devote much time to watching televised sporting events, but I remember seeing him cross the finish line. I wonder why I was watching the Olympic coverage the day Simon won? Maybe I was meant to see him win so I'd appreciate Australia now, years later. Odd.

I decide the sights I want to see are the opera house, Bondi Beach and the Royal Botanical Gardens. Perhaps I'll take pictures of the gardens and anonymously mail them to Cam and Pam. It might coax them away from lawn ornaments and toward foliage.

Taryn and I step out of the airport in Sydney. The plan is to take a cab to the Bondi Beach Bed & Breakfast where Taryn has booked us for a four-night stay. I'm wearing my — I shudder to think, yes, they are mine — Suzy Shier jean capri pants, a Garage t-shirt and the Payless flip-flops I resigned myself to wearing on Day 2 of Beachcomber. They are surprisingly comfortable, but I won't give Taryn the satisfaction of telling her so.

"Mother of Pearl!" I turn to Taryn, who has reached into her bag and is putting on a sweater. "Why is it so bloody cold?" I immediately start digging in my backpack to find anything warm.

"It's winter here, Mel, it may be cool, but it's hardly cold," Taryn laughs.

"But isn't Australia always *hot*?" I had no idea they had winter here. Until this moment I believed it was always hot and sunny. They have a desert for heaven's sake.

"No. They have seasons like us, only their seasons are opposite ours. When we have winter, they have summer. And it's hardly freezing. It's about ten degrees. So, it's actually more like our spring or fall."

"You took me away from Canada, when it's hot there, to bring me to a cold place? Why? Why would you do that?" I am shocked. Taryn knows my relationship with winter. Winter and I are not tight at all. I like sun. I drive a convertible. I suffer through winter only because I know summer will return. I would never voluntarily leave Canada when it's hot to come to a cooler place.

"It's not cold! You'll be fine. It will warm up as we head north anyway. Now, put your sweater on and let's get to the Bed & Breakfast," Taryn laughs.

Warm up north? Well, this is all just too much to take in.

When you head north from Toronto, you'll eventually get to the Arctic Ocean. So, not warmer — even with all the talk of global warming — but colder. Much colder. This continent seems to have everything backwards.

Admittedly, sitting in the comfort of the plane after leaving hot Fiji, I wanted to see Bondi Beach. But now that I find the weather is so cool, I really couldn't care less. We check into the B&B. Taryn wants to go for a walk, but I've never been so cold. Taryn keeps laughing at me, but it's not funny. I'm sure I'm going to get hypothermia. I even resort to wearing the awful hiking boots she made me buy — with socks. I have all my warm clothes on and insist we go shopping, as I want to buy more woolly sweaters.

"Two winters in one year is not what I signed up for!" I tell Taryn as I hold up a wool sweater.

"The temperature is springlike, and you're probably still feeling the effects of your heat rash. You'll be fine. Put down the sweater and let's go grab some dinner."

I do relinquish the sweater, but only because my bag is already full to overflowing and I can hardly lift it. I don't need the added weight.

"But you're sure it's going to get warmer as we go north?" I ask again, sceptically.

"Yes. It will get much warmer. I promise!" Taryn laughs. "But spring temperatures are fine. And with your propensity to get heat rash, you should appreciate the cooler weather."

Taryn grabs my hand and drags me from the store. "Hmmpf. One heat rash is hardly a propensity," I think to myself.

We spend the next day touring the sights. The opera house is a letdown. Oh, don't get me wrong; it's beautiful. The architecture is stunning and, when you admire it from across Sydney Harbour, it's breathtaking. Sadly, when you get up close, it looks like it's covered with fish-scale shingles. In all the pictures you see, the white peaks appear smooth, but up close, it looks like fish scales. I find the up-close view a bit disheartening.

"Mel, I think you're being awfully critical. It's a magnificent building, and the roof has to be covered in something," Taryn laughs. "You're just grumpy because you're cold and have to take public transit."

Taryn may have a point. I haven't taken the bus since I got my driver's licence at the age of sixteen. I'm not exactly a public-transit sort of gal. I also rarely get to travel in the carpool lanes on highways because it's generally just me and my stereo — turned up too loud. I think I might be a bit of a transit snob, but I won't give Taryn the satisfaction of knowing I *know* I'm a transit snob.

"I have no issues with public transit," is my pathetic comeback — not at all convincing.

"Yeah, whatever! Let's go. We have to catch the *bus*." She lifts her eyebrow at me.

I trudge towards the bus stop in my clunky hiking boots. I should break out my good boots; these ones are horrible. I do, however, appreciate the socks and will suffer anything to keep warm.

60

After a full day of sightseeing, Taryn and I return to the B&B to shower. I stay in the warm shower much longer than I should, but it helps to get me warm. In the shower, I notice my heat rash has magically disappeared. Which makes me happy but, since it's so bloody cold, I'm not surprised — how can heat rash exist where there is no heat? When I get back to the room in the hostel, Taryn turns to me and asks, "What do you think?"

"About what?" I ask absently while I dig in my backpack to find anything that might be remotely warm.

"These." I look up and examine Taryn. Her long blonde hair looks the same and I've seen her outfit before. I start to ask what the heck she's talking about, but then I notice she is wearing glasses.

"When did you start wearing glasses?" I honestly have no recollection of her getting glasses; surely my mother would have mentioned Taryn getting a permanent accessory like glasses.

"Today. Do you think I look smarter?" Taryn asks, assessing herself in the mirror.

"What? I was with you all day. When did you go to the optometrist for an eye test?"

"I don't *need* glasses. They aren't prescription. I just think I need to look smarter. People take one look at me and assume I'm dumb. Adam thought I was dumb enough not to notice he had traipsed off after the Swedish girls."

"But you *are* smart, and Adam is a hormone-driven boy. He's hardly worth making you feel dumb." I start to worry that Taryn is in the throes of a breakdown.

"No," Taryn laughs, "it's not just Adam. My teachers at school, people I meet, everyone just assumes I'm a blonde bimbo. I think the glasses will help when I start my internship."

"Don't be silly. I'm blonde, and no one thinks I'm dumb! What are you talking about?"

Taryn laughs. "No one thinks you're dumb because you are formidable. You walk with purpose and poise. You were born superconfident. I was not. I still feel like a little kid. Maybe because I'm a twin." Taryn shrugs and turns back to the mirror.

"Well, they look great on you and, if you'll feel more confident, I suppose they can't hurt. But don't tell the mothers. I don't think they'll understand."

"Agreed! They are the last two people I'll tell!"

"Well, let's get some food. I'll let you and all your smartness do the ordering."

As we are stepping out of the Bed & Breakfast we hear a familiar voice. "Taryn! I'm so glad I found you!"

It's Adam. He runs up to Taryn and gives her a huge hug. To her credit, she does not return it. She is obviously still angry with Adam.

"Oh, *you're* here," Taryn manages without showing a hint of pleasure while looking over the top of her glasses.

"Of course, I'm here. You left Beachcomber without saying goodbye. I've been hanging out on Bondi Beach; I figured you would come here eventually. Are you staying here?" Adam seems confused as to why Taryn isn't being very warm.

"Yes, we're staying here but only for a few days, then we're heading north. What do you care? Where are your little Swedish friends?" Taryn raises her eyebrow and gives Adam the "I'm less than impressed with you" look. I'm proud of her; so much for her feeling like a little girl. She's formidable now.

I touch Taryn's shoulder and say, "I'm just going to go for a little walk over that way." I point up the street. Taryn will be able to speak to Adam more freely without me being present. I then turn to walk away and hear Adam say, "I'm really sorry about taking off on you. It was totally disrespectful and I feel awful. I came on ahead to find you. Hey, I didn't know you wear glasses. They look really great on you."

I'm too far away to hear Taryn's reply but smile to myself. He has noticed the glasses, so points for him. "Came on ahead" sounds like Chazz stayed at Beachcomber with the Swedish beauties. He and Annika must be hitting it off despite any language barrier. I wander up the street, taking in the sights for a while, then head back toward the B&B after I've given Taryn enough time to deal with Adam.

"So, is everything okay?" I ask as I get back to the newly reunited couple.

"Mel, Adam has something to ask you," Taryn states matter-of-factly.

"Mel, I know I've been a jerk..." Adam starts.

"A horse's ass, actually," Taryn interrupts him.

"Okay, a horse's ass." Six-foot-tall Adam looks down at Taryn with "I'm really sorry" eyes. "I've been an ass, and you don't have to say yes. But I would love to hang out with you ladies while we're here, if it's okay with you?"

I smile and look at Taryn. I can tell by the look in her eyes she has all but forgiven Adam and would like him to tag along.

"Well, Adam, do you promise to treat my friend with all the respect she deserves for the rest of the trip?" I feel in control for the first time since arriving in the South Pacific.

"Absolutely. I adore Taryn. I'll be on my best behaviour," Adam smiles and takes Taryn's hand in his.

I know my fate is sealed now and travel with Adam is assured. My life should be fine though, so long as Chazz is occupied with his Swedish gal pal and not pestering me.

The next day, Taryn wants to go to the aquarium where she'll be doing some of her internship. I decide to stay back and let Adam and Taryn strike off on their own for the day. I think it will be nice for them to not have me hanging around. The cupid in me aside, the idea of spending the day looking at fish and other marine life gives me the chills — and not just because I'm already freezing.

I wander around and spot a cyber café. Seeing the café makes me realize I've gone an entire week without hearing a word from Kit. I'm suddenly completely homesick and can't log onto my email quickly enough. I sort through and delete all the junk mail, then start reading notes from home. Life in North Bay is perfectly normal. Mom's email is lengthy and gives a very detailed description of her new jewellery "expression," utilizing household materials such as garden-hose connectors. My dad's email, separate from my mother's, is a short note complaining about his grass not being up to par because my mother keeps taking his garden hoses apart. He requests my speedy return to "try and talk some sense into your mother." I smile as I close Dad's email and start reading the ones from Kit. There are ten, she has written at least once a day. Her life is the same with work, busy as usual during the summer construction season. The big news is that the radio play *Kevin* is getting is growing and the band's tour has been extended for several more weeks, maybe even the entire summer. I reply to Kit's email but wish I could actually talk to her and hear her voice.

I fill Kit in on the travels so far, of course, asking if she knew it was winter here; I express my happiness for Kevin's success and enquire if she'll be going on the road with the band? I fill her in on Chazz and Adam being on the same flight, but don't mention Taryn's budding romance. I believe it is Taryn's news to share, if she chooses to share it at all. I do mention Taryn's glasses, the Swedish girls and the heat rash. I then send off a quick note to my parents, copying Mr. & Mrs. Jennings, letting them know we are in Sydney and doing fine. I explain Taryn is at the aquarium getting acquainted with the area marine life and that I will have her send a note when she gets a chance. I *don't* mention boys, Swedish girls, glasses or heat rashes.

Before logging off, I scroll through my inbox again. Not one message from John. I hadn't really expected to hear from him; we did sever ties completely, after all. But I suppose a part of me wants him to apologize. When I say "apologize" I mean grovel on his knees, begging for my forgiveness while telling me I am the best thing to ever happen to him and not in any way "needy." Of course, I want this so I can say, "Ha! Not a chance, you philandering jerk!" Sadly, he hasn't even forwarded a joke. I suppose he's too wrapped up in eking out a living with Ursula since her husband cut off her funds. I wonder if "strong, independent" Ursula still embodies those traits without her husband's financial backing?

I log off and go for a walk on the beach. I have to wrap my sweater around me tighter, as the breeze off the ocean feels cool. But walking along the beach, I start to wonder if maybe a less stressful life wouldn't be so bad. I might be able to get used to living on a beach. Maybe.

61

"Hey man, where's Chazz?" is the first thing out of Pete's mouth. Pete is Adam's friend from school. He is Australian but went to the University of Western Ontario, my alma mater, with Adam and also presumably, Chazz. Subconsciously, I must have known Adam and Chazz went to school together, but I really haven't dwelled on thoughts of Chazz — and really don't care. I do feel a little less special, now I know Chazz went to the same school as I did. Apparently, they'll let anyone attend. Pete's parents own a large ranch outside of Sydney and had invited Adam to come spend some time with them when he was in the country. Adam had called to see if Taryn and I could join. Pete's family seemed thrilled at the idea of us coming with Adam, and I know Taryn wants to go, so I don't put up a fight. I do, however, hope it is much warmer in Orange than it is in Sydney. Orange is the town closest to Pete's family ranch, two hundred and sixty kilometres west of Sydney.

"He's coming in late tonight, but he'll be here before we leave tomorrow," Adam replies to Pete. Of course, he is! I would never have agreed to the ranch idea if I thought Chazz would be there. I had just assumed he was going to continue his travelling with the Swedish delegation.

"Forget Chazz. Who is this sweet little Sheila?" Pete steps

forward and puts his arm around me, running his hand down my back to squeeze my butt cheek.

"Eek!" I shriek and jump away from his octopus hands.

"The name's Mel, actually," I put out my hand to shake Pete's. "And where we come from, you have to know someone longer than thirty seconds before you squeeze their ass. I know, call us crazy!"

"Oh, I like this one, Adam! She's feisty." Pete ignores my outstretched hand and gives me a bearhug, enveloping me in his oversized, oilskin jacket.

"Let's get a drink, shall we? I don't get to this part of the city very often. So, little lady, what do you do back in Canada?" Pete drapes his arm over my shoulder and leads us a few blocks to the Beach Road Hotel. Either Pete is downplaying the amount of time he spends in the Bondi Beach area of Sydney or he can sniff out beer from miles away. I suspect the latter.

The plan is for Pete to drive us all to the ranch in the morning for a five-day stay. Up until now I thought "all" meant me and Taryn and Adam. I now understand "all" includes Chazz. I wonder if "all" will be expanded to include the lovely Annika and, if so, will she be bringing other Swedish girls. I suddenly regret my "what the hell?" decision to tag along to Pete's family ranch. Taryn is going to owe me huge for this one. I glance over my shoulder — the best I can, with Pete's substantial arm resting on it — and see Taryn and Adam walking along behind us, giggling. Yes, she's going to owe me huge.

The four of us drink into the night. Pete can hold his own

in the alcohol department, but I really had no doubt he could. Adam fills Taryn and me in on Pete. According to Adam, Pete is the nicest guy in the world; he does like the ladies and, despite his uncouth appearance, is quite respectful deep down. I wonder how deep you have to go as I look to where Pete is standing at the bar with his arm draped around one poor young girl while he chats up another. To Pete's credit, he will not let Taryn or me buy any of the drinks. I suppose I should allow him the odd grope in light of the amount of beer he feeds me. Luckily, he's busy entertaining almost every other woman in the bar, so he leaves me alone for the most part.

The next morning, slightly hungover, Taryn and I manage to pack our bags and stumble down to the curb at the appointed time to meet Pete and Adam. I half-expect Pete's van to have a bumper sticker stating, "If the van is rockin', don't bother knockin'." But surprisingly it's quite decal-free. The van pulls up, and I immediately see Chazz sitting in the passenger seat. True to his word, he did arrive in time to join the excursion to the ranch.

"Hey, Boots! Did you miss me?" Chazz smiles.

"Almost as much as I miss my heat rash. What happened to your sleazy friend? Oh, sorry, I mean Swedish friend?" It's my turn to grin.

"Do I detect a hint of jealousy?" Chazz and Adam are out of the van and helping Taryn and I load our bags in the back.

"Hardly" is my weak retort after my great start. Damn! I can never think of good things to say when Chazz is around.

"Well, you've got me all to yourself this week. Just you and me on the ranch. Sounds quaint, doesn't it?" Chazz opens the door and shoves me none too gently into the back seat.

"Quaint? That's a big word for you, isn't it?" I grab the seat so I don't fall over.

The drive is uneventful. Adam, Chazz and Pete chat the whole way and I'm able to curl up and sleep off my hangover. The ranch is stunning, not what I expected at all. It's more like an American Southern plantation than any ranch I've ever seen. The manor house is a two-storey brick mansion with columns across the front and a wraparound porch. The approach is a half-kilometre-long paved driveway lined with palm trees.

Pete's mother meets us on the front porch and is very welcoming. I can't imagine what my mother would do if I showed up with four friends for a five-day stay. I think she'd have a heart attack, or worse. Taryn and I are led upstairs to one of the guest rooms; Chazz and Adam are shown to the outer guest house, which is adjacent to the pool. Unfortunately, it's too cool for swimming. Orange is no warmer than Sydney, but I'm starting to acclimatize to the winter temperatures. Taryn does have a point; it's nicer than our fall or spring can be, with sunshine and ten to twelve degrees.

After we get settled in, Pete takes us for a walk around the property. The ranch is three hundred acres with several outbuildings, including stables that house the thirty horses. Across one of the fields, I spot movement. It's two kangaroos playing. I point the kangaroos out to Taryn who is more excited than I am and wants a closer look. Pete loads us into his four-wheel-drive ranch truck — which is definitely more like what I imagined Pete would drive. The truck has oversized tires, a row of floodlights across the roof, a roll bar in the back, and a gun rack in the back window — complete with guns. Pete was probably loath to leave this one at home while he drives the van in Sydney. The van must belong to his parents.

Pete insists the ladies sit in the front with him, and Chazz and Adam are pointed to the open box. I try to push Taryn in first, so she is squished beside Pete, but she's wiry and gets away from me. I have to get in first or I would look like an idiot just standing by the open passenger door. As I slide in, I notice Pete's truck lacks seatbelts. Of course, there are no seatbelts. Pete takes us on a bumpy ride over the fields and explains the kangaroos are considered cute and cuddly to tourists but, in actual fact, farmers and ranchers consider kangaroos pests because they eat the crops. Pete tells us the female kangaroos can reproduce year-round. There is no one breeding season, so most are pregnant their entire adult lives. The female kangaroo can have a youngster at her heels, another one in her pouch and an embryo waiting to start to grow. The kangaroos can breed fast, and a mob of them — Pete tells us a "mob" is what a group of kangaroos is called — can eat the best part of a crop in short order.

Pete stops the truck on a crest, where we can look down at a pond on the property. We see a mob of kangaroos standing by the pond, looking at us. They all stand on their hind legs with their little arms in front of them, like little soldiers.

"Oh, they are so cute!" Taryn exclaims.

"You sheilas!" Pete laughs, "Always taken in by how cute they are."

"Well, they *are*! Just look at them." Taryn defends her first opinion.

I have to agree the kangaroos are cute and sort of regal, standing there by the pond. "So, since they're pests, what do you do to control the population?" The question is out of my mouth before I can stop it. I suspect the answer isn't something I want to know.

"We shoot them!" Pete exclaims. Taryn gasps and covers her mouth. I manage not to show much emotion, but the thought of Pete out here with his truck and guns, shooting kangaroos, makes me a bit queasy.

"We're going hunting tomorrow night, in fact. You can see the action first-hand." Pete seems to think "we" includes Taryn and me. I glance over at Taryn, who looks a bit pale and slightly green. I recognize the shade of green. It's the same colour Kit turns just before she vomits.

62

Back at the house, I am able to log onto Pete's computer and I manage to catch Kit on MSN. It's late afternoon here and early afternoon, yesterday, for Kit. It's strange to talk to someone who's still living in yesterday and not in the delusional "I used to walk five miles to school, uphill both ways" sort of yesterday, like my dad. It feels a bit like a time-travel movie.

Seems Tia has quit her job and is going to go on the road with Ben and the band *Kevin*, acting as their road manager. I am completely surprised by Tia's new job title and change in direction. I know Tia likes music, but this seems a bit drastic. Kit tells me her parents are completely losing it. The thought of Tia being on the road with a rock band while Taryn is halfway around the world is not sitting well with them.

Tia leaves with the band a week from Monday. They are picking her up in New York then moving west. The plan is to be on the road for at least eight weeks.

How is she coping? I immediately feel homesick. Taryn and I left. Now Tia is leaving Kit as well; she'll be completely alone. I ask her if she wants me to come home.

Don't be silly. You'll be home in seven or eight weeks anyway. I'm fine. Besides, I'm spending most of my time trying to keep my mother calm. She's mailed me a box of cookies every day for the past week. I think she's in Betty Crocker overload. Ask Taryn to email her. Hearing from Taryn will make her feel better.

I assure Kit I will have Taryn email her and sign off. What the heck am I doing in Australia on a ranch with the likes of Pete and Chazz?

I find Taryn by the pool chatting with the boys. Pete's dogs are playing on the grass — Tim the Rottweiler and Tara the Australian Shepherd. Tim is the sinewy more muscular of the two; but Tara seems to be smarter. I sit down beside Taryn and Tara comes to me immediately to be petted. I oblige willingly. It's nice to have a dog around. I had no idea I was a dog person until Mr. Klein dropped Burton in my lap, but now I quite like dogs. I fill Taryn in on Tia's new job description and tell her she should email home soon. Taryn doesn't seem surprised by Tia's change of career direction and agrees, yes, her mother could very well be going insane.

"You look a bit down in the dumps, Boots! What's up?" Chazz is so annoying.

"Nothing. I'm fine. Just need to stretch my legs. Can I take the dogs for a walk?" I direct the question at Pete.

"Sure, just don't travel too far and get lost. Dinner's in an hour." I get up and start to walk toward the gate, calling Tim and Tara, who follow obediently. Two metres from the gate I hear heavy footsteps behind me, look over my shoulder, and see Chazz. He is relentless.

"I don't think I should let a city girl hike around by herself." Chazz throws his arm over my shoulder and I twist to escape it.

"I think I'll be okay. Thanks anyway."

"Nope, I'm coming with you. Did you get bad news from home?" Mr. Inquisitive won't let the home thing go.

"No. Well, sort of. Tia is travelling now as well, and my friend Kit is alone in Toronto. I just wish I were home with her. I should just be home, period. I should be getting my life back on track," I blurt out way more information than I want Chazz to know.

"Your life will still be there when you get back. Why the rush? Kit is a big girl. She'll be fine."

"But I'm not like you, Chazz. I don't take vacations. I work. Work is what I do and I'm good at it."

"You are wrapped a bit tighter than most people, for sure! But I think you're doing vacation pretty well, for a first-timer." Chazz laughs. "Well, aside from the panic attacks, the motion sickness and the heat rash."

"Exactly my point! I'm hardly cut out for this lifestyle." I feel tears starting to well up. I gulp and turn my attention to the dogs. I do not want to cry in front of Chazz.

"You're as cut out for it as anyone, if you'd just let yourself enjoy it." Chazz picks up a stick and throws it for the dogs.

I feel the tears subsiding. At least I didn't cry. What does Chazz mean I'm wrapped tighter than most people? I wonder if I should be insulted by his remark. I probably should; if Chazz said it, it must be derogatory. What's wrong with being a little more intense and driven than other people?

Pete's parents are warm, wonderful people. Pete's dad used to lead excursions in the Outback and has a million stories to entertain us with over dinner. The evening wraps up early. I'm still feeling the effects of the late drinking night last night and am a bit emotional after my e-chat with Kit. I'm worried about Kit alone back home all summer, with Tia and Kevin being on the road. Lying in bed, in the dark, my mind starts to work overtime. It's been less than two weeks since John's naked-dance exploit. John and Ursula, the breakup, quitting my job, Burton, the seal television commercial, the wedding, deciding to and actually coming to Australia. My life has been a non-stop whirlwind for the past month. No wonder I'm wrapped a little too tightly — if Chazz is right — who wouldn't be, in my position? So much has happened, I haven't really had time to process most of it, let alone come to terms with it.

63

I sleep fitfully, tossing and turning, thinking too much about the events of the past month. When I finally register, it's morning. I realize I have a pounding headache and my jaw is throbbing. I try to open my mouth in order to move my jaw and try to stop the pain, but the pain just increases, shooting from my jaw to my brain. It is excruciating, and I can't open my mouth. Mother of Pearl! I cannot open my mouth. Fully awake, with the realization there is something very wrong, I jump out of bed, my head pounding, and make my way to the washroom, where I inspect myself in the mirror. I look fine, no bruises or puffiness, but still I am unable to open my mouth. I rush back to the guest room and wake up Taryn.

"I can't open my mouth," I manage to say between my clenched teeth. Thankfully, my tongue and lips are working so I can communicate my very painful situation.

"What?" Taryn is still groggy from sleep.

"I can't open my mouth," I repeat.

Taryn sits up in her bed and I try to open my jaws. The stabbing pain shoots from where my lower jaw meets my upper jaw and into the top of my skull a second time. I shriek between my clenched teeth.

"Holy crap!" Taryn is fully awake now and is starting to panic just a little. She grabs my hand and pulls me along behind her, making her way downstairs to the kitchen. No one is around. Taryn spots movement outside, near the pool-side guest house. Pete is just coming from the guest house, making his way to the kitchen. Taryn drags me outside, towards Pete. I'm holding the left side of my face in an attempt to stop the jarring created by my walking from shooting pain into my head. I realize, too late, that Taryn and I are both still dressed in our pyjamas — mine being boxer shorts and a purple tank top — both from Old Navy.

"Pete, I think we need a doctor. Mel has lockjaw or something!"

"What? Let me see." Pete takes my hand away from my face.

"I can't open my mouth," I say from between my clenched teeth. The headache is agonizing. My eyes start to water as I speak.

"Get her back in the house; she's freezing. I'll get Chazz." Pete turns and jogs back to the guest house. Chazz? What the heck is stupid Chazz going to do? I'm certainly not going to let him anywhere near my non-functional jaw and pounding head.

I'm sitting at the kitchen table when Pete, Chazz and Adam rush in.

"What's up, Boots?" Chazz says, while rubbing his eye. It appears Pete had to wake him up.

"I can't open my mouth," I say for the fourth time this morning, causing pain to shoot to the top of my head again.

"Well, as much as you not being able to talk might be a bonus, we should fix you up. Let me take a look," Chazz starts to walk toward me.

"No. Uh uh. Doctor." I ignore Chazz's dig about me not talking and start to stand up but have to grab my jaw, which throbs with every movement I make.

"He is a doctor," Pete says at the same time Chazz laughs, "I am a doctor."

"Yeah, right," I manage from between clenched teeth and stand up.

"No, really. I'm a dentist. I just graduated: Dr. Chadwick Zadzilko, D.D.S. Now, let me take a look."

Chazz doesn't seem to be lying. In fact, this is the most serious I've ever seen him look in our short acquaintance. But I'm still not inclined to believe him. I look at Taryn and she shrugs her shoulders. She's never heard the dentist story before. I look at Pete, who nods. But two days ago, Pete was grabbing my ass.

"Really?" I ask Adam; he seems to be the most trustworthy of the bunch.

"Really. He's starting to work with his dad when he gets back to Toronto. His dad's a dentist too. Cross my heart." Adam seems convincing and does make an X over his chest.

"Are *you* a dentist too?" I ask Adam.

"Nope, Pete and I both just finished our engineering degrees. We can't help you."

"Really?" I find the idea of Chazz being a dentist too surreal and cannot get my head around it.

"Really! Why would anyone lie about being a dentist?" Chazz replies and looks very sincere. He has a point, why *would* anyone lie about being a dentist?

"Fine." I surrender my locked jaw to the likes of Chazz — anything to relieve the pain. Chazz directs me to lie on my back on the kitchen table; I do, and make a mental note to wipe it thoroughly after I get off it. No one should be lying on tables from which people eat. Chazz stands at my head and takes my tender jaw in his hands and gently starts to feel around where the lower and upper jaw meet.

"Boots, I believe what we have here is a classic case of one stressed-out lady who clenches her teeth when she sleeps. I saw it a couple of times at school during exam season. Just a second… this might hurt before it feels better…" Chazz pauses, then presses on my face close to my ears and starts to massage the jaw area. The shooting pain increases and makes me cringe, but then it subsides.

"Okay, try now. Can you open?" Chazz looks down at me. He appears upside down.

I slowly try to open my jaw, and it works. The area where it was catching has magically let go and, although it's still tender, the searing pain has stopped.

"Oh, my God. Thank you." It feels good to actually open my mouth while speaking. "Are you *really* a dentist? You don't look old enough to be a dentist." I'm still lying on the table looking up at Chazz, who is bending over me.

"Yep. I'm the real thing. Dr. Zadzilko; it's the last name that got me the 'with two *Zs*' business. Old enough? Yeah, I'm six years older than these guys. I just don't act it most of the time. Back to you — I'm going to have to keep an eye on you. If you aren't going to learn to relax I'm going to have to get you a night guard when we get back to Sydney." Chazz walks around the side of the table and helps me sit up. I feel the tension in the room evaporate as everything returns to normal. "I'm going to have to teach you how to meditate or, better yet, why don't you just find someone to have sex with you? A good roll in the hay will alleviate a lot of your stress — for a while, anyway!"

"If you decide to go the second route, I'll be right outside," Pete pipes up.

"Thank you for fixing my jaw," I look from Chazz to Pete, "but you are both still social deviants."

"I think she's starting to warm up to me," Pete says as he puts his arm around Chazz and the three guys start back to the guest house.

I watch them walk away, laughing and talking. Chazz is wearing only long pyjama pants, no shirt. I hadn't really registered he was half-naked when I was in severe pain, but now I notice how fit Chazz is. His back and arm muscles ripple as he and Pete push each other and start to wrestle. He is quite chiselled, and I have to admit, very nice-looking. I suppose, now that I'm actually giving it some thought, he is older than the other two guys. I wonder why I hadn't noticed before now? I had just assumed they were college kids the first time I saw them on the balcony. Just as I start to mentally reprimand myself for staring at Chazz, he turns back toward the garden doors and sees me watching him. Damn it. I can't believe he caught me watching him.

64

I spend the day quietly resting my jaw, which is still very tender, writing postcards to myself and addressing one to my parents for good measure. I'm sure my mother is freaking out almost as much as Mrs. Jennings. Taking off to Australia was fairly uncharacteristic of me; she must be wondering if I've completely lost my mind. Who knows? Maybe I have. I check my email and find out Kit has stepped up her jogging and is thinking she should run a half-marathon in the fall. Aside from running, she is completely bored and is considering redecorating her condo. I tell her about the lockjaw but not about getting caught staring at half-naked Chazz — way too embarrassing to share on email; it will have to wait until I'm back home.

"Here, use this," Chazz's voice says from behind me as I sit at Pete's computer in the den. A small notebook lands on the desk beside me.

"What for?" I turn to Chazz, who is standing behind me.

"Ahhh, to write in," Chazz answers in his trademark smart-ass fashion.

"Ahhh, about what?" I ask back at him.

"You know, to write about your trip. Or, wait, here's a crazy idea. You could write down the stuff in your life causing you to stress out when you're sleeping. Maybe you can even give those issues some thought and you can figure out how to deal with them while you still have a working jaw."

"I thought you were a dentist. Now you're a part-time psychologist too?" I ask.

"I am a dentist. Your jaw is my only concern. Give it a try. Who knows? You might like it," Chazz says over his shoulder as he's leaving the room.

I feel my jaw tense up again. Why does he make me so mad? No wonder I have lockjaw, having to hang out with the likes of him. Talk about tension! I open the little notebook and write, "I have a sore jaw because I have to travel with Dr. Chazz, with two bloody *Z*s and he makes me crazy!" on the first page. There. I feel better already. Maybe there is something to this writing-down-my-feelings crap.

True to his word, Pete rounds us up after dark to go hunting. Kangaroo hunting. My initial thought is I do not, under any circumstances, want to be anywhere near Pete with a gun. I'm starting to formulate excuses to get out of the excursion in my head, when Chazz says, "You know what, Boots? With your jaw, I'm not completely sure you should come out with us tonight."

"Why? Isn't my jaw related to clenching when I'm asleep?" My initial worry is Chazz isn't telling me everything about my jaw. What kind of flunky dentist is he?

"The bumping around in the truck might make you clench. I'm just worried you'll exacerbate an already tender area."

I stare at Chazz, confused. I can't tell if he's really worried about my jaw or if he just thinks I'm not cut out for hunting. "You just think I'm too much of a girl to go hunting, don't you?"

"Well, you said it, not me…" Chazz pauses and looks down my body.

I'm wearing my jean capri pants, a cashmere sweater, and my turquoise boots. The hiking boots have been rubbing on one of my heels, resulting in a very large blister. I have no choice but to wear my heels or suffer severe foot issues. "Oh, no, you don't! I can hunt as well as the next girl!"

Chazz looks over at Taryn who is dressed in hiking boots, a hoodie and camouflage cargo pants. "Boots, there is no shame in admitting you may not be cut out for hunting."

"I am so cut out for hunting! Hmmpf!" I storm away from Chazz and start towards Pete's four-wheel-drive hunting truck, thinking, "Chazz thinks I'm too much of a girl. I'll show him who's the girl!"

I hear Pete behind me say, "Is she going hunting with those boots on?"

"Apparently," Chazz laughs. "She is one tenacious woman!"

Damn it, I had an out. Why didn't I just agree with Chazz about my jaw? I didn't even have to come up with an excuse; he had handed me a perfectly good one. What is wrong with me? Why am I so determined to prove myself to the likes of Chazz with two *Zs*?

Sitting in the front of Pete's truck, in the middle between Pete and Taryn, I realize the error of my judgment. I *am* too much of a girl to be out hunting any of God's creatures. I could be back at the mansion emailing Kit and sipping tea.

"Okay, when I say 'now,' flip on all the lights. Make sure the big light is turned toward the trees," Pete says quietly out the driver's window to Adam and Chazz who are riding in the open box of the truck. Pete reaches behind my head and takes down one of the rifles from his gun rack, steps out of the truck, and rests his elbows on the hood of the truck, lining up something in the darkness.

"Now!" Pete yells and the treeline in front of us lights up like a football field. Kangaroos stop still in their tracks, mesmerized by the light, staring into it. Pete's gun explodes — one shot then another — and the two kangaroos closest to us drop where they were standing. The rest of the kangaroo mob scatters. Adam and Chazz jump out of the back of the truck after Pete's dogs, hooting. Taryn doesn't jump out of the truck; she slips out of her seat and walks toward a clump of trees, away from the action. The dogs are barking at the carcasses on the ground. I slide over to the door, feeling like I need to gulp in large quantities of air. I can't catch my breath. No air seems to be getting to my lungs. Why didn't I stay at home, nursing my jaw?

"Hey, Boots. What do you think so far? Pretty cool, eh?" Chazz isn't tormenting me as much as just commenting on the experience. But I can't muster a reply. I start to climb out the truck and stumble into Chazz, still unable to catch my breath.

"Whoa there, Boots!" Chazz turns to look at me, sees I'm close to hyperventilating, and grabs my arm to hold me up. He then leads me to a flat, grassy spot on the edge of the lit area, a good distance from where the dead kangaroos are lying.

"You're going to be just fine, my little hunter," Chazz laughs and unceremoniously drops me on the ground, then pushes my head between my bent knees, like he did the day we were on the beach on Beachcomber Island. "Take deep breaths and think happy thoughts. Oh, and turn your head if you're going to throw up."

"Chazzman! We need your muscles, buddy!" I hear Pete yell and feel Chazz walk away from me. At the same time Taryn plops down beside me and puts her arm around me.

I glance up at the action. I see Pete has deftly sliced one of the dead kangaroos down the middle with his knife and has made cuts through its fur around its ankles and wrists. The tail also has a ring of blood about halfway down the length. Adam takes Pete's knife and starts to cut the second kangaroo in the same fashion, while Pete gets Chazz to help him secure a length of chain to one of the nearby trees, then lift the already prepared kangaroo and attach one if its hind feet to the chain. Pete then affixes a hook through the animal's fur, near the tail; the hook is attached to a second chain, which is mounted onto the truck. Pete hops into the driver's seat and drives a few feet. The skin of the kangaroo peels off as easily as a banana peel.

"Why did I look up?" I am horrified and feel queasy again.

My eyes start to go black. "I will not faint!" I command myself to stay conscious and jam my head between my knees. But then I hear Pete's truck moving again and know the second kangaroo has been skinned. "I will not pass out! I will not pass out!" becomes my mantra as I sit in the cool grass with Taryn's head buried in my shoulder. I try not to visualize images to match what I'm hearing.

I hear Pete say, "We just take the skins. Leave the meat for the dingoes."

I don't look up until I feel Chazz lifting me by the arm.

"How do you like hunting so far, Boots?" Chazz asks.

"Good. I think I've got it all figured out," I manage, but I know I'm not convincing anyone as the boys start to laugh.

65

"Owww," I moan through clenched teeth. I can't open my mouth again. My jaw locked the same way it was yesterday morning. I stumble out of bed, noticing it's only six o'clock in the morning, but I can't stand the pain shooting to my head. I stumble downstairs and out the kitchen garden doors to the guest house. I knock quietly on the door, and then louder a second time as no one hears me. I'm not sure what time the hunting party returned last night. They had driven Taryn and me back to the house after the first two kangaroos and went back out.

"It's a bit early, isn't it, Boots?" Chazz mumbles through the crack in the door. "You change your mind about that sex?"

"Ha ha..." I start, but trying to speak normally causes the pain to shoot through the top of my skull. I shriek and almost fall over.

Chazz wakes up immediately and helps me to the kitchen table, where he lays me down and massages my jaw like he did yesterday. It hurts more today, and my eyes start to water — partly from the pain and partly from frustration.

"Am I hurting you?" Chazz stops what he's doing when I

feel tears falling down my cheeks. I shake my head. He starts working on my jaw again.

"Give it a try." Chazz leaves his hands gently resting on my cheeks so he can feel when I open my mouth. It opens and I'm relieved. I have no idea what I'm going to do when Chazz isn't my on-call dentist.

"Good. You should be good for the rest of the day, but we're going to have to look into a night guard," Chazz says, looking down at me. "You're not getting rid of any of the stress — and that isn't good." He walks around the table and helps me sit up so my legs are dangling over the side.

"Maybe I should just go home," I quietly say what I've been thinking in the back of my mind since I started this whole travel experience. Tears start to fall down my face involuntarily. I don't cry — and I certainly don't want to cry in front of Chazz — but I can't stop the flood of tears.

"Not like you to give up, Boots," Chazz states matter-of-factly.

"I'm not cut out for this, as you can plainly see. I do better with structure."

"So what? You want to go home now, go back to your job and keep doing the same old thing, day in and day out, until you die?" Chazz asks.

"Technically, I'm in between jobs!" I groan and drop my forehead. My tears are a torrent now.

"So you have no job, I know you dumped the ballerina boyfriend. What the hell are you in such a hurry to get home to?" Chazz takes my cheeks in his hands and lifts my face to look at him.

"You're right. I have nothing... *anywhere*!" The flood of tears starts again.

"Now you're just being melodramatic. You're travelling with people who care about you. You've been to Fiji, which is one of the most beautiful places in the world. You've touched the Sydney Opera House and, well, let's face it, you're a hardened hunter now! You can't go hunting back in Toronto. Well, legally, at any rate," Chazz smiles and almost seems nice.

"I just feel like I'm letting everyone down by running away," I get out between tears.

"Who? Your parents? They'll survive. If the worst thing that happens to them is you go travelling for a couple of months, I think they'll recover. My parents were none too happy when I told them I was putting off work until the fall. My dad's head almost exploded," Chazz states.

"Really?"

"Really. I'm supposed to be taking over his practice, and he's anxious to get me in the office learning the ropes. He also mentioned something about my 'owing him because he paid for my education.' Nothing your parents are feeling even comes close to the heart palpitations my dad's having." Chazz laughs again and sits down beside me on the kitchen table.

"Why did you come, then? Don't you feel like you should have started work?" I ask Chazz. I don't think I could have left if my dad was angry with me.

"I have my whole long life to work, and I know I will. If I hadn't come on this trip, I'd be back in Toronto right now, resenting my father, and growing ulcers, regretting my decision *not* to travel with Adam. We don't regret the things we do, Mel; we regret the things we don't do. The things we don't try."

"I think I may regret the hunting thing a little bit," I laugh through my tears.

"You didn't like it. True, but at least you know you didn't like it because you *tried* it. You won't regret the knowledge you gained and you certainly won't regret having the story to tell your friends when you get back. You went kangaroo hunting last night; what do you suppose your friends back home were doing?"

"I can guarantee they were *not* kangaroo hunting."

"See? You're going to have months' worth of stories and things you'll never regret. Let go of the fear. You've already done the hard part. You got on the plane. You're here now. Make the best of it and just have fun. Have you ever just had fun, Boots?"

"Don't be silly. Everyone's had fun… I've…" My brain goes blank. I don't remember the last time I had fun. John and Ursula interrupted my brother's wedding. The bridal shower was a drunken fiasco. My job hasn't been fun in months; I can't remember the last time I was really excited about a deal. My neighbour accused me of stealing her lawn ornaments and my boyfriend dumped me for a chubby, naked dancing queen.

"Oh, oh… I had fun babysitting Burton." There, I thought of something.

"Who's Burton? A friend's baby?"

"No. Well, yes, he is a big baby. But he's a Great Dane. He was fun. He attacked one of my neighbour's lawn ornaments and bit the leg off it. I had fun with him."

"Well, it's a start. If you had fun with him, I'd like to meet this Burton someday." Chazz stands up and brushes hair from my cheek. "Relax and have fun. You're here already, so enjoy it."

"If you think I should do things so I'll have no regrets, why did you try to talk me out of hunting yesterday?" It strikes me Chazz is saying one thing but doing the complete opposite.

Chazz grins, "I knew if I told you not to, you'd do it to spite me."

I punch him on his muscled shoulder. He laughs and starts to walk to the door.

I turn and watch Chazz make his way beside the pool to the guest house, his muscled back rippling when he walks. He doesn't turn around and catch me staring this time.

Later that afternoon, I look up from the computer and ask Taryn, "Horseback riding? Are you serious?" I know in my heart she must be joking.

"Yep, everyone's going. You have to come." Good Lord. She *is* serious.

"Taryn, sweetie, do you even know me at all? I've never been on a horse. The closest I've been to a horse was when

Pete gave us the stable tour, and they were all in stalls. Besides, I have lockjaw." Taryn can't argue the lockjaw point.

"You only live once. Besides, Chazz is coming too so you'll be safest coming along in case the lockjaw comes back. Chazz can fix it."

I start to object further to Taryn's suggestion but hear Chazz's voice from this morning in my head, "*You're here already so enjoy it.*"

"Is horseback riding fun?" I ask, catching Taryn off guard because she was mentally figuring out her next argument.

"Absolutely!" Taryn laughs.

"Okay, then, what are we waiting for?" I save the email to Kit I am working on and stand up from the computer to follow Taryn to the stable. "I'm here now, I might as well have stories to take home," I think to myself, trying to work up my nerve. "Mel Melrose on a horse? Definitely the potential for a funny story." I grin to myself as Taryn and I walk behind the guys to the stable.

66

"Lightning? Do you think I should ride a horse named Lightning?" I ask Pete for the second time. "I've never done this sort of thing before. And Lightning sounds like he might be a little too much for me."

Pete places a helmet on my head and laughs. "Lightning is a she, and on this ranch, it's Bob you have to watch out for — and Chazz is on Bob. You will be fine on Lightning."

It turns out Pete does indeed know the animals on the ranch. Lightning, I discover during the course of our ride, is short for Lightning Bug. And she's a twenty-five year old whose main desire is to eat. I have to keep pulling her head up every time she spots something she thinks she might like to nibble. Bob, on the other hand, gives Chazz his money's worth, galloping around us in circles, racing ahead, then turning around and coming back, with athletic Chazz holding on for dear life at some points. We even hear Chazz squeal like a little girl when Bob takes off and jumps a low fence. Chazz vehemently denies squealing, but the rest of us are certain we have heard him.

"My butt is going to be sore tomorrow. I haven't ridden since I started university," I hear Taryn say behind me. She's riding with Adam.

"I hear you on the butt. When did you horseback ride?" My butt has been sore for the past hour, but I can finally see the stable on the horizon.

"Every Thursday and Saturday from the time I was six! Honestly, Mel, you practically lived at my house. Don't you remember the trophies with the horses on them? The saddles in the garage? Any of this ringing a bell?"

"Saddles in the garage?" I honestly have no recollection of saddles. Surely I would have noticed saddles in Kit's garage.

"Yes. Tee and I both rode. She's better than I am. You and Kit were obviously too busy being teenagers to notice!" Taryn laughs.

"Well, that's awful of me. I can't believe you even speak to me after I ignored you all those years." I suddenly feel like a horrible person for not noticing the twins when they were growing up.

"Don't lose any sleep over it, Mel. We are ten years younger than you. You were sixteen and learning to drive a car when I started horseback riding. You had more important things to think about than your friend's little sisters."

"But, still, it makes me seem a bit self-absorbed, doesn't it?" I'm pondering my own question, when Chazz and Bob come charging up from behind. Bob is still raring to go after a long afternoon's ride. Chazz manages to slow him to a walk beside me. I look over at Chazz and he looks exhausted, still pulling on Bob's reins to keep him from taking off again.

"Okay, you win, Pete. Bob is too much horse for me! My arms are killing me," Chazz jumps down from Bob's back.

Bob immediately stops pulling and trying to run, and slows to a walk behind Chazz's lead.

"You walkin' back?" Pete asks Chazz.

"Yeah, you win! I buy the beer when we get back to Sydney."

"Do you want me to walk with you?" I ask Chazz. "My butt is killing me; I could use the break from the saddle."

"Sure."

I jump down off Lightning Bug and fall into step with Chazz. Pete, Adam and Taryn, still on the horses, start to get further ahead of us.

"I think Taryn likes your buddy Adam," I comment casually.

"You think?!" Chazz laughs. "I know he definitely has it bad for her. He was devastated when he missed her leaving Beachcomber. He couldn't get off the island fast enough to try to find her."

"Well, she's very glad he did," I smile. Chazz and I are actually having a normal conversation. It's a nice change from being constantly flustered in his presence.

The sun has started to fall and dusk is starting to settle. "Check out the moon, Boots." Chazz is looking up.

The moon is just a sliver but still seems to light up the cloudless sky. I look up at the stars and realize something is strangely amiss. "Does the sky look funny to you?" I ask Chazz.

"Absolutely. We're in the southern hemisphere now. The sky is completely different; all new constellations. No Big Dipper. Down here, they have the Southern Cross," Chazz explains, looking around to see if he can find it.

"If you'd asked me before I came here if I ever paid attention to the sky, I would have said no. But the minute it's different, you notice right away," I laugh. "Maybe I do absorb more than I give myself credit for."

"I think you're going to be just fine. You did great today — tried something new and didn't faint. I'm proud of you." Chazz drapes his arm over my shoulders.

"I didn't have to faint because today all the animals kept their skin on!" I laugh. I suddenly don't mind being this close to Chazz or having him touch me. If I'm completely honest, I think I like it when Chazz touches me.

We spend the next two days on the ranch. And, both mornings, I wake up with movement in my jaw. I can move it with no pain shooting into my skull. I quietly hope I've finally started to get over my stress of not being a productive member of society and vow to enjoy every day of the rest of my travels in Australia. Life on the ranch is very relaxing and laid-back. We spend the days helping with the horses, playing with the dogs and hanging out. In the evenings, we drink beer under the unfamiliar array of stars. Taryn, Adam, Chazz and I make dinner for Pete and his parents the night before we leave to thank them for their amazing hospitality. I'm sitting in the dark near the pool, after the dinner dishes have been cleared away, and am joined by Chazz and Pete; Taryn and Adam are taking a walk.

"How's the jaw, Boots?" Chazz asks.

"Great. Feels almost back to normal. Just a bit tender."

"Keep doing what you're doing to manage the stress and you should be fine," Chazz reassures me.

"So, Pete, are you going to take over the ranch someday?" I ask Pete after he hands me another beer.

"Maybe. I have a job in Sydney, so I live there now. This is just a break. I couldn't miss having the boys here when they were in the country."

"How did you guys meet?" I ask.

"We were roommates at university. I was in my first year, and Chazz was in his first year of dentistry. We were both a couple of years older than the other guys, so they bunked us together. It was a great match," Pete explains. "I took a couple of years off after high school to help out here. Chazz, what did you do, again?"

"I took a year off before I started dental school and went skiing. Drove my dad insane, knowing I wasn't in school," Chazz laughs an evil little laugh. "I had to give in finally. I knew I'd need an education, but it is just the means to allow me to do the things I want to do."

"Like what?" I ask.

"Everything except be a dentist," Chazz laughs again. "I want to climb mountains, hang-glide, kayak — you know, all the stuff that costs money but doesn't make you much if you do it for a living."

"So, you're only going to practise for a while, then give it up?" I ask, surprised.

"No, I'm not completely insane. Dentistry will be my career. But I'll take lots of extended holidays and do the things I want to do. It'll be my career but not my life."

"Sounds like a good plan. Maybe you are smarter than you look," I laugh, standing up to dodge Chazz's punch. "I'm going to the washroom. Can I grab anyone another beer?"

67

Pete drops us off at the same B&B we had stayed at before the ranch excursion, and this time Adam and Chazz check in as well. The plan is to spend one more day in Sydney, then head up the coast to Port Macquarie. Taryn and Adam claim some "mystery business" and take off, leaving Chazz and me in charge of booking our bus seats — everyone travels north by coach bus in Australia, by far the easiest and most economical way to travel — and hostel rooms for the next night.

"I think Taryn and Adam's 'mystery business' is having sex," I laugh as Chazz dials the Ozzie Pozzie Backpackers hostel and secures rooms for the next night.

"I know. Not much of a mystery, really!"

The bus booking takes another two minutes, then Chazz and I are free for the day. We start walking toward the beach.

"I think I can get used to this," I mention casually.

"What? *You*? Not doing a million things at once in your four-inch heels. *Mel Melrose* could get used to a calmer way of life?"

"Ha ha! You are a complete jerk, you know that?" I punch Chazz on the shoulder.

"So, maybe I'm right about travelling?" Chazz asks.

"Okay. Yes, before you start being smug, *you were right*!"

"Smug is one of my signature qualities. You'd miss it if I gave it up completely," Chazz laughs. "So this is where I have to say, 'Told you so!'"

"Remind me again why I talk to you?"

"Taryn and Adam are off having sex in some alleyway, probably on a garbage bin behind a dance studio, and I'm all you've got." Chazz and I laugh and continue down the beach.

The next day, we travel to Port Macquarie and check into the hostel in the early afternoon, grab some lunch and head to the Koala Hospital for the three o'clock tour. I've never really been one who gets into tourist attractions but, I must admit, as a tourist I feel quite comfortable in the role. I wonder if maybe I shouldn't check out some of the tourist destinations in Toronto when I return.

Taryn and Adam are walking ahead of Chazz and me as we approach the Koala Hospital. Taryn is just getting to the door when I hear a giggly squeal from behind.

"Shazza! I've missed you!" Annika leaps forward out of a group of three of her Swedish friends and at least six men.

I feel the gust as she rushes past me and slips under Chazz's arm, slinking all over him in seconds, ignoring the fact that I am standing there. I look past Chazz and Annika to find Taryn and Adam. Adam immediately looks uncomfortable and reaches out to hold Taryn's hand. Chazz, admittedly, looks a bit startled but rallies quickly.

"Hey, Annika! How have you been?" he asks as he puts his hand on the small of her back.

"Dreadful! I've been missing you sooooo much!" Annika runs her finger down the side of Chazz's face and presses closer to him.

The Swedish contingent moves in closer to Chazz, surrounding him and Annika, pushing me off the sidewalk.

Yuck. I've seen enough; I'd rather watch another kangaroo get skinned.

"It looks like Chazz has a better offer than the koalas," I say quietly to Taryn after I manage to get around the Swedes and reunite with my friend. "You know what? I think I'm going to pass on the hospital and just take a walk." I don't wait for Taryn's objection. I suddenly just want to be very far from Chazz and Annika.

"But..." Taryn rubs my arms and looks at me sadly.

"I'm fine. You guys go." I turn quickly so Taryn won't see the look on my face.

"Be careful. Come back for dinner, okay? We'll grab something together," Taryn yells after me but she doesn't try to stop me as I walk away.

My stomach has dropped, and I know I look pale despite my tanned face. I start to walk toward the beach realizing I'm on the verge of tears.

Seeing Chazz with Annika draped all over him has caught me completely off guard. I have to get a grip. I'm being totally insane. I have no claim on Chazz. In fact, up until a few days ago, I thought he was a complete cad — for lack of a better phrase involving profanity. It's none of my business what he gets up to, or into... or onto. "Stupid Chazz. What kind of name is Chazz, anyway? Stupid name, that's what it is!"

I get to the beach, trying to block Annika and Chazz from my thoughts, and settle to watch the waves. I wrap my sweater around me for protection from the breeze. The weather is still spring cool. No swimming until we get farther up the coast — "we" being Taryn, Adam and me, I suppose. Chazz will, no doubt, start travelling with the Scandinavian delegation. He is attractive enough to hang out with them. Oh no, now I think Chazz is attractive. Well, admittedly, he does look like Brad Pitt and I do, sort of, have a thing for Brad, so my opinion is probably a bit skewed.

I see a windsurfer jumping out on the waves. Watching him takes my mind off Annika and Chazz... for a few seconds. I bet Chazz windsurfs. Of course, Chazz windsurfs. Now, I'm picturing Chazz and Annika with their matching windsurfing boards and wetsuits. "Kill me now!" I say out loud and start to laugh. I throw myself back on the beach, stretch out my legs, cross my turquoise leather-clad feet and close my eyes. The warm sun feels incredible on my face. When was the last time I did absolutely nothing? I can't remember. I wonder why I don't do this more often. There's an amazing calmness in doing nothing. I smile.

I start to think about my life and how my outlook has changed so drastically in the past two weeks. Wow, I've only been here for two weeks and all the issues that drove me to uncharacteristically jump on a plane seem much less important. The Sunset Disaster — trust me, after seeing a *lot* of sunsets since arriving here, I have yet to see one the colour of my bridesmaid dress — is a distant memory. My job? If I'm totally honest, I was hard on Astrid. Maybe I deserved the whole Sesame-Cecily-translator-thing. Back then, I thought my issues with Astrid stemmed from her incompetence. But maybe not; maybe it was my narrow-mindedness. My entire world had revolved around my work. Astrid's didn't. She considers her life outside of Jim's office more important than work. Her job is just the means to an end. My job, on the other hand, was both my means and my end.

John and Ursula? I still don't like this one, and I get a knot in my stomach when I think about it. But I have to come to terms with it at some point. Was the downfall of the relationship partly my own creation? I remember him calling me "needy" and I cringe. Me? Needy? Could I have been acting that way? Did my life revolve totally around John, with my only other outlet being my job? Did I put too much pressure on him to be my whole life? Maybe. Maybe the pressure of having to be everything for me outside of my job was too much for him. It doesn't excuse his subsequent behaviour, but if he did feel like I was clinging to him like a life preserver, of course he'd run the other way. No one wants to feel like they are being dragged under by the weight of someone else.

Do I miss John, the person? Honestly, miss him? No, not

really. When I had started wondering about the affair, I think I was more upset to be losing the life I was striving to make more than losing him. I had no idea of what my life should be, but believed it revolved around work and being in a relationship. With the removal of the relationship, the idea crumbled. Now, I find myself here, halfway around the world, lying on a beach with no preconceived ideas of what my life will be when I return home. I smile at the uncertainty; with no plans carved in stone, or my thick skull, anything can happen.

I smile to myself again. It really is funny how far I've come in such a short time, and it's Chazz I have to thank. Chazz. Who would have guessed? I hate it when he's right — and he is often right. I also hate the idea of Chazz with Annika but, really, what can I do? She does have prior claim — I thought he was an arrogant ass when she hooked up with him. Let's not forget she's stunning, taller than me and has an exotic accent. Of course, Chazz should be with Annika. They should scamper off together and make beautiful blonde, blue-eyed babies named Björn and Brigitta.

Besides, I couldn't live with a man who calls me Boots all the time, anyway. I'm sure it would get on my nerves... after thirty or forty years. I laugh out loud at my own joke. No, I'm better off without him — or any man, at this point. I have a whole new life path to figure out and a tendency to come across as "needy" that I must address. I certainly don't want a man hanging around, screwing up my personal growth, right? Besides, now that Chazz has helped me figure out there is more to life than work, there would be no living with him. No, I am better off on my own.

68

I make my way back to the hostel and meet up with Adam and Taryn. Chazz is nowhere to be seen.

"Hey, we were worried about you? Are you okay?" Taryn asks.

"I'm fine. Nothing a walk on the beach couldn't cure," I smile and try to look sincere. I don't want Adam running off and telling Chazz I'm pining for him or anything.

"Okay, but I checked my email while you were at the beach and Kit needs you to call her." Taryn looks a bit worried.

"What? Call her? Is everything okay?" I immediately start to panic and start digging in my backpack for my credit card.

"I'm not sure; she just sent an email asking you to call, no matter what time. Do you want me to come to the phone booth with you?"

"No, I'm good," I yell over my shoulder, starting to sprint towards the door.

International telephone calling is not my forté and it takes three tries to get connected to Kit's condo in Toronto.

"Mel, is that you?" Kit sounds hoarse and stuffed up. She has obviously been crying.

"What's wrong? Are you okay?" I immediately jump into protective-mother mode.

"I'm fine..." Kit starts but gasps and the tears start.

"Kit, you're not fine. Are your parents okay? My parents?" My first thought is to our families.

"No, they're fine. It's... it's... the groupies..." Kit starts to blubber again.

"Sorry sweetie, you lost me. Did you say 'groupies'?"

"Yes... *Kevin*... groupieeeeees..." Kit disintegrates into sobs.

I've known Kit my whole life and can translate the previous three, almost incoherent, words combined with her emotional distress perfectly. It seems Kevin, her boyfriend of seven months, has done something unwholesome while on tour with his band.

"Do you want me to come home? I can be on a plane tomorrow..."

Kit snuffles. "No. No. I'll be fine. I just feel all alone with you and Tia both gone and now this..."

"How did you find out about the groupies? What did he do?" I ask Kit now that she seems a little more able to speak.

"Nothing. Well, nothing that I know about. He called and we talked, and it just makes sense that we break up. He's away and will be for the rest of the summer, and Tia says all the girls are all over him all the time. Tia hates the groupies, but they're the ones making the band popular, right? Breaking up makes sense, but it still sucks. I really like him..." Kit blows her nose.

"I'm so sorry, Kit. But, I hear you on the groupies. Chazz has attracted a whole pack of them!" I laugh.

"Chazz? Your last email said he'd ditched the Swedes?"

"Seems when you're travelling in the same direction as everyone else, your paths cross continually. They're back in full force," I state, trying to sound unaffected.

"Oh, that's a drag. Just when you were starting to warm up to him." I can tell Kit is smiling her little "I know a secret" smile.

"No I wasn't. He's still the same obnoxious..."

"Yeah, yeah. Even half a world away, I can tell when you've got a crush." Kit sounds better.

"Well, I don't. I am worried about you, though. Do you want me to come home?"

"No. Don't be silly. I'll be fine. Really. This too shall pass, and I feel better just talking to you."

Kit and I talk for a few more minutes but don't stay on the line too long because it is an expensive call. I walk slowly back to the hostel, missing Kit and home. When I tell Taryn about Kevin, she suggests, "When I get home, I'm going to put on my glasses, march up to Mr. Groupie Kevin, and tell him what I think of him!" I do believe Taryn's glasses have given her a whole new level of confidence.

69

We spend another full day at Port Macquarie, and Chazz seems to have completely disappeared. I don't ask Adam but overhear him tell Taryn that Chazz has moved his backpack to the Port Macquarie Backpackers hostel, where, presumably, Annika and the Swedish contingent is staying. I try not to show any emotion when I overhear this information, but I suspect my face shows more sadness than I would like. Later, when Adam is snorkelling and Taryn and I are alone on the beach, she mentions, "It's too bad Chazz moved. We were just starting to have fun, the four of us."

"Yes, but the magnetic draw of the Swedish girls is a force unto itself. You've seen it in action." I smile but can't laugh. I am a bit sad at the thought of being the constant third wheel for Adam and Taryn. Having Chazz around did even up the numbers. The truth be told, even numbers aside, I quite miss the challenge of conversing with him. Taryn smiles and pats my arm. I'm sure she suspects I'm jealous but she doesn't force the issue; instead, she suggests we move on tomorrow to see what else the east coast has to offer. It's an offer I readily accept because Taryn's words are still hanging in the air when I hear the laughter and accents of the Swedish contingent as they walk up behind us and settle on the beach twenty feet away from where we're sitting. Annika is draped over Chazz like a tight-fitting spandex dress, and it's all I can do not to throw up. Taryn excuses herself to go to the water and meet up with Adam, and I settle back on my towel, close my eyes and turn up Kings of Leon on my iPod to drown out the gaiety going on next to me.

Moving north up the coast and putting some distance between Chazz and me is a great idea. Adam, Taryn and I fall into an easy routine for the next couple of weeks. We move to Coffs Harbour and spend a few days there, the highlight of which is canoeing — on a creek, not in the ocean. Yes, I go canoeing. But not without a great deal of convincing from Taryn and Adam. As much as I'm now a little more open to the idea of trying new things, canoeing involves a very small, tippy boat and is, therefore, not the place I should be. Surprisingly, once I'm in the canoe and Adam gives me a few pointers, my control-freak nature takes over and I discover I'm actually fairly proficient with a paddle. Not only do I manage to keep the canoe upright and keep myself out of the water, I actually have fun. Well, it's fun until the very end, when I try to beach the canoe and get myself out of it without getting wet, wherein I immediately fall into the water, landing on my butt and soaking myself from the waist down — including my turquoise boots, which I had insisted on wearing for the canoeing excursion. Sitting in the water, I register Taryn and Adam being completely silent, having no idea what to say to me.

"Well, I suppose I had to break the boots in properly at some point," I start to laugh, and Taryn and Adam both let out audible sighs of relief. Taryn even snaps a photo of me sitting in the creek.

"You've come a long way, Mel! There was a time, not too long ago, when this sort of thing would have put you into a tizzy," Taryn laughs as she helps me up.

"Yes, well, after you see your boyfriend dancing naked in front of hundreds of people, you get a little better perspective on things," I laugh and we wrestle the canoes out of the creek and onto the shore.

70

In Byron Bay, our next stop up the coast, we walk to the lighthouse — the most easterly point of the Australian coast — and for the first time we see dolphins swimming in the ocean. Marine life and I are good together as long as there is a distance between us. I am absolutely awed by the dolphins jumping and playing in the surf. The path we are standing on is deserted, except for us. The overcast day and occasional drizzle is obviously keeping fellow travellers from hiking too far from the hostels. I stand quietly watching the dolphins, and a feeling comes over me I barely recognize. I realize the feeling is calm. I haven't felt a calm like this one in as long as I can remember — perhaps, ever. For the first time in weeks, I realize I can't feel the throb in my jaw. The throb has been a dull constant since my first bout of lockjaw, but now seems finally to be abating.

"Mel! Are you listening?" Taryn touches my arm, and I realize she has been speaking to me but I haven't heard her.

"Oh, sorry. I am completely enthralled with the dolphins," I laugh. "I didn't even hear you."

"Adam and I are going to head back to the hostel. Are you coming?" Taryn asks, taking Adam's hand and starting to walk back from where we came.

"No, you guys go on ahead. I'm going to watch the dolphins for a while. I'll be back before dark; we can grab some dinner together?"

"Sounds great. Don't get lost!" Adam laughs and he and Taryn start to walk away from where I'm standing.

I find a bench and sit down, the amazing feeling of calm still within me. Calm. If you'd asked me a few months ago, while I was running around making real estate deals if I was calm, I would have answered, "Yes" — and I would have been wrong. There is nothing calm about my life at home. Maybe I do have it all wrong? Maybe the fast-paced world of chasing deals while wearing high-end suits and expensive boots isn't the answer? I assess my hiking boots as I cross my legs underneath me and smile. Mel Melrose, sitting in the drizzle, wearing hiking boots, Old Navy and Suzy Shier — and being okay with it. Who could have predicted this? I watch the dolphins for another hour, until the drizzle turns into a torrential rain shower and forces me to start back to the hostel to meet up with Adam and Taryn.

Surfer's Paradise is the next stop in our trip, and it's an experience like none other. The waves are huge. The weather is too cool for me to venture into the water, but Adam and Taryn dare the chill and play in the surf for an hour before succumbing to blue lips and pruning fingers. Adam and Taryn return to the hostel to warm up, but I venture to stay on the beach, watching the surf to give them some time alone. They have been absolute troopers, including me in all their activities, so I like to give them alone time whenever possible. I start to take my book out of my small pack but decide against it. I don't really feel like reading. Instead, I lie back on the sand and close my eyes, listening to the surf.

"You've got to be careful sleeping on the beach, Boots. You might get accosted by a really good-lookin' guy." I feel Chazz plop down beside me.

"Whew, then it's a lucky thing you're here. You can warn me if any come along." I open my eyes and grin at him. My stomach is all butterflies and somersaults. Honestly, what is wrong with me? I sit up in an attempt to settle my stomach.

"Whatcha doin' out here all by yourself?" Chazz asks.

"Oh, you know, working on my tan." I look down and start playing with the sand between my knees.

"Fully dressed, head to toe?"

"You don't want to rush into these things. I am prone to heat rashes." I smile at Chazz. "What did you do with the Swedes?"

"The girls have gone shopping. Not really my cup of tea. They'll be fine for a while without me," Chazz pauses. "I'm sorry I didn't get to say goodbye in Port Macquarie; I didn't plan on meeting up with Annika again."

"You don't have anything to be sorry about. She's a beautiful girl. You'd be crazy not to want to be with her."

"Yeah, she's a great girl. Her friends can be tough to take sometimes. How is the travelling going? Still having new adventures?" Chazz asks sincerely.

"It's been great. Oh, and my jaw is a lot better. Almost one hundred percent — no more episodes." I smile at Chazz, and my stomach finally stops the fluttering and flipping. It's just know-it-all Chazz; my stomach should be able handle a conversation with him standing on my head.

"Excellent. I knew you'd find your stride here. I just wish I'd been around to witness the Mel transformation," Chazz laughs.

"Are you staying in Surfer's for a while? Maybe we can catch up. I think Taryn, Adam and I are staying for three days."

"A few days, I think. Maybe we can hang out," Chazz smiles, and we fall into a conversation about our travels and experiences since last seeing one another.

Forty minutes later, Chazz starts checking his watch every few seconds, indicating he has overstayed his time away from Annika.

"You have somewhere to be?" I ask, although I suspect the answer.

"Yes. Well, no, not really. I told Annika I might catch up with her. But I can stick around if you want company," Chazz backpedals.

"No, you go ahead. I'm going to get back and catch up with Taryn and Adam." I smile but have to lower my head to look at the sand in case Chazz sees the sadness in my eyes. "Go. Have fun."

"Are you sure?" Chazz asks but has risen to standing and is brushing the sand off his shorts.

"Absolutely," I look up. "I'll head back myself in a few minutes."

"Catch you later, then," Chazz turns and starts to jog away, obviously anxious to get back to Annika.

I watch Chazz's back as he increases the distance between us. What is wrong with me? I don't even like Chazz. Okay, maybe I like him. But I shouldn't be getting tied up in knots whenever he's around, and I certainly shouldn't begrudge him the chance to hang out with beautiful Annika. Who wouldn't want to hang out with Annika? If I were Chazz, I'd pick Annika over me, hands down. She seems to have it all together, while I hardly recognize myself anymore and am still trying to pick up any recognizable pieces of the "in-control person" I was six months ago.

Walking back to the hostel, berating myself for having a crush on know-it-all Chazz, I realize I haven't even thought about John or the naked dance business in days. Getting out of Toronto and away from it all really does seem to be helping with the healing process. If only I can now purge thoughts of Chazz.

71

Taryn and Adam are dry and relaxed when I get back. They tell me they had met up with Chazz as well — they told Chazz I was on the beach, apparently — and are planning to join him and the Swedes for a pubcrawl later. My brain starts to swim; Chazz came to find me at the beach on purpose? Well, that must be something, right? Of course, he couldn't wait to get away from me and back to Annika. No, Chazz was just killing time. I'm not going to read anything into our meeting on the beach.

My first response about joining the pubcrawl is "No, not my cup of tea." But Taryn makes the excellent point that there will be no tea involved, and I do like beer and wine, which will be involved. Avoiding Chazz is my sole motivation for not joining. But honestly, if I spend the entire rest of my time here avoiding Chazz and Annika, I may only see the inside of hostels. The Gold Coast of Australia is like one huge grocery store, wherein an annoying lady runs her cart into the back of your legs as you start your shopping and you continually see that same cart-wheeling maniac in every aisle of the store for the rest of your shopping experience. Having a silly crush on Chazz should not keep me from enjoying the second half of my trip. It is decided verbally I will join the pubcrawl. Internally I decide Chazz will not get to me in the least.

By the third pub of the crawl, I can honestly say I am drunk. Chazz is too occupied with Annika and company to even acknowledge my existence in the group. I spend the best part of the evening with two very interesting guys from England, Nigel and Simon, who have been travelling for six months of their one-year, around-the-world travel plan. Taryn and Adam check in with me regularly but have met up with a couple from Texas and are partying with them. Nigel and Simon decide at some point it would be a good idea to try every shooter known to man and convince me to join them in their adventure — a decision I will regret later despite Chazz's ideology that you only regret what you *don't* do.

I enjoy a tequila shooter occasionally but, for the most part do not consider myself a shooter connoisseur. By the time we get to the last club on the pubcrawl, I've ingested every liqueur I can name and some I've never heard of before. Nigel and Simon seem to be in much better shape than I am in when we enter the last club, mid-foam party.

I am startled by the foam-party concept, even in my drunken haze. The sunken dance floor is enclosed in plywood walls, about four feet high, and lined with a pool liner, then the interior is filled with foam. It's like a gigantic bubble bath, and what appears to be hundreds of bar patrons are dancing *in* the foam. I have never witnessed anything like this and my first thought is "Wow, there must be a lot of germs in there."

Nigel and Simon are thrilled with the foam concept and immediately drag me to the edge of the vat, trying to coerce me into the foam. I balk and remain firmly on dry ground as they dive in, showing no fear. Taryn comes up behind me laughing, also amazed by the concept but at least she'd heard of it before. Nigel and Simon are having the time of their lives, slipping and sliding up to their armpits in foam. Simon is completely soaked, he must have fallen and been completely submersed at some point. I see Chazz and Adam across the dance floor-slash-bubble bath, standing with Annika and some of her friends. Chazz and Adam are obviously planning to go into the foam and Chazz appears to be trying to persuade Annika to join him. She is flatly refusing — even stamping her foot for good measure. I can tell by the look on her face Chazz is fighting a losing battle. Chazz shrugs his shoulders and starts toward the foam, while Adam comes over to Taryn and grabs her hand to lead her to the foam.

"But what about the germs?" I grab Taryn's shoulder and ask her, puzzled no one in the bubble vat seems concerned about the diseases they will surely catch.

"You only live once!" Taryn laughs.

"Well, you won't live very long after going in there!"

"I'm not thinking about the germs — you shouldn't either! Come on!"

Standing on the side, I see Annika across the way starting to pout like a petulant child because Chazz isn't doing her bidding. I don't want to be like Annika. Besides, I'm here to try new things and have stories to take home. I'm going to do it. With the courage one can only acquire from the amount of alcohol I've ingested, I think "Germs be damned! I'm going in."

I manage to get Nigel's attention, and he comes to the side of the vat, takes my hand and leads me down four steps into the foam. When I'm fully immersed and up to my armpits in foam, I realize my feet, up to my knees, are in water, spilled beer and Lord-only-knows-what-bodily-fluids. Of course, they need water to create the foam, I hadn't thought about it before venturing into the slippery pit. But now I've figured it out and realize I have voluntarily walked into the water and foam wearing my turquoise boots. Sadly, by the time I realize the magnitude of the situation, I'm in the middle of the pool, dancing with Nigel and Simon, and the damage is already done.

"Oh, my God! I've just totally ruined my boots this time!" I laugh to Taryn, who dances over when she sees me in the foam.

"Well, if that's the worst thing that happens, we'll be okay. I've already slipped twice and fear I might break a leg!"

"No broken bones! Destroying the boots is…" I start to say but am cut off as I spot Nigel falling out of the corner of my eye, then feel myself being dragged down into the foam and water and germs. Flailing and sputtering under the foam, I try to stand up but can't get my boots to hold me without slipping. I feel Nigel doing the same beside me and I start to laugh under the foam. I bump into legs and feet and finally feel strong hands grab my arm and lift me up out of the murk, back to the air above the foam. Laughing, I wipe the foam off my face and open my eyes. "Oh, my God, that is so disgusting!"

"Boots! Are you okay?" The concerned voice comes from Chazz, who hadn't been anywhere near me when I fell.

"I'm fine, just grossed out by the germs," I laugh.

At this point, Nigel has righted himself and is standing beside me. "Sorry about dragging you down… oh no, did I do that?" Nigel asks, looking down at the side seam of my Old Navy sundress that is now torn open and would be exposing my naked side to the entire bar had I not been mostly covered in foam.

Before I can completely register my almost public display of nudity, Nigel has removed his dripping-wet t-shirt and is putting it over my head. "Here, this will keep you decent for the rest of the night."

I register Nigel standing in front of me with a naked torso. I also register that I like the look of his naked chest.

"Let's get out of here and dry off a bit," Nigel says. "I'll buy you a beer. The least I can do after tearing your dress."

"Sounds good," I laugh. "A break from the foam might be a good thing."

Nigel leads me out of the bubbles and helps me up the slippery steps leading to drier ground. In my drunk, germ-covered, torn-dress, soggy-booted state, I don't even realize I have let Nigel whisk me away from Chazz without even thanking him for picking me up.

Shortly after my drenching in the vat of foam and only

halfway through the beer Nigel has purchased for me, I get the distinct feeling that I should no longer be in public and have the dizzy, stomach-churning knowledge that I've ingested more alcohol than is good for me.

"I have to go now, Nigel," I slur and touch Nigel on the shoulder, which is now covered in his windbreaker, before darting towards the door. I realize I must appear quite rude, but my only thought is I must get outside to some fresh air before I throw up.

"Hey, wait up. I'll come with you." Nigel falls into step and opens the door for me.

"Are you okay?" Nigel asks as I lean against the wall of the building, mentally willing my head to stop spinning.

I just nod and try not to think about throwing up.

Nigel grabs my shoulder. "I'm going to go back and tell Taryn that I'm walking you back to your hostel. Will you be okay for a minute?"

I nod again, not able to form words. I manage to hold it together and not vomit, but it takes all of my concentration while I wait for Nigel to return. Nigel is very cute, although several years my junior — closer to Taryn's age, I'd guess. He has beautiful blue eyes, is tall and slim and, well, the polar opposite of John; maybe that's why I feel so immediately comfortable around him. I intuitively know Nigel would never voluntarily dance naked in front of an audience.

Nigel holds me up for most of the very long, zigzagging walk to the hostel. I am very glad Nigel is there to help me walk straight — well, straighter.

"You are not like anyone I've ever met before," Nigel laughs as he grabs me and rights my direction so I won't venture into a hibiscus shrub — I only know its name because Taryn has been quizzing me on the flora and fauna in our travels.

"I get that a lot, but it sounds nicer with your accent… oops!" I giggle as I stumble over an uneven patch of sidewalk and tumble into Nigel's chest. Luckily, Nigel is not nearly as unsteady as I am and is able to hold me up. Nigel then does something most unexpected. He holds my shoulders and kisses me. The kiss is nice — soft and sweet — but he catches me completely off guard and my muddled brain goes into immediate overload. The last person I kissed was John, and we were together for over two years. It's been a very long time since I've had a first kiss, and I'm not completely prepared for the flood of emotions — good and bad — that sweep over me.

"Ahh…" I manage as I pull away. I imagine I resemble a deer in headlights.

"Mel, I'm sorry. I just… well, I just wanted to kiss you… and, well, there you were…" Nigel stumbles over his words.

"No. It's okay. Fine. I just…" I pause to find words that won't sound ridiculous, "I just recently broke up with someone, that's why I'm here in the first place, and I haven't even given any thought to… well, I'm just not ready to be with someone else. Sorry." I look down at my feet, feeling a little less drunk than a few moments ago.

"No. No. That's fine. I'm sorry." Nigel takes my arm and steers me toward the hostel. "Let's just get you home."

The rest of the walk is quiet, rightly so, as I've just inadvertently hurt Nigel's feelings. I think about the kiss. It was nice. I like kissing. I just didn't see it coming. Don't get me wrong — Nigel is a wonderful, sweet guy, but there's just no spark. I hadn't considered him as someone I would ever kiss. I wonder if I'll ever be ready to kiss anyone after John's betrayal and subsequent accusation of being needy. I then wonder what my reaction would have been if the kisser had been Chazz.

72

Standing in the shower the next morning, desperate to scour off the germs, I try not to think about the damage the germs from the foam did while I slept. I make a mental note to wash my sheets. I come back to the room I'm sharing with Adam and Taryn. Taryn is lying on her bed, and I flop down beside her.

"Adam has gone to get some food. I can't even lift my head," Taryn laughs weakly.

"I feel terrible myself but had to get the germs off me." I close my eyes and think a nap will be a good thing, even though I've just woken up. I drank way too much last night.

"You were very popular last night," Taryn laughs.

"What do you mean?" My eyes pop open immediately. I wonder if Taryn knows about my kiss with Nigel. I immediately feel quite nauseous. The way I feel is very reminiscent of the morning after John's dance exhibition.

"Nigel was completely smitten with you, obviously. And did you see Chazz come to your rescue?" Taryn tries to ask casually, but I can tell she isn't really being casual at all.

Chazz? Whew, Taryn doesn't seem to know about my walk home with Nigel. "Hardly a rescue. Chazz grabbed my arm and picked me up. He's not exactly lifeguard material," I answer, my eyes still closed.

"Oh, it was a rescue, all right! He practically knocked over three people, getting across the foam, and had you lifted before I could. And I was standing right there!" Taryn laughs. "And when you walked off with Nigel, he looked like someone had punched him in the stomach. He gathered up Annika and her friends, and they left shortly after that."

"Really?" I am very surprised by Taryn's recounting of the past evening's events. I don't remember it that way, but I was under the influence of alcohol and several feet of foam at the time. "Well, the point is he left with Annika. And you have to admit they make one extraordinarily handsome couple."

"Attractive couple or not, Chazz has a thing for you," Taryn laughs. Just then Adam returns to the room with chocolate milk and breakfast sandwiches from Hungry Jack's — just what a hangover demands.

I try not to dwell on what Taryn had said about Chazz having a thing for me but I find myself coming back to it several times over the course of the day. What if Chazz does have a thing for me? Do I want Chazz to like me back, or would it be better for all involved if it remains as is? If kissing Nigel tells me anything, it's that I'm not ready to be interested in anyone new. Have I recovered enough from my relationship with John to get involved with someone new? Even if I have, should it be know-it-all Chazz? I wish Kit were here.

I claim a severe hangover and manage to escape Taryn's

plans for a nature walk. I do enjoy the outings, but I need to talk to Kit. I find a cyber café and log on to my email to discover several messages from Kit having issues with her condo redecorating and paint colour selections.

ME: Hey, I thought you were doing a red wall in your living room? What happened to that? The colours I used are in a file in my office marked "renovation." All the paint chips are there. Feel free to pilfer the file.

I send the email, then start one to my parents and Mr. and Mrs. Jennings when a response from Kit pops into my inbox.

KIT: Hey, Are you still online? I will definitely pilfer your file. I think I want to paint my living room the same colour as your bedroom. Maybe? I've already painted it twice. The red looked horrible and the blue was no better. I have no idea what I'm doing. Fill me in on your travels! You know I live vicariously through you these days.

ME: I went to a foam party last night and got kissed by an Englishman!

KIT: What? What is a foam party? Who is the Englishman?? And?? What happened??

I describe the foam party the best I can and fill Kit in on the kiss from Nigel.

KIT: So? Any potential with Nigel?

ME: No, I don't think so. Too soon and no spark. Oh, and he's much younger than me.

KIT: Well, all that and he's not Chazz.

ME: What? Hardly. Chazz is a know-it-all blowhard. Definitely not what I need in my life. Besides, he'd be impossible to live with and he's currently sporting a stunning Swedish girlfriend.
KIT: LOL. Whatever! I do believe you profess too much. You've been emailing about him since you met him. And let's face it, he is stunning! (and I know you're going to say he isn't...)
ME: He may be considered attractive by some but not me. Don't you have some painting to do? ;-)

Wandering back to the hostel, I ponder Kit's comments about Chazz. Okay, maybe I have a crush on Chazz. He did save me when I had lockjaw, but surely it's just the normal fall-for-your-saviour, knight-in-shining-armour sort of thing. It doesn't matter anyway. Chazz only has eyes for Annika — which is hardly avoidable, when Annika is constantly hanging off him like a bad Mexican poncho. I smile at the mental picture and wonder if they even wear ponchos in Sweden.

73

The next day Taryn, Adam and I, accompanied by Nigel and Simon, head north up the coast to Hervey Bay. Nigel and I are fine after the "kiss" and are both choosing to ignore the incident and not speak of it.

"So, we rent camping gear and camp on Fraser Island! According to the guidebook, Fraser Island is 'the largest sand island in the world and the only place rainforests grow on sand.'" Taryn then repeats this animatedly, as I had asked, "Pardon?" even though I had heard her words the first time. I was hoping I had heard them incorrectly.

Camping. Wow. I assess my outfit down to my flip-flops and realize I have certainly come a long way in five short weeks. I've embraced average clothing and am now going to experience camping. I weigh the pros and cons. Sleeping in a tent for several nights versus seeing this amazing place — the awe of beauty wins over my disapproval of the theory of camping. Even despite the fact it turns out Adam and Chazz have arranged for their excursions to the island to coincide. Chazz, Annika and three other Swedish delegates will be joining us in a second rental SUV. I have been doing well to convince myself Taryn is wrong about Chazz's feelings toward me, but have yet to convince myself I don't have a crush on Chazz — whether it's good or bad, I very clearly do. The idea of spending three nights on an island in close vicinity to Chazz and the Swedish poncho is not exactly in my plan, but it seems to be the way it's working out. Thank goodness we'll be in separate vehicles.

The first day on Fraser Island, after what I consider a very harrowing ferry ride but the others thought was nothing, we explore some of the sand dunes and rainforest and set up camp at Lake Boomanjin in a designated campsite. We have two small tents, so decide Taryn, Adam and I will share one and Nigel and Simon can have their own. Chazz and the Swedes set up next to us but far enough away that we can't make out what they are saying. I, for one, am glad for the distance. Close enough for Adam to visit his friend but far enough that I don't have to deal with any of them.

Our first dinner on Fraser Island is bread, cheese and beans. I start to laugh as I begin my meal. Mel Melrose happily dining on bread, cheese and beans? Not something I could have imagined a few months ago — but here I am, and I'm enjoying it. After dinner, Taryn and I use maps and the guidebook to determine the itinerary for the next day. Huddled together, while the guys chat quietly around the campfire, we hear very loud voices — an obvious argument — coming from the direction of the Swedish camp. No one says anything and, when the voices die down, we return to what we were doing prior to the interruption. Taryn and I have decided we would like to explore Lake Wabby and Eli Creek tomorrow and are just deciding where we should consider camping tomorrow night when Chazz plops himself down with a great "huff" beside Adam at the fire.

"Hey, man, trouble in paradise?" Adam asks Chazz. I try not to listen, but the guys are in close proximity and I'm infinitely curious, so I fail miserably.

"No. It'll be fine tomorrow. None of the girls have ever camped before and they aren't very happy. I'll just hang out with you guys tonight until they get used to the idea, if that's okay?" Chazz asks in a defeated manner.

"Sure, no worries. We have Mel the non-camper, but she's doing okay. Right, Mel?" Adam laughs.

"I'm a natural-born camper, so I don't need experience," I laugh, proud of myself for coming up with such a witty retort in Chazz's presence.

"Yeah, well, I wish I had some natural, or even good-natured, campers in my truck!" Chazz rolls his eyes and pops open a beer.

The next morning, we pack up camp, despite my back screaming in pain due to a rather large rock I had slept on, and head to Lake Wabby. I glance over at Chazz's camp a couple of times during packing up, but there seems to be no movement. I don't want to ask Adam what he thinks, as he doesn't seem too fazed by last night's argument and it's really none of my business. We spend the morning at Lake Wabby, an amazing freshwater lake surrounded on three sides by lush rainforest with a huge sand dune making up the fourth side. It is breathtaking, and I even venture into the water.

"Do you feel that?" Taryn says as we stand knee-deep in the water close to the sand dune.

"What?" I ask innocently, having no idea what she's talking about.

"The tickling on your legs. I think it's the fish nibbling on us!"

And just then, I realize I do feel something tickling my legs — and it is fish. My shriek draws attention, but I don't care about being embarrassed. My only concern is how fast I can get out of the water and back on dry land. Adam, Nigel and Simon, who are all swimming in the lake, laugh hardily as I scurry up the sand dune to safety. I knew fish would find me appetizing! I make a mental note to tell Chazz when I see him next.

After the morning at Lake Wabby, we head to Eli Creek, the longest freshwater stream on the island, and decide to go for a hike. We all change into sensible footwear and trek off into the rainforest following the creek, laughing and joking and having a great time. Occasionally, we take off our shoes or hiking boots and walk in the water. Not being an exercise enthusiast, I may not have signed up for a long hike but, because it's scenic and social and we are all having so much fun, I don't even register the amount of exercise I'm getting. Two hours into the walk, Taryn suggests we may want to turn around, as it will be late when we get back to the SUV and none of us has realized how long we've been walking. We are thirty minutes into the return walk — Nigel, who is walking in the creek, is giving me a piggyback ride around a muddy patch of shore too large to jump over because I don't want to remove my boots again — when I see Chazz tromping up the centre of the stream towards us.

"Hey, Chazz! Where are the girls?" I hear Adam ask, as Chazz walks closer to us, Nigel still carrying me.

"They went back to the mainland. Seems they aren't really the camping type." Chazz looks at his feet. "I was hoping I could crash with you guys for the rest of the island?"

"Ahh..." Adam wants to say yes, of course, but turns to the rest of us.

"Sure, man!" Nigel says from in front of me. "The more the merrier, right, gang?"

Everyone answers affirmatively, except me. I just nod, and Chazz turns around and falls into step with us. Having Chazz around without Annika might be fun, but I'm sure she'll be waiting to pick up where they left off the minute he sets foot back in Hervey Bay. I can't let myself get too excited about the lack of Swedes; I'm sure it will be short-lived.

"Isn't that thing getting heavy, Nige?" Chazz motions his head toward me.

"Ha ha!" I answer sarcastically.

"Some hiker you are, making Nigel carry you," Chazz laughs.

"Yeah, well at least my friends didn't abandon me!" I laugh back.

"How did you find us anyway?" Adam asks Chazz.

"I got the girls to hit a few spots I thought you might be before they 'abandoned' me." Chazz shoots me a look. "And when I saw the SUV with the dilapidated turquoise heels on the front seat, I knew I'd found you."

"They aren't just boots anymore; they are a beacon for lost souls," I laugh. "See, Taryn? And you didn't want me to bring them."

The SUV is a bit crowded, but we make the best of it for the next two days. Chazz fits in easily with our group, even becoming very close with Nigel and Simon — both figuratively and literally speaking, because the three of them are forced to share a very small tent.

74

Travelling in Australia's winter has its chilly downside, but the upside is the timing for the whale migration. From Indian Head, the lookout point on Fraser Island that rises sixty metres out of the water, we can see for miles. The six of us sit in a row, searching the horizon for signs of life. Sadly, aside from a few seabirds, we are disappointed. After thirty minutes, the boredom sets in despite the glorious view, and we start discussing what to do next because it's apparent we won't be seeing any whales. Nigel and Simon stand up and start to make their way back down towards the beach. Chazz stands and extends a hand to help me up.

"Oh, man! What did I sit on?" I realize I have something sticky on the butt of my pants and am trying to look behind me to see what it might be. "Did anyone else sit in something sticky?"

"Boots…" Chazz says quietly and reaches for my arm.

"What? Are you sticky…"

"Boots, shhh. Be quiet." Chazz points towards the ocean and I see the shiny back of a whale glisten in the sun as it breaches the surface.

I stand frozen, forgetting anything is stuck to my backside.

One of the whales jumps and flips, landing in a thunderous crash, and I gasp out loud. My skin is covered in goosebumps but not from being cold, from being in the presence of such magnificent beauty. Nigel and Simon hadn't made it very far from us before Chazz spotted the whales and they are standing with us again. Never in our time on the island have all six of us been silent, spellbound by whales as they breach the surface while making their way south. At one point I am so moved by the sight of the whales, I think I might start to cry but manage to control myself. The urge to cry is very new to me, but despite the frequency in which it creeps up on me these days I'm still not completely sure I want to embrace it fully. Taryn gets her wits about her and starts taking some pictures. We discover later that none of the photos could ever capture the awe of seeing the whales in person.

I sit down at one point — completely forgetting I might sit in something gooey — near the lookout's edge. I'm afraid that I'm so engrossed in the whales that I might accidentally take a wrong step and topple down the cliff. Sitting on top of Indian Head, watching the whales disappear on the horizon, I feel calm and happy. I realize I don't care what happens next. This is the best moment in my life so far — and I didn't plan it, or even expect it. It just happened. All the time I've been working hard, planning the next deal, making money to buy a better car, planning to be married because marriage is the next logical step, it has never occurred to me there might not be any next logical step.

Why do I want to get married? Certainly not because I can't live without John. I'm living without him just fine, and haven't even given him one thought in days. I'm happier now than I ever was with him. I only considered marriage because it was the next thing on the list. Now the list has been erased. There is no list. I'm free to do whatever I want, whenever I want. I don't need to adhere to anyone else's idea of what I should be or where I should be at a certain age; not even my own.

"I can march to my own drummer!" I say out loud, breaking the silence and surprising myself.

"Oh, you already do, Mel Melrose. Trust me, you already do!" Chazz laughs, and I register for the first time that he is sitting beside me. I look around me and see no one but Chazz.

"Where did everyone go?" I don't remember them leaving.

"They went for a hike. But you seemed to be in your own little world, and didn't answer when they asked you to join them, so I stayed back to make sure you didn't wander off the cliff," Chazz laughs.

"Well, thank you. I don't know where I was just now, but I don't remember everyone leaving so I might well have fallen to my death." I am surprised I was not aware of my surroundings. It's a bit startling to think you can be so deep in thought you don't notice people moving around you.

Chazz and I sit in silence for a while, but I can't think of anything now except him sitting beside me. We haven't been alone since he joined our group, and I find myself unable to control the flippy stomach and butterflies. I try to think of something to say, but all I can think of is how good Chazz smells despite being on an island camping for three nights.

"Annika and her friends didn't abandon me to go back to the mainland," Chazz states quietly.

"Pardon?" I believe I heard him correctly but can't be sure. Why would he say they went back when they didn't? Why is he camping with us if they are still on the island?

"Remember the day on the beach in Surfer's Paradise? When you told me I'd 'be crazy not to want to be with Annika'? Well, you can call me crazy. I told her I'd rather be with you." Chazz leans and bumps his shoulder into mine. "She's a really great girl, but I'd rather be with a sharp-tongued spitfire in four-inch heels."

My sharp tongue goes instantly dry and I can't say anything. Well, I generally can't find the right thing to say in Chazz's presence anyway, but this time it's in a good way. My stomach butterflies increase to a crescendo, and I know I'm grinning from ear to ear.

"When I saw you with Nigel at the foam party, I thought I was going to lose it. I don't want you to hang out with Nigel, or anyone else who isn't me." Then Chazz pauses.

"Nigel is just a friend…" I look up at Chazz, surprised he would think otherwise.

"I know. Well, my brain knows it, but my heart doesn't like it. When I left Annika and the Swedish girls, I came to find you and tell you I want to be with you. Then I saw Nigel giving you the piggyback in Eli Creek and I thought I was too late. Oh, and I wanted to punch him. It's taken me these past two days to get the nerve to talk to you."

After a short pause, while I try to calm my excitement, I say, "Sharp-tongued girls in four-inch heels aren't easy to live with. Are you sure you're up for the challenge?" I bump Chazz's shoulder in reply.

"*Up* for it?" Chazz laughs, "I'm looking forward to it. I've *been* looking forward to it since the first time I saw you with your skirt hiked up around your waist, trying to get on the garbage bin. I knew right then and there, you were the girl for me."

"Really? You didn't think I was some kind of crazy woman?"

"Oh, you *are* a crazy woman. But you're the crazy woman I want to be with." Chazz puts his arm around me and pulls me to him. "I didn't like seeing you with that Nigel guy. I don't want you to be with anyone but me, okay?" Chazz leans around and kisses me. He kisses me hard, like he's been waiting to do so for a long time. I kiss him back. I realize I *have* been waiting a long time to kiss him.

I pull away from Chazz. I have been hoping to kiss him for a long time, and it's nice. Very nice. I want to keep kissing him and forget the self-doubt caused by my recent breakup that is ricocheting around my brain. But I have yet to figure out what I did to make John feel I was "needy and smothering."

"I'm not sure I can just jump into this… I mean us…" I realize this statement sounds ridiculous as soon as it's out of my mouth. I've wanted to jump into something with Chazz since he fixed my jaw the first time.

"What do you mean?" Chazz stiffens.

"My last boyfriend — the 'ballerina' as you call him — said I was 'needy and smothering.' And since I still can't figure out what I did to make him feel that way, I'm afraid I will inadvertently do the same thing again. I wouldn't want to make you, or anyone else, feel that way." I look down at my hands. Sitting here with Chazz's arm around me is exciting and scary. I feel happier and more sexually aroused than I ever remember feeling with John — even at the very beginning — but my fear of being clingy holds me back.

Chazz starts to laugh. A long, hard, from the gut, belly laugh.

"What?" I am instantly hurt and offended. When you share my deepest concerns with a man, laughter is not the response you expect or hope to get.

"It's not funny!" I try to pull away from Chazz, all the excitement of kissing him a few moments ago fast evaporating. Maybe my initial opinion, of him as an obnoxious know-it-all, was accurate.

"Sorry. Sorry…" Chazz holds my shoulder firmly so I can't get up. "I shouldn't have laughed. It's just that *you* are the most frustratingly independent woman I've ever met. For someone to refer to you as 'needy' just seems… well… it's just really funny."

I start to laugh as well. "Well, if you put it that way, I suppose I'll take it as a compliment." I punch him lightly in the side.

"Good, I meant it that way." Chazz laughs again and wipes his eyes. "You? Needy." He laughs again. "I really want to meet this guy. He doesn't know you at all."

"Well, I guess we are even, then. Seems I didn't know him either. He was having an affair for two months before I even had an inkling, and then it took me two more months to get up the nerve to do anything about it."

"If he was having an affair, that's where he got the needy thing from. He was doing something wrong, so he was paranoid and defensive. You were probably just being normal, asked how his day was, and his dishonesty made you seem like you were prying because he had something to hide." Chazz laughs again.

"Really? You think that's what happened?"

"I think it's more probable than the idea of you hanging off his leg and begging for attention." Chazz smiles at me.

"Yeah, that never happened, nor is it likely to." I crinkle my nose, imagining the scene Chazz described — reminiscent of John clinging to Ursula's leg at the end of "Free Bird."

"So…" Chazz turns and takes both my hands in his, "if I promise to tell you immediately if any of your 'neediness' starts and you promise not to cling to my leg begging for attention, do you think I could kiss you every now and then?"

"Okay, but you have to give up all Swedish girls. Oh, and

no modern dance. Ever!" I laugh, my stomach doing somersaults and my head swimming, but in the good way.

"Deal." Chazz kisses me again and leans into me, pushing me onto my back. Chazz continues kissing me, and I kiss him back, then he rolls on top of me. That's how I ended up making out with my dentist on the top of Indian Head with an amazing view of the ocean and something sticky on my pants.

75

I giggle quietly at the computer terminal as I get Kit's response.

KIT: See? I told you. I knew you had a thing for Chazz with two Zs! I knew it. How is the kissing? *wink wink nudge nudge* Tell me you are coming home soon. I've made a mess of my living room. It's green now.

ME: Green? You hate green! I'll be back in three weeks. Chazz and I both have open-ended tickets and managed to get on the same flights. The kissing is exceptional but there are some things you can't share in email. We'll go out for a "nice dinner" when I get back and I'll fill you in.

KIT: Green is meant to be calming but I think I picked the wrong green. I feel like I'm in a pot of peas. I can't have peas with our "nice dinner." I may never eat peas again, actually.

ME: Well, we can figure out your living room. It will be good practice for me. I'm considering a career change—interior design—what do you think?

KIT: Wow! You'll be an amazing designer. I look forward to being your first assignment... well, if you can find time with the new love interest! ;-)

ME: I can absolutely find time. I'm not going to make the same mistake of smothering this one. I'll live my own life and meet up with him when I can. I'm going to maintain my independence this time. No driving him to naked dance and the likes of Ursula!

The next three weeks fly by. I fall into travelling with Chazz like I'm actually good at being a backpacker. The weather improves every mile we travel north, and I'm able to work on my tan and get wet in the ocean on occasion. When we get to Airlie Beach, the Whitsunday sailing debate starts. Taryn and Adam are definitely going sailing and investigate companies that let you sail with them. Apparently, the Whitsunday Islands are some of the most beautiful in the world and, according to Taryn, "need to be experienced." I, on the other hand, feel the need to experience dry land more than I need to experience a sailboat for three days and two nights, and I am adamant that they should go without me.

"But look, Mel. You can't miss this." Taryn throws a pile of postcards on the table in front of me. The top postcard is an aerial view of Whitehaven Beach. The picture is spectacular; lush green lines the beach on one side, while the turquoise ocean — at least four identifiable shades of turquoise, none the same as my dilapidated boots — butts up to the other side. The beautiful sky is yet another shade of blue.

Taryn reads from the brochure she's holding. "Whitehaven Beach is a definite 'must-see' in the Whitsundays. The crystal-clear aqua waters and pristine silica sand of Whitehaven stretch over seven kilometres along Whitsunday Island, the largest of the seventy-four islands in the Whitsundays. It defines nature at its best and provides the greatest sense of relaxation and escape." Taryn looks up at me, pleading with her eyes.

"Wow, it is beautiful, and you make a tough sale, Taryn." I glance down at the postcard. "But you have to get there by boat, and I can't do it."

"Mel, you can't let this boat thing keep you from seeing one of the most beautiful places in the world. You've been on so many boats since we got here, surely you're over the boat thing!"

At this point, Adam and Chazz, who have remained quiet, decide to jump in on Taryn's side.

"She has a point, Boots. You've been on lots of boats..." Chazz starts.

"...including a very tippy canoe! Remember? In Coffs Harbour. A canoe is way more treacherous than a huge sail-boat. The boat is eight-eight feet long..." Adam joins the sales pitch.

"Eighty-eight feet is a huge boat, Boots. I think you can do it," Chazz continues.

"Guys, I appreciate you want me to come with you, but I might ruin it for all of you. If I freak out when we're in the middle of Lord-knows-where, what are you going to do with me?" I really would like to see Whitehaven Beach but am well aware of my limitations.

"Drug you," Chazz says at the same moment Taryn says, "Keep you drunk!"

"What?" I laugh nervously. "Drug me? Keep me drunk? That's hardly the support I'll be looking for in the middle of the ocean!"

"Boots, you'll be fine. You've been fine with everything we've done here. Trust me, you'll regret not coming when we get back with our stories and photos. Besides, I already paid for your way. We're leaving tomorrow morning."

I am in shock. I'm being bamboozled — if that's even a word — into going sailing. "I hate you." I glare at Chazz. "All of you." I extend my glare to Taryn and Adam, who just grin back at me. I stand up to demonstrate my displeasure further and gather up the postcards. "They better be really good drugs, and however much wine you have isn't enough!" I huff and storm away as the plotters laugh behind me.

76

"Boots, you're going to pass out if you don't start to breathe," Chazz laughs as he plops down beside me, where I've been sitting since this journey began, wearing a life jacket and wrapped around the centre mast, clinging for life. We had to take our shoes off — apparently, it's a sailboat thing — and are all barefoot. Chazz has stepped it up a notch and removed his shirt. I could be distracted by the chiselled chest I've come to know intimately had I not been so frozen with dread and fear.

"I'm fine." I try to sound casual but know I'm not even close to pulling it off.

"Mel, we're still using engine power to get out of the harbour. We haven't even put up the sails yet. You may have to let go of the mast when we do. Do you want some Gravol before we get going?" Chazz holds out a little pink pill and an open bottle of water.

"I can't believe I let you talk me into this..." I start but gladly take the pill and down it with a swig of water. "Should I take two?" I start to panic.

"No. One is plenty, and you're going to thank me. I know you are. Your boat thing is completely in your head. When we get home, you're going to want to buy a boat!" Chazz unclamps my hands from the mast. "Here, I'm going to walk you to the front, where Taryn is, so you can enjoy the view."

"Not likely," I manage between letting go of the mast and clamping onto Chazz's arm.

"Not likely you'll want a boat? Or not likely you'll enjoy the view?" Chazz grins at me.

"Both!"

Taryn stays near me as the crew, including the paying passengers, get ready to switch from engine power to wind power. Chazz and Adam seem to love the unwinding of sails and tying of sailor knots. Adam is particularly versed in tying knots. I make a mental note to ask Taryn if Adam's knot tying extends into any other aspects of life, and smile at my own internal joke.

The theory of wind power and the actual experience are two very different things. When the boat goes under wind power it tilts — in the case of this boat, dramatically — to one side. Being on a boat when the deck is parallel to the water is one thing; being tilted so the water readily splashes up on deck, because the edge of that deck is actually in the water, is entirely another. I don't remember shrieking, but Taryn affirms later that there was plenty of it. I vaguely remember clinging to Chazz and telling him, "If we live through this experience, I'm going to kill you." I will later pinpoint this statement as the low point of my sailing career.

Luckily, the Gravol kicks in shortly after my low point

and I get semi-relaxed with the tilted boat — although I still maintain an iron grip on the cleat I've assigned to myself. Adam, who apparently has been sailing since he was a kid, keeps reminding me that the sailboat has a huge keel on the bottom that extends into the water on the opposite side so the boat will not tip over. Since I know nothing about sailboats, and the boat hasn't tipped over, I have no choice but to believe him.

I watch the other sailors and crew walk around the boat like they are on dry land, and I marvel at them. How can they not be afraid of toppling over the side into the ocean? Most of them aren't even wearing life jackets. Clinging to my cleat in my cumbersome life jacket I watch Taryn sitting beside Adam, who is showing her how to tie a knot. Taryn is laughing, and the wind is blowing her hair around her face as she tries to concentrate on her knot. Adam reaches around behind her and puts his hands on hers to show her what to do. I sit completely lost in the scene — calmed by it — and forget for a few moments that I'm surrounded by ocean and cannot see any land.

Chazz sits behind me and curls his legs around my life jacket, hugging me.

"I'm proud of you, Boots. You're sailing," Chazz whispers in my ear.

"You can hardly call clinging to a cleat for dear life sailing!" I laugh, turning my head so I can see his chin above me.

"You've only been at it for a few hours. Wait until tomorrow you'll be a hardened sailor by then."

"I hope so." I rest my head on Chazz's chest and close my

eyes. The motion of the boat is quite relaxing if I can forget that we're miles out to sea and likely to perish.

By the next day, when we anchor the boat near Whitehaven Beach and start to load into the dingy to go to shore, I am much more relaxed. Sleeping on the boat was fine, as it was anchored and thus not tilting, and Chazz held me close all night — which was really the only thing he could do, as I insisted on sharing his single bunk.

We spend the afternoon on Whitehaven Beach and I have to admit that Chazz was right, although I actually have yet to tell him he was right — I refuse to give him that kind of ammunition. Standing in the ocean, off the beach, up to my armpits, I can still see my feet in the water. The water is so clear and clean that even I feel safe. I've spent over twenty-four hours on a boat to get here, and now I'm comfortably standing in the ocean, not worrying about sea creatures coming to get me. Chazz's theory that the "boat-thing is all in my head" may be accurate. Although I probably won't mortgage the house when I get home to purchase that boat Chazz mentioned. Lake Ontario isn't nearly as clean and inviting as the ocean off Whitehaven Beach.

I hear splashing and turn to see Chazz running into the water behind me. He dives into the water, and I can see him as he swims up to me and grabs my legs. I scream but in a good way, because I knew he was coming. Chazz's head pops up in front of me and he grabs me around the waist. My legs wrap about him voluntarily. Chazz kisses me with his wet, salty lips.

"You've come a long way, Boots!"

"I know! Conquering the boat-ocean thing is the first step towards the new me. I can't imagine what else I'll be able to accomplish now that I've done this."

"Then imagine what we can accomplish together!" Chazz kisses me again, and I completely forget I'm armpit-deep in a scary, fish-filled ocean.

77

"You're absolutely sure, man?" Chazz asks Adam for the third time. "We can probably still get you on the flight."

Adam had originally planned to return to Toronto with Chazz, now us, but all the mystery business in Sydney was Adam applying for jobs and internships. Shortly after he hooked up with us at Bondi Beach, Adam had decided he'd rather stay in Australia with Taryn than return to Toronto. He's already lined up two interviews, and is in the process of exchanging his visa. He and Taryn are going to travel for another month before returning to Sydney. They are leaving for Ayers Rock tomorrow.

"No way, man. Leave all this? Are you crazy?" Adam laughs and hugs Chazz. "Have a safe trip."

"Oh, my God. I don't want to leave you." I hug Taryn again and can't let go.

"I'll be fine. Adam's staying with me. We'll both be fine!"

"Make sure you email loads." I finally let go of her.

"Give my love to Kit, Tia and my parents. Tell Mom I want her to mail me some cookies as soon as I'm settled in Sydney." Taryn takes a step back. "Oh, Mel, thank you so much for coming with me."

"I wouldn't have missed it for the world. I love you." I hug her one more time.

"You ready to go, Boots?" Chazz takes my hand and we start toward the departure check-in.

"Do you remember when I asked you to please, not call me that?" I look up at Chazz.

"Yep, and you must remember me laughing and saying, 'If the boot fits, zip it up and go for a stroll.'" Chazz winks at me. I may have to concede on the nickname.

Walking to the departure gate, hand in hand with Chazz, I know that even though I have no idea where my life will lead me, I'm exactly where I'm meant to be.

Sitting on the airplane, somewhere over Middle America, Chazz turns to me and asks, "What was your favourite part of the trip?"

"Hmmm... let me think. Ahhh? Fraser Island in general, Indian Head in particular," I laugh.

Chazz laughs and kisses me, "Good answer. But seriously?"

"Seriously?" I pause. "Seriously, it wasn't the places so much as the people, and being able to figure out who I am and what I want to do with my life. I can't pick one favourite part. I'm just happy I had the entire experience."

"Better answer." Chazz kisses me again and we start talking about the reality at hand: returning to Toronto and getting back to real life.

Chazz is going to start working the week after next, but is taking a week off to get acclimatized to Toronto again. He's going to come home with me and stay at my house for a few days before looking for his own place.

I'm going to call Morty and track down my new signs and business cards. I had totally forgotten I'd ordered them until I booked my flight home and thoughts of home and work and "real life" started to flood back. My plan is to sell real estate to pay the bills while I take courses toward an interior design diploma. I can't say for sure that I will leave the real estate world completely but, in the meantime, I want to experience more than what I already know. I want to live my own life while enhancing Chazz's, not controlling it. I don't want to repeat the same mistakes I've made in previous relationships.

As the plane starts its descent, I look out the window at the city below. I can't believe we're home already.

Standing by the luggage carousel, holding Chazz's hand, I realize I don't ever want my backpack to slide down the chute. I want to be back in Australia, on the beach, living a carefree life with Chazz. I want my biggest concern of the whole day to be whether I want cheese or peanut butter for lunch. I know my life has been changed forever, for the better.

"I wish it wasn't over," I whisper to Chazz.

"You and me both, Boots. But it will be nice to see family and friends again. It's the only good part about coming home." Chazz reaches out and hauls his backpack off the conveyor.

"Well, I guess we'll just have to get to work and save for the next trip," I laugh.

"I knew I'd make a traveller out of you. How do you feel

about hiking in Peru?" Chazz laughs, puts his arm around my waist and kisses my forehead.

My bag finally slides down the chute and we start towards the door leading to the terminal. I stop Chazz just before the door and kiss him. "Thank you for being a part of my Australia."

"No, thank you!"

We walk out the doors and there's a sea of people waiting to meet loved ones. I search the crowd for Kit — we had prearranged for her to meet us — as we start to walk down the ramp. I hear Kit's squeal of excitement before I feel her run up beside me and wrap her arms around my neck. We're hugging, squealing and jumping when Marc catches up to Kit.

"Oh, my God. Don't ever leave me for so long again!" Kit says when she can finally speak.

"Next time, you'll have to come," I answer, catching my breath and hugging Kit again. I can't hug her enough. I didn't know how much I missed her until I saw her again.

"Chazz, you remember Kit, I'm sure."

"Absolutely!" Chazz laughs and shakes Kit's hand.

"Welcome to our little family, Chazz. Mel has been gushing about you on email for weeks. Thanks for taking care of her."

"The pleasure was all mine. She is truly one of a kind."

"He means that in the good way!" I laugh at Kit, then turn to Marc. "Marc, this is Chazz. I'm sure Kit's filled you in on Chazz and how we met him."

Marc and Chazz shake hands.

Kit stands back and assesses me. "Mother of Pearl. What happened to your boots?" I had decided to wear the now mostly dilapidated heels for the trip home as their last send-off. I won't be wearing them in public again.

"Everything! If these boots could talk," I laugh.

Marc laughs. "We'll have to take the boots out for beer and get their version of the story." Marc finishes his sentence, then most uncharacteristically puts his arm around Kit and, more to my surprise, Kit puts her arm around Marc and leans into him.

My backpack slides from my shoulder, where it was only precariously perched, and my jaw drops open. I am at a complete loss for words. My head turns from Kit to Marc and back as I point, not knowing what to say even if I could form words. Kit giggles and Marc is grinning ear to ear. Marc leans over and kisses Kit's forehead and Kit puts her hand on Marc's chest.

"Oh… my… God!" I manage, having finally realized the magnitude of what I'm seeing. Kit and Marc have finally, after what seems like decades, gotten together — in the dating sense of the word.

"Are you two finally… ?" I ask, my brain still unable to comprehend what my eyes are seeing.

Kit nods and a gigantic smile spreads across her face.

"Oh, my God! Oh, my God!" I shriek and wrap my arms around them both.

"Yes, finally! You shouldn't leave me alone for so long. Redecorating the condo got overwhelming. And one thing led to another between the green living room and the purple bathroom!" Kit laughs, unhooks herself from Marc and hugs me back.

"Yeah, she was driving herself and me insane with decorating. I was tired of listening to paint drama, so I dragged her out of the condo for dinner and a movie. And then... well, here we are!" Marc squeezes Kit, and Kit just grins.

"You have a purple bathroom? Why didn't you email me immediately?" I grab Kit's shoulders and shake her. My thoughts are disjointedly rampaging through my head.

"Well, Mom and Dad came to help. Enough said. It's really fuchsia..."

I cut Kit off, "No. Not the bathroom. I mean about you guys. Why didn't you email me about this? You and Marc? This is news!"

Kit laughs, "It was just a couple of weeks ago, and we knew you were coming home so we thought we'd surprise you. Did it work?" Kit laughs agains.

"Absolutely." I hug Kit again then turn to a very puzzled Chazz. "I've been waiting for these two to figure it out for years."

"Sorta like I had to wait for you!" Chazz smiles and grabs my hand as we follow Marc and Kit to the parking garage. We get to Marc's truck and I try to throw my bags in the open back, but it's too tall for me to lift my heavy backpack into.

"Here, Boots, give me your bag before you hurt yourself." Chazz takes my bag from me and easily hoists it into the back of Marc's truck.

"Boots! Good one, Chazz! I like it," Marc laughs.

"Oh, *no*! Don't you start too!" I give Marc my best angry eyes, but he just laughs and pats my shoulder.

"Too late, Boots. I only wish I'd thought of it."

We hop into the truck and start toward my house. I tell Kit I want to hear all about her and Marc finally getting together as soon as we get home and open some champagne.

"Oh, dear, do I even have champagne? I left in such a hurry I couldn't tell you what's in my kitchen," I wonder out loud.

"Yes, we stocked your fridge with all the staples. And champagne is one of your staples. You're all set," Kit laughs.

78

For the remainder of the ride home, we chat about what I missed while I was away. Kit tells me Tia is in Missouri with the band and has found her niche as their road manager. I am surprised by Tia's new-found career but, hey, I'm a world traveller now, so stranger things do, indeed, happen. Kit also mentions she's bumped into Cam and Pam a couple of times while checking the house. She has filled them in on John "borrowing" the lawn ornaments, even showing them the video.

"Mother of Pearl, Kit! I'm trying to stay friendly with my neighbours! Seeing Ursula's vision may not encourage the end result I'm looking for."

"They thought it was hilarious. Pam did mention she may disinfect Goldilocks, though," Kit laughs. "Oh, and they're pregnant! Cam wanted me to tell you Pam is feeling better and everything is back to normal, so it's safe to come home now. We'll have to find the perfect lawn ornament to commemorate the baby's arrival," Kit laughs.

We pull into the driveway of my house — I love my house. My car is spotless and shiny in the afternoon sun.

"Did you wash my car?" I ask Kit as I jump out of the truck.

"Marc did, this morning. It was pretty dusty from just sitting while you were gone."

I don't have to point out the lawn ornaments to Chazz. He spots them immediately. I had warned him, of course, but you can't fully explain them really. They have to be experienced.

"That is one wicked display of tacky," Chazz states quietly, staring across the yard.

"But at least they are all present and accounted for," I laugh. I had explained the lawn-ornament theft ring to Chazz one night in Australia over a bottle of Shiraz.

I start to take a bag from Marc, but he says, "You go ahead with Kit and open the champagne. I'll grab these."

"Thank you!" I give Marc another hug. "I can't believe you and Kit are finally going to give it a try. I can't tell you how happy I am."

"If you're half as happy as I am, I can imagine," Marc laughs as I walk toward the house where Kit is unlocking the door.

I bend down to right the groom squirrel who has not gotten any steadier on his feet during my absence, when I hear Kit yelling, "What did you do, mister?"

Who is she talking to? I step into the kitchen to see what she's doing and look through to the living room. The living room floor is covered in foam stuffing, once belonging in the five decorative cushions on the sofa, and, in the middle of the mess — which looks like the bad fake Christmas snow you see in store windows at Christmas time — a black-and-white head pops up with stuffing in his mouth so that he looks like he has a beard. The bearded, black-and-white head looks at Kit in a familiar head-tilted "Huhhhh?" I immediately recognize.

"Burton?" I ask, knowing it can't be Burton because this head is too small and the ears have not been clipped. The colouring of this dog is almost identical to Burton's, though — the same black spot over his left eye that looks likes he's questioning something. At a quick glance, with the nose covered in foam stuffing, it's an easy mistake to make.

When the dog hears my voice, he jumps up and lumbers towards me. He's a smaller version of Burton, a harlequin Great Dane puppy. When he runs, his feet go higher than his head in the most awkward fashion. He is completely gangly and slips on the kitchen tile, sliding on his bum.

"Bad dog!" Kit says as she bends to start picking up the stuffing. The puppy is paying no attention to Kit as he scurries towards me.

"Where did he come from?" I ask Kit as I pick him up and he starts licking my face with a sizable tongue. I remove a wad of foam stuffing from his mouth.

"Mr. Klein called the other day when I was here... oh, just a second." Kit stands up and comes over to the kitchen island. Marc and Chazz are now in the kitchen.

"Hey, is this the famous Burton?" Chazz asks.

"He escaped from the bathroom, I see," Marc says.

Kit hands me a note, written in Calvin Klein's distinctive handwriting, and I read out loud:

Missy, he got his father's good looks but sadly his mother's taste in music. The only band he likes is called Kings of Leon. Ever heard of it? His registered name is Harry Connick, Jr. Jr. but he won't answer to it. He only responds to Leon.

"Leon? Oh, my God! So cute. He's mine?" I set the note down and look at Kit, surprised.

"All yours, baby! Mr. Klein called the other day and as soon as he said Kings of Leon, I knew this puppy was meant for you. Mr. Klein dropped him off this morning." Kit hands Marc a bottle of champagne out of the refrigerator. "Can you do the honours, please?"

Kit kisses Marc as he takes the bottle. I feel a tightening in my chest like I might start to cry. I'm so happy. Chazz. Leon. Kit and Marc. I'm almost overwhelmed.

Kit opens the cupboard to get the champagne flutes. "We can pick up the pillow mess in a minute. Right now, first things first." Kit places four glasses in a row on the island.

"It looks like you might have your hands full with that one, Boots." Marc nods at Leon as he pours the champagne.

"Probably," I laugh, "but we'll figure it out. Won't we, Leon?" I hold the puppy up by his armpits — are they called armpits on a dog? — and give him a kiss on the nose, which is returned with a puppy lick. Marc pops the cork on the champagne.

"He's one mighty large puppy!" Chazz takes Leon from me and cuddles him, and I hug Chazz around the waist.

Marc hands out the glasses of champagne, and I make a toast. "Here's to life's greatest adventures. They are the ones you can't plan for because you just don't see them coming."

Burton's Expenses (May 9 — May 13)

$500	Office stereo receiver
$100	Food, Stella stuffy and rawhide bones
$200	Bang & Olufsen A8 headphones
$400	2 iPod Shuffles and extra headphones
$1,400	Prada boots (really great deal!)
$100	Leotard (men's medium-flesh colour)
$300	Prince Charming and horse lawn ornaments
$3,000	

Leon's Expenses (September)

$300	Puppy food (large-dog variety)
$100	Doggie bed (giant size), Stella stuffy and rawhide bones
$400	3 iPod Shuffles and 2 earphones (not Bang & Olufsen)
$105	Black leather collar (large) with "LEON" in rhinestones (custom order)
$300	Five decorative sofa pillows
$ 56	Television remote controller (original missing and presumed eaten) — Leon has his father's constitution
$ 0	No replacement for the tangerine Prada handbag (original partially eaten) — there's more to life than Prada
$1,261	

Watching Chazz wrestle Leon off the bed when he stays over so Chazz can sleep beside me... priceless!

Don't miss out
on Kit's adventures in
It Would Be Funny...
If It Wasn't My Life

What Readers are Saying

"What a great easy, funny read! A book that will get passed around to many girlfriends!!!"

"If you like the 'Shopaholic' series, you'll enjoy this book. Likeable characters and funny plot twists."

"A **wonderfully funny** and well written novel! I loved it the first time and it was even better the third time. Make sure you hang on for this ride... you will not be disappointed!"

"I really enjoyed this book. I loved that it was set in Ontario and that it was Canadian and that I related to the references. **I couldn't put it down.** I loved everything about it."

"Funny and kept me intrigued the whole time...it was really neat to see you naming places in your book (that) I could identify with."

"I was hooked and could not put the book down."
"My husband kept telling me that if I was going to 'chortle' while reading I had to at least read it out loud."